Graham Lord has pu[illegible]ost notably *The Spider and the Fly*, *Time out of* [illegible] and *A Party to Die for*. He is also the biographer of Jeffrey Bernard and James Herriot. He was for many years Literary Editor of the *Sunday Express*, where he interviewed a wide variety of writers, from P.G. Wodehouse and Muriel Spark to Ruth Rendell and Graham Greene.

Books by Graham Lord

Novels

Marshmallow Pie
A Roof Under Your Feet
The Spider and the Fly
God and All His Angels
The Nostradamus Horoscope
Time Out of Mind
A Party to Die For

Autobiography

Ghosts of King Solomon's Mines

Biography

Just the One: The Wives and Times of Jeffrey Bernard
James Herriot: The Life of a Country Vet

Sorry, We're Going to Have to Let You Go

GRAHAM LORD

A *Warner* Book

First published in Great Britain in 1999
by Little, Brown and Company

This edition published by Warner Books in 1999

A CIP catalogue record for this book
is available from the British Library.

ISBN 0 7515 2011 X

Typeset in Janson by
Palimpsest Book Production Ltd,
Polmont, Stirlingshire
Printed and bound in Great Britain by
Clays Ltd, St Ives plc

Warner Books
A Division of
Little, Brown and Company (UK)
Brettenham House
Lancaster Place
London WC2E 7EN

For Mandy

with love and admiration

CONTENTS

PART ONE

CHAPTER 1

The Wrinkly

Peter Hallam stood on the patio in his thin summer dressing-gown, sipping his orange juice and sniffing the air. He sighed with pleasure. Nothing at all could ever go wrong on a day like this. This was the sort of day that was built for memories.

It was eight o'clock on a beautiful summer Sunday morning, and already the dawn was promising a breathless day. Fudge padded towards him across the paving-stones, panting and wagging his tail. The air was as still and clear as a mirror. Jezebel stalked away from him across the little lawn, carrying her tail as high as a banner, paddling in the dew. On the trellis beside the kitchen door the honeysuckle flirted with the rose and teased it with its fragrance. Sunlight glinted purple on the water-lilies in the pond, touching the fat goldfish with a hint of bronze and glistening on the damp spiders' webs that stitched the shrubs together.

Hallam took a deep breath. The air tasted sweet, of pine and petals. He felt like singing. He wanted to hug the world. How good it was, so good, to be alive.

Fudge pressed his wet nose against his hand and licked his fingers. In the bushes beyond the little greenhouse Jezebel was shadow-boxing with a lilac bush. *What have I done to deserve so much good luck?* He looked and felt much younger than forty-five. Strangers refused to believe that he had two big teenagers. He loved his wife and he had for twenty-two years and they still made love every Sunday night and sometimes on Wednesdays too. He adored their sixteen-year-old daughter, Susie, and the way she sparkled when she smiled at him. He enjoyed his job, his games of golf and tennis, the swimming, gardening, the pontoon and poker school on Saturday afternoons, the weekend lunches with friends. He envied no one, not even the rich, even though he knew that he was never likely to be rich himself. Who needed to be rich? He needed only to have enough. So his house was undistinguished, just an ordinary little suburban box, but why should that matter? It was home. His closest friends – Jim Donaldson, Pinky Porter, Bob Lambert – were as warm and close as any friends could be. His colleagues respected him, acquaintances liked him. He made people laugh. His wife was proud of him. What more did any man need? So what if his routine was predictable? So what? It made him feel warm and safe, the familiarity of it, the ordinariness. Life was a joyous gift and he was grateful for it.

There were flaws in Hallam's life, of course. It was difficult sometimes to appreciate fully the hidden charms of his glowering nineteen-year-old son Matthew, who had decided two years previously to stop smiling and to dedicate himself instead to a lifelong career of idleness. And there was Hallam's mother-in-law, Jenny's mother, Monica Partridge, a tough old bird aged seventy-one going on fifteen, who had come to stay for a couple of weeks a year ago and still showed no sign of moving out of the spare bedroom.

But what were two little niggles against the great good fortune that graced every other aspect of his life? Other men all over the world were cursed with wives they disliked, bosses they hated, jobs they loathed, colleagues they despised, disloyal friends and faithless lovers, enemies who made their lives a misery. Millions were tortured daily by loneliness, depression, pain, poverty, hunger, hurricanes, disease. Ninety-nine point nine per cent of the population of the world would envy him if they knew of his existence. So why had God been quite so kind to him? Perhaps he had been a saint in some previous life and this was his reward.

He touched wood hurriedly, the garden table on the patio, to appease the pagan gods. But maybe the gods were still asleep that lovely summer day.

The greenhouse winked at the rising sun. Jezebel danced out from behind the little compost heap and strutted back towards the patio, leaving damp pawprints across the lawn.

It was going to be a glorious day. Perhaps it was going to be a glorious summer.

He smiled and patted Fudge, fondling his velvet ears, and went back into the kitchen to feed the animals and to make the early-morning tea, and as the sun came up above the trees the pagan gods awoke and rubbed their eyes and stretched themselves and grinned as if they were looking for mischief.

Jenny was still asleep. He was not surprised. They had had the Donaldsons and Litherlands for dinner, and she had spent most of the day preparing for it and afterwards they had spent an hour after midnight clearing up the mess together. She must be exhausted.

He gazed at her for a moment, savouring the fact that she did not know he was there. Her essence was somewhere else, beyond his reach. He looked at her, relishing the quiet rhythm of her breathing. She's still so beautiful, he thought, somehow so pure even though she's forty-two. She was lying on her side like a child, with one hand raised like a benediction on the pillow beside her head: a strong hand with capable fingers yet when they touched him, even now, even after twenty-two years, his skin tingled. The lines of middle age had started to track across her brow, wrinkles ambushed the edges of her eyes and tiny crimson veins fluttered like butterflies across her cheek. But why should they make any difference? She was still the woman he had always loved ever since that first startling glimpse of her so long ago when suddenly he had known without any doubt that he wanted to spend the rest of his life with her. Her hair was tousled dark and fine across the pillow, hints of silver glinting here and there amid the strands. He placed the cup of tea gently on her bedside table and bent towards her. He kissed the corner of her mouth. It was damp. He wanted to climb inside her, into her body, into her head. He wanted to clamber into her dream and share her fantasy. She smelt delicious. He had always loved the way she smelt. She smelt of happiness.

She moved on to her back and groaned softly. 'Pete?'

He smoothed her brow with his fingers. 'And who else were you expecting, I'd like to know?'

'Mmmm.' She smiled. 'Nice.'

'Tea.'

'Lovely.'

'So are you,' he said.

Her eyelids flickered. She looked at him with eyes as slow and soft as chocolate.

'Just stay where you are,' he said. 'There's no hurry. It's Sunday. I'll bring you breakfast in bed and then I'll do Monica's and mine.'

She sighed and smiled. 'I don't deserve you,' she said.

He saw himself reflected in her eyes. He hoped that when he had to die it would be before she did. He could not bear to think of life without her. But neither could he bear to think of her alone and vulnerable. He tried not to think of it: Death would find them soon enough without him anticipating it.

He kissed her eyelids.

She looked suddenly haunted, as though she had just read his thought, as lovers do eventually.

'I love you so much,' he said.

Susie was away, spending the weekend with a schoolfriend in the country, so he carried just one cup of tea upstairs for Monica along with the scandalous Sunday tabloid that she insisted on having delivered every week. Today's huge front-page headline shrieked about some unfortunate actor who had been having a secret affair with his best friend's wife. Why should anyone want to read about it? Who cared, except for the three or four people most closely involved? How odd it was that the newspapers seemed to be at their grubbiest on the one day of the week that was meant to be holy.

The stairs creaked as he mounted them.

He knocked at Monica's door.

'Cuckoo!' she called from inside, as she always did. 'Is that you, Peter?'

Who the hell does the old bat think it is?

He opened the door and entered her room. It stank of tired gin fumes and dead cheroot butts. She was sitting up in bed with a board across her knees, doing a jigsaw, a tiny figure smoking yet another cheroot and wearing her leopardskin hat, a pair of matching leopardskin gloves, a pink chiffon scarf tied tightly under her chin, a strip of sticking plaster between her eyebrows and an orange tracksuit top.

'Why do you wear a hat and gloves in bed?' he had asked her once.

'In case I die in the night, of course,' she had said.

The real reason was probably to keep her warm as she and Jezebel rode a broomstick high above the rooftops every night, surfing the icy skies on silver shafts of moonlight.

The chiffon scarf, she had once explained, was to tighten the chin and prevent the development of flabby jowls; the sticking plaster between the eyebrows to stretch the forehead and smooth away the possibility of frown lines. She seemed completely unconcerned that neither measure had been successful: her jowls and frown lines were exactly what you would expect on the face of a woman of seventy-one.

She beamed at him with an expression of delighted discovery. 'It *is* you!' she exclaimed, with apparent amazement, as though she had expected instead the arrival of the Dalai Lama, a delegation of Japanese Sumo wrestlers and the entire brass section of the Boston Philharmonic Orchestra.

It would have been pointless to ask her why she always seemed so surprised to see him. Had he done so she would probably have answered with some crushingly unexpected reply. He had once asked her why she stuck strips of sticky tape over the holes of the electricity power points in her room. She had looked at him as though he were a moron. 'To stop the electricity leaking out, of course,' she had said.

'Morning, Monica,' he said. 'Tea. And your revolting scandal rag.'

He handed her the cup and placed the paper on the bedside table beside the overflowing ashtray and half a dozen bottles of different sorts of pills. She swallowed so many pills each day – uppers, downers, heart-starters, bladder-stoppers – that she could have opened a chemist's shop of her own.

'Three spoons?' she said suspiciously.

'I always give you three spoons,' he said. 'You know I do. I'm amazed you haven't got cavities in every tooth.'

'Just old wives' tales,' she said.

'What?'

'Things like that, about sugar being bad for you. It's nonsense. They're always going on about things being bad for you: sugar, booze, fags, meat, sex. Never did me any harm.'

She gave a filthy laugh. It sounded like a diesel truck starting up on a cold morning.

'What about your Mad Old Cow Disease?' he said.

She gave him one of her Looks. 'You catch that from your in-laws,' she said.

She stubbed out her cheroot and peered suspiciously into the cup of tea. She sniffed it, as she always did.

He folded his arms and watched her. 'Yes, I've put some rat poison in it today,' he said. 'Yesterday I tried arsenic but obviously that didn't work so if you're still around tomorrow I'm going to try some weed-killer.'

She gazed at him with an angelic expression. Beneath the brim of the leopardskin hat her pale blue eyes were bottomless and disconcertingly translucent, as though they had seen everything that there was to be seen in the world. She smiled sweetly. 'You wouldn't dare,' she said.

'Oh no? And what makes you think that?'

'I'd come back and haunt you.'

'Only at night,' he said. 'At least we'd have the days to ourselves.'

She adopted her martyr's expression. 'You ought to be kind to me,' she said. 'I'm seventy-four.'

'I'm always kind to you. I've just brought you a cup of tea and the Sunday paper, and now I'm going to cook you an unforgettable breakfast. What more do you want?'

'A glass of champagne would be nice.'

'So would a million pounds. And you know very well that you're only seventy-one.'

'It's not polite to discuss a lady's age in front of her.' She nodded towards the plant pot on the table by the window. 'Say good morning to Hank.'

He glanced across the room. The cactus sat morosely in a pot of pebbles on the table. Its spines bristled. It did not look happy.

'Don't be ridiculous,' he said.

'Go on, Peter, don't be a brute,' she said. 'Be nice to him. He's not feeling himself this morning.'

'I'm very glad to hear it, considering the number of pricks he's got.'

'What?'

'Never mind.'

'Be nice. Hank's had a bad night. He needs to be loved.'

'He needs to be back home in Arizona, where he belongs, not cooped up here in a fuggy, smoke-filled room with you.'

She looked hurt. 'Don't be horrid. He loves me. He told me. I saved him from a lonely life in the desert.'

'Has he also told you that he has a serious hangover every morning because of all the gin you give him every night?'

'Nonsense. Arizonans are renowned for being able to hold their liquor.'

'Not when they're only eighteen inches high and they drink a third of a bottle of gin a day.'

'Now you're being a bore. Don't exaggerate.'

'I'm not. The level in the gin bottle seems to drop by several inches every day.'

'It's this heat. It evaporates.' She sniffed and tightened the scarf under her chin. 'I only give Hank a drop or two. He needs his little treats. It's terribly dry being a cactus. And I have to hide him in here with me: he's on the run from the police, you know.'

'What on earth are you talking about?'

'Hank. He's an illegal immigrant, isn't he? There are laws against bringing illegal cacti into the country. I smuggled him in past Immigration in a plastic bag. Now that's quite enough about Hank. He'll be getting a swollen head if we talk about him any more. *Pas devant le cactus.*'

'I bet that's not a proper French word.'

'Oh yes it is, Mr Clever: Brigitte told me.'

'Brigitte?'

'Bardot.'

'You knew Brigitte Bardot?'

'But of course.'

'Come off it, Monica.'

'I did. In St Trop in the fifties. We were the first to take our tops off on the beach.'

True? False? Who knows? Maybe not even Monica herself.

She reached for a piece of paper on the bedside table. 'Now I need some literary advice,' she said.

'Not another limerick, please.'

'Of course. They come to me in the middle of the night. I suddenly wake up and there's a new one in my head, all neat and tidy: tee-tiddly-tiddly-tum, tee-tiddly-tiddly-tum, tee-tiddly-tum, tee-tiddly-tum, tee-tiddly-tiddly-tum.'

'So the limericks are as tiddly as the cactus.'

'Now you're being facetious.'

'No one will ever publish them, you know, Monica.'

'Of course they will. This book is going to make me a fortune.'

'They won't. Most of them are far too filthy.'

'Rubbish, they're just a little *risqué*. That's the whole point of limericks: they have to be naughty otherwise they don't work. Now, listen to this and tell me what you think.'

'Not now, Monica. I've got to go. I've got a lot to do.'

'Nonsense, it's Sunday. Just listen to this and give me your opinion:

'There was a young feller named Price
Who dabbled in all kinds of vice.
He had virgins and boys
And mechanical toys
And on Mondays he meddled with mice.'

Hallam laughed. 'That's disgusting,' he said.

She beamed. Her eyes glittered. 'Do you really think so?'

'Yes. But you can't put that sort of thing in a book, Monica.'

'Why not?'

'We'd never be able to look the neighbours in the eye again.'

She patted the top of the leopardskin hat. 'Stuff the neighbours. Po-faced lot. It would do them good to shake them up a bit. People need a bit of a laugh. There are far too many misery-gutses wandering around these days with long faces not smoking or drinking or laughing or eating meat or having sex or reading rude limericks. They need cheering up. I'm doing clerihews too, you know.'

'What on earth is a clerihew?'

'They're wacky little four-line verses about famous people that rhyme but don't scan. I've just done one about the Queen.'

'Dear God, you're not going in for *lèse-majesté* as well now, I hope?'

'Certainly not. HM would love this one. Listen . . .'

'Not now, Monica.'

'Elizabeth the Second
Was resigned to her fate when Destiny beckoned,
But Phil the Greek
Thought it was a hell of a bloody cheek.'

'Monica! You can't put that in a book. They'll hang you for treason.'

'Stop being such a wimp, Peter, there's a dear. Now, what are you going to do me for breakfast?'

'Egg and bacon? Poached eggs on toast? Scrambled?'

She cocked her head to one side like a wary sparrow and gave him a sharp look. 'I'll have a kipper,' she said triumphantly.

'There aren't any kippers.'

She flirted with him. 'Couldn't you go and buy one?'

'It's Sunday.'

'The Pakistani will be open.'

'He doesn't sell kippers.'

'The supermarket, then.'

'It doesn't open till nine.'

She nodded decisively. 'I'll wait till nine, then.'

Hallam grunted. 'Monica,' he said, 'I love you dearly but I am not going to go out early on a Sunday morning to drive for ten minutes to the supermarket and then to stand in a queue for another ten minutes just to buy you a kipper.'

She batted an eyelid at him. 'You could get two,' she simpered. 'I could always manage the other one tomorrow.'

'I'm doing poached eggs,' he said firmly. 'They'll be ready in about ten minutes.'

She sighed. She looked very small propped up on her pillows. The leopardskin hat drooped over one eyebrow. 'I'm only a poor old widow woman with no one to protect me,' she said.

'One egg or two?'

'Nobody cares about me,' she said.

'One egg or two?'

'I ought to be dead, I suppose. Everyone else is. I'll have two.' She reached for the newspaper on the bedside table. 'I wonder what my stars say today.'

'Twinkle,' he said, 'I expect.'

The curtains were still drawn in the living room and a pungent odour of sweat and cheap scent anointed the gloom. Matthew was asleep and snoring loudly on the sofa, wearing shoulder-length hair, one earring, a mangy sort of fur coat and designer stubble. In the sixties you might have taken him for a pop millionaire but now he just looked ridiculous. Two of his friends were curled up in the armchairs like foetuses. They smelt of unwashed feet.

'He's just going through a phase,' Jenny had suggested nervously, but the phase had lasted nearly two years and showed no sign of passing.

'I'm not gay, you know,' Matthew had said on one

occasion. 'I just like wearing girls' things sometimes. Okay? God, you're so *judgemental.*'

'But you look so – *silly*, Matt.'

Matthew had looked him up and down. 'Not half as silly as you look in a suit and tie.'

Hallam opened the curtains. Sunlight stabbed the carpet. He released a couple of windows. A gasp of fresh air hovered by the window-sill and retreated. The room was littered with discarded clothes: a couple of donkey jackets, a pair of underpants, three socks, two stained pairs of trainers, a sweater, a peaked cap, a comic, several old sweet wrappers. Scattered across the coffee table were several dirty cups and plates, a knife coated with butter and jam, a carpet of toast crumbs, two sticky brown patches of spilt coffee, a hard piece of dead chewing gum and a jagged assortment of horny yellow toenails.

Matthew stirred on the sofa and farted. Lipstick smudged the stubble on his chin. Dear God, thought Hallam, what woman in her right mind would want to kiss Matt? Even a nymphomaniac with defective eysight would be repelled by the smell.

'Tea,' said Hallam.

Matthew opened one eye, closed it again and grunted. 'Tea!' he muttered. 'Christ!' He broke wind again. 'Sod off,' he mumbled, 'and close the bloody curtains.'

Hallam took a deep breath. He had never been a violent man but one day Matt was going to go too far.

'I'll thank you to mind your manners when you talk to me,' he said.

Matthew snorted, rolled over on the sofa and faced away from him.

'I'm getting breakfast,' said Hallam. 'Poached eggs on toast. If you and your mates want some I shall expect to see you at the table in about ten minutes. If not, I want you up and out of this room by nine o'clock, please, and I want it left clean and tidy. It's an absolute mess, Matt. You've got your own bedroom for sleeping.'

'Ach, don't be so bloody anal,' growled Matt. 'It's only a bit of mess.'

'In future I'll thank you to make your mess somewhere else. I mean it, Matt. Ten minutes, that's all.'

Hallam left the room and went into the kitchen to prepare the breakfast.

There was silence for a moment in the living room.

'Bourgeois prat,' said Matthew.

Hallam gave Jenny breakfast in bed: egg, toast, marmalade, orange juice, an apple, another cup of tea.

She sat up, protesting, as he set the tray across her knees.

'You deserve it,' he said. 'You were at it all day yesterday. You didn't stop. Just take it easy.'

He ate with Monica at the kitchen table. She was wearing scarlet lipstick, faded blue jeans, bright red trainers and a yellow T-shirt decorated with a clenched fist and the slogan THE OLD ONES ARE THE BEST ONES. She smelt of nicotine and mothballs but she ate, as always, as though she had not eaten for months, doggedly chewing her daily sandwich of raw onions and then putting the eggs and toast away as though she were a builder's navvy. How could someone so small eat so much? There was never much wrong with her appetite. In fact there was never much wrong with any part of her, even though she drank and smoked like a navvy too. How was it that some people could ignore all the rules and still have so much energy? he wondered. She must have been overdosing on HRT for years. Sometimes he felt quite exhausted just looking at her.

The sun splashed gold across the kitchen floor, promising a perfect day. The air outside was absolutely still, as though the morning were waiting for something. A heavy silence drifted from the living room, punctuated suddenly by a rumbling snore. How could they waste such a beautiful morning? He would give Matt and his scrofulous friends another ten minutes, he thought, and then he would roust them out and send them packing. He hated having to play the heavy father. Why should he have to do it, to be forced to play the ogre? Why didn't Matt understand that he and his friends were simply not entitled to annex the entire house and to leave every room in it looking like a rubbish dump? And why were they so *disgruntled* all the time, as though the world had done them down and owed them something? Matt and Susie were so different that it was barely credible they were descended from the same parents. Sometimes Hallam wondered whether Matthew might have been the unfortunate result of an unsavoury fling Jenny had had twenty years ago with some recidivist or tramp. What other explanation could there be? Yet Susie was a constant delight: always smiling, cheerful, keen to make other people happy. Susie was Jenny all over again. When Susie smiled at him the sun came out in his head.

Monica pushed away her plate, poured herself a second cup of coffee, lit another cheroot and took a hearty swig from her usual morning glass of port and brandy, which she drank at breakfast every day 'to prevent diarrhoea'. Hallam had never quite liked to ask whether it worked.

She blew a cloud of smoke. 'And where is Madam?' she enquired.

'Sorry?'

'Her ladyship. Your dearly beloved wife.'

'She's having breakfast in bed.'

'Oh dear. Is she ill?'

'No, she's just having a lie-in.'

Monica made a rubbery noise with her lips. 'You're far too good to her, you know,' she said, blowing more smoke.

'What?'

'You spoil her. Women don't appreciate it, you know.

They start to get suspicious if their husbands are too kind to them.'

'Come off it, Monica. All I've done is give her breakfast in bed.'

'Women think their men are having affairs and feeling guilty and trying to compensate if they treat them too nicely. Or they begin to suspect that they've married a wimp, which is even worse.'

'What balls!'

Monica sniffed. 'You'll see,' she said. 'Don't say I didn't warn you. Women need to be dominated. They hate being put on a pedestal.'

She reached for the leisure section of the second Sunday paper. She rustled her way through a few of the pages, was silent for a moment, and then gave a whoop of delight.

'Listen to this!' she said. 'My stars! It says, "This week your forceful, dominant personality will sweep everything before you."'

Hallam looked glum. 'What a depressing prospect.'

'Don't be cheeky. Here, listen to this: "You have the potential to challenge the universe and change your eternal destiny. Your every wish will be granted."'

'Unless you want kippers for breakfast,' he said, 'in which case you will be told to go jump in the lake.'

She gave him an old-fashioned Look.

'Who writes all this astrological cobblers?' he said. 'The same people who make up mottoes and jokes for Christmas crackers, I suppose. Here, why don't you have a go at it yourself, Monica? You could do crackers with dirty limericks in them, and cleri-things. You could start a new fashion: filthy crackers for Christmas Day. Yes! And pornographic carols: "Oh Come, All Ye Faithful"; that sort of thing.'

Monica sniffed. 'You've got no soul,' she said. 'I feel sorry for you.'

She returned to the paper, puffed at her cheroot, swigged

her coffee and suddenly cackled. '*Your* stars are terrible,' she said. 'Just listen to this . . .'

He rose from the table. 'I'm not listening to anything,' he said, 'and certainly not to that mumbo-jumbo. I'm off.' He carried the dirty plates towards the sink. 'I'm going to play tennis,' he said.

She looked up from the paper. 'You'll be going past the chemist, then.'

'It's Sunday, Monica.'

'It's Sunday *morning*,' she corrected him. 'They're always open on Sunday morning. For emergencies.'

He sighed. 'Oh, very well. What emergency is this, then? What do you want me to get?'

'Thank you, Peter. How very sweet of you to offer. I need some haemorrhoid cream.'

'Hell's bells, I'm not going into the chemist to ask for that. They'll think—'

'Don't be so precious,' she said. 'I don't want it for my bum, it's for my eyes.'

'I beg your pardon?'

'It helps to remove the wrinkles and bags under the eyes. It shrinks the skin, you see, and tightens it.'

'Good grief, isn't that dangerous? I mean, doesn't that stuff have cortisone or something in it? If you—'

'Oh, do stop being such a wuss,' she said impatiently. 'Why is everyone so *afraid* of everything these days? Dear Lord, if we all avoided everything that might be a little bit dangerous we'd all have been dead long ago. We'd never get out of bed. Like your precious wife.'

Matthew suddenly loomed in the doorway, still wearing his old fur coat, with stubble, bleary eyes and bare feet. His hair was long and tangled and looked as if it had not been washed for weeks.

'Cor, it stinks in here,' he said, waving a hand in front of his nose. 'D'you really have to smoke so much, Gran?'

'Yes.'

'But it's disgusting.'

'At my age, Matthew, you have to do everything you can to keep the germs away,' she said. 'Tobacco kills germs better than anything else.'

'It kills you, too.'

'Not yet, it hasn't, and I don't intend to let it. And they say that smoking stops you getting Alzheimer's disease.'

'Only because smoking kills you before you're old enough to get Alzheimer's,' said Hallam.

'And brandy at breakfast,' said Matt, wrinkling his nose. 'Brandy's revolting anyway, but at *breakfast*.'

Monica stuck her chin out with defiance. 'Brandy is excellent for the arteries,' she said, 'as well as diarrhoea.'

'Oh, yeah?'

'Certainly. That's what Graham Greene told me, anyway.'

'Graham Greene?' said Hallam. 'The author?'

'Of course. Who else? Dear Graham.' She sighed and gave a little private smile. 'Happy memories.'

'You knew *Graham Greene*?'

'Intimately.'

'You've never mentioned him before.'

'Why should I? One doesn't go around gossiping about one's famous friends. That would be vulgar.'

'You're always dropping names about famous people you say you once knew.'

'I am not.'

'Yes, you are. Last week you said you knew Laurence Olivier.'

'Well, of course I did. Larry was a great old chum. In Dorking.'

'*Dorking?* What the hell was he doing in Dorking?'

'Larry was born in Dorking,' she said. 'I knew him for years. And Viv.'

'Viv?'

'Vivien. Leigh. His wife.'

'There you are, you see, you're at it again. And last month you said you knew Francis Bacon.'

'Well, not the philosopher, Peter, just the painter.'

'Of course you didn't know the blasted philosopher, Monica. Not even you are quite ancient enough for that. The philosopher died more than three hundred years ago, for God's sake.'

'Well, there you are, then.'

'Is there bacon for breakfast?' said Matthew.

'You really expect us to believe that you knew Francis Bacon?'

'And why not?'

'A bacon sarnie would be great,' said Matthew.

'How did you meet him, then?'

'In Soho in the fifties. We used to get pissed together in the French and the Swiss and the Colony club with Dylan Thomas, Dan Farson, Jeff Bernard, all that lot. And Muriel Belcher. Dear old Muriel: what a bitch she was.'

'Dear God, so now it's Dylan Thomas as well, is it?'

She stared at him with those pale, piercing blue eyes. Was she telling the truth? Was she lying? Fantasising? Was her memory beginning to go? And how would he ever find out?

'Yes,' she said, 'and he wrote a poem for me once as well.'

He shook his head and made for the door.

'Here!' said Matthew, aggrieved. 'Where's my breakfast, then?'

'Still inside the eggshells,' said Hallam.

'But you said you were doing breakfast. With bacon.'

'I was. Half an hour ago.'

'Charming. That's really charming. So I've got to get it myself, have I?'

'Not at all. We couldn't possibly allow you to go to so

much trouble. I'm sure your grandmother would like nothing better than to do it for you.'

She rustled the paper and took another slug of port and brandy. 'I wouldn't bank on it,' she said. 'And don't forget the haemorrhoid cream.'

'You got piles?' said Matthew. He scratched his crotch. 'I thought only gays got piles.' He sniggered. 'Here, you're not gay, Gran, are you?'

She looked up from her paper and gazed at him with cold appraisal. 'No, Matthew, I am not gay, but if all men looked like you then I probably would be.'

Hallam grinned.

'Sod breakfast, then,' said Matthew. 'I never really wanted any, anyway.'

Hallam stopped in the doorway. 'Monica,' he said, 'if you're thinking of helping Jenny to get the lunch, go easy on the eye of bat and tongue of toad.'

'I never use toad,' she said. 'I always think spleen of lizard is so much more effective.'

The sky was cloudless as he drove the three miles to the tennis club. The roads were almost empty so early on a Sunday morning, the trees lush. He loved this time of the day, especially at weekends when people were still in bed and the world was fresh and almost his alone. A breeze caressed his naked arm as he propped it out of the driver's window. The metal was already warm on his skin. A dog lay sunbathing on the pavement. A child's laughter drifted across a hedge. What could go wrong on a day like this? He hummed to himself as the car swung into the club driveway, the tyres crunching across the gravel towards the lawns. '*Oh, what a beautiful morning, Oh, what a beautiful day!*' The flower-beds in front of the clubhouse shimmered with whites and yellows. The steps gleamed a deep red.

Oh God, it's good to be alive, he thought.

Pinky Porter spotted his arrival and emerged from the clubhouse as pink as ever, waving his racquet. 'Fantastic day,' he called.

'Magnificent.'

'You're a bit late, Pete.'

'Sorry. Mother-in-law.'

Pinky looked mournful. 'Ah. Well,' he said. 'No contest, then. Good game yesterday afternoon.'

'Only because you were banker. How much did you win in the end?'

'About sixty quid.'

'Half of it from poor old Charlie, I think, you jammy devil. I think we'll settle for a mild game of Canasta next week.'

They played tennis for an hour and a half – 6–4, 6–7, 3–0 – before they had to stop when a foursome turned up to claim the court. There were days when everything seemed to go right with Hallam's tennis and this was one of them: his serves were fast, deep and low, his volleys sure, his killer backhand as true and straight down the tramline as it had ever been. His muscles sang with the warmth of physical exercise. His blood rejoiced in the harmony of body and mind. His skin tingled. Sweat ran honest down his spine. It felt good to be damp and loose.

'Good game,' panted Pinky, by now more puce than pink, as they walked back to the clubhouse. 'You're getting better, damn it! How the hell do you get *better* as you get older?'

'Just one of those lucky days.'

'Rubbish. You're actually getting *better*.' Pinky grimaced. 'Quite frankly it pisses me off.'

They showered, swam for twenty minutes in the club pool, showered again, dressed and collapsed on the terrace with a couple of early beers, slumping into wicker chairs beneath a fat white sunshade. The club was full of members now and noise and laughter, the sun high, casting stubby shadows. Pinky was back to his usual colour again, as rosy as an alcoholic's elephant, flirting with the barmaid, greeting

Barry White's wife with a kiss and a lingering pat on the bottom, winking at one of the girls in the clubhouse, following another with his eyes as she crossed towards the courts in her skimpy little white skirt and frilly knickers.

Pinky sipped his beer and shook his head. 'It's a bloody tragedy,' he said.

'What is?'

'All the gorgeous women all over the world that we'll never have time to shag.'

'I wouldn't have said that you go exactly short,' said Hallam. 'You've had more crumpet than the Tiggywinkle Tea Rooms in Turnival Street.'

'No, it's not that. It's just such an awful *waste*.'

So how did he do it? Enthusiasm, that was all: Pinky loved it, and women, and that was enough; they could never resist such dedicated eagerness. He had been married four times and divorced four times, each time for his philandering, but so successfully on the last occasion that he was now the happy recipient of monthly alimony payments from his rich fourth ex-wife and consequently extremely reluctant to marry again. He was so keen on women that it made no difference what they looked like. 'What am I supposed to do?' he said. 'They keep throwing themselves at me.' He would spend a month pursuing the ugliest of girls with such persistence that they always succumbed in the end. And he was generous too. There is nothing that turns a woman off more than meanness and you could never say Pinky was mean. Just over a year ago he had borrowed a thousand pounds from Hallam to pay off some disgruntled creditor who had started to make serious threats and he had then proceeded to fly off to Monte Carlo for the weekend with Norman Litherland's glamorous thirty-two-year-old niece. At first Hallam had been furious: it was not that he feared he would never get the money back – of course he would, Pinky was a good old friend – it was just that he felt he had been conned. And Pinky had still not paid it back. Perhaps it was time to remind him again. Whenever he had raised the matter Pinky had asked for another week or two to pay. 'Cash flow, old boy,' he had always said. 'Next month, for sure. Scout's honour.' But next month had always become the next and then the next, and Pinky was hardly broke, considering the amount of maintenance he was paid by his ex-wife. It was time he paid the money back.

But not now. Not today. Why raise something like that on such a lovely day? It was too perfect to talk about money. Hallam's skin glowed with the memory of effort, exercise, cold water. His sinews throbbed with delicious weariness. The beer tasted as if it had been brewed by a god. Not now. Some other time.

'The other half?' said Pinky.

Hallam drained his glass. 'You bet,' he said.

Oh God, it's bloody marvellous to be alive.

On his way home he stopped off at the bank to cash a cheque – how odd it was that banks were open nowadays on Sundays – and then he popped into the chemist to buy Monica's haemorrhoid cream. Back at home he parked the car in the garage, and as he walked up the path to the front door he could hear her up in her room loudly playing her old vinyl LP pop records, the scratched, crackly hits of the sixties: the Beatles, the Who, the Rolling Stones. As he approached the front door he could hear her singing along with the music in a disconcertingly gravelly voice: *I can't get no. I can't get no. I can't get no. Satisfaction. Satisfaction. SatisFACTION. SATISFACTION!*

Hallam grinned: poor old Hank must be cowering in his gravel.

Jenny was in the kitchen preparing the lunch and looking wonderful in a light summer dress. Her legs seemed to go on for ever.

He crept up behind her and put his arms around her.

She jumped. 'God, you gave me a shock.'

He pressed up against her back, feeling her buttocks soft against his groin, touching her breasts, kissing the back of her neck.

'You look wonderful, Mrs Hallam,' he said.

She smiled. 'You don't look so bad yourself, Mr Hallam,' she said, 'and now go away or we'll never get anything to eat.'

'Who cares? You'll do.'

'Get off.'

He poured three glasses of white wine and took one up to Monica along with the haemorrhoid cream. Then he sat outside on the swing-chair beside the goldfish pond with the respectable Sunday paper on his lap and Fudge lying in the shade at his feet. Matthew and his friends had disappeared, probably to the gym as usual to spend several hours punishing their bodies. It never ceased to amaze Hallam that Matt and his friends could be so scruffy and disorganised and yet so dedicated to exercise and keeping fit. With impressive self-control they pumped iron for hours, did press-ups, ran, jumped and strongly disapproved of smoking, drinking, drugs and eating meat – except for ham and bacon, which Matt had decided were not really meat at all. Yet they resented any other sort of discipline or authority, and seemed to spend half their lives asleep and the other half leaving a trail of grunge behind them wherever they went. The two sides of their lives seemed to be utterly inconsistent and illogical. Nowadays there was an entire generation of youngsters dedicated to outer filth and inner cleanliness – unlike Monica, whose body was immaculately clean but whose mind was like a sewer.

'I can't get no,' growled Monica upstairs. 'I can't get no. I can't get no.'

Hallam smiled.

Satisfaction.

Yes.

He sat in the sun and wondered whether he had ever been happier in his life. It did not seem possible.

At one thirty Jenny served one of his favourite summer lunches out on the patio: cold salmon with salad and new potatoes, a bowl of strawberries, a bottle of chilled Viognier, a creamy Brie that was leaking all over the cheeseboard; a lunch that was good enough to silence even Monica for nearly half an hour.

Afterwards Monica disappeared to her room for her afternoon rest, Jenny sat in the living room and flicked through the Sunday colour supplement, and Hallam lay on the sofa and gazed at the sunlight in her hair until he too fell asleep, warm with a glow of wine, security and contentment.

Somewhere a bee was buzzing. It sounded in his sleep like the humming of the gods.

He woke more than an hour later to find Jenny looking at him.

He blinked and stretched. 'Penny for them,' he said.

She shook her head. 'No. Nothing.'

'Come on. Why so sad?'

'Sad? I'm not sad.' She rose from the chair. 'Cup of tea?'

'Lovely.'

Later he washed the car, mowed the grass and he and Fudge did some weeding, Fudge nosing about in the flower-beds like a truffle hound as the sun began to slide down towards the river and cast pale shadows across the little lawn. At seven o'clock Susie arrived back home from her weekend away and hugged him hard and laughed, and he felt complete again. He poured the evening drinks: a vodka and lime for Jenny, gin and tonic for Monica, a Coke for Susie, a Famous Grouse for himself, and the four of them sat outside with Fudge and Jezebel stretched out and basking on the patio and they talked and talked until the sun had been swallowed by the tallest pine trees. There was still no sign of Matthew. Sometimes he disappeared for two or three days at a time, staying with friends, squatting on their sofas, making someone else's life a misery. Jenny was never happy about these absences, which came without warning and were never explained, and she always worried about Matt, but Hallam considered his sudden evaporations to be his most charming feature.

At eight o'clock Jenny and Susie served up a chilled vichyssoise, some warm French bread, a cheese soufflé, a bowl of fresh peaches, two bottles of red Château Timberlay and after supper they listened to CDs – Celine Dion, Phil Collins, Annie Lennox – while they played a game of Canasta. Hallam watched them from behind his cards: Jenny so serene, Susie grinning and making faces, Monica looking crafty as she moved the cards about surreptitiously in her hands; his family, his closest friends; even Monica, the old witch.

How lucky I am, he thought. Don't ever forget it.

They went to bed at ten o'clock, soon after the moon came up. There was still no sign of Matthew and his friends.

Hallam sighed as he slipped into bed. He held Jenny's hand. 'What a perfect day,' he said.

She wrapped her legs around his. 'Just one more thing to make it even better,' she whispered.

He relished the way she made love with him, the way they moved together on a tide of affection and lust and joy and memory. He loved the way she touched him, the feel of her, the warmth, that smell of hers, the way she kissed him, the way she whimpered. He loved the way she made him feel twenty-five again and omnipotent.

At the final moment she cried.

They were asleep when the telephone rang.

Hallam fumbled for the light-switch beside the bed. *Bugger it!* He looked blearily at the clock: 23.02.

He reached for the receiver. 'Yes?'

'Pete?'

'Yes?'

'Jim.'

Donaldson.

'Jim.'

Jim hesitated. 'Pete? Did I wake you?'

'Yes.'

'Hell, I'm sorry. I didn't think . . . It's only eleven o'clock . . .'

He propped himself up in bed. 'Don't worry.' He rubbed his eye. 'I'm awake now.'

'Hell, I'm sorry. I would have waited till the morning but I thought you should know as soon as possible.'

Hallam sat up. 'Know what? Bad news?'

Jenny stirred in the bed beside him. 'Who is it?' she muttered.

'Not . . . *bad* news. Not exactly . . .'

'What do you mean?'

'It's just . . .'

'Yes?'

'What is it?' said Jenny.

'This is off the record,' said Jim, 'but it's only fair that you should know before you go into the office tomorrow. Andy Unwin has been sacked.'

'What?'

'Andy. Bertie's just called me.'

'Hell's bells! Why?'

'Who knows? The usual thing these days, I suppose. Too old, I expect. He's fifty-seven next week. They probably think he's past it. Perhaps he is. I've been called to an emergency directors' meeting first thing tomorrow morning. Mulliken's already appointed a new MD, some thirty-one-year-old whizz-kid called Skudder.'

'Thirty-one!'

'They're taking them straight out of kindergarten these days.'

'Who the hell is he?'

'Jason Skudder. I don't know much about him. He used to be at Fitzgerald and Parsons, some sort of whizz-kid trouble-shooter. Bit of a shit, they say. Ruthless. Unprincipled. Bertie says Skudder wants to get rid of everyone who's over forty-five.'

A pagan drumbeat echoed at the back of Hallam's mind.

'Apparently Skudder says that anyone over forty-five is past it. He calls them wrinklies.'

Hallam hesitated. 'Them?' he said. 'What do you mean, *them*? I'm forty-five myself.'

The telephone line was silent.

'My God,' said Jim. 'So you are. I'd forgotten.'

'So where the hell does that leave me?'

'You don't look even forty,' said Jim. 'You look as if you're still in your thirties. You'll be OK. Of *course* you'll be OK.' He sounded hearty. 'You'll be fine. Of *course* you will. Don't worry about it. Must go. Let you get your beauty sleep. Sorry to wake you but I thought you'd want to know.'

'Yes. Thanks, Jim. Thanks.'

'See you in the office in the morning.'

Hallam replaced the receiver.

'What is it?' said Jenny. 'Trouble?'

'No, no,' said Hallam. 'Nothing at all. Just an early meeting tomorrow. Go back to sleep.'

He switched off the light and laid his head on the pillow. His heart was pounding inexplicably as though he had just run a mile.

Wrinklies. He calls them wrinklies.

Them?

Not them. Us.

Something seemed to stir in the darkness, the quiet clink of a hoof on stone, a shadow flitting across the window.

He turned over in the bed and moved towards Jenny and wrapped his arm around her.

'I love you so much,' he said, but she was already asleep.

Somewhere in his imagination he thought he could hear a distant voice calling him.

CHAPTER 2

The Whizz-Kid

Andy Unwin had always been renowned as an early riser so Hallam had no hesitation in telephoning him at seven o'clock to commiserate about his sudden departure from the company.

'That's jolly nice of you,' said Unwin breezily, 'but there's really no need to feel sorry for me.'

He sounded surprisingly cheerful. He sounded like a man who has just collected a very fat cheque. He probably had.

'I'd been meaning to take it a bit easier soon anyway,' he said. 'Now I can play golf every day. No more endless dreary meetings or moronic memos from Willie Mulliken. Just eighteen holes every day and long lazy lunches. I'm going to love it.'

'We'll miss you.'

'Nice of you, but I doubt it. Nobody's indispensable. Just watch your own back, Peter, that's all. I'm told this Skudder bugger is a vicious, underhand little bastard. Be careful.'

'I will.'

Unwin chuckled. 'Skudder,' he said. 'Unusual name. German, I suppose, or Scandinavian. Nasty, anyway. Skudder, half skunk, half adder. Most appropriate, if all the rumours are true. Not that you'll have anything to worry about. You're far too good at your job for that. Even a fully paid-up bastard like Skudder wouldn't dare to try to get rid of you. The directors would be up in arms. They wouldn't allow it.'

'Andy . . .'

'Yes?'

'Thanks . . . you know . . . for everything. Over the years. It's been a privilege to work for you.'

'Kind of you to say so. Feeling's mutual. I've been lucky to have you on my staff. Now, I really must go. Caroline wants me to take her off to the Caribbean for a couple of weeks to get over the shock.'

'Good idea. I envy you.'

'She's rather upset about it all, actually. Funny, that. I don't give a damn but she's taken it rather badly. I suppose women like being the wife of the managing director – gives them some sort of status. Anyway, I need to fix the tickets. Mulliken's going to give me a farewell lunch in a month's time, so maybe I'll see you then. In the meantime, good luck. And watch your back.'

Matthew and two of his friends had returned at some time during the night and were asleep once again in the darkened living room, which rumbled with the sound of snoring. Hallam felt a surge of irritation. Who were these people? He didn't even know their names. Once, when Matthew had brought three of them home one night, he had asked him what their names were. Matthew had sniggered: 'Mark, Luke and John,' he had said. But whoever the hell they were, why didn't they have homes of their own? Why couldn't they go and annoy someone else's family? And how did they manage to collect the dole yet make no effort at all to find a job? Nowadays the unemployed were meant to sign a Jobseeker's Agreement promising to look actively for work and to be flexible about the kind of work they were prepared to do, and they were supposed to keep records and evidence of their efforts. And if they were still unemployed after six months on the dole they were supposed to go on serious retraining courses. The bad old days when scroungers had been able to live for years on unemployment benefit were meant to be over, yet somehow Matt and his friends had managed to find huge loopholes in the system. How did they get away with it? he had asked Matt once. Matt had smirked and tapped the side of his head with his finger. 'Brains,' he had said.

And why did they always come back here to empty the fridge and fill the house with junk? He opened the door and peered into the room. It stank of sour cooking smells, cold congealed curry, the sweet whiff of something sickly. It looked like a doss-house. Shadowy figures were draped over the chairs, one was curled up on the floor, which was littered with discarded items of clothing, the coffee-table with half-empty Chinese takeaway cartons, empty fizzy-drink cans, dirty mugs. Matt was on the sofa as usual but this time he had a waif-like figure tucked into him. Male? Female? Who could tell? The young all looked the same to him, these days, as though they were of a different race.

Hallam was really going to have to put his foot down: enough was enough. But not now. He had to get to work. He did not have time for a row with Matthew now.

He showered, shaved and drove to the office an hour earlier than usual, telling Jenny only that Unwin had been sacked. Why worry her unnecessarily? There was nothing to worry about yet. He *was* good at his job, damned good, so why should anyone want to sack him? But there were other people in his department who might well be vulnerable. George Pringle was nearly fifty and poor old Elsie Benson was fifty-four and a natural victim: even the droopy way she walked suggested that she was on her way to the scaffold. Yet both were invaluable to the department: their knowledge of the company over the past thirty years was astonishing and either of them could lay hands on any file within a couple of minutes. He had to protect them. If necessary he would fight to keep them.

But who would speak up for *him* if the going got really nasty? Good men in their forties were being fired nowadays all over the country to make way for younger people, and it did not seem to matter how good they were at their jobs. Younger staff were much less expensive – their wages and overheads were lower, their perks and expectations fewer, their pension contributions much smaller – and the fact that they knew so much less as well seemed to make no difference. Bosses nowadays were only too happy to sack highly experienced, hard-working, middle-aged employees and to replace each of them with a couple of cheap, raw youngsters. One plus one no longer equals two. In the world of modern corporate accountancy 1 + 1 = 1.

Some of the directors might try to protect him if Skudder began to cull the middle-aged staff, but how successful would they be? Jim Donaldson would speak up for him, of course: Jim was an old friend. But who else? Amanda Young? Perhaps. Paul Rampton? Maybe. Bertie Small? Doubtful. And after that . . . the others would do whatever they were told if they felt that their own jobs were threatened. Hallam had no illusions: if the new MD wanted to get rid of him he could be out by the end of the day.

The car park was already packed with the directors' company vehicles: Jim's Rover, Amanda's Clio, Bertie's small Merc, Paul's Granada. Parked in Andy Unwin's space beside the entrance to the building was a newcomer: a dark green, hand-built Morgan with a broad, polished leather strap across the bonnet. The new MD's car. A Morgan. Of course. Typical.

Hallam grabbed his briefcase and loped up the front steps, taking them two at a time. Just inside the swing doors the security guard was sitting in a glass cage, looking morose, like an elderly unemployed tart in Amsterdam.

'Morning, Mr Hallam,' he said.

'Morning, Ron.'

The guard emerged from his glass box, shuffling sideways like a crab. 'Met the new boss yet, sir?'

'Not yet. Is he in already?'

Ron nodded. ''E come in 'alf an hour since, sir,' he said eagerly. 'Gaw! Never seen nothing like it.'

'Yes?'

'Young geezer, no more'n his thirties, but he's bald, sir, only a youngster but bald as a coot, like one of them skinheads. And 'e were wearin' a cloak with a red lining, and 'e 'ad a walking stick with a silver 'andle.' He sucked his teeth like a plumber about to give an outrageous estimate. 'And 'e wears a bow-tie, sir, 'e does.'

'Ah!'

Ron lowered his voice and leaned forward confidentially. 'A *spotted* bow-tie, sir!' he said, with distaste. 'And a matching waistcoat. A *yellow* spotted bow-tie and waistcoat, an' all.'

'Thank you, Ron.'

Ron looked over his shoulder. 'An' 'e don't talk proper neither, sir, nor does 'e. Not like what gentlemen does.'

'*Thank* you, Ron.'

'Thank you, sir.'

Hallam ran up the stairs to the second floor and took the left-hand corridor towards his office. Thirty-one years old. A green Morgan. And a cloak, for God's sake, and a silver-topped cane. Not good news. And a yellow spotted bow-tie, and a matching waistcoat. Not good at all.

His office door was unlocked.

He frowned. His door was always locked at night and only he, Doreen and the security staff had keys.

He pushed the door open.

She was already there, squatting on her heels in front of a filing cabinet.

'Doreen!' he said. 'What are you doing in so early?'

She stood and smiled. 'Morning, Peter,' she said cheerily. 'I thought you might need me in a bit earlier than usual, what with the new boss arriving and everything.'

He gazed at her. 'You knew? About Skudder?'

'Well . . . yes.'

'How the hell did you know?'

She blushed.

'When?' he said.

'Yesterday morning. I got a phone call. A friend.'

'I see.'

'Was it meant to be secret?'

Hallam dumped his briefcase on his desk. 'Hardly,' he said, with a trace of irritation. 'Everyone else seems to have known about it except for me.'

'Should I have phoned you?' she asked anxiously. She was so eager to please. She had always been a superb secretary. 'I'm sorry,' she said. 'I assumed you would know already.'

'Never mind,' he said. He shook his head. 'It's nothing to worry about. It's just . . .' He laughed. '. . . a bit funny, that's all. Here I am the head of the sales department and everyone else in the building, from the office boy to the tea lady, seems to know that the managing director has been sacked before I do. I expect the telephonists have known all about it for weeks. The night caretaker probably even had a hand in choosing the new MD.'

She giggled. She had a nice giggle: it made him happy to hear it, like water gurgling down a plughole. They had been together for nearly twenty years. It was almost a marriage.

'Sorry to be a bit bolshie,' he said, 'and thanks for coming in so early. You're right. There'll be a lot to do today and I really appreciate it. Have you seen him yet? Skudder?'

'Yes. I bumped into him on the stairs ten minutes ago.'

'And?'

'He's completely bald.'

'So I'm told.'

'I've never seen anyone quite so bald. You know what I mean?'

'No.'

'Well, there's not even a hint of hair anywhere. His skull's like a billiard ball. It glistens. He's almost *aggressively* bald. And he wears a yellow bow-tie and a yellow waistcoat.'

'I know.'

'I thought he was a new messenger boy at first. He talks like some flash little git from Whitechapel, all glottal stops and dropped Hs and Gs and swallowed syllables. You know: instead of bottle he says baa-ooo, instead of house he says arse. Then he commended me for being in the office so early and I suddenly realised who he must be. His praise was so over-the-top it was quite embarrassing. He wanted to know my name, where I live, whether I'm married, how much I'm paid, who I work for, what I think of you, what I thought of Andy Unwin, everything.'

'Bloody hell!'

'He even asked me why I got in to work earlier than you do.'

'Oh, great.'

'I told him I couldn't sleep last night. He even asked if I smoke.'

She grimaced.

'You didn't like him, then?' he said.

She hesitated.

'He made my skin crawl,' she said. 'He smiles too much. He smiles like a man without any sense of humour.'

Hallam tried to keep busy all day but it was difficult to start on anything new in the fetid atmosphere of rumour and counter-rumour that infected the entire building. An uncomfortable silence loitered like fog in the corridors as the directors met the new MD behind the closed doors of the main conference room on the third floor. Elsewhere in the building people spoke in low voices, as though they were in church.

The sackings started just before noon. Nathan Solomons was the first to go, summoned at eleven fifty-two and out of the building by eleven fifty-eight. Nathan was fifty-one. He was also Jewish. Perhaps Skudder was not only ageist but also anti-Semitic.

Jim Donaldson telephoned, using an outside line. He spoke hurriedly in a hushed voice. 'I've just had a call from Nathan. He can hardly believe what's happened to him. It was all over so quickly he didn't have time for it to sink in. Did you see him leave? Skudder insisted that Security should see him off the premises.'

'You're not serious!'

'Absolutely. Two security men were standing outside Skudder's office and as soon as Nathan came out they closed in on each side of him and walked him to the lift and out of the building. You'd have thought he was a criminal. He might just as well have been handcuffed. Skudder wouldn't even let him clear his desk or say goodbye to anyone.'

'My God! Why Nathan?'

'The word from Fitzgerald and Parsons is that Skudder hates Jews as well as anyone over forty-five, blacks, cripples, homosexuals and men with beards. He calls them kikes and yids quite openly. He didn't even give Nathan a reason for firing him, he just told him that he had big new plans for the company and that the plans didn't include him.'

'Hellfire! I hope he got a decent pay-off.'

'Six months' pay, that's all.'

'Six months! After all the years he's been here?'

'It's the maximum legal requirement, no matter how long you've been with a company. Unless you've got a better contract that's all any employer is obliged to pay you.'

'So what about Nathan's contract? He must have had one.'

Donaldson was silent for a moment.

'Jim?'

'He never bothered to sign one. When he joined the company twenty-eight years ago he was never given one and he trusted Andy and the three previous MDs so he never pushed the issue.'

'Good grief. Poor devil.'

'Nathan says that Skudder even insisted that he should hand over the keys to his company car immediately.'

'That's insulting. What a bastard. So what's he like? Skudder? In the flesh?'

'Bouncy little man, completely bald, big chip on the shoulder. Never went to university and resents anyone who did. Talks like an East End gangster. Swaggers when he walks. Punches the palms of his hands a lot. Cracks his knuckles all the time. He's a yob, Peter. He could be a barrow-boy, one of those Thatcherite yuppies from the City.'

'Bloody hell! How do these people get these big jobs?'

'Because they're utterly ruthless and they have no morals, so they get things done by trampling all over everybody in their way. They're never hampered by principles or decency, so the banks and accountants love them: they get results; they ruin people's lives and careers but they reduce overheads and make profits. They're asset-strippers, really, but the assets they strip are people. But why should the banks give a damn about people? All they care about is the bottom line. In fact, Bertie tells me it was the bank that eventually insisted that Andy Unwin should be sacked and replaced by Skudder. Apparently the bank thinks Skudder is brilliant. And maybe he is. Who knows? But after meeting him I feel like I need a hot bath.'

'So who's next for the chop?'

'He's got a hit list of about twelve people . . .'

'Am I on it?'

Jim hesitated. 'I don't know.'

'Come off it, Jim. Just tell me straight.'

'Really. I don't know. Honest. Promise. He only discussed half a dozen names with us, including Nathan and Bill Collins.'

'Why Bill?'

'He's forty-nine.'

'So it really is about age.'

'Who knows what it's about? It may be about nothing more than a stroppy young man flexing his muscles and showing who's the boss. I *think* you'll be OK. Honestly. I'm sure you'll be OK. He did mention your name but only in passing, and three of us spoke up for you. I ran through the most recent sales figures but he knew them already and seemed to be impressed. I'm sure it'll be all right, Pete. Really.'

At twelve forty-five Skudder's secretary rang to say that Hallam should not go out for lunch because Skudder would want to see him in his office at some time during the lunch hour. Hallam cancelled his lunch with Joe Roberts and settled instead for a slimy cheese sandwich in his office and a cup of 'coffee' that tasted like the polystyrene mug it came in. For an hour and a half he fidgeted at his desk, unable to settle to anything, unable to concentrate, tapping his fingers, fiddling with his biro, staring out of the window. A cloud of foreboding hung low over him. Nathan's departure had been followed swiftly by those of Bill Collins, Mike Jenkins, Belinda Daniels, Asoke Gupta, Mary Wheeler, all in their late forties or fifties, all escorted out of the building by the security men without being allowed back to their offices to clear their desks. At one moment they had had titles, salaries, status, expense accounts, company cars, at the next they were 'taking early retirement' and the bus back home. So why shouldn't he be next? He tried to look on the bright side: if the worst came to the worst they would have to give him a decent pay-off. Wouldn't they? After twenty-four years with the company? He ought to get two years' pay, at least. Surely. Even three years', maybe? At least he had a contract, unlike Nathan, the poor devil. And it would actually be a relief to take a break, have a decent holiday with Jenny, the Caribbean perhaps, like the Unwins; to relax completely for the first time in years; to take three or four months off to rethink his priorities. And he wouldn't have any trouble finding another job when he decided it was time to get back to work again. Of course he wouldn't. He was bloody good at his job. Everyone said so.

The afternoon passed in a haze and still the call to Skudder's office did not arrive. Of Skudder himself there was no sign: he sat like some invisible god behind the closed doors of Andy Unwin's office and did not come out even for lunch. Word came down from on high that he had not emerged even once, not even to use the executive washroom. 'The man's a zombie,' said Dave Gordon, when he dropped in to see Hallam about the export figures. 'He doesn't even need to pee.' Throughout the office the tension was at snapping point. Rumours were born, grew, mated and became monstrous. *What's he like? Have you seen him yet? Does anyone know anything about him? Is he married? Kids? Is it true that when he left his last place a couple of days ago the staff fell into the pub across the road with gratitude and drank the place dry, every bottle of champagne and then every bottle of wine? And what's he* really *like?*

The security men were said to be emptying the contents of the desks of those who had been fired into big black plastic bags and sealing them ready for delivery later to Skudder's office. Someone in Accounts said she had heard that Skudder had done the same thing in his previous job and that he had spent the first fortnight there trawling personally through every item in the black plastic bags to look for any evidence of malpractice or disloyalty that might allow him to wriggle out of making any pay-offs to the people he had fired. It was said that Skudder had ordered that the contents of every waste-bin in the building should be collected each night, labelled and delivered to him. Someone in Dispatch started a rumour that Skudder had bugged all the telephones at his previous office and liked to record telephone conversations at random. One of the drivers reported that a cousin of his sister's best friend's next-door neighbour had worked for Skudder two years ago and had discovered that he had installed security cameras even in the women's lavatories.

A couple of men in their thirties were fired at tea-time and escorted from the building by the new afternoon security shift. For the first time Hallam felt a flicker of hope. Perhaps Skudder's venomous gaze had passed him by. If Skudder had been going to sack him, surely he would have done it before getting rid of a couple of comparative juniors? Wouldn't he? It stood to reason. Perhaps the danger had passed, at least for the time being. Perhaps Elsie and George, too, were safe for a while. Perhaps it was going to be all right after all.

Skudder sent for him eventually when it was nearly six o'clock. Although Hallam had been well prepared to meet a man whose head was completely hairless he was still quite shocked to see the extent of Skudder's baldness. It was an unrelenting, unforgiving baldness, sharp and sinister with the strangely angular shapes of Skudder's skull. There was nothing smooth and gently rounded about Skudder's skull, nothing softly pink about it. Skudder's skull was threatening. It dipped into a concave hollow in the middle and stuck out at the back, and each temple was crowned by an uneven ledge of bone. There was not a trace of eyebrow or stubble, nothing but smooth, off-white flesh. He had no eyelashes at all: his eyelids flicked up and down like a lizard's. His ears were very small and without any lobes, the forehead jutted low above the eyes and the fluorescent lighting in his office seemed to glint on it with particular malevolence. It made Skudder look at least as old as he did. No wonder he hates having older people around him, thought Hallam. They remind him too much of himself. And yet Skudder's eyes were undoubtedly those of a young man: they burned with a cold energy, suspicion and contempt that only a young man could possibly maintain. Skudder's eyes were the eyes of a hater.

'Skudder,' Andy Unwin had said. 'Unusual name: half skunk, half adder.' It was also half skull, half shudder; like a skeletal rodent scurrying through the sewers.

Skudder was lounging in the big black leather chair behind Andy Unwin's desk, casual in shirtsleeves and scarlet braces. He had jettisoned the yellow spotted bow-tie and waistcoat and was now wearing a striped bow-tie in what looked suspiciously like the colours of some exclusive school or club. Eton? Balliol? The Guards? Surely not: Skudder did not look at all the sort of man who had ever been the member of any exclusive school or club. He looked more like an undertaker, or perhaps a barker in a fairground, or a bouncer in a sleazy nightclub. Perhaps he had simply adopted some exclusive tie to wear especially when he was about to sack someone, like the terrifying old-time hanging judges who used to wear a square of black silk on their heads when they were about to sentence you to death.

Skudder jumped out of Andy Unwin's chair and bounced round the desk towards Hallam. He was surprisingly small and smiling broadly, his smile almost as wide as his face, his teeth alarmingly strong and white. *He smiles too much*, Doreen had said. *He smiles like a man with no sense of humour.*

He bounced constantly from one foot to another as though his shoes had springs in them.

'Pee, Pee,' he said, dropping the 't' in 'Pete' with a flourish of glottal stop and clasping Hallam's hand firmly between both of his and looking up at him, deep into his eyes. 'Ex'lent!'

A chunky gold ring dug into Hallam's fingers.

'Mr Skudder. How do you do?'

'Nah, nah! Caw me Jyson, *please*. Or Jyce. All me mates caw me Jyce.'

Skudder's eyes were almost colourless. He smelt strongly of some powerful aftershave.

'Sorry to of kept you waiting so long, skipper,' he said.

'You've had a lot to do today, I'm sure,' said Hallam.

Skudder gazed up at him. His pallid eyes were bottomless. He shrugged. 'Yeah!' he said slowly. 'Yeah! You're right, I have. There you go! I been *mega* busy. Still, being busy keeps you outta mischief, eh? Hard graft never hurt no one.'

He said the words *hard graft* as though they were in quote marks and simultaneously raised two fingers of each hand and drew inverted commas in the air.

He clenched his fists and cracked his knuckles: the sounds were like pistol shots. 'I been *mega* busy,' he said again. 'Yeah! But I also been mega keen to meet wiv you to interface together personal, Pee. I've heard so much about you. You was almost the first person what Bertie Small verbalised at the directors' meeting this morning. Yeah! You was! Bertie said you was one of the few invalual, 'completely irreplaceaboo' guys on the staff.'

He raised his fingers again and twitched quotation marks around the words *completely irreplaceable*. It made them seem an allegation rather than a truth, as though Skudder did not believe them for a moment.

'Free other directors agreed,' said Skudder, nodding vigorously and smiling so much that his lips curled back to expose angry purple gums and strong yellow teeth. 'Yeah. Straight up. Free of them agreed you *was* "completely irreplaceaboo".'

Was irreplaceable? But not any more?

'Paul Thing "sang your praises" too,' said Skudder, twitching his fingers in the air. 'What's his name?'

'Paul Rampton.'

'Right. Special friend of yours, is he?'

'Not especially. We're good colleagues.'

Skudder stared at him suspiciously, then suddenly grinned. 'Ex'lent,' he said, smacking his right fist loudly into the palm of his left hand. 'Plus Tim Brothers said you was ex'lent at your job. Plus Mandy Young too.'

And Jim, of course. What about Jim?

Skudder laughed. 'I fought for a mo you must of bribed the lot of them to "sing your praises".'

He rubbed his thumb and forefinger together as though he were a miser feeling the thickness of a banknote and laughed again, like a machine gun, *ack-ack-ack-ack*.

Skudder stopped laughing then and leered instead. 'Wooden half mind giving her one, that Mandy Young. Not bad, eh?' He clenched his fist and bent his elbow, jerking his arm upwards. He winked. 'Great knockers, eh? Not half! And I wooden mind giving her a tongue sandwich, neither, eh? What about you?'

'Well, she's . . . quite attractive, I suppose.'

'*Quite*?' Skudder stared at him. 'Not a poof, are yer?'

'No.'

Skudder looked at him with suspicion. 'Yeah, well,' he said, 'they was all full of praise for your work, all free of them.'

'That's very good of them.'

Not Jim?

Skudder frowned. '*Good* of them? What you mean, 'good' of them? Wasn't they telling the troof, then?'

'Well, I hope so . . .'

'If they was just doing you favours, Pee . . .'

'No, I mean . . . Well, I do think I'm good at my job. Yes. Of course.'

'Ex'lent. I like a guy what knows his own wurf. Be proud of your achievements. Blow your own trombone. The directors was so flattering about you your ears "must of been burning". So I reely been looking forward to this meeting. Sit. Sit. There. Right. Ex'lent!'

Skudder bounded back around the desk to Andy's chair and dropped himself into it with an extravagant flourish. He propped his feet up on the desk, exhibiting the hard soles of a pair of black, steel-capped boots. He steepled the fingers of one hand against those of the other.

He gazed at Hallam appraisingly.

'You Jewish?' he said suddenly.

'No.'

'You'd deny it if you was.'

'Of course not. Why should I?'

Skudder's face was a mask. 'Peter,' he said. 'Good Jewish name, that. Like Simon Peter, the one what got his ear cut off.'

Hallam shrugged. 'Maybe originally, perhaps, I don't know.'

Skudder stared at him. He cracked his knuckles. 'Hallam,' he said. 'Sounds like Allah.'

'That's Muslim.'

'Yeah. Hallam. Sounds like *halal*, too, like them Jewish butchers.'

'They're Muslim too. Arabs, not Jews. *Halal* is Muslim.'

Skudder leaned forward. 'You know a lot about Jews and Muslims, then?'

'Very little, actually.'

Skudder stared at him, rolling his biro around in his fingers, then seemed to make a decision. He smiled hugely and reached for a silver cigarette box on his desk. He flicked it open and pushed it towards Hallam.

'Ciggie?' he said. 'Help yourself.'

Hallam shook his head. 'No, thanks. I don't.'

'Cigar?'

'I don't smoke at all. Thanks.'

Skudder nodded solemnly, then smacked his palm with his fist, threw back his bald head and clattered with laughter again: *ack-ack-ack-ack-ack.*

'Just playing "devil's adjutant", skipper,' he said, clawing the air again with the two fingers of each hand. 'Just "testing the temperature". Jyson Skudder can't stand smoke, see. He can't stand smokers, either. He had to "let them go" at his last company. Can't work wiv smokers – untidy peopoo, scruffy. So just "flushing out the enemy".'

He chuckled again – *ack-ack-ack-ack* – and raised his right hand, palm forward, with fingers and thumb extended wide, like a man about to take an oath. *Why does he keep waving his arms and fingers about?* You'd think he were playing charades or *Give Us A Clue*. Hallam would not have been at all surprised if Skudder had suddenly laid his hand on the pages of an open Bible while secretly crossing the fingers of his other hand.

Skudder punched the air with his fist and pointed a forefinger at him. 'You passed the test, Pee. Well done! Wicked! Well done, Pee! You passed the test wiv "flying colours". Ex'lent! Right! Nah! Tell me all about yerself. And I mean *every*fink. I wanna get to know you, Pee. I want us to be mates.'

'Well, I . . .'

Where to start? Skudder would have seen his personnel file already. He would know everything about him. So what was this for? To trip him up? To lure him into some indiscreet revelation or discrepancy?

'Well, I'm married . . .'

'Great!' said Skudder. 'Ex'lent! Can't stand poofs meself.'

'I've got two kids, boy and girl, nineteen and sixteen. I play tennis and golf . . .'

'Brilliant! We must have a game. How long you been here?'

Hallam cleared his throat. 'Twenty-four years,' he said.

Skudder's eyes were like lasers. He whistled. 'Strewth!' he said. 'Twenny-four! You never fought of moving somewhere else?'

'Not really. I've always been very happy here.'

Skudder stared at him. 'Twenny-four years! Bloody hell! You must be older than what you look. How old you, Pee?'

'How old?'

'Yeah. 'ow "old"?'

There was a special glint of contempt in Skudder's eyes as he twitched his fingers around the world *old*. He must know the answer already, the devious little so-and-so. Of course he knew it already. It was on the personnel files.

'I'm forty-five.'

Skudder gave him a huge grin and smacked his palm with his fist. 'A "wrinkly"!' he said jovially, twitching his fingers. 'Wicked!'

'I beg your pardon?'

'You're a "wrinkly",' said Skudder, throwing his arms wide, reflections of light dancing across his bald head and bouncing off the angles of his skull. '"Wrinklies" is old peopoo what're over forty, see, like you. You're a "wrinkly". Then "crumblies" start at fifty. And anyone over sixty . . . You wanna know the word for people what're over sixty?'

'Please.'

Skudder smacked his hands together. '"Oven-dodgers"!' he cried. '*Ack-ack-ack-ack-ack.*'

'Oven-dodgers.'

'Yeah. Great, innit? "Oven-dodgers"! Ex'lent! *Ack-ack-ack-ack-ack.*'

Skudder stood up and came around the desk. He put his arm around Hallam's shoulders and walked him towards the door. 'I like you, Pee,' he said, and patted his shoulder. 'I like you a lot. And I respect your 'bilities. Yeah. Straight up. We're going to work together well, I know that. Plus I hope we get to spend some "quality time" together too, as mates. You don't have to be the same age to be mates. Course not. I know lots of guys what got friends what are wrinklies. Yeah. Plus you got a great future here.'

'Thank you, Mr Skudder.'

Skudder looked at him earnestly. 'Jyce, *please*,' he said. 'Caw me Jyce.'

'Jyce.'

'Great! Brilliant! Ex'lent!'

They reached the door. Skudder clasped both of Hallam's shoulders as if he were about to kiss him on each cheek. He looked up at him, staring him firmly in the eye. His smile was as wide as ever. 'Mind you,' he said, 'there's one fing I gotta talk to you about, skipper. Your secketry. Doris.'

'Doreen.'

He waved a hand. 'Doreen, Diana, Doris, whatever. Now hear this, Pee: she's much too gone on you.'

'I beg your pardon?'

'I fink she's got the hots for you. You're too kind to her, Pee, too gentoo. I met wiv her on the stairs this morning and she talked about yer wiv stars in her eyes. If I didn't know you was an 'appy family man I would of guessed you was giving her one. Slipping her a length, like.'

He clenched his fist and bent his elbow again.

'Straight up. It's always dead dodgy if yer secketry likes yer. Much better if she's afraid of yer.'

'*Afraid?*'

'Course. Only way they'll ever work proper is if they're afraid. Give her an 'ard time. Give her a major bollocking nah and then. Make her work froo her lunch hour. Make her work late. Put the fear of God into her. Make her cry.'

'Make her cry?' said Hallam.

'Yeah. Course. That way yer get the best out of her – hard work, value for money, proper respect. P'raps I better send you on wunna them management motivation courses. Yeah, good finking. She called you *Pee*, too. Now that's not on, my son, not on at all. Bad news, that. She oughter call you *sir* or *Mr Hallam*. Christian names makes them too familiar. You reckon Peter's a Christian name, yeah?'

'As far as I know, yes.'

'Right. Well, they get cocky when you let them use yer Christian name or kike name or whatever it is. Take liberties. Know what I mean?'

'Make her cry,' said Hallam.

'Ex'lent! You got it! Ex'lent! I can see yer gonna be one of me main men, I can see that.' He flashed a huge smile again, then patted Hallam's shoulder and opened the door. 'I want you to feel free to come and see me any time. Jyson Skudder's door's always open. Any problems you have, you must come to me. Jyson Skudder's in the Peopoo Business, see, he is. And you can say anyfink to me, Pee, however "offensif" you fink it might be, however "criticoo". Jyson Skudder won't be offended, I promise yer. We can only work together if we're completely open wiv each uvver. Yeah? So I wanna fink you'll speak yer mind to me, "in confidence", whenever you fink it's nessary. Yeah? OK?'

'That's very good of you. Thank you.'

'Jyce. Please. Jyce.'

'Jyce.'

'Right! Great! Ex'lent!'

He clasped Hallam's hand between both of his. The chunky ring dug into Hallam's fingers.

'It's been ex'lent meeting yer,' said Skudder. 'We're going to have great fun together.'

'Just one thing,' said Hallam. 'As head of the sales department I'd like to know if you're planning to – uh – remove anyone from my department.'

Skudder gave him yet another huge grin. 'You wanna sack someone? Ex'lent! Just gimme the guy's name and I'll chuck 'im "down the plug'ole" first fing tomorrow.'

'No, no,' said Hallam hurriedly. 'I didn't have anyone in mind. I just wanted to know if you're thinking of getting rid of anyone yourself.'

Skudder looked disappointed. 'Not as of this moment in time,' he said. Then he smiled brilliantly. 'But there's still plenny of time. I plan to be around here for a few more years yet.' He patted Hallam on the shoulder. 'Nah you get off to that lovely wife of yours, skipper,' he said. 'It's been a long day.'

Outside Skudder's office Hallam suddenly felt hot. His face was burning. Sweat was trickling down his back like a thin waterfall of relief. He went into the gents' lavatory on the second floor and bent over the wash-basin, splashing his face several times with cold water.

It was going to be all right, after all. They were right about Skudder, everything they said about him. He was a rough, unprincipled, bigoted little yob but at least Hallam's job was still safe. And Elsie and George were still safe. And things would work out. He would find a way of working with Skudder. He could always find a way of working with anyone: it was simply a matter of time, decent behaviour and diplomacy. In the end he and Skudder would get along fine. Why shouldn't they? They both had the same goals in mind: good management, increased sales, the success of the company. He would never like Skudder. He would always distrust him. But who said you had to like the boss or even trust him? If he played it right everything was going to be fine.

* * *

Skudder picked up his telephone.

'We're gonna have to get rid of Hallam as well,' he said. 'Hallam. Wiv a haitch. The sales manager. Well, the poor old bugger's past it, inn'e? Forty-five, set in his ways, stupid old fart, don't know nuffink. He's lost the plot. Yeah, I know, but he's gonna be trouboo. I fink he may be a yid, too.'

Skudder listened for a few moments.

He shrugged.

'OK, skipper,' he said. 'So we can't just sack him, not just yet. OK. Fair enough. So we just get him to resign. Make his life a misery. Freeze him out.'

Skudder cackled. '*Ack-ack-ack-ack-ack*. We give him the Maxwell Treatment.'

CHAPTER 3

The Maxwell Treatment

Monica was in the hallway, talking on the telephone, when Hallam returned home that night. The little room was hazy with smoke from her cheroot. As he came in through the front door she was standing in the far corner of the hall, six feet from the cradle, with a cheroot in one hand and the receiver in the other with its curled flex pulled so tight that the kinks were almost completely flattened out. One day she was going to pull the flex right out of the telephone. Dear Lord: how often had he told her that it made no difference at all whether the flex was curly or not? She still refused to believe him. 'It stands to reason,' she said. 'If the flex goes round and round and round then your voice must go round and round and round as well. Consequently the person at the other end can't possibly hear you properly.'

'It just doesn't work like that, Monica.'

'Prove it.'

To make matters worse there was always a terrible sort of logic about her barmy theories. When she wanted to listen to the radio – she still insisted on calling it the 'wireless' – she would always open a window 'to improve the reception'. When he remonstrated gently with her about it she was defiant. 'It's perfectly obvious,' she said. 'How can you be so obtuse? How can wireless waves go through glass, eh? You tell me that, Mr Clever Clogs.'

Good question. How *do* radio waves go through glass? And through brick, tile, concrete?

A couple of months ago she had sulked for a day and a half because he refused to cut down the trees at the end of the garden, as she had asked, 'to improve the television reception': she was convinced that there were 'leafy shadows' flickering all over the screen and now, when watching TV, she had taken to wearing a red peaked golfing cap 'to cut out the branches waving around at the top of the screen'.

Tonight she was dressed in an orange T-shirt with the slogan ANCIENT MONUMENT, baggy grey leggings and bright green trainers. She gave him a wink and an animated thumbs-up as he came in through the door and tipped her cheroot hand towards her mouth several times as though she were signalling that she wanted a drink. As he looked at her he felt suddenly exhausted. *Forty-five? I feel ninety.*

'Yes,' she told the telephone eagerly, 'Purple Heather in the two thirty at York, and Mulligatawny in the four fifteen at Newbury. Would you believe it? Ninety-three pounds forty after tax. Yes! Ninety-three pounds! I'm taking them all out to dinner for a Chinese to celebrate.'

Hallam closed his eyes. No. Please. Not tonight. I'm knackered.

She gave him a grin and another thumbs-up. He ducked under the telephone flex and slipped into the house. At least she'd got one thing absolutely right: a drink was a damned good idea. A large drink. A very large drink indeed.

Jenny was in the living room, sitting in an armchair and watching the TV news. How fresh she looked, how clean and unsoiled, a beautifully fragrant antidote to all the grubbiness, scheming and backstabbing of office politics. Here was his oasis and she was his mirage. He smiled to see her. Just to look at her lightened his heart. He bent and kissed her.

'You look tired,' she said.

'I'm knackered.'

'Bad day?'

'Not much fun.'

She stood. 'Here, give me your jacket and tie and sit down,' she said. 'I'll get you a drink and then you can tell me about it. The usual?'

'That'd be wonderful. And the Battleaxe wants one too.'

'How surprising.'

He shed his jacket and tie with relief. 'Susie home?'

'Yes. She'll be down in a minute. She's doing her homework.'

Susie. He smiled. Jenny and Susie: how lucky could any man be?

Jenny took his jacket and tie away to hang them in his cupboard. On the television screen some earnest face was glaring at him and haranguing him about Saddam Hussein and the latest crisis in Iraq. He had heard quite enough about Saddam Hussein and Iraq over the past few years to last him several lifetimes. He never wanted to hear a word about either of them again. *Saddam both*. He reached for the remote control and zapped the TV off.

A fizzing noise.

Silence.

Bliss. He closed his eyes.

Skudder.

It wasn't all over, was it? It wasn't that simple. Just because he still had his job, just because George and Elsie hadn't been sacked yet, it didn't mean that the problem had gone away. The problems were only just beginning. When he really thought about it, how could he possibly work with a man like Skudder? He rarely made snap judgements about people he had only just met. He had always thought it was rubbish to say that first impressions are usually right. But even after just one meeting he knew that Skudder had to be one of the most unpleasant men he had ever encountered. He was shallow, vulgar, bigoted, unprincipled, brutal. Skudder could probably give Saddam Hussein a few lessons. So how was Hallam ever going to be able to work with him? Skudder had just sacked twelve employees in one day, twelve *good* people, excellent workers, without reason, without blinking, without a qualm. And who was to say that that was the end of it? It might be the end of the sackings but why should it be the end of the mindless viciousness? Each day could bring with it another example of Skudder's ruthlessness, another moral dilemma to be faced, another challenge to everyone's integrity. How long could Hallam tolerate such a regime without sticking his neck out and making a protest? Even if Skudder left him alone to run the sales department as he wanted – and why should he leave him alone? – how was Hallam going to be able to ignore what was going on elsewhere in the company? How would he and his conscience both survive? One of them was going to have to go.

'Mummy's taking us out for a Chinese,' said Jenny, handing him a wonderfully deep, tanned Scotch and sitting on the sofa. 'She's won again on the horses.'

Hallam took a mouthful. 'Ah,' he said, 'that's nectar.'

He leaned back in the chair and closed his eyes. 'That's the third or fourth time she's won this month, isn't it?'

'Fifth.'

'Good God. How does she do it?'

'She spends an hour or more every morning reading the racing pages in the papers, listening to the racing tips on the radio and studying form in some horsy book she's got in her room. She never bets more than a pound but she's really getting rather good at it. Today she had a twenty to one and a five to one.'

Hallam chuckled. 'Well, good for her. I must confess, though, Jen, I don't know if I can face going out again tonight. It's very generous of her and I don't want to be ungracious but the thought of a Chinese meal . . .'

'Oh dear. She's so looking forward to it.'

'Yes, but frankly . . . Well, you know I'm not much of a Chinese freak at the best of times, and today . . .'

She put her hand on his arm. 'She really does need to get out tonight. It's the anniversary of Daddy's death.'

He grimaced. 'Oh, hell. I'm so sorry. I should have known. I'd forgotten.'

'So you see . . .'

Hallam sighed.

'It's four years now, but even so . . .'

'Of course.'

'She still misses him terribly, you know.'

'Of course she does.'

'She doesn't show it. She's awfully brave. But inside . . .'

'I know, Jen. I know.'

Will you miss me as much when I am dead? I hope so. No I don't. I hope not. Yes I do. Oh God.

She smiled. 'I've even managed to persuade Matt to join us tonight.'

Hellfire! That's all I need.

Jenny looked at him with a sort of longing. 'We don't often get the chance to go out all together as a family. I don't think we've all been out together for nearly two years. So you see . . . Pete?'

Her eyes were full of hope, awash with memories: Matt giggling as a fat baby, Matt as a scrawny little boy with big ears and gawky knees, Matt when he still used to smile. Such nostalgia. So little to ask. How could he refuse?

'Yes. Of course. Of course I'll come. I'm sorry I was a bit . . . well, you know.' How could I possibly say no? By being a bit of a shit, that's how. By being utterly selfish for a change.

I should try it some time. Skudder would never say yes if he really meant no. That's why people like Skudder become managing directors and why people like me don't.

She leaned across the sofa and squeezed his hand. 'You're so sweet, Peter. Thank you.'

Sweet? Skudder would go ballistic if anyone called *him* 'sweet'.

He settled back into the armchair and gave a huge yawn. 'Sorry.'

'You poor darling.'

'Just give me ten minutes to enjoy the drink and pull myself together, then I'll be with you.'

'Oh, I'm so sorry, darling. Your bad day. Tell me about it. What's happened? What's the new boss like?'

Hallam sighed. 'Well, he's an absolute bastard, actually. He's one of the nastiest people I've ever met in my life.'

'God, that's not like you, Pete. Why? What's he done?'

He took a deep sip of his whisky. 'He sacked twelve people today.'

'Twelve!'

Hallam snapped his fingers. 'Just like that. Twelve. Already. On his first day. Without any justification at all. Just like that. Out.'

'Twelve! You're—'

'Don't worry, Jen, not me. I had a meeting with him a couple of hours ago and it's OK. I've still got a job. He seems to rate me.'

'I should damn well hope so.'

'But Nathan Solomons has gone, and Bill, and Mike, and Belinda Daniels, Asoke Gupta, several others. It's been a bloody awful day, quite frankly.'

'But how terrible. Poor Annie. And Laura. I must ring them.'

'It was like sitting in prison and hearing the condemned on Death Row being dragged away one by one to the gallows.

And not one of them made a sound, that's the terrible thing. Not one of them cried out or shouted or argued. They went in silence. That's what makes it even more horrible. They went as though they'd had their tongues cut out.'

'Ugh!'

Hallam sat up suddenly. 'I've just realised something,' he said. 'He's got no ear lobes, Skudder, no ear lobes at all. Not even the tiniest bulge. His ears just go straight down into his neck. I read somewhere that people without ear lobes are probably psychopaths. Good God!'

'Cuckoo!' cried Monica, coming into the room. 'Cuckoo!'

Cuckoo? Hellfire, you can say that again.

The Chinese restaurant was almost empty. The lighting was far too bright. Two young couples sat at tables far apart and gazed morosely at each other and at the red flock wallpaper, which depicted sulky-looking mandarins and sullen dragons. The walls were decorated with silky pictures of precipitous snow-capped mountains, buffaloes in rice paddies, Chinese junks. From the tinny loudspeaker above the door there came discordant noises that sounded vaguely Oriental. A couple of red and green lanterns hung at each end of the tiny bamboo bar. In the corner a spindly rubber plant was leaning towards the doorway as if it were trying to make a run for it.

'Well, isn't this nice?' said Monica brightly. She was bright all over: to the orange T-shirt, grey leggings and green trainers she had added an orange anorak and the red peaked golfing cap. Dear God, thought Hallam, she looks like a miniature traffic light. But even that's a damned sight better than Matt. Matt looks as if he has just crawled out of a garbage tip. Susie looks lovely as always – clean, wholesome, *happy* – but Matt looks as if he hates the whole world.

A young Oriental waiter approached them and bowed slightly.

How do I know he's young? They all look the same, whatever age they are. They all look so smooth, even in middle age, as though they have just been hatched from eggs. The waiter could be fifty, for all I know. He could be old enough to be on Skudder's hit list. Bloody Skudder. I must stop thinking about Skudder. This is meant to be a family celebration of Monica's win on the horses. We're supposed to be enjoying ourselves.

'Hello,' said Monica cheerfully.

The waiter gazed at her without expression. 'Herro?'

'I've booked,' said Monica.

'Prease?'

'I rang.'

'Laing?'

'Yes, on the telephone.'

'Terry Fone.'

'About an hour ago.'

He consulted an appointments book with tired, pencilled pages that lay on the bar counter, running his finger down it. He frowned and shook his head slightly, as though to clear it of some obstruction. He looked again at the top of the page and ran his finger slowly down it again.

'No Laing,' he said.

'What?'

'No Booker. No Herro. No Terry Fone. Onry Porridge.'

'Porridge?'

The waiter hissed.

'Porridge?' said Monica. 'I'd rather hoped we might have some of that nice duck you do with pancakes.'

He looked baffled. 'Punkase?'

Hallam interrupted. 'May we have that table there?' he said. 'That big one?'

'Ah. Yes. Table.' The waiter went ahead of them, busily bowing and beckoning them towards it. 'Table. Yes. You come, Miss Porridge. Mr Porridge. All Porridge. You book.'

Monica gave a deep growl of laughter. 'Miss Porridge! Not Laing, Porridge.' She rumbled with mirth. 'Oh, what a hoot! He thought my name was Laing. When I said—'

Matthew sighed with theatrical emphasis. 'OK, Gran, we got it, all right? We got it the first time. There's no need to sneer at him just because he's foreign.'

'Sneer?'

'Just because he doesn't speak English very well.'

'I wasn't sneering. It was just—'

'I don't suppose you speak much Mandarin, do you?'

'Matt,' said Hallam.

'Or Cantonese either, come to that.'

'That's enough, Matt,' said Hallam.

'It's just racist,' said Matthew. 'The imperialist mentality. I hate it. Cultural colonialism. It's disgusting. And xenophobic. You just think of him as a funny little Chinky-chonk, don't you? Just because he's slightly yellow and his eyes are a little flatter than yours and he doesn't speak much English. Well, your time is over, I'm glad to say. The world has changed. Just because he doesn't speak much English doesn't mean he's not just as good as you are.'

'Well, of course, Matt,' said Monica, 'but I—'

'Stop being a pain,' said Susie, 'and leave Gran alone. I thought it was funny, Gran.'

Matthew looked at Susie with contempt. 'You would,' he said. 'We all know you're a fully paid-up Fascist.'

'I'm not!'

'Yes, you are. You're against immigration—'

'Only too much of it.'

'Only if they're not white, you mean. You hate the unemployed.'

'Only lazy scroungers like you.'

'That's enough, both of you,' said Hallam.

'You're against Kids' Lib,' said Matthew.

Susie's face was reddening. 'I just don't think kids know enough to run schools and things,' she said.

'Well, you certainly don't. You're even in favour of capital punishment.'

'Only for really terrible crimes.'

'Like what?'

'Like raping or murdering a child.'

Matthew shook his head slowly. 'I can't believe you said that,' he said. 'You'd think we were still living in the Middle Ages. Have you never considered that rapists and murderers might need help? Understanding? Counselling?'

'You're mad,' said Susie, her face glowing. 'You're bad as well.'

Matthew looked at her with a condescending expression. 'You're just an old-fashioned Nazi and you know it.'

'That's quite enough now, Matt,' said Hallam.

Matt gave him a supercilious look. Even his long tangled hair seemed to radiate contempt. 'Who says?'

'I do.'

'I can't believe you said that.'

'What?'

'That paternalistic crap. "Who says?" "I do." I'm nineteen now, *Father*, or hadn't you noticed? I got the vote. You can't boss me around any more.'

'Stop it, Matt,' said Jenny. 'This is supposed to be a happy family evening.'

'That'll be the day.'

Jenny looked as if she might weep.

Why do you always have to spoil everything, you little sod? Little? He's six foot two. Something has to be done about Matt. We can't go on like this.

A dapper little Chinese man, immaculate in a smart grey suit, appeared suddenly beside the table. He rubbed his hands together and smiled. 'Good evening,' he said, with perfect pronunciation. 'Welcome to our humble establishment. What seems to be the trouble?'

'No trouble,' said Monica brightly, sitting at the big round table. 'No trouble at all. Everything's just ticketyboo.'

They ordered a bottle of white wine and more than a dozen dishes to share between them – the spring rolls, the shredded duck with pancakes, the chicken with cashew nuts, the pork with soy, the beef and beansprouts, the special fried rice, several vegetable dishes. Matthew glowered at them, ate only the vegetables and drank only water. The atmosphere was strained.

'I can't believe you're all still eating meat,' he said, 'and poisoning yourselves with booze. In this day and age.'

'Not now, Matt,' said Hallam.

'Do you know how they kill the ducks?'

Jenny looked at him with beseeching eyes. '*Please*, Matt.'

He shrugged. 'Suit yourselves. If you don't want to face the truth.'

'I heard a good joke at the hairdresser's the other day,' said Monica, with loud determination.

Matt sighed and wrinkled his nose. The others looked at her: anything at all to lighten the atmosphere.

'Go on, Gran,' said Susie.

Monica chuckled throatily. 'Well, it seems that St Peter was due to go off on holiday and there was no one left in Heaven to man the Pearly Gates while he was away, so Jesus volunteered.'

'Blasphemy,' said Matthew.

Monica ignored him. '"What does the job involve?" asked Jesus. "Well," said St Peter. "You just sit here at the registration desk and whenever anyone turns up you ask them a few questions about themselves and if you think they deserve to come in you unlock the Pearly Gates, get them to sign the registration book and then you send them off to Housekeeping Stores to get their wings."'

'Profanity,' said Matthew.

Monica cleared her throat. It sounded like a digger excavating a ditch. She took a sip of wine. 'So St Peter goes off on his hols and Jesus takes over for a couple of weeks, and on the third day this old man arrives at the Pearly Gates and asks to be let in. "And who are you?" says Jesus.

'"I'm just a poor old carpenter," quavers the old man, "but I've seen some really miraculous things in my time."

'"Oh yes," says Jesus. "Like what?"

'"Well," says the old carpenter, "I had an amazing son once. He was born in a very special way and he was quite different from everyone else in the world. He went through a great transformation even though he had holes in his hands and feet, and although I lost him many years ago his spirit lives on and will for ever. All over the world people tell his story."

'By now, of course, Jesus has unlocked the Pearly Gates and thrown them wide and is hugging the old man with tears in his eyes. "Father," he cries, "it's been such a long time."

'The old man steps back and stares at him. He frowns, takes off his glasses, cleans them, puts them on again, looks at Jesus in bewilderment and says: "Pinocchio?"'

For a tiny moment there was silence and then Hallam, Jenny and Susie burst into laughter.

'That's sacrilege,' said Matthew angrily. His eyes blazed.

'Well done, Monica,' said Hallam, chuckling. 'So who says women can't tell jokes?'

Matthew banged his head three times with his fist. 'I can't *believe* you all thought that was funny.'

'Come on, Matt, of course it was.'

'It wasn't at all funny. It was blasphemous. And evil.'

'*Evil*?'

'Evil. It took the name of the Lord in vain and it made

fun of an ordinary old carpenter, a sad, bereaved, partially sighted, working-class, old-age pensioner. I can't believe you can all just sit there swilling your disgusting booze and chewing your revolting animal corpses and jeer at some poor deprived old bloke like that.'

'Dear God.'

'Ah, Matt.'

'Matt.'

'Grow up, Matt,' said Susie. 'Jeepers.'

'There you go again,' said Matt fiercely. '*Jeepers*. Do you know where the word jeepers comes from? Of course you don't. You don't know anything, do you? Well, I'll tell you: it's a corruption of *Jesus*, that's what it is. Every time you say jeepers you're blaspheming and taking His name in vain.'

They gazed at him in silence. There seemed to be nothing that anyone could say.

'Oh, Matt,' said Jenny softly. There were tears in her eyes.

'So when did you become so religious all of a sudden?' asked Susie.

'I'm not. I just can't stand spoiled, bourgeois cynics like you making fun of other people's beliefs.'

'Spoiled?' said Susie, with spirit. 'You're a fine one to talk, lounging around all day and scrounging on the dole.'

'I don't have to listen to this.' He pushed his chair back roughly and stood up, looming over them, a towering monument of resentment. Why is he always so *angry*? thought Hallam. With his loose, untidy clothes and his long, matted hair and his wild eyes he looked like some Old Testament prophet.

'In fact I can't stand sitting with people who make fun of other people's race and beliefs,' said Matthew tightly. 'I'm going. I'm not sitting here a moment longer with a bunch of sneering, blaspheming, pampered, middle-class, neo-Fascist cannibals. I'm off.'

He turned away and marched towards the door. They watched him go, indignation even in the shape of his ankles.

'Sod off, then,' growled Monica, with sudden ferocity. 'And don't worry about the bill: it's my treat, you miserable little shit.'

The tiny waiter scurried towards the door to open it. Matthew turned, looked down at him, and suddenly bent down and gave him a tight hug.

'We're not all like them,' he said loudly. 'We're not all racists. And I'm sorry about the Opium Wars. And Shanghai. And Hong Kong. I want to apologise.'

He hugged the waiter again, put him down and marched out of the restaurant, slamming the door behind him. The waiter nodded at the closed door, shot his cuffs, straightened his jacket and dusted at the sleeves. He smoothed his trousers. He seemed completely unperturbed.

What amazing people they are, thought Hallam. He had read somewhere once that in Peking during the 1920s dozens of Chinese rebels were made to kneel in rows to be beheaded and that those who still had only a few seconds to live had laughed uproariously as they watched the hilarious spectacle of their comrades' severed heads bouncing in the dust. How can Matt pretend that such people are no different from us? What is this modern madness where the truth is not only denied but considered immoral?

The natty little proprietor materialised again beside the table, rubbing his hands, his face full of concern.

'What seems to be the trouble?' he asked anxiously. 'Is there something wrong?'

Monica pushed her plate away and reached for a cheroot.

'Yes,' she said, 'too right there is. Unlike you, my grandson does not appear to be too keen to worship his ancestors.'

The evening improved. It's always much better when Matt's not around, thought Hallam, making a determined effort to give Monica a cheerful evening out. 'So tell us, then, Miss Porridge,' he said, 'how do you always manage to win on the horses?'

She chuckled. 'I always ask Hank.'

'*Hank?*'

'Of course. Who else? Arizonans are all geniuses with horses, you know, and Hank is no exception. When he was little and living out in the desert he would watch the cowboys galloping by so he soon became an excellent judge of horseflesh.'

Susie giggled.

Monica gazed at her coolly. 'You think I'm barmy, don't you?'

Susie giggled again. 'No, Gran, not barmy, just lovely and funny.'

Monica leaned over and squeezed her hand. 'Thank you, dear. I'll choose to take that as a compliment. Now, there were several good horses running today that I reckoned were possible winners – Purple Heather, Mulligatawny, Popocatapetl in the two forty-five at Ascot, Sherpa Tensing in the three twenty-five at Ayr – so I put Hank on the window-sill so that he could see what the weather was like outside and then I sat in front of him and read the name of each possible winner out to him slowly to see if there was any reaction. He didn't move a muscle when I said Sherpa Tensing and Popocatapetl, but when I said Purple Heather and Mulligatawny he trembled slightly each time so I knew those were going to be the winners.'

Hallam gazed at her. 'Fascinating,' he said.

She looked at him sharply. 'You don't believe me.'

'On the contrary,' he said, 'I believe every word of it. You asking a cactus for racing tips? Oh, yes. I believe every word of it. Absolutely.'

She sniffed. 'Now you're laughing at me.'

'Would I ever do that?'

'And anyway,' she said forcefully, 'remember what my stars said yesterday? "Your every wish will be granted," they said.'

'Except kippers for breakfast.'

She grinned. 'Except kippers, as you say. And now, before we all mosey on back to the ranch, as Hank would say, I've got a new limerick to try on you.'

Not again, Monica. Not now. Not here. But be nice. It's her party. Be nice to her.

'OK,' she said. 'Here goes:

> 'There was a young lady named Gloria
> Who was had by Sir Gerald du Maurier
> And then by six men
> And Sir Gerald again
> And the band of the Waldorf-Astoria.'

'Mother!' said Jenny. 'Really!'

Susie snorted, hiding her mouth with her hand and starting to giggle. Hallam laughed. It was really quite funny. And clever: the rhymes, the scansion. But he laughed mainly because the limerick was so perfectly *Monica*, set as it was in that never-never thirties world of hers where gels were called Gloria and bounders were called Sir Gerald and hotels still had their own big bands. 'Excellent,' he said, clapping.

'And I've written another Alternative Nursery Rhyme,' she said.

Not now, Monica. Please. Not again.

'Just one, I promise. It goes like this:

> 'The grand old Duke of York
> He had ten thousand men . . .
> Which made Oscar Wilde ever so jealous.'

Susie chortled. Hallam laughed. He could not help himself. It was not so much that the thing was particularly funny, it was simply that she was so absurd and outrageous. And by laughing at her jokes he was thanking her for her generosity and rescuing the evening. Matthew was a cloud that had already passed. For now.

'Honestly, Mummy,' said Jenny, 'you've got the filthiest mind.'

Monica waved the hand with the cheroot. 'All old women have filthy minds, dear,' she said. 'You will too, just you wait and see. My own mother became quite disgusting once she reached seventy. I suppose it's because old women finally realise at last the truth about sex – what an awful lot of silly fuss it all was about very little.'

'Very little?' said Hallam. 'Speak for yourself, Miss Porridge.'

'Peter!' said Jenny.

Monica gave her gravelly laugh. 'You men! So proud of a little bit of gristle.'

'Mummy!'

'So I suppose you were an intimate acquaintance of Sir Gerald du Maurier as well, were you?' said Hallam.

Monica smiled sweetly. 'Sadly not. I was only seven when he died. But I knew his daughter Daphne very well.'

'Daphne du Maurier? The novelist? You knew her?'

'Of course. When I lived in Cornwall. She told me once she wished she'd been a shepherdess instead.'

I don't believe a word of it.

'And what about the band of the Waldorf-Astoria?' he said. 'Did you know them too?'

'Peter!' said Jenny. 'You're just as bad as she is.'

Monica gazed at them both with her pale blue eyes. She gave a tiny smile. 'Oh no he's not,' she said.

Hallam had drunk no more than two glasses of white wine at dinner but he had a restless night, sleeping in fitful snatches, waking with a start several times in a sweat, feeling queasy, hearing voices in his head, dreaming time and again that Oscar Wilde was marching ten thousand Chinese waiters to the top of a hill accompanied by the band of the Waldorf-Astoria, none of whom was wearing any trousers. Why did so many English people pretend that they enjoyed Chinese food? It might, perhaps, be delicious in China but when you ate it in an English restaurant it taught you precisely the meaning of Chinese junk. All that fried gunge and monosodium glutamate squatting on his ribs all night: no wonder he felt queasy. They said that the trouble with a Chinese meal was that you needed another one an hour later. Not so: an hour later you were likely to be taking a second look at the one you had just eaten.

He woke with a headache, swallowed a couple of Nurofen and went to work in a mood of foreboding.

Skudder.

As he drove he tried to be optimistic and to persuade himself that he had been exaggerating the problem. Could Skudder really be as bad as he had seemed last night? Surely not. Skudder, too, must have been pretty tired after his long first day in the office: he had obviously not been at his best. And in any case it was pointless to resent Skudder's appointment as MD, even if he was not at all the sort of man that Hallam himself would have chosen. Skudder had been appointed and that was the end of it; it was useless to whine about it. And maybe the company really did need a brash, vigorous, ruthless young hand to run it. Perhaps indeed they had become a bit set in their ways under Andy Unwin without realising it. Maybe they did need a shake-up. Maybe even some of the sackings were necessary. Take Mike Jenkins: you had to admit that he hadn't really come up with a decent idea for several years now. And dear old Mary Wheeler: she had always been something of a passenger. Perhaps it was right that they should go.

And did it really matter how Skudder spoke? Hardly anyone nowadays speaks the Queen's English any more, thought Hallam, not even the Royal Family. Not even Oxford undergraduates speak Oxford English any longer. And who was to say that Hallam's version of English was 'better' than Skudder's? It was probably only snobbery that made him think so. The English language had been changing and adapting constantly for centuries. Hallam's mid-twentieth-century, middle-class version of it bore little resemblance to the English of Shakespeare or Chaucer. Hellfire: Shakespeare's accent, once he had spent a few years in London, may well have sounded just like Jason Skudder's.

Hallam drove into the car park and left his Cavalier in his usual space. Skudder's Morgan was sitting already in Andy Unwin's old slot by the entrance. Well, that was one thing in Skudder's favour: he started early; he was obviously not afraid of work. He deserved co-operation. He deserved to be given a chance.

Hallam reached for his briefcase, locked the car, loped up the steps and vowed to try to be tolerant, to work smoothly with Skudder. Skudder was the new boss and if Hallam didn't like it then he could always find another job somewhere else. Put up or shut up. Anything less than his best effort would be dishonourable.

'Morning, Mr Hallam,' said the commissionaire, as he went in through the swing doors.

'Morning, Ron.'

The commissionaire sidled out of his cubicle and adopted his conspiratorial tone. 'They're bright pink today, sir.'

'Pink?'

'The boss's bow-tie, sir, and weskit. Bright pink, sir. Thought you oughter know. Advance warning.'

'Right. Thank you, Ron.'

'Thank *you*, sir.'

He jogged up the stairs.

Warning? Why should pink be a warning? Was this some sort of working-class proverb? *Pink tie in the morning, porter's warning?*

His office door was unlocked again.

Odd. Was she in before him again? She had rarely been this early before.

'Doreen?'

She was emptying her desk, cramming papers and notebooks into a plastic carrier bag. Her face was white and drawn.

He went towards her. 'Doreen? What's the matter? What are you doing?'

The rims of her eyes were red.

'What is it?'

'I've been moved to the typing pool,' she said.

'*What?*'

She thrust a sheet of paper towards him, a computer printout of an internal e-mail memo. Hallam took it. 'What's this?'

'My marching orders,' she said bitterly. 'Skudder seems to think that you don't need a secretary any more.'

He read the memo with disbelief.

MEMORANDIUM

TO: Doreen Jones, Sales Departmint Operative Grade 2
FROM: Jason Skudder, Managing Director
SUBJECT: *YOUR CONDITIONS OF EMPLOYMINT*
DATE: 9 June

(1) Due to the currant Reorganization of the

Company you will no longer be required to work for Mr Peter Hallam Sales Manager.

(2) You will report immediately to your new Work Station in the Typing Pool where you will in future be required to service any other Member of Staff to who you are allocated.

(3) Mr Halla'ms sectarial requiremints will in future be met on a causal basis by any Employee Unit in the Typing Pool allocated to him by the Personal Manager.

(4) Your present Work Station in Mr Hallams' Office will be re-dezignated a Managerial Work Station and will be allocated to Mr Hallams new Deputy Sales Manager Mr Shane Gorman who, will be joining the Company next week.

ends

Hallam stared at the memo. If anyone ought to be 're-dezignated' it was Skudder's secretary, whoever she might be: her spelling and typing were atrocious. And who the hell was Shane Gorman, the 'new Deputy Sales Manager'? Skudder had said nothing at all about that. How dare he appoint a deputy sales manager without any consultation?

'There must be some mistake,' he said. 'We'll soon see about this.'

He dropped his briefcase on his desk and left the room, climbing the stairs briskly and walking with purpose along the corridor towards the personnel manager's office. It was only just after eight o'clock but almost everyone was already at work. The odour of fear drifted through the building.

The personnel manager looked up nervously. He waved the memo at her. 'Fiona . . .'

She flinched. 'I know, I know. I'm sorry, Peter. It's—'

'What the heck's going on?'

'It's Mr Skudder. He says you don't need a secretary of your own any more.'

'He does, does he? We'll soon see about that. I've always had a secretary. For twenty-four years. I couldn't function without one.'

'I told him that. He almost spat at me. He said that if you couldn't do your job without a secretary then he'd find someone else who could.'

'He said *that*?'

'Yes. He says that now we all have computers you only need occasional help from the typing pool.'

'Occasional help? Hellfire, Fee, Doreen never stops. You've seen her – always arrives early, always leaves late. She's the best and hardest-working secretary in the entire building.'

'I know, but—'

'How am I going to manage with only a temp for an hour or two every now and then?'

'I know, Peter, but what can I do? He *is* the MD.'

'Even his bloody memo is illiterate.'

'I know. He's brought in two girls with him from Fitzgerald and Parsons to be his secretaries.'

'Two? Why does he need two? What happened to Barbara?'

'She was sacked last night.'

'Good grief, this is a disgrace. I'm going to see Mulliken about this.'

Fiona looked apprehensively over her shoulder. *Hell's bells: you'd think she was living in a police state.* She lowered her voice. 'I wouldn't if I were you, Peter. Percy Langan went to see Mulliken last night to protest about Bill Collins being fired and Skudder rang him later at home and told him not to bother to come in today because he was sacked as well.'

'Dear God.'

'I made the mistake of hinting that his new secretary's spelling and punctuation were not quite up to the mark and I thought he was going to bite me. He actually snarled like an angry dog. He said I was out of date, that nobody gives a damn about spelling and punctuation any more. He said I was old-fashioned, past it. He asked me how old I am.'

'Dear Lord.'

She looked at him pleadingly. 'I know it's not going to be easy, Peter, but please don't make waves. I'll do everything I can to make sure you have plenty of backup even without Doreen.'

She looked frightened. He remembered what Doreen had told him once about Fiona: a single mother living with two small children in a tiny flat way out in the suburbs; an ex-husband who never paid enough maintenance and never on time; an hour each way commuting into work; all the cost and guilt of having to pay child-minders so that she could earn a living. How could he think of asking her to defy Skudder even for an hour or two?

'I'm sorry, Fee,' he said. 'I didn't mean to get so steamed up. Look, Doreen had better come to you for an hour or two until I can get to see Skudder and sort this out, but please don't insult her by loading her with a pile of audio-typing or anything like that. She's far too good for that. She's been a senior secretary for a dozen years or more: she can't just be dumped back in the typing pool with girls of sixteen and seventeen.'

Fiona's face lit up with relief. 'Thanks, Peter,' she said.

'One more thing,' he said. 'What about this Shane Gorman? This guy that Skudder's bringing in to be my deputy?'

She shrugged. 'Search me. I don't know anything at all about him.'

'But surely as personnel manager—'

'I don't think I'm going to be that for much longer.'

'What? Don't think like that, Fee. You're—'

'I think the skids are under me,' she said. 'The way he looked at me. With contempt. The way he told me I was past it. I'm only thirty-eight but he looked at me as if I was an old woman. I know I look a bit older than my age. It's – all the worry and – a bit of a strain.'

She bit her lip and reached for a tissue.

'He wouldn't get away with that,' he said encouragingly.

'Yes, he would,' she said. 'And I hate to say it, Peter, but I think the skids are under you too. It's quite obvious that he's determined to get rid of everyone over forty.'

'So why hasn't he got rid of me yet? Or Elsie Benson? Or George Pringle?'

She wiped her nose. 'He's run out of redundancy money so he can't get rid of George or Elsie until he persuades the bank to cough up a bit more. Anyway, they're just small fry, he can take his time over them. But you – you've got a nice fat two-year contract. You're too expensive to sack: he'd have to give you two years' pay. Unless, of course, he can manoeuvre you into a position where he can claim that you've been guilty of some sort of misconduct or gross incompetence or negligence, in which case he could sack you without paying you a penny. Or unless he can make it so difficult for you to do your job that you resign.'

'He won't get me to resign, I can promise you that.'

'I wouldn't bank on it,' she said. 'Skudder's an animal. I wouldn't bank on it at all.'

There were two new secretaries sitting in the little office outside Skudder's office, both in their early twenties, both strikingly good-looking: one with black hair and the darkest blue eyes, the other a spiky redhead with skin like cream. The redhead was chewing gum and reading a glossy magazine. She glanced at him without interest and looked away.

He smiled at the dark-haired girl. 'Hello,' he said. 'I'm Peter Hallam, the sales manager.'

'Oh yeah?' She had a little silver stud in her left nostril and a tiny blue dolphin tattooed on the back of her delicate wrist. Her eyes were the deepest blue he had ever seen but she looked at him as if he were made of glass.

When do girls stop looking at you properly? he thought. *Noticing* you? When you turn forty? Bloody forty-five?

A uniformed security guard sat to attention on a chair beside the door that led into Skudder's inner office. Why on earth did Skudder need a security guard in his office? The redhead was staring out of the window and chewing gum with the slow sideways rhythm of a sheep extracting the last drop of moisture from a blade of grass. Why two secretaries? Andy Unwin had never needed more than one. Barbara. Poor Barbara: sacked as well.

'Mr Skudder is not available today,' announced the dark-haired girl. She sounded bored. She really was incredibly pretty.

Hallam smiled. 'I do need to see him rather urgently, please,' he said, 'If that's at all possible.'

She looked at him with mild amusement, as though noticing him for the first time. 'I jus' told you,' she said. 'I said he's not available, din' I? Jyce said specific not to disturb him.'

'When will he be free, then, please?'

She sighed almost imperceptibly, a little sound like a rustling leaf. She turned to her computer terminal, clicked her mouse a couple of times and looked at the screen. Her fingers were as white and fragile as china.

'Fridy afternoon next week,' she said. 'Six thirty.'

'Friday! I can't wait that long. I'm his sales manager, for goodness' sake. I have to see him much sooner than Friday.'

She shrugged. 'He's chocker. Fridy, six thirty. Yes or no?'

'No,' said Hallam.

She shrugged. 'Suit yourself.'

Calm down. What's the point of getting tetchy? It's not the girl's fault. She's only doing her job.

He smiled at her. 'Look,' he said, 'I really would be most grateful if you could tell Mr Skudder when you next see him that I really do need to talk to him before next Friday. Ideally some time today, if that's at all possible. It really is pretty urgent. I'd be very grateful.'

She tossed her head. Her dark hair danced about her perfect face. 'You'd best send him a memo, then,' she said.

'A memo?'

'A memorandium, like. You never heard of memorandiums?'

'Memoranda. Well, of course I have.'

'Well, then.'

'A memo just to ask for a meeting?'

'Yeah.'

'If I did that I'd be writing him memos asking for meetings every other day.'

'Jyce likes memorandiums.'

'But won't you be speaking to him yourself some time today? Couldn't you just give him a quick message for me?'

'He likes memorandiums best.'

Hallam appealed to the other secretary. She was chewing languidly and flicking through the magazine. 'Excuse me.'

She looked up. 'You what?'

'Could *you* perhaps pass on a message to Mr Skudder for me, please?'

She thought about it. 'Nah,' she said. 'Melody's Jyce's number-one secry. 'Sup to 'er.'

Melody. Yes, of course: she would be.

'I see,' said Hallam tightly. 'Well, thank you both so much for all your help. I really appreciate it.'

Now I'm getting sarcastic. I'm *never* sarcastic.

'Look, if either of you gets a chance, just tell him I really do need to see him, please,' he said. 'Hallam's the name. Peter Hallam. I'm the sales manager.'

He turned and walked away towards the stairs.

'Well, he is at the moment,' said Melody, 'leastways till Shine arrives.'

Hallam sat at his computer terminal and composed a reasoned memo to Jason Skudder. It was cool and rational, pointing out that the smooth running of the sales department depended on an efficient, full-time secretary and that Doreen was excellent at her job and extremely hard-working. He also asked politely for information about the arrival of the new deputy sales manager, Shane Gorman, and the nature of his job.

Melody was filing her fingernails. They were tiny, the palest pink. She looked up. Her eyes engulfed him. 'You again,' she said.

He smiled. 'Yes. Me again.'

'Wotcha want, then?'

'Here's the memo for Mr Skudder.'

He handed it to her.

She gazed at it. She shook her head. 'Gaw, I don't believe it,' she said. 'You takin' the piss?'

'I beg your pardon?'

'You takin' the piss, sendin' Jyce a memo on *paper*?'

'Sorry?'

'You deaf?'

'I don't know what—'

'Doncha know nuffin, Grandad?'

Grandad?

'No one sends *paper* memorandiums no more. Where you bin the lars twenny year? You should of sent Jyce a *computer* memorandium on 'is e-mail, not a memorandium what's printed on paper. You know 'ow to use a computer?'

'Of course I do.'

'Just lots of old guys dunno 'ow.'

'I'm not a complete idiot, you know.'

Melody sniggered. 'Jus' practisin', then, is yer?'

The other girl looked up from her magazine and chortled. 'Nice one, Mel,' she said.

Hallam smiled. '*Touché*,' he said.

They looked at him blankly. 'You what?'

'Never mind.'

He turned and walked away.

In their eyes I'm just a dreary old drone with no sense of humour, he thought, of no interest at all, long past his best, devoid of all passion. To them I'm just a silly old bore.

He felt a sudden deep pang of loss.

As he walked away towards the stairs their voices drifted down the corridor after him.

'Sarky ol' fart,' said the red-haired girl. 'Borin' ol' git.'

'Don't worry, 'e won't be 'ere long,' said Melody. 'Jyce is gonna drop 'im down the plug'ole.'

On the Wednesday morning there was still no reply to Hallam's memo. Neither was there any response on the Wednesday afternoon, nor on the Thursday. Hallam telephoned Skudder's office six times on the Thursday only to be told that Skudder was 'in conference' or 'at an important lunch' or 'on the phone' or 'with a client' or 'with the bank manager' or 'still with the bank manager'. He sent Skudder a second electronic memo asking for an urgent meeting. He left telephone messages with both of Skudder's secretaries. To no avail. Skudder, protected by his own personal security guard and his two killer bimbos, was as silent and unapproachable as a Trappist abbot.

Without Doreen to help him, Hallam found that the paperwork was piling up alarmingly on his desk. He tried to borrow her from the typing pool for a couple of hours to stem the flow but the invisible Skudder kept dumping so much extra work on her and demanding that it should be done immediately that she did not have a moment to spare. Hallam's telephone seemed to ring constantly but there was no one around to answer it for him. Fiona did send a young black temp called Charity to help him out for a couple of hours in the afternoon, but although she was cheerful and obliging she simply did not know where anything was. How could she? And after two hours she was called away to help someone in Accounts.

Doreen's desk sat empty and forlorn in the corner of his office. Its loneliness reproached him. Could he really do nothing to rescue her from the ignominy of the typing pool? Was he really so feeble and powerless? He felt ashamed of himself.

He telephoned Jim Donaldson to ask his advice. Jim's secretary sounded hesitant and distant. 'I'm afraid Mr Donaldson is in a meeting,' she said.

'Will you ask him to call me, please, when he's free?'

'I'm afraid he's in meetings for the rest of the day.'

'Perhaps he could phone me at home tonight, then.'

'Perhaps.' She sounded doubtful.

Hallam replaced the receiver.

So now even my best friend is avoiding me. No, surely not: not Jim. Not *Jim*.

Jim telephoned him at home at seven thirty. 'Sorry about that, Pete,' he said, 'but we have to be bloody careful. The phones in the office are bugged.'

'You've got to be joking.'

'I'm absolutely serious. It was almost the first thing Skudder arranged when he arrived. You must never call me in the office again unless it's actually about business. If you need to speak to me personally then wait until we're both at home. Skudder is bugging calls at random – and in your case every single call you make.'

'I don't believe this.'

'You'd better, Pete, I'm telling you. He's hired an outside security firm to police the building and they're going through your wastepaper basket every night, too.'

'This is unreal.'

'Unfortunately not. Welcome to the real new modern corporate world. It's positively medieval: those security guys of Skudder's are like some private feudal army in the Middle Ages and they owe allegiance to no one except Skudder himself.'

'Hellfire, Jim. So what do I do? He's already making it damned difficult for me to do any work. He's taken Doreen away, he won't see me, he won't even answer my memos.'

'That's the way it works. All you can do is to keep your head down, do your job as well as you can, don't let it get to you and hope that eventually the storm will pass. If you sit it out long enough he'll move on to some more rewarding target. Just batten down the hatches.'

'But it's almost impossible to get any work done.'

'For God's sake don't let Skudder know that, it's just what he wants to hear. He's trying to find some reasonable excuse to fire you without having to pay you off. If you tell him that you can't get any work done he'll say you're not up to the job any more and there'll be nothing that any of us can do to save you.'

'But when I saw him on Monday evening he told me how much he appreciates what I do.'

Jim gave a cynical laugh. 'That's all part of the technique,' he said. 'They call it the Maxwell Treatment, courtesy of that old shit Bob Maxwell, the patron saint of bastard bosses. First they lull you into a false sense of security, then they remove all your support so that it becomes increasingly difficult for you to do your job properly, then they make increasingly impossible demands and finally, when you fail to meet their targets or deadlines – *bingo!* – they can claim that you're utterly inefficient or lazy or both, and out you go. You've given them the excuse they need. Goodnight, Vienna.'

'Hellfire.'

'You'd better believe it, Pete. This is for real. And this new so-called "deputy" of yours: I'm told that he's a dangerous little sod. He used to be Skudder's office spy and arse-licker at Fitzgerald and Parsons. You're going to have to be bloody careful if he's sitting in your office all day listening and reporting back.'

'Hell's bells, Jim! Can't you do anything about all this? You and the other directors? What about telling Willie Mulliken what's going on?'

'He knows already. Tony went to see him.'

'And?'

'Willie says that management must be allowed to manage.'

'Good God, this isn't management, this is rule by terror.'

'Willie says Skudder has the confidence of the bank and that he must be given a chance to make the changes he thinks are necessary.'

'So none of us has any protection at all?'

'Only your contract, Pete. That's all there is between you and me and the dole queue.'

'Oh, great. That's just wonderful. After all these years.'

Jim hesitated a moment. 'Pete . . .'

'Yes?'

'Uh . . . when we're in the office . . .'

'Yes?'

'We'd best . . . well, I think we ought . . . to keep our relationship there sort of . . . well, businesslike, you know.'

'What do you mean?'

Jim coughed. 'Well, I – I don't think it would be awfully good for either of us if Skudder thought we were friends.'

'Jim?'

'For both our sakes. For the time being. Till things settle down.'

That's it, thought Hallam, in a moment of sharp insight. The end of a beautiful friendship. I'm a leper. He's afraid he'll be tainted by me. He's given me up for lost. Jim Donaldson, one of my oldest friends. He's going to dump me.

'There's something wrong at work, isn't there?' said Jenny.

They were sitting in the living room after dinner watching television. Matthew was out as usual, Susie upstairs in her room doing her homework and Monica had gone to bed early for a change.

Jenny reached for the remote control and zapped the TV off. 'You're not watching this at all,' she said. 'You haven't taken in anything for at least ten minutes. Come on, Peter, tell me. There's something wrong at work. What is it?'

'Nothing.'

'Yes there is. I can tell. My God, we've been married long enough. I *know*. What is it?'

He stared at the blank black television screen. He had wanted to protect her, not to worry her. He had always tried to protect her. But of course she had to know. She had a right to know.

'I think I ought to resign,' he said.

Her face froze. 'Resign? From what?'

'The job.'

'The *job*? What on earth are you talking about?'

'I think I may have become too old for it, Jen. Perhaps I've been stuck in a rut too long.'

'Too *old*? What in God's name are you talking about? You're *brilliant* at your job. Everyone says so. Even the new boss. What's his name?'

'Skudder.'

'Didn't he say how good you are? On Monday?'

'Yes.'

'There you are, then.'

'It's not that simple. And things have changed since Monday. It's become quite obvious to everyone that he's gunning for anyone who's over forty-odd. The only reason he hasn't sacked me is that I've got a two-year contract. That's the only protection I've got.'

'And you want to throw it away by resigning? You must be mad.'

'It's only a matter of time, Jen. Even Fiona Wilson knows that he's determined to get rid of everyone over forty within a couple of years.'

'He can't do that.'

'He can. Who's going to stop him?'

'There are laws against that sort of thing, aren't there? Discrimination. Ageism.'

'There aren't.'

'There *must* be.'

'No. You're not allowed to fire someone just because she's a woman or black or disabled or a Mormon but you can sack anyone you like because of their age.'

'That can't be true.'

'It is.'

'That's disgraceful.'

'And even if there were a law against it, how would you prove that you'd lost your job just because you were too old? Skudder would simply tell any industrial tribunal that you'd been fired because you were no good. It would be almost impossible to prove.'

She was worried now. This was not like him. Hallam was usually so positive and optimistic.

'Don't resign,' she said. 'Please, Pete. Sit it out.'

'That's what Jim says too.'

'He's right. Is he in danger too?'

'Not yet. He's only forty-four. He's probably OK for

another year or two. Maybe Skudder won't even last as long as that. These corporate sharks often savage everything in sight for a couple of years and then move on to savage somewhere else.'

'All the more reason for hanging on, then.'

'I don't know if I can. Things are getting pretty nasty at work already. There's a smell in the air. Fear. And what's the point of doing a job where you hate going in to work? What's the point of staying somewhere that you're not wanted? I'd get another job soon enough.'

'Of course you would, but that's not the point. If you resign it means you've given up. You've never given up in your life. Why should you resign just because some little twerp has been made the managing director? You've been there for twenty-four years! It's your life. You've poured your soul into it. It's just as much your company as it's his. It's much *more* your company than it's his.'

Hallam took her hands in his. 'If I stay he'll make my life a misery,' he said. 'He'll give me impossible things to do. He'll watch every move I make, hoping to catch me out. Going to work every morning will be awful. The tension and stress will be dreadful. It'll be hell in that office for months, maybe years. Is it all worth it?'

'You can do it, darling.' She squeezed his hand. 'You're a fighter. You've always been a fighter. You don't give up. Please don't give up.'

She came and knelt on the floor at his knees. She rested her head in his lap. He stroked her hair. Such pretty hair. Sometimes he thought he knew every single strand.

She was right. Of course she was right. Why should a little upstart like Jason Skudder ruin his career and undermine everything he had done for the company? He would see the little bugger off.

'It could get very nasty,' he said. 'I could find myself having to work very late, at weekends, bringing piles of papers home every night. Without any help from Doreen it would—'

Her eyes flashed. 'I'll help!' she said eagerly. 'I can type. I can learn to use the word-processor. I can file and catalogue. Make telephone calls. Whatever you want.'

He bent forward and kissed her. This is all that really matters: this woman, this family, this home, this way of life. Skudder is not going to take all this away from me. No way. 'God, I love you,' he said.

'OK,' said Skudder. 'Now we "turn the screw".'

He twitched his fingers in the air.

'So we take his company car next, then his office. Shift him out into the open-plan sales department with all the erks. Cut his exes down to nothing. Make him clock in and out each day. Tell him he can only have half an hour for lunch. Give him piles of crap jobs to handle. Make him work late. Make him work weekends. Give him a hard time. Give him a bollocking whenever possiboo.'

'Good thinking, boss,' said Shane Gorman. 'Just like what we done to that coon at F and P.'

'Just like that,' said Skudder.

He laughed: 'Ack-ack-ack-ack-ack.'

'Ex'lent!' he said. 'Ack-ack-ack-ack-ack.'

CHAPTER 4

Turning the Screw

On the Monday morning there was a bad accident on the motorway and Hallam arrived half an hour late for work.

A plump young man was sitting at his desk: deeply tanned, curly-haired, in his late twenties, with sharp black eyes too close together, a thin black moustache, a gold chain around his neck and a blue open-necked shirt with the cuffs turned casually back to the elbows to display a huge gold watch on one wrist and a thick gold chain on the other.

'You must be Shane Gorman.'

'Alimentary, my dear Watson,' said Gorman, in a disconcertingly falsetto voice. 'And you must be Shylock Holmes.'

He stood, shorter than Hallam expected, no more than five foot four, and offered his hand.

'Peter Hallam.'

'Hi there, Pete.'

Gorman's handshake was limp, his palm soft and damp. Hallam wanted to wipe his fingers. 'Welcome aboard,' he said. 'I hope you'll be happy here. That's a wonderful tan you've got. Been away?'

Gorman simpered. 'Yeah, me and me friend just come back from holidy in the Seashells.'

'The Seychelles?'

'Yeah, them. Three weeks. You been on 'olidy yet?'

Hallam propped his umbrella up in the coat-rack beside his desk. 'Not yet. We're going to Portugal for a fortnight in September.'

'Is that all? Just one a year?'

'Well, yes, I'm afraid so. There are five of us, so . . .'

'I couldn't be doing with that,' said Gorman. 'I'd go beresk if I only had one holidy a year. Yeah, beresk, I would. I gotta genital weakness for travel, I have. It brawns the mind, see. Oh, yeah, me and me friend done trips all over the world. We done Monica in the South of France plus we done Italy and Cecily where they got that Mount Edna volcano. Plus we done skiing in Shammernicks.'

'Shammernicks?'

'That's in France, that is, up in the Alps, near that Mount Blonk.'

'Chamonix.'

'Yeah. Right. Plus we done the Serviette Union a few years back – Moscow, Red Square – before that Maurice Yeltsin come in.'

Dear God: and this is the man Skudder thinks should be my deputy, perhaps my replacement.

'Fascinating,' said Hallam, moving towards his desk. 'We must have a long chat some time about your travels. In the meantime perhaps we ought to get down to some work. Your desk is that one over there.'

Gorman looked at Doreen's desk and made a face.

'Nah, I rather fancy this one,' he trilled, 'with me back to the window.'

'I'm afraid this one's mine.'

'I gotta have me back to the window. It's me eyes.'

'What's wrong with your eyes?'

'I got sensuous eyes. They can't take too much bright. I gotta have the light behind me.'

'Then we'll have your desk turned to face the wall,' said Hallam firmly, sitting behind his desk and opening his briefcase.

'I can't do that neither,' whined Gorman. 'I got cluster phobia.'

'Just from facing a *wall*?'

'Yeah. I get panic attacks. They just come on. I get pulpytations.'

'Then we'll pull your desk away from the wall and face it away from the light as well. That should do the trick.'

Gorman looked doubtful. 'Then I got no view,' he piped.

'Well, I'm very sorry, Shane,' said Hallam, briskly emptying his briefcase, 'but that's the best I can suggest. Now, tell me, I'm still not sure what exactly your job here is meant to be. Do you know?'

'Course. No sweat.' Gorman approached Doreen's desk apprehensively and settled at it as though it might suddenly savage him. 'Jyce's been in for a rabbit already this morning. Me and him's old mates, used to work together at Fitzgerald and Parsons. He come in half an hour ago to give you instructions with regards to me job only you wasn't here. He were a bit pissed off you wasn't here yet, tell the truth.'

'I was delayed by a crash on the motorway.'

'Yeah? Jyce said you was getting lazy.'

'Oh, he did, did he?'

'Yeah. He don't like no unpunctility, Jyce don't. You wanna watch it with Jyce: he's as tough as old boobs, he is. He told me to tell you he 'spects you at your desk by eight thirty sharp every day.'

'Did he, indeed? And what did he tell you about your job?'

'Well, he's changed his mind. He don't want me to be deputy sales manager no more, he wants me to be associable sales manager so I gotta report to him, not you.'

'I see. And what exactly does that entail?'

'Come again, squire?'

'What exactly does an associate sales manager do?'

'Well, the same as what you does. He give me a couple a jobs to get started on.'

'Oh, yes? And what are they?'

Gorman looked shifty. 'Can't say. Sorry, squire, they're comfydental.'

Hallam felt a sudden surge of irritation. Confidential? How could the associate sales manager's work be kept confidential from the sales manager?

'Confidential?' he said. 'From *me*?'

'Swot Jyce says.'

'I think I'd better speak to Mr Skudder about it as soon as possible. Like right now.'

'Oh, you won't catch him today,' trilled Gorman, smiling winningly. 'He's just went out to see the bank manager and he won't be back all day. You should of come in earlier. He were a bit pissed off with you, tell the truth.'

Hallam telephoned Skudder's office.

'Yeah?'

'Melody?'

'Yeah. Oozat?'

'Peter Hallam.'

''Oo?'

'Peter Hallam, sales manager.'

'Oh, you again. Wotcha want nah?'

'I really *must* see Mr Skudder as soon as possible, please. It's urgent.'

'Gaw, not again. Look, you already got a 'pointment with 'im Fridy week.'

'I *have* to see him before then.'

She sighed dramatically. 'Look, I told ya, he's chocker. He carn' do nuffink till Fridy week.'

'This really is urgent, Melody—'

Her voice rose. 'Nah, look 'ere, Grandad, if yer don't stop pesterin' me I'll tell Jyce yer 'arissin' me. Right? He don't like people 'arissin' 'is secries. Right? Nah, naff off.'

She slammed the telephone down.

A secretary. Just Skudder's secretary. But she slams the phone down on me. This is something else and I'm not standing for it.

'I said, didn't I?' squeaked Gorman. 'Jyce's got a lot on his play these days. He's more busy than the Chancer of the Exchequer and the Arsebishop of Canterbury put together.'

Hallam sent yet another computer memo to Skudder, politely but firmly insisting on a meeting before the end of the week. He spent the rest of the morning ploughing through a mountain of papers and mundane details that would normally have been handled by Doreen. This situation was impossible. And Doreen: how was the poor girl coping? He had to get her out of the typing pool some time, somehow.

Gorman worked in silence at Doreen's desk all morning, gazing at his computer terminal, pulling up files and studying them intently. *What the hell is he up to?* Now and then he would make a loud sucking noise through his teeth and would print out some document and lock it carefully in his top drawer. Once or twice Hallam saw Gorman smirking at the screen. *What the hell is he up to?*

Soon after midday Gorman grunted, switched off his computer, stood, stretched and reached for his jacket.

'Well, I'm off for lunch,' he said.

Hallam looked at his watch. 'Already?'

'Yeah.'

'We usually take lunch between one and two thirty.'

Gorman looked smug. 'I gotta date with an important

new client. Always likes a bottle a shampoo before lunch. Friend of Jyce's.'

'Who's that?'

Gorman tapped his forefinger against the side of his nose. 'Carn' say, can I? Jyce said it gotta be comfydental.'

Hallam leaned forward, his elbows on his desk, his fists pressed together. His knuckles were white. 'Let's get this straight,' he said. 'You, the deputy sales manager . . .'

'Associable sales manager.'

'. . . associate sales manager, are going off to lunch with an important new client but the managing director will not let you tell me, the sales manager, who that client is. Right?'

'Got it in one, squire. See ya later. If anyone needs me I should be back by three thirty, three forty-five.'

Three and a half hours for lunch!

Gorman winked. 'It's the other side of town, see,' he said, 'and me company car hasn't arrived yet.'

So he's getting a company car, too, is he? Already. On his first day. Only the directors and departmental heads are given company cars.

Hallam could not resist it: he had to know. 'So what sort of car are you getting?'

Gorman smirked. 'TVR Griffith five hundred,' he said. 'Coming next week. Pearlyscent silver, soft top, cream leather seats, mohair roof, tinted glass, hallo wheels, power steering, heated seats, air-conditioning – the works. Brand new, in Christine condition.'

Good grief: a Griffith 500? That costs – what? Thirty-eight, thirty-nine thousand. Hellfire: nearly £40,000-worth of company car. Sex on wheels.

'What sort a car you got, then?' said Gorman.

'A Cavalier.'

Gorman stared at him. He grimaced. 'A Cavalier? Bloody 'ell, I wooden stand for that, mate. I wooden stand for that at all. You oughter have a word with Jyce about that. Now,

I better be off. Have a nice lunch: *bonn happy teeth*, as the Frogs say in Monica.'

A Griffith 500? And three-hour champagne lunches? If Skudder won't see me soon I've *got* to go to Mulliken, face him with what's going on. Something has to be done before it's too late.

When Gorman had gone to lunch Hallam telephoned Doreen in the typing pool. She sounded harassed.

'How's it going?' he said.

'It's horrible,' she said, in a low voice. 'That bastard is making Fiona give me all the really lousy jobs: long, unintelligible audio-tapes to transcribe, letters to be done over and over again even though there's nothing wrong with them, work to take home at night. It's driving me mad, Peter. I don't know how much longer I can take all this. I'm not sleeping . . .'

'Look, Dor,' he said, 'don't do anything hasty. Not yet. I'm trying to get to see Skudder, to sort it all out.'

'You'll be lucky,' she said.

He wandered down the corridor to show his face in the sales department. The open-plan office was weirdly quiet. Usually there was a quiet hum of activity and banter but today the staff were bent in silence over their terminals. The air was stiff with apprehension. Even Keith Smith seemed to be rooted to his desk beside the main door: Keith the jester, always ready with a quip or a joke, Keith who could make almost anyone laugh just by looking at them with his manic expression, his wild hair and those huge, bulbous, lugubrious eyes. Today he was silent. He looked morose.

Hallam stopped at his desk. 'How's tricks?' he said. 'You're all very quiet today.'

Keith leaned back, pushed his chair away from his desk and ran his fingers through his jungle of hair. He sighed.

'You can say that again, *bwana*. It's like a bloody morgue in here these days. Nobody dares to breathe. They're all terrified.'

'Of what?'

'Of being sacked. Getting something wrong. Just catching Skudder's eye. God, he's an ugly bastard, isn't he? I mean, I know I'm not exactly an oil painting myself but this bugger deserves some sort of prize. Stick him in a beauty contest with Quasimodo, King Kong and the Elephant Man and Skudder would come fourth. And that bonce of his: bloody hell, if he wandered into a cemetery at midnight with the moon behind him all the stiffs would sit up with their hands in the air.'

Hallam laughed.

Keith rolled his vast eyes. 'It's not funny, *bwana*. It's a tragedy. This place used to be great to work in, thanks to you and Andy Unwin, but not any more. People hate coming to work now. Everyone gets in half an hour early and they're afraid to leave at night in case they're accused of slacking. People sit around till eight, eight thirty, pretending to be busy. And no wonder: Skudder came in this morning and saw Mary and Donna getting themselves some coffee from the machine and, of course, they were having a bit of a chat while they waited for the coffee to come out, but Skudder just went ballistic. He nearly went into orbit. And his language! Jesus! "Get back to your effing work stations, you effing slags," he yelled. "If I catch either of you effing gossiping again you're out." Jeez, you'd think he'd caught them giving blow-jobs behind the filing cabinet. And since when was a desk a bloody "work station", anyway?'

'He's been in today? Skudder? This morning?'

Keith nodded. 'Yeah, sure.'

'When was this?'

'An hour and a half ago, maybe two.'

'Damnation. They told me he wouldn't be in at all today.'

Keith looked at him with sympathy. 'You too?'

Hallam nodded. You could trust Keith. A good man. Loyal.

'Oh, boy. Then we might as well all pack up and go home.'

This can't go on. People can't be expected to work their best in conditions like these. Something has got to be done to raise their morale.

He raised his voice, clapped his hands twice and addressed the whole room. 'Would you all gather round, please?' he said.

They turned to look at him. His people. Twenty-two of them. They needed him. They depended on him.

'Yes. Here, please. Now. Yes. That's it. I've got something to say.'

They left their desks and gathered round, forming a circle beyond Keith's desk. Hallam waited until they were all within easy hearing: George Pringle looking frightened and older than his forty-nine years; Elsie Benson as nervous as a mouse; and the younger ones apprehensive too – Ian Forbes, Molly Unwin, Paul Yallop, Leila Roberts, Bill, Simon, Mary, Donna, good people, all of them. They did not deserve this. They deserved to be nurtured and encouraged, not bullied and harangued.

Hallam cleared his throat and nodded. 'I just want to say one thing,' he said, looking at several of them in turn. 'I know you're all worried about the recent changes and that's only natural. A lot of things have changed very quickly and some people have had to go and that's always unpleasant. But I'm glad to say that no one has gone from this department – quite rightly, because you're all great at your jobs – and I want to reassure you that none of you is going to go, either. Mr Skudder has assured me of that, quite categorically. So let there be no doubt about it: no one here, not one of you, faces the sack. Your jobs are all safe so long as I am here.

I give you my word. That's a promise. So let's get back to enjoying our jobs again, as we did before. Work can be hard and earnest – it *should* be hard and earnest – but it ought to be fun as well.'

They stared at him.

They don't believe me. I'm not sure if I believe myself. But it had to be done. Something had to be done.

Keith started some gentle clapping and six or seven of them took it up, giving him a ripple of applause.

'And now let's get back to work,' he said. 'And if any of you has any particular personal worries, anything at all, you have only to come to me and I'll see if I can help. My door is always open.'

They stared at him. Two or three smiled. Others still looked worried. Elsie was fiddling compulsively with a button on her cardigan. George's left eyelid was twitching uncontrollably.

'OK,' said Hallam. 'That's it. That's all.'

They don't believe a bloody word of it.

He met Rupert Johnson for lunch in the Toad in the Hole on the corner of Darwin Street: a pint and a half of bitter each, a couple of cheese and chutney sandwiches, the genial buzz of a City pub at lunch-time, the relief of an hour nattering with someone who worked elsewhere, who knew nothing about the nightmare of Skudder.

He returned to the office at two o'clock and saw that Skudder had returned his two most recent claims for expenses. The forms were lying in his in-tray with almost every other item crossed out with a red pen. His claims had been slashed by more than half without any explanation. *How dare he?* Every single claim was absolutely genuine, of course it was: he had never in his life fiddled his expenses. How *dare* he? He had to see Skudder as soon as possible. This couldn't go on.

He switched on his terminal. Across the top of the screen

there flashed a line of type telling him that there was a new message waiting in his internal e-mail. He retrieved it. Melody's beautiful, incompetent fingerprints were all over it from the very first word:

MEMORANDIUM

TO: Peter Hallam, sales manager
FROM: Jason Skudder, Managing Director
SUBJECT: *CHANGES IN YOUR DEPARTMINT*
DATE: 15 June

(1) Mr Shane Gorman, is appointed Associated Sales Manager with immediate affect and will answer only to me.

(2) For health reasons you will swop Work Stations with Mr Gorman so that he faces away from the light.

(3) You will stop harissin my sectries immediately. You will not enter my sectrie's Office exept when I want you.

(4) Why wasn't you in your office this morning when I come to see you? In future you will be at your Work Station by 8.29 every day. I will be checking.

(5) I notice your work is piling up on your Work Station. This is against company Polisy. I expect your Work Station to be cleared every night before you leave the office. Work that canot be completed in office hrs must be done at Home.

J S

Hallam stared at the memo. He scrolled it back down the screen and read it again. He could barely believe it. He read it a third time.

How *dare* he?

Hallam stood up. His heart was hammering. His face in the mirror beside the coat-rack was pale and strained.

Calm. Be calm. The last thing I need now is a heart-attack. What an irony that would be: Skudder would have got rid of me for nothing.

He dug his fingernails into his palms. The sharp pain diverted his anger.

The telephone rang. He lifted the receiver.

'Pete?'

Sid Thomas, the transport manager. He had always liked Sid: good man, nice wife, played a neat game of golf, did conjuring tricks at children's parties.

'Sid?'

'I'm so sorry, Pete,' said Sid. 'Skudder says you no longer need your company car. I've got to have the keys. I think this place is going mad.'

Hallam took the steps two at a time, running up both flights to the top floor and striding briskly along the corridor to Skudder's office.

He pushed the door open.

''Ere!' said Melody. 'You carn' come in 'ere.'

He walked towards Skudder's inner door. The security man stood up and moved in front of the door to bar his way.

'Let me in, please,' said Hallam.

'I'm sorry, sir. I got my instructions.'

'I'm the sales manager. I need to see Mr Skudder.'

'I'm sorry, sir. Mr Skudder said no visitors till six o'clock. He's in a meeting.'

Melody glared at him. 'Jyce said specific you wasn't to come in,' she said.

'Very well,' said Hallam. He sat on the sofa and picked up a magazine from the glass table. 'I shall sit here and wait until six o'clock, or however long it takes before he comes out.'

'You're gonna be in trouble for this,' said Melody, with satisfaction. 'Jyce won't like this at all, he won't.'

Hallam looked at her and smiled. 'Shut it, sweetheart,' he said.

He sat in the waiting area for more than two hours, flicking through magazines and a couple of newspapers. Melody disappeared into Skudder's office for fifteen minutes and Hallam could hear a hurried conversation inside. She emerged with a smug expression. 'You're for it, you are,' she said.

Hallam gazed out of the window. People were working on several floors of the building opposite, each window framing some drama, achievement, unhappiness, the inhabitants of each unaware of those above and beneath. How small they all look from here, he thought, how trivial their hopes and fears and endless jostling for position. We're just modern cavemen, that's all, each one of us cooped up in a shadowy hole in the side of some steep mountain, unaware that the sun is shining outside and the air is fresh and free.

He studied the ugly modern pictures on the walls. He glanced at Melody. She really was stunningly good-looking: what a shame she was such a little bitch. He glanced at the other girl: not bad either. Skudder certainly knew how to pick the lookers. Her skin was like milky silk. Shame about the voice. Whenever she answered the telephone she sounded like a duck quacking.

He looked at his watch. He folded and unfolded his arms. He crossed and uncrossed his legs. The minutes dragged. A clock ticked loudly above the doorway. Every now and then a telephone rang. The security guard kept clearing his throat and looking at his watch.

At six fifteen the intercom buzzed. Melody answered it. 'OK, Jyce. Right. Yeah. Wicked.'

She put the receiver down, switched off her terminal and began to clear her desk. 'Come on, Liz,' she said. 'He says we can go.'

The women both disappeared along the corridor towards the ladies' lavatory. Hallam eyed the security guard.

Any moment now. At last.

After six or seven minutes the secretaries returned. They collected their coats and handbags. Melody smiled at the security guard.

'OK, Steve,' she said. 'You can go now, too.'

She looked at Hallam with contempt. 'And so can you, Grandad,' she said.

'I'm not going anywhere until I've seen Skudder.'

She laughed unpleasantly. 'He's gone already,' she said, and laughed again. 'He'll see you Fridy unless you go on playing silly buggers.'

Of course. How bloody stupid. The other door.

He had forgotten how unpleasant it was to travel to and from work by train during the rush-hour. The pavements leading to the nearest station were jammed with thousands of commuters scurrying and jostling home towards the barriers and elbowing towards the edges of the platforms. Men and women pushed and shouldered each other like pigs stampeding into an abattoir. By the time Hallam boarded his train the seats had all been taken and he had to stand for forty-five minutes wedged between a fat woman who stank of garlic and kept sniffing, coughing and prodding him with her umbrella, and the sweaty, open armpit of a huge, hairy man wearing a vest but no shirt who hung from a strap by one hand like a chimpanzee. Somewhere in the packed carriage the heavy metallic beat of a personal CD player rattled and pounded on and on. The train moved like a hesitant tortoise, stopping often for no apparent reason, jolting whenever it started so that all the standing passengers had to hang on tightly to anything that might stop them skittling each other down the aisle.

And people do this every day, he thought. Twice a day, five days a week. This is the twentieth century. This is civilisation.

He was hot, tired and irritable when he reached home after a fifteen-minute walk from the railway station. His back was sweaty, his shirt and suit damp and crumpled, his tie twisted out of shape.

I can't do this every day, twice a day. Not for long. It's not so bad now, in the summer, perhaps, but in the winter . . . I'm too old for all this malarkey, all this rushing and pushing and shoving. *Too old?* Yes: old. Maybe Skudder is right.

'Cuckoo!' called Monica, as he opened the front door. 'Is that you, Peter? Cuckoo!'

So help me, if she recites another limerick tonight I shall bite her ankles and then throttle her. Slowly.

She was sitting in the living room watching some raucous game show on television, shouting at the contestants, smoking and sipping at a cut-glass tumbler of gin and tonic that clinked with chunks of ice. She was wearing blue jeans, a white T-shirt with the slogan GRANNIES LIB and the red peaked cap.

She looked up. 'It *is* you, Peter!' she exclaimed. 'How nice!'

'Hallo, Miss Porridge.' He shrugged himself out of his jacket. 'Who did you think it might be, then? Cary Grant?'

'Oh, no, dear, not Archie. You couldn't have been Archie – he died more than ten years ago. His real name was Archie, you know, Archibald Leach.'

'Come off it, Monica.'

'It's true,' she said. 'He was born in Bristol. I knew him well in Hollywood.' She gave a private little smile and sipped her gin. 'Very well indeed,' she said.

Cary Grant? What rubbish. How did she hope to get away with it, the lying old trout? Well, easily: most of these people she claimed to have known were dead, so nobody could actually prove she was lying. Perhaps that was one of the few advantages of growing old: you could tell outrageous fibs about your life.

'If I'd stayed on any longer in Hollywood,' she said, 'I think he might have married me.'

'I need a drink,' he said, 'a very large one.'

Susie bounded down the stairs, came into the living room like a gust of wind and gave him a big smile and a hug. Her eyes shone. 'Hi, Dad,' she said, and kissed him on the cheek. She hugged him again. 'It's lovely to have you home.'

She loves me. She really loves me: this delightful child-woman, this beautiful person who is always suffused with laughter and warmth. How did I get her to love me? I never tried. What did I do to deserve her? And Jenny.

'Gran won on the horses again today. Isn't it great?'

'Well done, Miss Porridge,' said Hallam.

'It came as no surprise,' said Monica. 'My stars said I was in for a bit of luck.'

'Where's Matt?'

Susie shrugged and tossed her head. 'Out.'

'Where?'

'Who cares?' said Monica. 'I wouldn't mind another little drinkie if you're going that way.'

He took her glass.

'You're a sweet boy,' she said, 'despite the rumours.'

Sweet again. Sweet. I don't want to be sweet, I want to be a ruthless bastard like Skudder.

Monica reached into the sleeve of her sweater, retrieved a handkerchief to blow her nose and stopped, staring at it. She frowned. 'Now why did I tie that knot in it?'

'To remind you of something?'

'Well, of course,' she said, 'but to remind me of what?

I've forgotten. Dear Lord: another little Senior Moment. Hi there, Uncle Al Zheimer.'

'Perhaps you'd better smoke a bit more. And tie another knot in the handkerchief to remind you to remember what it was you wanted to remember.'

She gave him a sharp look. 'Don't be cheeky,' she said.

She collects bits of string, too, and elastic bands, and paperclips, pieces of cardboard, old envelopes, half-used paper, hoarding them on shelves and in cupboards, and none of them is ever seen again.

Jenny was in the kitchen, creating miraculous fragrances of cooking, herbs and spices. He kissed her.

'Hello, darling,' she said. 'I didn't hear the car.'

I'm not going to tell her yet about the car. Why worry her unnecessarily? Once I tell her what's happened it'll mean I've accepted it and given up the fight and that would be disastrous. I haven't accepted it. I can't. I won't. If necessary I'll leave and sue the bugger.

'It broke down. It's in the garage. I had to get the train.'

'Oh, no. How long will it be?'

'Two or three days. They need to order a part.'

'What's wrong with it?'

'God knows. Something technical. You know me.'

She laughed and hugged him. 'Do you want to use mine tomorrow?'

'That'd be nice. You sure you don't need it?'

'Oh, damn. I've just remembered: I promised to give Paula and Ginny a lift to the Red Cross charity lunch.'

'Never mind, darling. Don't worry. It won't kill me to get the train again.'

'You sure? I'm so sorry.'

She turned back to the stove.

'Nice day otherwise?' she said. 'At work?'

'Not too bad.'

'Oh, I *am* glad, darling. I've been so worried about you.

About us all. You know, you talking about resigning. It frightened me. What would we do if you did? How would we live?'

'I'd get another job, of course. But it won't come to that.'

'You look tired. I'll pour you a drink. The usual?'

'That'd be great. Please. But first I need a shower. I feel all wrung out after the train.'

'I'll pour it for you. Dinner's in half an hour.'

This is it. This is what really matters: my women, my family, my home. This is my haven. Nothing that Skudder can do can change all this.

A sound of devilish, pagan laughter came from the television set.

Upstairs, before he undressed to go into the shower, he looked up Cary Grant in *Chambers Biographical Dictionary*. 'GRANT, Cary,' it said, 'originally Archibald Leach (1904–86) British-born American film actor, born in Bristol.'

The TV laughed again.

'I'm so sorry, Peter,' Sid Thomas had said, when he came to collect the car keys.

'It's hardly your fault. But can't you let me keep the car until I see Skudder on Friday?'

Sid had looked embarrassed. 'I wish I could but it's more than my job's worth. He's already bawled me out when I queried Gorman's new company car. Do you know what he's getting? A Griffith five hundred!'

'So I hear.'

'A Griffith five hundred! It's a bloody disgrace. This place is going mad. I'm so sorry, Pete. And you heard the latest rumour? They say Skudder's bringing in his girlfriend to be the new personnel manager.'

'But that's Fiona's job.'

'Not any more. He's demoted her to deputy personnel manager.'

'But he can't do that.'

Sid gazed at him. 'Who's going to stop him?'

I will. Hellfire, I bloody well will. I'm going to go and see Mulliken, put a stop to all this.

'I bloody well will,' said Hallam.

Sid looked at him sadly. 'I wish I could believe you,' he said.

Hallam came out of the shower, dried himself vigorously and felt renewed. He wrapped a towel around his waist and consulted his diary. Mulliken, Willie. He reached for the bedside telephone and dialled the number.

'Mulliken.'

'Mr Mulliken. It's Peter Hallam.'

'Hallam?'

Hell's bells, he doesn't even remember who I am.

'Sales manager.'

'Ah, yes, of course. Hallam. What can I do for you?'

He took a deep breath.

This is it. Percy Langan has already been sacked for complaining to Mulliken but someone has to do it. Somebody has to stop the rot.

'I need to see you urgently, sir,' he said. 'Tomorrow morning, if possible.'

'What's all this about?' said Mulliken, with a trace of irritation in his voice.

Damn. Perhaps I've caught him in the middle of dinner.

'I can't really say over the phone,' said Hallam. 'It's . . . ah . . . confidential. There are people . . .'

Another lie.

'It's urgent, sir. I'm sorry to bother you, but . . .'

'Very well, but it'll have to be early. Seven thirty. I have a meeting at eight. Yes?'

'Seven thirty. Fine.'

'In my office in Southery Street.'

'Fine. Yes. I'll be there. And thank you.'

'I very much hope this is not about Jason Skudder,' said Mulliken, and put down the telephone.

'Was that you on the phone?' said Jenny. 'I heard it ping.'

'Just a quick call. Business. Jim Donaldson.'

Yet another lie. Why am I lying? To protect her. To stop her worrying until it's really necessary. But I never used to lie. Now Skudder's turned me into a liar as well. Skudder is turning me into someone I don't like at all.

He dressed, went downstairs, retrieved his drink and sat in the living room. The TV had been switched off.

'I've got a brilliant new limerick for you,' said Monica.

CHAPTER 5

Up a Gum Tree Without a Paddle

He caught the 6.32 a.m. train into the City. It was another glorious morning and the carriage was not nearly as crowded at this time of day. The passengers were clearly in a different social class from those who travelled during the rush-hour. They were labourers, workmen in overalls, messenger boys, cleaning women: people who did not spend their lives cooped up in offices like battery hens. They smiled more than the middle-class crowd and they made jokes, bantered with each other, laughed. They seemed happier and more relaxed.

Maybe there's more warmth at the bottom of the pile.

During the journey into town he rehearsed what he was going to say to Mulliken, trying out different approaches. None of them seemed quite right. Most, in fact, sounded pathetic, as though he were some whingeing six-year-old snivelling in the playground: 'Daddy, Daddy, that horrid boy's taken my toys away and he won't let me play any more.'

He took two buses to reach Mulliken's office in the City, becoming increasingly apprehensive. It was high in a tower block and slick with the usual trappings of commercial success: vast windows, a stunning view across the river, thick white carpets, huge polished wooden desk, expensive paintings, open fireplace with flames flickering among a few small logs, huge TV, real antiques, an elegant secretary who spoke with a crystal accent. Even her smile seemed genuine. 'He'll see you now, Mr Hallam,' she said.

His heart was pounding. This is ridiculous. Why am I so nervous? He's only the chairman, just another human being. 'I very much hope this is not about Jason Skudder,' he had said.

Mulliken was at his desk in his shirtsleeves, one of those sleek, slim men in their late fifties who look ridiculously fit and impossibly expensive: £1,200 suit, £300 blue-striped shirt, £90 tie, £850 shoes, £75 haircut. Even the discreet hint of aftershave suggested a man with a bank manager who bows from the waist. It was probably thirty years since Willie Mulliken had last had to catch a train or a bus.

Mulliken rose from behind his desk. 'Hallam,' he said, in a silky voice. 'Good to see you again. What is it? Two years? Three? And how's that lovely wife of yours? Jenny. And the children? Matthew? Susan?'

I had an efficient secretary like yours once, too, and I want her back again.

Mulliken came towards him and shook hands. His palms were soft but firm, his fingernails immaculately manicured. He waved Hallam towards an armchair by the fireplace and sat in another on the other side.

'I won't offer you coffee, if you don't mind. I've got this blasted meeting at eight. So what's it all about, eh? What's the problem?'

How to start? What do I say? I've rehearsed it all, over and over again, and I still don't know the best way to tackle it.

'I'm afraid it *is* about Jason Skudder,' he said.

Mulliken's genial expression slipped. A cloud passed across

his eyes. He folded his arms. A pair of sleek platinum cufflinks winked in the sunlight. *He doesn't want to know. He's not even going to listen.*

'Go on.'

Hallam swallowed. His throat was dry. 'This is not a personal matter,' he said. 'Well, not entirely.'

Mulliken stared at him.

'What I mean is, I believe very strongly that I'm coming to you for the good of the company as a whole. I feel certain that what I am going to say would be supported by ninety per cent of the staff, if not more.'

I must look Mulliken in the eye. I've only got the one chance. He has to take me seriously. He has to believe me.

He looked Mulliken in the eye. 'I'm sure that Mr Skudder will turn out in the end to be an excellent appointment but—'

'But what?' Mulliken's expression was cold.

It all sounds so pathetic. So feeble.

'I truly believe that he's started off on the wrong foot,' said Hallam. 'He's only been with the company just over a week but already he's sacked nearly twenty people.'

'Dead wood.'

'Well, yes, some of them, maybe—'

'That's what he says.'

Well, he would, wouldn't he?

'It's not only that, it's the atmosphere of the place. It used to be such a happy place but now . . .'

'What?'

'Now it's . . . well, it's incredibly *un*happy.'

'We're not running a holiday camp, Hallam.'

'No, of course, but . . . morale is incredibly low. Skudder frightens people. He bullies them. He lashes out. Everyone is terrified that they're going to lose their jobs.'

Mulliken looked at his watch. 'They won't if they're any good.'

He doesn't want to know. He doesn't give a damn.

'Well, perhaps I should be more specific, give you a particular example,' said Hallam.

Mulliken gazed at him. 'You, I suppose.'

'Yes.'

Mulliken's nostrils twitched. 'I thought it might be.'

I'm losing this. I'm getting nowhere.

'I've been the sales manager for fifteen years now, but within days of taking over Skudder has deprived me of my secretary, my company car and my expense account, making it almost impossible to do my job. He refuses to speak to me or even to answer my memos. In addition he has brought in a young man over my head who knows nothing whatever about the business but who is apparently to be my superior.'

Mulliken tugged at his ear. As a gesture it seemed horribly dismissive. 'So it *is* personal,' he said. 'You obviously have a particular grudge against Skudder.'

'Well, no, not a grudge. I just—'

'I thought you said you were coming to me for the good of the company.'

'Well, I am.'

'It seems to me that you are more concerned with complaining about your own minor problems with the new management.'

'No, that's—'

Mulliken fixed him with a stare. 'Listen to me, Hallam. I shall do you a favour by not mentioning this visit to Skudder. Should he hear of it he would undoubtedly be extremely angry – and justifiably so – that you have seen fit to come complaining to me behind his back. If you have a specific complaint to make then I suggest you go through the proper channels and the proper complaints procedure: the personnel manager first, then the personnel director and finally, if necessary, to Skudder himself.'

'But that would be—'

Mulliken raised his hand. 'Don't interrupt me, Hallam. What you do not do if you have a piddling personal complaint is to come to the chairman and waste my time. Good God, man, I've got better things to do than to listen to your whining.'

Hallam stood. 'If that's your opinion of me then I shall not waste any more of your time.'

'I'm pleased to hear it.'

I can't just let it end like this. This is our last chance: my only chancc. If I lose Mulliken I might as well give up.

'You're obviously not prepared even to consider that Skudder should treat his staff with more consideration and encouragement.'

Mulliken stood and moved smoothly back to his desk. 'Management must be allowed to manage.'

'My argument entirely,' said Hallam desperately. 'And since I am the sales manager I should be allowed to manage Sales.'

Mulliken sat behind his desk. 'And Skudder is the managing director and therefore entitled to manage the sales manager, no matter how long he may havc worked for the company. Times have changed, Hallam. It's a young world out there nowadays and we of the older generation have got to accept that we must be prepared to welcome younger talent, even if necessary to make way and step back to let them take the reins.'

You smug old bastard: when did you ever step back for anyone?

'Those are the facts and it is useless to resent them. They are *facts*, Hallam. Young men must be given their head. Skudder is an energetic and resourceful young man who comes to us highly recommended and with a superb track record and some excellent ideas. Do you think I would have appointed him had it not been so?'

'Of course not, but—'

'But nothing, Hallam. Perhaps Skudder is a little brusque, even ruthless, but difficult times demand ruthless measures. As you say yourself, he has only been in the job for just over a week: he must be given time to settle down and prove himself. Now I have a meeting to go to. Good day to you, Hallam.'

He did not offer his hand.

'He's sacking everyone over forty-five. Is that with your approval too?'

Mulliken stared at him. His eyes were brilliantly clear. *But still he just can't see.*

'How old are you, Hallam?'

'Forty-five.'

'Has Skudder sacked you?'

'No.'

'So he can't be sacking everyone over forty-five.'

'Not yet, but he's trying to get rid of me, trying to drive me out.'

Mulliken sighed and looked at his watch again. 'I cannot go on bandying words with you, Hallam,' he said. 'We've wasted quite enough time and I have an important meeting in fifteen minutes. If you have some personal problem then you must take it up with the personnel manager.'

'That would be a complete waste of time. Skudder's just appointed a new one, his girlfriend.'

Mulliken looked up sharply. 'Is this true?'

Hallam faltered.

'You have proof?'

'No. Not actual proof, no. I've just been told—'

Mulliken's face was reddening. 'I suggest you should be exceedingly careful with your slanderous allegations, Hallam. Coming here, wasting my time with wild accusations and idle gossip. Go away, Hallam, and count yourself extremely fortunate that I have decided not to tell Skudder about this meeting.'

Hallam nodded. 'I'm sorry you are not prepared to listen to me,' he said, 'but thank you for seeing me. And I will say just one more thing. If Skudder is allowed to continue to behave as he is he will ruin the company. Not one of your employees will be able to give of his best in the present atmosphere. The best people will leave and those who are left will be a bunch of petrified incompetents. One day you will deeply regret your refusal to take me seriously.'

Mulliken stared at him.

'Go away, Hallam,' he said.

So now we're all on our own, with no defence, no support. It's every man for himself and to hell with the women and children.

Gorman was sitting at Hallam's desk when he reached the office. He was tapping at Hallam's computer keyboard.

'Out!' said Hallam.

Gorman looked defiant. 'No,' he trilled. 'Jyce said. I've moved all your stuff. From your draws.'

'Out, Gorman! This has been my desk for years.'

Gorman hugged himself nervously. 'No. And Jyce said if you was difficult I gotta call Security and they'll chuck you out a the building all together.'

Dear God. Like children in the nursery, and all because of a desk. And it's only a desk. Why should I make a scene about it? It's only a bloody desk. There are other ways to deal with this. Skudder. On Friday. Somehow I have to persuade Skudder to see reason.

'Jyce were here half an hour ago,' said Gorman. 'He left some papers on your work station over there.'

'It's a desk, Gorman, not a work station. What the hell is a work station?'

Gorman sniffed. 'He were right pissed off that you was late again.'

A pile of papers four inches deep lay on Doreen's desk. Stuck to the top sheet was a message scrawled in childish writing on a yellow Post-It label. 'Hallam:' it said, 'Urgent. See to these today. JS.' And then, underlined: 'Late again. Why? I'm fed up of your excuses.'

For a moment he was threatened by a small wave of despair. There was nothing left now but rebellion or surrender. He dumped the new pile of papers on top of another pile that had also come from Skudder and was still left over from yesterday. He would never get through them all this week, not on top of everything else, not even if he worked sixteen hours a day, not even if he took them home every night.

Come back, Doreen, I'm drowning.

'I don't give a stuff about Skudder,' he said, sitting at Doreen's desk.

'You what?'

'You heard.'

'You'll be up a gum tree without a paddle, mate, if you go on like this,' trilled Gorman. 'He'll have you doing penile servitude for life.'

Hallam pulled the new pile of papers towards him. Until now he had always enjoyed his job, but for the first time in his working life he felt inadequate. He leafed through the papers with increasing bewilderment. None had anything at all to do with his job or with the sales department. They referred to forward planning, product alteration, financial estimates, ultimate projections. What did Skudder expect him to do with this lot? It did not make sense. Of course it did: Skudder expected him to be upset by them, to stumble, falter, make mistakes. He would not give Skudder the satisfaction.

He spent the morning working slowly through the sheaf of unlikely papers, telephoning colleagues when he was baffled and passing the documents on to the departments that ought to be dealing with them.

At twelve fifteen Gorman left for an early lunch.

'Another new client?' said Hallam.

Gorman smirked. 'Nah, Jyce is taking me to the Ritz to celebrate my arrival.'

'How jolly nice of him. I thought he was terribly busy this week, no time for anything.'

'He's always got time for me, squire. Him and me's old mates.'

When Gorman had gone Hallam telephoned Doreen in the typing pool.

'Can you talk?' he said.

'No.'

'Doreen? You there?'

Silence.

'Doreen?'

She had cut him dead. *Doreen*.

Gorman's telephone rang.

He ignored it. Why should he answer it? Let the bloody thing ring.

After half a dozen rings the telephone fell silent again and a few seconds later there was a tap at the door. Doreen poked her head into his office.

'Has he gone?'

'Gorman? Yes.'

'For lunch?'

'Yes.'

She came in quickly and closed the door. She was jittery.

She noticed where he was sitting. 'What on earth are you doing at my desk?' she said.

'I've been moved. Skudder.'

'So who's . . .'

'Gorman.'

'Oh, no. Oh, Peter, I'm so sorry. Skudder must be out of his mind.'

She looked nervously over her shoulder. 'Look, I've got to be quick. I'm sorry about hanging up on you but Skudder has forbidden me to have anything to do with you, even to speak to you. And your phone is bugged.'

'So I've been told. I still can't believe it.'

'You'd better. Stan Norman in Security told me. And beware of Gorman. He's poison. He stays on late at night after you've gone. He's going through your desk, your files, your wastebin, everything he can find. He's trying to find something to trip you up, anything.'

'But that's ridiculous.'

'No, Dick Johnson saw him in here last night. Dick was working late, went past in the corridor, saw the light on in here, peeked in through the glass panel and there was Gorman sitting at your desk – right there – and all the rubbish from your wastebin was spread all over it and he was reading it.'

'Hellfire.'

'What's more, your desk drawers were open too.'

'Would Dick be prepared to go on record? Give evidence?'

'Of course not. Come on, Peter, how could he? He wouldn't last another day here if he did. And now Fiona's been demoted.'

'I heard. Bloody disgrace. What's the new woman like? I'm told she's Skudder's girlfriend.'

Doreen laughed sourly. 'Dawn Francis. I wouldn't be at all surprised. She's almost as ugly as him: small eyes, mean little mouth, smell under her nose. She looks like she hates everyone. They don't spoil a pair.'

She looked hurriedly at her watch. 'I'd better go,' she said. 'I've got a mountain of stuff to do.'

'Look, stick with it, Dor,' he said. 'Chin up. Don't let

them get you down. We'll see this through together. Just don't weaken. OK?'

'I'll try.'

She opened the door a fraction, stuck her head out, checked the corridor, and was gone like a phantom.

What has Skudder *done* to us all?

A small rage was beginning to burn at the back of Hallam's mind. How could even Skudder treat people like this? How could he look at himself in the mirror? How did he sleep at nights? This was no way for any company to be run. Yes, times had changed and office life had become very different from what it had been in the seventies and early eighties. In those days the balance of power had been tilted towards the workers and their trade unions, but now it was the employers who were completely in control. Ordinary workers nowadays were little better than feudal serfs. *Thank you, Lady Thatcher*. What had happened to all those promises of shorter working hours and greater leisure? Anyone who still had a job was working harder and longer than ever. Many of them had hardly any time for their wives, husbands and families. Nine out of ten were highly stressed and deeply unhappy. All those miraculous labour-saving devices – all those computers, modems, fax machines, photocopiers – had not made life any easier, they had simply put huge numbers out of work. And the fear of unemployment had spawned a new breed of brutal employer, an entire race of Skudders.

They have to be resisted and driven back, thought Hallam grimly. *We cannot let them get away with it.*

Gorman returned from lunch at five to four, his face glowing with alcohol and self-satisfaction. He was smiling to himself. He glanced at Hallam and smirked. He swayed slightly as he headed towards Hallam's old desk.

Hallam ignored him.

Gorman sat at the desk, gave a deep sigh, belched, switched on the terminal, pulled up a computer file and gazed at it glassily.

He's drunk. Nearly four hours for a drunken lunch – with Skudder, yet Skudder claims to be too busy to spare even five minutes for his sales manager. I get the message now, at last: there's no point at all in seeing Skudder on Friday or on any other day. There is obviously not the slightest chance of any compromise. This is a war with no truce and no prisoners. One of us is going to have to go – and after talking to Mulliken it's obvious that that one of us is me. It is simply a matter of how and why and when. I'm going to have to resign, maybe sue for constructive dismissal. My job has been taken away and given to Gorman instead. That's constructive dismissal, surely, without any doubt.

It was another hellish, crowded, sweaty journey home by train again that night, but once he was home and sipping his evening Scotch on the terrace in the twilight Hallam's determination to resign and sue Skudder for constructive dismissal began to evaporate.

It was a lovely balmy summer evening of birdsong. He and Monica sat on the terrace basking in the peace of the lengthening shadows. Jenny and Susie were singing together in the kitchen as they prepared the dinner, 'Happy Days Are Here Again,' Monica was doing the crossword and wallowing in a vast gin and tonic, Fudge was lying at his feet and Jezebel was stalking something at the end of the garden. Matt had disappeared again for a couple of days. How could Hallam possibly jeopardise all this? Everything he had worked for? How could he disrupt all their lives for the sake of his pride?

No, it wasn't just pride. Of course not. Much more was at stake than that. There were serious principles involved and other people's lives and careers. But what would happen even if he did win a court case against Skudder? At best he would be awarded no more than the maximum eleven or twelve thousand in compensation in an industrial tribunal and that could take months to come to court. And although it was true that he might eventually win two years' pay if he took Skudder to the High Court and demanded the terms of his contract, the legal costs would be horrendous and there was always the chance that he might lose and have to pay Skudder's costs as well. And he would be weighed down for months, maybe even years, by endless meetings with lawyers, by extra work and continual worry. And in the meantime there would be all the business of finding another job, maybe even having to move house.

Did he really need all that hassle? Wouldn't it be better to sit tight for a while, try to talk some sense into Skudder, make a real effort to retrieve the situation, perhaps compromise? Hallam had always prided himself on his calmness and tolerance, his ability to see the middle way. And it was foolish to be too hasty. After all, it was still just ten days since this nightmare had started. The situation was bound to settle down soon. And what about the sales-department staff? They depended on Hallam and his protection. How could he just walk out on them and abandon them? What sort of leadership was that?

Best to wait a week or two, he thought, see Skudder as arranged on Friday, apologise if necessary, mollify him, try to come to some sort of understanding. Yes. Definitely. Give it a little while longer.

'Eight letters beginning with P,' said Monica. '"Sweat by the tower."'

'Perspire,' said Hallam, emptying his glass. 'D'you fancy the other half?'

She glanced up at him through her half-moon glasses. 'Is the Chief Rabbi circumcised?' she said.

He grinned. 'I suppose you know him intimately as well.'

She drained her glass. 'Not *that* intimately,' she said.

He took her glass.

'I've got another limerick,' she said.

He sighed. 'Oh, all right.'

Why not? It gives her pleasure.

'Here goes,' she said:

> 'A mathematician named Hall
> Had a hexahedronical ball
> And the cube of its weight
> Times his pecker, plus eight,
> Was four-fifths of five-eighths of fuck-all.'

He laughed. He could not help it. 'You're quite impossible,' he said.

She beamed.

It really was a lovely evening. Why rush things? Much better to wait a week or two, see how it all turned out.

Hallam was early for work the next morning and at his desk soon after eight. There was no sign yet of Gorman. He was probably still in bed nursing a major hangover.

At eight fifty-five his telephone rang. It was Doreen. 'I've been sacked,' she said.

He felt the adrenaline surge through his veins. 'No!'

'Yes.'

'Hellfire.'

'That bitch Dawn Francis saw me coming in to talk to you yesterday. She rang me at home last night and told me not to come in today. Deliberate disobedience, she said. God, they haven't even got the guts to tell you face to face.'

'You're at home now?'

'Yes.'

'Ah, Dor . . .'

'Don't worry,' she said. 'I'll get another job, easy. And

quite frankly I'm damn glad to be out of the place. But what bastards they are. And I'm worried about you.'

'Don't be. I can look after myself. God, I can't believe this.'

'Nor can I, really. Not yet. We've worked together for so long.'

'Look, come to lunch on Sunday.'

'I can't. I'm going to see my folks.'

'Well, the next weekend, perhaps. I'll get Jenny to ring you. We'll fix something soon.'

'That'd be great.'

'And, Dor . . .'

'Yes.'

'I'm so sorry. You're a brilliant secretary. They're mad. Insane.'

'Thank you. And you're a brilliant boss.'

He replaced the receiver.

Doreen. How could they do it? All those years of dedication and experience just chucked out as though it were no more than garbage. It was absurd. Self-destructive. It was criminal.

At ten past nine Gorman's mother telephoned to say that he would not be coming in to work today.

So he still lives with his mother, does he?

Her voice was tinged with the whine of constant disappointment. 'It's his tummy,' she said.

I'll bet it is.

'My poor Shane. He's always been a martyr to his tummy, ever since he was a baby. And migraines. He gets terrible migraines.'

I'll bet he does.

'And his heart. He gets terrible palpitations. Quite worrying, really, but the doctor says it's normal at his age. Growing pains. And his athlete's foot. And his piles. He's never been really well, not really.'

'I'm very glad to hear it,' said Hallam.

'What?'

'I'm very sad to hear it.'

'Oh. Yes. Well.'

At nine twenty-five George Pringle called from a telephone box down the road to say that he and Elsie Benson had just been made redundant. 'That new personnel manager,' he said, 'the ratty-faced girl, Skudder's piece of skirt. She called us in this morning and said we're not up to it any more.'

Hallam was stunned. 'But Skudder promised there wouldn't be any sackings in Sales.'

'I know, you said.'

Oh, God, the promise I made to them all. I've let them down. I've failed them, and the promise is broken.

'They're not calling it sacking,' said Pringle, 'they're calling it early retirement, so they haven't even given us a month's notice pay. They haven't even enhanced our pensions.'

So Skudder had found a way of getting rid of them without it costing him a penny.

'I can't believe I'm hearing this.'

'Our pensions are going to be tiny, Mr Hallam. I'm not even fifty yet and Elsie's only fifty-four so our pensions haven't had nearly enough time to build up to be enough to live off.'

'Where's Elsie now?'

'She's here, in the phone box with me.'

'I'm not standing for this,' said Hallam. 'I'm going to see Skudder. Now. I'll call you both at home later.'

'She said we were useless. That girl. She said we ought to be in a museum.'

Hallam dropped the receiver on to its cradle and rose from his desk. His mind was whirling. He felt hot. His face was burning. Skudder could not be allowed to get away with this. This was war. This was deliberate provocation: to sack people in his department without even consulting him, without any warning.

He loped purposefully up the stairs to the top floor and strode along the executive corridor to Skudder's office.

He walked briskly past Melody's desk. Skudder was obviously in for a change: his cloak hung from a peg behind the door and his silver-topped cane was propped up in the corner.

''Ere!' she said. 'You! What . . . ?'

The security guard was sitting po-faced like a gargoyle on the straight-backed chair outside Skudder's office. But he wasn't one of Skudder's outside security guards: he was Ron, the car-park entrance commissionaire. What a bit of luck.

Morning, Mr Hallam. Morning, Ron. It's a pink bow-tie and weskit today, sir. Ah, pink, are they? Thank you, Ron. Thank you, *sir.*

Hallam nodded at him as he strode towards Skudder's door. 'Hi, Ron,' he said. 'Lovely morning. He's expecting me.'

Ron blinked, twitched, hesitated, and Hallam's fingers were on the door handle and the door was open.

He entered Skudder's office, closed the door and locked it behind him. He slipped the key into his pocket.

He could hear Melody's muffled voice in the outer office as shrill as a mating magpie.

''Ere, Ron! 'E carn' go in 'ere, not wiv Jyce. Jeez, Ron, 'e's wiv *Jyce*, yer stupid old wanker.'

Skudder glanced up from his desk. He was wearing a black shirt, a multi-coloured bow-tie and matching waistcoat, and he was speaking on the telephone. He waved an imperious hand at Hallam, motioning him away, ordering him out of the room as though he were some junior skivvy.

Hellfire, but he's ugly. I'd forgotten quite how ugly he is.

Skudder's bald uneven head jutted towards him as shiny and threatening as a mortar shell. His skin was pale, like the flesh of a dead fish, as though it never saw sunlight. His eyes burned with dislike beneath their non-existent brows.

This ugliness is not physical at all. There are plenty of men who are bald and less than good-looking but still perfectly pleasant. But this Skudder is something else: this ugliness seethes and bubbles somewhere deep inside.

Hallam strolled across Skudder's office to the second door, locked that as well, slipped the second key into his pocket, wandered back towards Skudder's desk and perched himself on the edge.

Skudder glared at him.

Hallam smiled nicely. 'Hello, *Jyce*,' he said. 'Nice day.'

'Just a mo,' said Skudder into the mouthpiece. He looked up at Hallam. 'What the fuck d'yer fink yer doing?'

'I've altered the time of our meeting on Friday. I've brought it forward. To now.'

Skudder's expression was malevolent. His bow-tie and waistcoat glinted like a dozen rainbows in a thunderstorm.

'I gotta problem,' he said, into the telephone. 'I'll call you back.' He crashed the receiver on to its rest.

He pressed the buzzer on his intercom. 'Mel?'

The intercom crackled. Her voice sounded twittery. 'I'm ever so sorry, Jyce, 'e jus'—'

'How did he get in?'

''E jus' barged past—'

'What about the security geezer?'

'Ron. 'E jus' walked pas' 'im.'

'Tell Ron he'd better get in here *nah* and get ridda this lunatic, if he wants to keep his job.'

'Right, Jyce, I'm ever so sorry, Jyce. I—'

'Stop rabbiting, for Chrissake, and get this lunatic outta here.'

He snapped the intercom lever back again and glared at Hallam. He clenched his fists, cracking his knuckles. His eyes glinted with hatred. Like a pirate's eyes, thought Hallam. All he needs is a knife clenched between his teeth. He's a corporate corsair, a cut-throat determined to make us all walk the plank.

'I'll have you for this, Hallam,' he said. 'What the fuck d'yer fink yer doing?'

'So it's "*Hallam*" now, is it?' said Hallam, mimicking Skudder by raising his hands and twitching his fingers around the word, 'not "*Pee*" any more?'

'Sod off, Hallam. You're starting to get on me tits.'

The door handle rattled. Muffled voices drifted from the other side.

'Jyce?' said Melody miserably, her words sounding as though they were spoken through cotton wool. ''E's locked the dowah.'

'Then break the bastard down!' yelled Skudder.

He rose from behind his desk, his face pale, his head gleaming. His eyes twitched from Hallam to the door and back again.

He's afraid! thought Hallam. *Good grief, he's afraid of me. He thinks I'm going to hit him, beat him up, perhaps.*

A warm feeling flooded his veins, a sensation of power. He knew that for just a moment or two he was capable of anything at all.

'This is it, Hallam,' said Skudder, his voice breaking with anger. 'You're finished here. Nobody messes wiv Jyson Skudder, no way. You're out.'

There was more muttering beyond the door. Somebody whispered hoarsely. The muttering resumed.

'Smash the bugger down!' yelled Skudder.

He danced across the room with rage and battered at the door with his fists. 'Get a batterin'-ram! Get a drill! Get a sodding screwdriver and unscrew the hinges!'

'We carn, Jyce,' said Melody plaintively from the other side of the door. 'The 'inges is yowah side of the dowah.'

'Ah, shit!'

'Settle down,' said Hallam gently, 'or you'll have a stroke. Calm down. I'm not going to hurt you. I just want a "little chat" and then I'll be off.'

Skudder looked hunted. He clenched his fists. He eyes were wild. 'Too right you'll be off,' he said viciously. 'Don't you worry about that, sunshine. You'll be off all the fucking way to the Job Centre.'

He circled his desk carefully and sat in his chair again. He picked up his telephone and dialled the switchboard. 'Call the pleece,' he said. 'There's a fucking manic in me office.'

Hallam slid off the edge of the desk and walked around it towards Skudder.

Skudder shrank in his chair. He looked alarmed. 'You're sacked,' he said.

Hallam shrugged. 'Of course, that goes without saying. But you're going to have to pay for the privilege, *sunshine*. I've got a two-year contract.'

Skudder laughed nastily. 'Not any more, you haven't, *sunshine*. That's null and void if yer sacked for misconduct and this is gross misconduct, this is – ignoring me orders, breaking into me office, interrupting me meeting, insubordurations. You'll get fuck-all from me, *sunshine*.'

Hallam laughed. The light tone of his laugh surprised him. He was actually enjoying himself.

'I'm not talking about myself,' he said. 'I can look after myself. No, I'm talking about the people in my department who you've sacked quite unfairly today – my secretary, Doreen, and Elsie Benson, George Pringle.'

Skudder sneered. 'So wotcha gonna do about it, eh?'

Hallam smiled at him. 'Unless you reinstate them,' he said gently, 'I'm going to take you to the cleaners, Skudder. I'm going to get everyone you've sacked together and we're going to find the very best lawyer in town and we're going to sue the arse off you, *Jyce*, me old chum. We're going to sue you not just as MD of this company but personally, individually, in your own private capacity, for every penny you've got and then some more. We're going to squeeze you until there's four-fifths of five-eighths of fuck-all left and then we're going to squeeze you again. OK, "*sunshine*"?'

Skudder smiled like a crocodile. 'Just you try it, Hallam. You'll get nowhere. Jyson Skudder knows his law.'

'I wouldn't bank on it. In the meantime I want the answer to just one question. I'll find another job easily enough and so will Doreen, but why sack Elsie Benson and George Pringle?'

'Fucking crumblies. Past it.'

'They're bloody good at their jobs.'

'Has-beens. Never-weres.'

'You promised me that no one was going to be sacked from my department. You gave me your word.'

Skudder stared at him. Then he leered. He cracked his knuckles. 'I lied, then, didn't I?' he said.

Hallam gazed at him. He shook his head. 'What a creep,' he said.

He turned and walked to the door. 'See you in court,' he said.

He unlocked the door, opened it, walked out into the outside office and locked Skudder's door behind him again. Melody and Liz were staring at him with horror. Ron was mesmerised.

I'm sorry about Ron: now he's probably going to get the bullet too. 'I'm sorry, Ron,' he said.

Hallam strolled across the outer office to the rubbish chute in the corner and tossed the keys to both of Skudder's office doors into it. They clanged in harmony against the inner metal lining of the chute like a stable door being bolted and fell five echoing floors into oblivion.

''Ere!' said Melody. 'You carn' do that!'

'I have,' he said.

''Ow's Jyce gonna get out?'

'Why not try the fire brigade? Or what about the council's rodent-control department?'

Skudder was banging on the inside of his office door. 'Let me out!' he yelled. 'I'll have yer, Hallam! Guard! Grab him! Arrest him! The pleece is coming.'

Hallam nodded genially at Ron and Liz, and gave them a little wave goodbye with his fingers.

'See you around,' he said.

I'm free, he thought, *at last, and it feels bloody wonderful.*

PART TWO

CHAPTER 6

A Golden Summer

Hallam revelled in being free of Skudder and all the stress of the office. How simple it had been in the end to break away, even after twenty-four years. No one has to be a prisoner: you just walk out. The weather that July was magnificent and Hallam basked in its warmth. One golden day followed another, and he relished the emptiness of that glorious summer, the fact that each day he had no timetable or responsibilities and he could do exactly as he pleased. Each day he woke with a smile, and each day he thanked the pagan god of courage for giving him the strength to walk out. Had he stayed in his job any longer he would by now have been cowed and miserable, dreading each new day and despising himself, but by leaving he had kept his dignity and integrity.

Every morning he went to the club to play tennis and swim, and there he found a dozen other men in their forties and fifties whose time was also their own and who never looked back on their business lives with regret. Some had been made redundant, some had been sacked, some had taken early retirement, but each had escaped the drudgery of office life with a hefty pay-off or pension to cushion his life.

Not one seemed to resent his empty days and idleness: they were all exhilaratingly cheerful, as if they were mischievous schoolboys playing truant.

Hallam's only regret was Jenny. 'You promised you wouldn't resign,' she said. Her voice trembled. Her lips were pinched. 'You promised you would stay on and fight.'

'I know, Jen, but eventually it became impossible.'

'You used to say there was no such word as impossible.'

'I was wrong. There is. It became impossible to stay on after Skudder sacked Doreen, Elsie and George.'

'Why?'

'Come on, Jenny. I'd promised them their jobs were safe. I'd given them my word. I was their boss, for goodness' sake.'

Her face was tight. 'So your promise to them is more important than your promise to me, is it?'

'Of course not. But I was supposed to protect them.'

'You're supposed to protect me, too. And Susie. And Matt. And how are you going to protect your precious staff by walking out on them?'

'They trusted me and I let them down, so when Skudder fired them I had to make a stand on their behalf. It's the principle of the thing, Jen. Can't you see that?'

She laughed mockingly. 'Principle! That's what people always say when they really mean something else.'

He reached out and touched her arm. 'Come on, Jen, be reasonable.'

She shrugged away his hand. A chill tested his spine. This was not like her. How could she possibly not understand? Surely it was obvious.

'You just don't know what it was like in that office,' he said. 'You can't imagine the horrible atmosphere, the animosity, the aggression. It was like a snakepit.'

She looked at him without affection. 'A lot of people have to work in jobs they hate. They cope. They put up with it. They don't just walk out on their responsibilities.'

He stared at her sadly. *Don't do this. I love you.* 'I can't believe you said that, Jen.'

'Perhaps you've had it too easy all these years.'

'I beg your pardon?'

'It was always a bit cushy under Andy Unwin, wasn't it?'

He felt a sudden pang of apprehension. She had never talked to him like that before. 'That's a horrible thing to say, Jen. And untrue. You can't really mean it.'

Her eyes were cold. 'I thought you were tougher. You said you'd stick it out. Instead you've just crumbled.'

'Hellfire, they trusted me – George, Elsie, Doreen.'

'And a fat lot of good it did them.'

Suddenly he was irritated. Why should he have to listen to this? Whose side was she on?

She was bitter now. He had never seen her like this. She was frightened, too: he could see the insecurity in her eyes. His irritation melted. Poor Jenny: of course she was bound to be worried. He was unemployed. The foundation of their lives had been shaken. She needed security and reassurance.

He held out his hand again.

She turned away.

Don't reject me, Jen. Not now. Not because of this.

'How are we going to live if you haven't got a job? Where's the money going to come from? How are we going to keep paying the mortgage? How are we going to eat?'

'Don't worry, darling. I'll get another job and the mortgage payments are covered by insurance, and in the meantime we've got a few thousand in the building society.'

'How much?'

'Fifteen, sixteen thousand.'

'We'll need a damned sight more than that.'

'Come on, Jen. Stop being so negative.'

She stared at him. 'You promised,' she said, and turned away.

She doesn't understand at all. I could have been talking to a stranger. Jenny, where are you?

A shadow moved across his happiness.

Jim Donaldson telephoned him at home that evening. 'My God, Pete,' he said, 'that was a brave thing to do.'

Hallam said nothing.

Where the hell were you when I needed you? Keeping your head well down in the nearest funk hole.

'You're a bit of a hero back at the ranch.'

'I doubt it.'

'It's true. You stood up for your staff. People are impressed.'

'Not enough for any of them to raise a finger themselves.'

There was an uneasy silence.

'Are you going to be OK?' said Donaldson. 'Financially?'

'I shouldn't have too much trouble finding another job.'

'Of course not.'

'And I'm going to sue Skudder for constructive dismissal. That should bring in at least a couple of years' salary eventually. Plus damages, with any luck.'

Donaldson hesitated. 'I wouldn't bank on it,' he said. 'Constructive dismissal's hellishly difficult to prove in court. And expensive. And Skudder'll claim that *you* walked out on *him*. He'll claim you were never actually sacked.'

'Yes, I was. In his office this morning. He said I was sacked five minutes before I left.'

'Any witnesses?'

Hallam thought about it. 'No.'

'There you are, then. And in any case he'd probably claim that by bursting into his office and locking him in you were guilty of gross misconduct and God knows what else, and a court might well agree with him. He might even sue *you* for breach of contract, for walking out without giving the proper notice.'

'Hellfire, I hadn't thought of that.'

'Take my advice, Pete,' said Donaldson, his voice smooth with concern and conciliation. 'Drop any thought of legal action. It's bloody expensive, almost impossible to prove, incredibly chancy and it could make Skudder retaliate by counter-suing. You could end up losing a fortune as well as your job.'

'So I just do nothing at all? Just wander off into the sunset without any pay-off? Without a bean, after twenty-four years?'

'It's rough, I know, but nowadays . . . Things have changed, Pete. The law is not on your side any more.'

And nor are you bloody lawyers. Why are you trying to talk me out of it? Because you're Skudder's legal director, that's why, and still on Skudder's payroll, and you need to brown-nose Skudder because you're getting closer and closer to forty-five yourself. Because you're on Skudder's side, not mine.

'Skudder asked you to pump me, didn't he?' said Hallam. 'See what my plans are.'

'Don't be ridic—'

'Well, you can tell your creep of a boss that I'm going to sue him until his bloody bow-tie revolves.'

'I wouldn—'

'And Jim?'

'Yes?'

'You're a treacherous sod. I never want anything to do with you again.'

As he dropped the receiver he noticed Jenny standing in the doorway. 'That was Jim?' she said.

'Yes.'

'You've told him you want nothing more to do with him.'

'Yes.'

'But he's your best friend.'

'Was.'

'Why *was*?'

'He let me down. He should have supported me.'

She stared at him and shook her head. 'Are you going mad?' she said. 'You're going to need all the friends you can get.'

'Not friends like that.'

She looked at him with something like disdain. She held her hand out with the palm up, like a beggar. 'I need some more money,' she said.

Hallam called several business contacts to put the word around that he was available if they heard of a suitable job. 'Good God,' said Harry Formby, 'you'll be snapped up within a week or two. They must be mad to let you go.' He wrote to Tom Roberts at Perkins and Lloyd, and to Donald Sanderson at Postlethwaite King, then sat back to wait for the offers to come in.

He went to see an employment lawyer who had been recommended by Pinky Porter and who had promised to study his case for constructive dismissal if he would write a full report on it and produce as many supporting documents as possible.

'You must be out of your mind,' said Jenny. 'Two hundred and fifty pounds an hour!'

'We'll get it back. He won a settlement of a hundred and seventy-five grand for wrongful dismissal for one of Pinky's friends.'

'I don't suppose they just walked out of their job, though, did they?'

Come back to me, Jen. Please. Come back, wherever you are.

He telephoned Doreen to see how she was coping. 'I'm fine,' she said cheerfully. 'I've found another job already, at Flanders and Charles.'

'Fantastic, Dor. I knew you would. Well done!'

'And you?'

'Not yet. It's early days.'

'Yes.'

He telephoned George Pringle and Elsie Benson, feeling guilty. He had let them both down. He had failed to protect them.

'I'm so sorry,' said Hallam.

'It's not your fault,' said Elsie.

'Skudder promised me.'

'I know. It's not your fault.'

But he felt that it was. Skudder had sacked them all to goad him into resigning, he was sure of it. Their connection with him had tainted them.

'I'm trying to apply for unemployment benefit,' said George Pringle hopelessly, 'but they say I'm not eligible because the company says I've taken voluntary early retirement. I've tried to explain that it wasn't voluntary but they won't listen. One arrogant young man in the Job Centre told me to come back when I'm sixty-five. I don't know how I'm going to make ends meet. Who gives a job to a man my age?'

'Something will come up,' lied Hallam. 'You'll see.'

I'm sorry, George, I'm so very sorry.

He started to read again: books, not just the newspapers. He spent an hour or two every day in the garden in the lovely summer afternoons, and as the evening commuters pushed and jostled to board their trains or sat in traffic jams, breathing carbon monoxide fumes, he was pouring himself his evening Scotch and listening to music.

He repainted the utility room: Jenny had been on at him to do that for ages. He started to help with the shopping and housework, doing some of the heavier jobs, and offered to cook the occasional meal, but Jenny seemed to resent his constant presence around the house. 'I'd really much rather do it myself,' she said, with thin lips. 'Just you concentrate on getting another job. Isn't it about time you signed on for the dole?'

He was disconcerted. 'The dole? Hellfire, Jenny, I wouldn't dream of it.'

'And why not?'

'Well, it's not meant for people like me.'

'People like you? What's different about you?'

Ah, God, Jen, you'd never have asked me that six months ago. 'I'd feel ashamed. It'd be a confession of failure. And the dole is really for people who can't help themselves. People who really can't find jobs. People who are helpless or handicapped or uneducated. And the layabouts and scroungers like Matt, of course, but it's not for people like me.'

Her eyes flashed. 'My God, you're an arrogant bastard. So you're Mr Perfect and Matt's just a layabout and scrounger, is he?'

'Come on, Jen, you know very well he is. Do you really think he's seriously looking for work? Matt doesn't know the meaning of the word. God knows how he gets away with it; legally he's meant to be out and about looking for work all the time but he doesn't even read the ads in the paper. He's quite happy to lounge about the place and collect the dole every fortnight and sneer at those of us who try to earn a living.'

She almost spat at him. He had never seen her lips in *that* shape before. 'So you think you're somehow better than everyone else, do you?'

This is ridiculous. 'Not better, Jen, just luckier – better educated, more self-confident, less desperate.'

'Well, you damned well ought to be desperate. It's been more than a month now and you still haven't got a job. How long do you think we can go on like this? How much longer is the money going to last?'

There was a pain in his heart.

How can you be saying such things to me? Oh, Jenny, my Jen, what's happened to us? 'I'm trying, Jen. I'm doing my best.'

'Well, it's not good enough, is it?'

Oh, Jenny, no.

'At the very least you could go and claim the dole and bring in *something*. It's your *right*, for God's sake. You're out of work, so you get the dole. There's nothing shameful about it. That's what it's for. Lord knows, you've paid enough national insurance over the years.'

'It's not for people like us,' he said.

'If you say that again . . .'

'It's for people who can't help themselves. People like us should stand on their own feet, not sponge off their fellow taxpayers.'

'My God, you're a snob. So you expect us to starve just because you're too proud to ask for help?'

'Who's starving?'

'We all will be quite soon if you don't do something about it.'

'Why's Mum being so horrible to you?' said Susie.

'She's not really, Suze. She's just worried, that's all. It's natural. We haven't got any money coming in at the moment.'

'You *will* find another job, Daddy, won't you?'

'Of course I will. It might take a few weeks but then we'll be fine.'

Monica was unexpectedly generous. 'I could pay a bit more towards my keep,' she said one evening, 'if that'll help.'

He squeezed her hand. 'That's kind of you,' he said, 'and thank you for the offer but you're paying quite enough as it is.'

'Well, if ever you need—'

'Thank you, Monica. That's really sweet of you, but there's no need. Something will come up soon, I'm sure of it.'

But as the weeks passed, and July leaked into August, he began to feel less certain. It was useless approaching anyone for a job now: people were taking their summer holidays and thinking of anything except hiring new staff.

He was probably going to have to wait until the middle of September, perhaps even October. And to make matters worse the insurance company was refusing to meet his monthly mortgage payments, arguing that it was not liable since he had not been sacked or made redundant but had walked out of his own accord. It seemed sensible to cancel the family holiday in Portugal, even though it meant that he lost his deposit. Jenny's face was even grimmer after that. The silences stretched further than ever.

Worst of all, the employment lawyer agreed with Jim Donaldson. 'I wouldn't advise it at all,' he said, after studying Hallam's report. He was one of those tall, thin, lugubrious legal men with the mournful air of an undertaker. 'Quite frankly, I don't think that you have any case at all. You walked out far too soon. Had you waited for six months and been able to list a much longer catalogue of humiliations and breaches of your contract you would have had a much stronger case. As it is, the other side would simply argue that you overreacted too quickly and this Skudder was sensible enough not to put any of his insults in writing. They would say that a new managing director is perfectly entitled to make changes, and that your contract stipulates that you should be flexible in your approach to your job and to any alterations in your working conditions. They would argue that you broke your contract by walking out so soon without going through any complaints procedure or arbitration. In fact I would have said that *they* have a very strong breach-of-contract case against *you*.'

'I don't believe this,' said Hallam. 'Are you really telling me that Skudder was perfectly entitled to treat me like dirt, to change my working conditions almost entirely, to remove my secretary, company car and expense allowance, to refuse to communicate with me and to make me subordinate to someone else?'

'Perhaps not. That would be for a court to decide. But one

thing is absolutely certain: you yourself were not entitled to break your contract by suddenly walking out without giving any notice or going through the company's grievance procedure.'

'So what do you suggest I do?'

The lawyer gave him a tight smile. 'Nothing at all,' he said, 'and just pray that they don't sue you instead.'

Bloody lawyers. Whoever said that British justice is the best in the world?

'What about all the others he sacked? Could we get them all together and sue as a group?'

'You'd be very foolish indeed to get involved at all. If you stick your neck out too far your head might get chopped off.'

Hallam thought about it, cursed, nodded.

He reached for his cheque book. 'Two hundred and fifty pounds?' he said.

'Per hour. Three hours. So that's seven hundred and fifty.' The lawyer smiled thinly. 'Plus VAT,' he said.

The days passed. September. Each day he awaited the arrival of the post with trepidation, fearing the dreaded writ accusing him of breach of contract, but it never arrived. Perhaps Skudder was still frightened of him, he thought. Perhaps they realised that he might actually win if they took him to court.

But why in any case should Skudder go to all the trouble and expense of suing? There'd be no point. He wanted me out and I'm out. Skudder has probably already forgotten my name.

Hallam telephoned Harry Formby and Tom Roberts again.

'Sorry, old chap,' said Harry, 'nothing yet, but it can't be long before someone bites. I've been putting the word round. Something will crop up. These things take time. You'll see.'

'Slight snag,' said Tom. 'Couple of bods I've spoken to say you'd be great but they're looking for someone . . . well, less expensive, not quite so experienced.'

You mean younger.

'Someone who wouldn't cost them quite so much.'

Younger.

'Someone who wouldn't upset the present pecking order too much.'

Yes. Someone younger.

'Still, chin up. It's only been three or four weeks, hasn't it?'

'Nearly eleven.'

'Good Lord. I hadn't realised. Still, plenty of time yet.'

But time and the savings were running out.

He telephoned three more contacts and wrote to half a dozen more. He waited. They replied. No luck. He started scanning the situations-vacant columns of the trade press and then those of the general newspapers, but most of the advertisements blatantly stipulated applicants between the ages of twenty-five and thirty-five. Forty was never mentioned, let alone forty-five. Forty had become a dirty word. How did they get away with it? he thought. It was illegal to specify the sex, colour or religion of potential employees but there was nothing to stop you specifying the age. He circled a few possibilities that made no mention of age and went for a couple of interviews but as soon as he walked into the room he could see rejection already on the faces of the interviewers: *My God, he must be nearly forty. We'd have to make huge contributions into his pension fund. He'll only be with us for a few years before he retires. He probably knows more than we do. How would he fit in? Too old.*

Summer died and autumn began to darken the hidden damp corners of the garden, plucking the leaves and scattering them brown across the lawn. Hallam's optimism started melting. His savings were dwindling with alarming speed.

He started to worry, and it did not help that Jenny's eyes were cold with accusation. It frightened him to realise how quickly she had distanced herself from him and how wide was the gulf now between them. He began to cut down on his trips to the club: it was becoming too expensive. When he did go for an occasional game of tennis with Pinky Porter he took to slipping away afterwards without stopping for a drink in the bar so that he would not have to buy a round. One Saturday he raised the question of the thousand pounds that Pinky still owed him.

'Sorry about that, old boy,' said Pinky. 'I'm a bit short myself this month. Pamela's a couple of months in arrears with my maintenance. God knows how she thinks I'm supposed to live if she doesn't pay my alimony on time.'

What about the fortnight's holiday you had in Florida with some floozie last month?

'Next month, for sure,' said Pinky. 'Or Christmas at the latest. Promise.'

Hallam tried to drink less at home as well, but it was difficult to resist a glass or two each evening as the autumn evenings fell with sudden gloom and the long nights stretched before him. Gradually, too, he reduced his occasional visits to Mike Gregory's regular Saturday-afternoon card school: he could no longer afford to lose. And every time he shut down another corner of his life he left himself with even more time to worry.

Why was nobody writing or telephoning? Where were the head-hunters? Somebody, somewhere, must need him, surely? How could he possibly be over the hill at forty-five? It was absurd: he was full of energy, ideas, enthusiasm. Perhaps he should start his own company, set out as a freelance. But how could he do that, without any savings, without any capital? And what sort of business could he possibly set up at his age? Perhaps they were absolutely right after all. *Too old. Past it. On the scrapheap.*

For exercise now he started to walk miles every day, braving even the wet and blustery afternoons, and he began to realise whenever he went out that the neighbours seemed not to notice him nowadays. Once they had always exchanged polite smiles and greetings across the garden hedges but now whenever he passed they seemed to be busy or looking the other way. Good manners? A desire not to be thought nosy? Embarrassment? Who could tell? Only the jolly West Indian family at the end of the road still greeted him as though nothing had happened. Perhaps they did not know that anything *had* happened. Why should they know? The middle-aged father – whose name was Junior – was always in his front driveway working on some battered old car and always gave him a huge grin and a jovial hello when he walked by. And if Junior's children – Winston, Everard, Wilhelmina – were home they would run down the road after Hallam, dancing around him and twittering like birds. But the other neighbours were silent shadows suddenly disappearing into doorways.

I'm a leper. They don't want to be contaminated. And how can I blame them? I infected Doreen and Elsie and George. Perhaps failure is contagious.

'You're going to have to sign on for the dole,' said Jenny. 'You're going to have to swallow your precious pride, whether you like it or not.'

He looked at her with misery in his eyes.

Hold me, Jen. Hug me. Please. I need you. Especially now.

She turned away.

'I know,' he said. 'I know.'

CHAPTER 7

Sharon and the Centre

The Job Centre was a grimy four-storey Victorian building that skulked down a drab back-street as though it hoped not to be noticed. *Me too*, thought Hallam. To avoid being recognised he had decided not to wear a suit but had dressed instead as if he were on holiday in pale summer trousers, a short-sleeved shirt, a pair of loafers and dark glasses.

What am I doing here? Me: the quintessential middle-class man, so careful, so stable, insured against everything except stupidity. I never thought it could ever come to this.

He peered through the main door and found himself in a foreign country: a huge grimy room with black linoleum floors, cream walls stained ochre with nicotine and eight long queues of jobless people shuffling slowly towards eight large glassed-in hatches at the far end where eight clerks were processing applications and signatures. On the far right-hand side three people queued at a window under the notice DECLARATION OF EARNINGS.

Just three honest people in the whole place and dozens of liars.

Here and there a few of the unemployed looked clean and respectable but most were soiled and scruffy, as though they had long lost all self-respect, the men unshaven, the women untidy in T-shirts, tracksuits, anoraks, trainers, one even wearing fluffy, soiled pink slippers. The room was thick with a haze of cigarette smoke, and several men were swigging at cans of beer or bottles of cider. Two were slumped on a bench that ran along the side of the room.

Drunk, at ten o'clock in the morning. How on earth can they afford it on unemployment benefit? And what am I *doing* here?

He joined the end of the shortest queue. In front of him a couple of men were chatting in Spanish or Italian. Further forward in the next queue an entire family of Greeks appeared to be about to come to blows.

Perhaps they're all foreigners. Maybe I'm the only Englishman here.

He shuffled forward with the rest, praying that he would not suddenly be spotted by someone he knew. How undignified it was, this begging for charity, this acknowledgement of failure. At the head of the queue an hysterical woman was shouting at an Indian clerk in French. He looked at her as if he were deaf.

It took twenty minutes to reach the head of the queue.

'Your first time?' said the Indian clerk. 'Sorry, mate, wrong queue. You have to go round the side door and register upstairs.'

Outside again and around the corner he found a door marked NEW CLIENTS REPORT HERE.

So the unemployed are 'clients' now, are they? What wondrous miracles are being wrought with the English language nowadays.

He climbed a flight of dingy stairs to the first floor and opened the door. The reception room was unexpectedly bright, furnished with comfortable chairs and carpeted in a soft oatmeal. It resembled the living room of a cheerful old folks' home rather than the grim barrack area he had expected. An old folks' home? How very appropriate.

He picked up a Jobseeker's Charter booklet from a table just inside the door. Three unemployed people – two men and a woman – were sitting patiently in a row of grey plastic chairs while two others were being questioned by Employment Service clerks at separate desks at the far end of the room. One of the men in the queue was dressed immaculately in a crisp, blue-striped shirt, smart tie and pinstriped suit. His black shoes gleamed. He was tall, thin and patrician, with a bony nose and an amused expression that seemed to say, 'I'm not really here, you know, not at all, I just came along for the hell of it.' The other man was short, fat, unshaven and wearing a grubby vest, an anorak and stained trainers. The woman was decked out in red hair curlers, a baggy sweater and soiled pink leggings with a hole in them. She was chewing gum. On her right hand the index and middle fingers were stained yellow with nicotine. Dear God, thought Hallam, so this is what I've come to.

He sat beside her. She smelt of sweat and cigarettes.

The two people who were being interviewed at the desks were sitting in front of two young clerks: one a gentle-looking black youth with dreadlocks, the other a pasty-faced white girl with tiny black eyes, pudding-basin hair, brown dungarees, chunky boots and a piercing voice. On one strap of her dungarees she wore a red Aids ribbon and on the other a plastic badge that said, 'HI THERE! I'M SHARON, YOUR PERSONAL JOBSEEKER COUNSELLOR (Grade 3b).'

Above each desk a large sign promised 'COMPLETE CLIENT CONFIDENTIALITY GUARANTEED'.

'So is 'e shaggin' you or not?' bellowed Sharon.

The woman 'client' shrank into her seat.

'Well? Come on, now, Mrs Feeney, yes or no? Eiver 'e is or 'e isn't. Simportant. Makes a difference to yer benefit. So is 'e givin' yer one or not?'

The man in the pinstriped suit caught Hallam's eye and swiftly looked away, ashamed to be seen to be here. He pretended not to notice him, as nonchalant as two heterosexuals ignoring each other in a public lavatory.

'What you mean, 'e only shags yer once a mumf?' squawked Sharon, fingering an angry cluster of acne on her chin. 'Makes no difference how often it is. Shaggin' is shaggin' whevver it's once a mumf or five times a day.'

Hallam flicked through the advice in the Jobseeker's Charter booklet. 'Telephoning employers,' it suggested. 'Have a pen and paper ready. If you use a pay phone, have plenty of change. Say why you are phoning, what the job is and who you want to speak to. Be ready to answer questions about your background and work experience.'

Hellfire: can anyone who is intelligent enough to read really need such simple advice?

'Going for an interview,' suggested the booklet. 'Make sure you know how to get there.'

After several minutes the cringing woman appeared to have satisfied the pasty-faced Sharon's interest in her sex life, rose from her seat, retrieved her shopping bag and left the room. The Pinstriped Suit gave a purposeful sniff, rose brisk and lanky from his seat in the queue and strode towards Sharon, who was scribbling on a pad. Like clockwork crabs the rest of the queue shuffled sideways one place to the left and sat again. Sharon glanced up, spotted the Pinstriped Suit advancing towards her, frowned furiously and waved him back. 'Wait till I call yer!' she barked.

'Sorry?'.

She flapped both hands at him. 'Back! Back! Sit down! I'm not ready! Wait till I call yer!'

'Sorry,' he said. 'Sorry.'

She could have been his daughter, thought Hallam. He could have been her boss. But here he's just about to become no more than a name on a numbered file.

The Pinstriped Suit retreated towards his previous seat at the head of the queue, dislodging the squat, fat man in the vest, who rose, scratched an armpit and shuffled one place to the right again, in turn dislodging the woman in the red curlers who in turn dislodged Hallam.

'So sorry,' said the Pinstriped Suit with a crooked smile to no one in particular, looking vaguely over their heads. 'Much obliged. Awfully sorry. Very good of you. So sorry.'

The backbone of England and now reduced to this.

After several minutes Sharon stopped doodling, looked up, gazed without interest at the expectant queue as it sat and watched her like roosting vultures, picked her teeth, sniffed, wiped her nose on her sleeve, rose from her seat, turned away and disappeared through a door at the far end of the room. For several more minutes muffled conversation and laughter wafted from the other side of the door.

Her coffee-break, I suppose. Or a trip to the ladies'. Or – most likely of all – just bloody-mindedness.

The queue sighed, scratched its heads, crossed its arms, shuffled its feet, shifted the weight of its buttocks, crossed its legs. Two more 'clients' entered the room and joined the end of the queue. The dreadlocked clerk droned on and on in a muted voice. The Pinstriped Suit smiled to himself yet again and examined his cuticles for the fifteenth time. He looked at his watch.

Why bother about the time? thought Hallam. What's the hurry? We're not going anywhere, any of us, are we? This is a world that is outside time, and you and I are about to become permanent residents.

The Pinstriped Suit started humming tunelessly to himself.

It was nearly an hour before Hallam finally reached the head of the queue and Sharon's desk. She looked at him with belligerence. 'Yes?'

'I would like to sign on for the dole, please,' he said.

'Well, I dint think you was 'ere for the champagne

and caviare,' she said. She cackled. 'Anyway, it's called Jobseeker's Allowance now. How long you been outta work?'

'Five months.'

'Five mumfs! Gaw, what took yer so long?'

'Well, I didn't like to come before. I thought I could manage without.'

Her eyes narrowed. 'I see,' she said. 'Thought you was too good fer us, didja?'

'Not at all. I just—'

She sniffed and handed him a printed form. 'Go away and fill this in,' she barked. 'Come back tomorrer.'

'Tomorrow? But—'

She waved him away imperiously. 'No! I don't want an argument! That's it! Back! Go on! Go away! Just do as yer told.'

'But—'

'Go on! Off you go! We're closed. Lunch-time. And we're closed all arternoon. It's Wensdy, see.'

'Ah, well,' said Hallam. 'That settles it, then. Of course. *Wednesday*, eh? Well, in that case . . .'

She leaned aggressively towards him and jabbed her forefinger towards his nose. 'Don't you get all sarky with me, mister,' she said, 'or I might just 'appen to lose yer file.'

So this is it, now: threatened by a female yob with acne. Humiliated by a teenager in brown dungarees and bovver boots. How much lower can you get?

Oh, much lower than this, me old son, said a vicious whisper at the back of his mind: sinister, sibilant, the voice of Jason Skudder. *Oh, yes – much lower. You ain't seen nothing yet, sunshine. It's only just begun.*

When Hallam returned home Matthew and three of his friends had annexed the living room. They were playing rap music so loudly that the windows were rattling in their frames.

Hallam grimaced. Music? It sounds more like a dozen dinosaurs dancing on a thousand pieces of corrugated iron.

He crossed to the music centre and turned the noise down.

'Oh, great,' said Matthew. 'Thanks a lot. Thanks very much.'

'The neighbours,' said Hallam.

'Shit, you're always so worried about what the neighbours think. You're so . . . *anal*.'

'It's not what they think, Matt, it's just simple good manners, consideration for others.'

'*Saint* Peter,' sneered Matthew, 'I don't think.'

They seemed to be sprawled everywhere, surrounded by scattered items of clothing, crushed cushions, dirty cups and plates, toast crumbs, open jam jars, empty sardine tins, soft-drink cans. Dirty teaspoons lay in pools of spilt liquid on the coffee table. Something sticky was smeared along the side of the heavy silver table cigarette lighter.

How do they always manage to take up so much room? thought Hallam in despair. How do they always manage to make so much mess?

They seemed like a different species, like aliens. One of them – Ben? – was wearing one vast earring, a striped sort of kaftan and green eyeshadow. Another – Nigel? – was dressed in a stained vest, skimpy running shorts, socks and brown open-toed sandals. What *is* it about people who wear socks with sandals? The androgynous one who appeared to be suffering from anorexia, Mickey, was lying on the sofa with his/her head nestling in Matthew's lap and his/her trainers smearing mud on the covers of the sofa.

Hallam had made the mistake once of asking Matt whether Mickey was male or female.

'I can't believe you said that,' Matt had snapped.

'I only asked.'

'But why should it matter?'

'Just curious, that's all.'

'So what's your problem, then, hey? God, you're so sexist. And homophobe. You're so judgemental.'

'Mickey,' said Hallam now. He gestured at the trainers. 'Please.'

Mickey sighed and moved his/her feet slowly and reluctantly, leaving his/her legs protruding over the edge of the sofa but settling his/her head more firmly into Matthew's groin.

Is Mickey a male person? If so, is my son homosexual? And why should it matter?

'You're so bloody anal,' said Matthew, lounging back and resting his long, greasy, matted hair on the back of the sofa. 'What's wrong with a bit of dirt? It's only Mother Earth.'

'And it's only Mother Hallam who has to wash the covers. Don't you ever think of her?'

'Yeah, whenever I realise the poor woman's married to you.'

'Charming.'

Matt grinned slyly. 'I hear you're on the dole,' he said.

Bloody Jenny.

'I'm applying, yes.'

Matt leered. 'I thought you disapproved of people going on the dole.'

'Not if they're in genuine need. If they've got no savings and they're genuinely trying to find work.'

'And who decides if they're genuine, then? You, I suppose – the great Peter the Perfect, Hallam the Magnanimous.'

Hallam sighed. 'I really don't want an argument, Matt.'

Matthew sneered. 'No, of course not, not when it's one you're bound to lose.' He jeered. 'You're a hypocrite, *Father*. It's not so easy finding a job, is it?'

'No, not at my age.'

'Not at any age, mate, not yours nor mine. But you've been patronising me for months about not being able to get a job and now you can't either. That's poetic justice and I love it.' He snorted. 'Here, *Father*, we'll be able to go down to the Job Centre every fortnight to collect the dole together, all nice and cosy, just you and me. That'll be nice, won't it? Daddy and son together again, holding hands, bonding.'

Hallam felt suddenly very tired. 'Why do you hate me so much, Matt?' he said.

Matthew laughed sarcastically and put his feet on the coffee table. Mickey's little head bobbed in his lap. The heels of his boots smeared spilt coffee across the wood.

'Hate you? Don't flatter yourself, *Papa*. I just think you're pathetic, you and your middle-class values, you and your bourgeois so-called standards and principles. They haven't done you much good, have they?'

'Good enough, thank you.'

'Like what?'

Character, determination. But you wouldn't understand.

'There's no point in trying to explain it.'

'That's pathetic. A cop-out. But then you always did cop out, didn't you, *Pater*?'

Hallam made for the door. He was not going to fight with Matt in front of his friends. No way.

'I'm going to do some gardening,' he said, 'and perhaps you'd be good enough to clear up in here by six o'clock when your grandmother will want to watch the news.'

Matt grunted. 'When you'll want to start swigging your usual nightly bucketful of whisky, you mean. Why do you middle-aged, middle-class prats all drink so much? To try to forget what arseholes you are?'

'To try to forget our graceless sons,' said Hallam.

When Hallam returned to the Job Centre the following day there were four 'clients' waiting on the queue of plastic chairs: a pretty Asian girl wearing a green sari and a red spot in the middle of her forehead; an elderly man with a fierce white beard; a young black man in a Tyrolean hat and sunglasses; a red-faced tramp, who kept cursing under his breath and muttering, 'Holy Mother,' and 'Wouldja fockin believe it?'

Pasty-faced Sharon was at her desk as usual haranguing a client. She was wearing a faded ochre tracksuit top, the red Aids ribbon, threadbare leopardskin leggings that bulged over her ample thighs and scuffed yellow trainers.

'Wotchar mean yer got six kids?' she was bellowing at a tiny, grey-haired woman, who looked about seventy.

The tiny woman leaned forward and whispered to her.

'Bloody 'ell,' screeched Sharon. ''E should've 'ad 'em chopped off, then, dirty bugger. 'Ow old yer, then?'

The tiny woman leaned forward and whispered again.

'Fordy-seven!' squawked Sharon. 'You look abaht an 'undred an' ten!'

Hallam joined the end of the queue and sat and waited, rising every fifteen or twenty minutes, whenever another 'client' left the room, to move to the left, one chair at a time. He had brought his *Daily Telegraph* to pass an hour or two and to hide behind if necessary but there was no one there who knew him and in any case it was impossible to concentrate amid the yakking from Sharon and the coughing, sniffing, sneezing and fidgeting of the other 'clients' beside him.

Eventually, after waiting for more than an hour, he reached the head of the queue, and ten minutes later Sharon looked up from her desk and beckoned him with a bony finger.

'Nex'!' she boomed. 'Yeah, that's right: you, Grandad! Get a move on! Come on, come on! I 'aven' got all day!'

Hallam sat in front of her and slid the completed form across the desk. 'Good morning,' he said.

She grunted and extended her hand. 'Yer P45,' she said.

'I'm sorry?'

She snapped her fingers. 'Yer P45.'

He stared at her. 'P45?'

'Gaw, doncha know nuffing? It's a bit of paper what yer company give yer when yer left, says 'ow much wages you earned, 'ow much tax yer paid.'

They never gave me one.

She snapped her fingers again. 'Come on, come on!'

'I haven't got one.'

'Yer what? Course you 'ave. Yer must of. Yer personnel manager would of given yer one.'

The personnel manager: Skudder's girlfriend; Dawn Thing. Of course. She never sent me one. They knew that something like this would happen.

'No, I was never given one.'

'But everyone's gotta 'ave one.'

'Not me. They've never sent me one.'

She stared at him balefully. Her eyes were as cold as pebbles. Why did she loathe him so much? He was too middle-class: he spoke too well; Matt would have understood immediately.

'OK,' she said brusquely. 'Yer P60s, then.'

'What?'

A small smile spread across her lips, as though she could hardly believe her luck. Her little black eyes almost twinkled. 'Yer not got nuffing, 'ave yer?'

'I've got my national insurance number and my national health service number.'

'Snot enough,' she said with satisfaction. 'Yer need yer P45 as well, or all yer P60s.'

She looked at him with a smug expression. Frustration surged through him like a tidal wave. He was no longer the master of his fate, no more the captain of his soul. His life was bobbing on an open sea, a rough and unforgiving ocean infested with pirates. Reflected in the blackness of her eyes he saw, suddenly stretched out in front of him, an endless vista of daily new frustrations, of long, cold, wet, wasted bus journeys, of pointless telephone calls and fruitless letters, of malice and misunderstandings, and always at the end of it there was Sharon's smug little face with its pudding-basin hair and self-satisfied nostrils and nasty little eyes glinting with pleasure at his discomfort.

'I've probably got my old P60s in a file at home.'

She regarded him with pleasure. 'You better go an' get 'em, then, incha?'

She looked over his shoulder. 'Nex'! Nex'!'

He drove home in a fog of irritation.

The waste of time. The endless bureaucracy. The self-importance of these jumped up little people.

Back at home he found Jenny pacing impatiently up and down outside the garage. 'About bloody time,' she said furiously. 'Where the hell have you been?'

'The Job Centre, trying to sign on.'

'You've taken your time about it. I need the car. I've got an interview for a job in twenty minutes.'

'A job? You're going to get a job?'

She looked at him with contempt. 'Somebody has to,' she said.

'What sort of job?'

'Just a school-dinner lady,' she said bitterly. 'That's all. What else am I qualified for?'

'Jen . . .' Let me hold you. Let me hug you and smell your neck again, your hair. Let me hear you laugh again. I can't bear this. Please. Jenny. Please, Jen.

'I've got to go,' she said.

'Could you wait just a sec? Give me a lift into town? I've got to go back to the Centre. They want some tax documents that I'm supposed to take.'

She opened the car door and climbed into the driving seat. 'No time,' she said. 'You'll have to get a bus. I can't wait.'

'Couldn't you drop me off on the way? I won't be a mo. They close at twelve thirty.'

'Too bad. You've held me up quite enough already.'

She switched on the ignition, revving the engine more than necessary, shooting backwards out of the driveway, roaring away up the road.

Jenny looking for a job. Just a humble school-dinner lady. Another gulf between us. Another reason for resentment. Another failure.

The living-room curtains were still drawn. At eleven o'clock! Bloody Matt and his layabout friends. Why did they sleep so much? What did they do all day that was so exhausting? And why always in the living room, for God's sake?

He went upstairs to look for the P60 forms in his tax and salary files. Monica was playing a record in her room: the jaunty rockabilly sound of country and western music leaked beneath her door and flooded the landing.

'Cuckoo!' she called. 'Is that you, Peter? Cuckoo! Come in.'

'I'm in a bit of a hurry, Monica. I've got—'

'I won't keep you long, dear. Come in, come in.'

He knocked at her door and opened it. Tammy Wynette on the old-fashioned record player: 'Stand By Your Man'. What an excellent idea. *Will you play it to Jenny, please?*

Monica was lying on her bed, an elfin figure wearing cowboy boots, leather trousers, leather jerkin, a Stetson tipped over her forehead and used teabags pressed deep into her eye sockets. She was snapping her fingers in time to the music.

'What on earth are the teabags for?' he said.

'They're excellent for tightening the bags under the eyes.'

'*Tea*bags?'

'But of course. They have to be cold, though, straight out of the fridge. Everyone knows that.'

'I thought you swore by haemorrhoid cream.'

'I do, only I've used it all up. Would you get me some more? There's a dear.'

'If you insist. Now—'

'Don't you just love country and western music?'

'Not much.'

'Come on, Peter, it's so jolly and rollicking, so full of life.'

'So miserable, you mean. They always seem to be whining about something – mah baby done left me, don't go with ma woman, that sort of thing.'

'But the tunes are always so bouncy. Hank loves them all, of course, coming from Arizona. He's very fond of the gramophone.'

'No one calls them gramophones any more, Miss Porridge. They call them music centres.'

'How very boring of them,' she said. 'I want to recite another limerick for you, see what you think.'

He backed towards the door. 'Not now, Monica. I really do have to go.'

'Don't be horrid. Just listen.'

'I'm going, Monica. I have to get back to the Job Centre.'

> 'In the Garden of Eden lay Adam,
> Complacently stroking his madam . . .'

Hallam left the room and closed the door firmly behind him.

Her muffled voice followed him along the landing:

> 'And loud was his mirth,
> For on all of the earth . . .'

He closed his bedroom door behind him and looked at his watch. Five past eleven – less than an hour and a half to get back to the Job Centre before they closed. Damn Jenny.

He rummaged in his tax files, found the P60s for the last five years and set off at a trot down the road to the bus stop. It was bitterly cold outside and now it had started to rain.

He returned to the house, found his heavy winter overcoat, gloves and furry Russian hat and pulled them on. He plucked a small, folding brolly from the umbrella-stand beside the front door. He opened the door. The cold fingered his cheeks and ears.

Bloody Jenny.

Bloody Jenny. She could at least have taken him some of the way.

He buttoned the overcoat to the neck, pulled on the Russian hat and gloves and headed out. The raindrops pricked at his face like needles of ice. He tried to open the umbrella but the wind gusted against the fabric, trying to tug it inside out. He folded it again and jogged towards the bus stop, bending his face downwards and into the wind.

Bloody Jenny.

Yes.

It took him over an hour to reach the Job Centre again: first a long wait in the rain at the draughty bus stop, then a short ride into town, then another wait, another ride, and finally a breathless five-minute jog in a freezing breeze to arrive gasping and sweaty at twelve twenty, just ten minutes before the Centre was due to close.

The place was empty except for the two clerks.

He approached Sharon's desk and as he did so three other 'clients' walked in behind him and jostled for places in the queue of plastic chairs.

'I've found the P60s,' he said.

She made a rumbling noise through her nose, took the P60s and his application form and cast her eyes down the answers he had given, running a forefinger slowly down the page.

She looked up at him. Her eyes were like little black stones. She smiled unpleasantly. 'You left yer job voluntry,' she said.

'Well, that's not quite—'

She jabbed the form with her finger and raised her voice. 'It says 'ere you jus' walked aht of yer job.'

'Well, yes, but—'

'You also got mortgage insurance, unemployment insurance.'

'Yes, but they won't—'

'Insurance always 'as to be deducted from yer benefit.'

'But they won't—'

Her eyes glittered with accusation. 'You tryin' to pull the wool over me eyes, Grandad?'

'Sorry?'

'You ain't qualified for benefit. You jus' walked out of yer job. You wasn't sacked or nuffing. You jus' walked out. And yer got insurance. You ain't entitled.'

'No, I—'

She raised her voice to the pitch of a road drill. 'Look 'ere, Grandad!' she yapped. 'Pay attention! Watch my lips, right? Yer says in yer form what you walked aht of yer job, right? Yer wasn't sacked, yer wasn't made redunt nor nuffink, yer jus' walked aht. Anyone what jus' walks out of 'is job is not entitled. Them's the rules. See?'

She tossed his application form into her wastebin and waved him away. She clapped her hands and looked over his shoulder towards the queue. 'Nex'! Come on! 'Oo's nex'? I 'aven't got all day. It's near me lunch-break.'

He lowered his voice. There was no point in getting heated.

'Sharon,' he said quietly. 'This is the situation. I've been out of work for five months—'

'Gaw, you still 'ere?'

'—and whether it's my own fault or not I've used up nearly all my savings so that soon I won't even be able to pay the mortgage. I've been paying national insurance contributions for more than twenty years and now I need help. I would have come to you earlier if I hadn't had any savings but I think it's wrong for people like me to go on the dole so long as they can rely on themselves.'

Sharon gazed at him with menace. Her nostrils twitched. 'Wotcha mean, people like you?'

'Well, you know. Sort of better-off people—'

'So yer fink yer better than what the rest of us is, eh?'

'Not at all. Of course not. I just—'

'Yer jus' too soddin' snooty, that's wotcha mean, Mr 'Oity-Toity. Well, let me tell you somefing for nuffing, Grandpa. You ain't qualified for Jobseeker's Allowance. Right. That's it. Off yer go. Nex'!'

'Of course I qualify,' he said irritably. 'You people are constantly dishing out wads of cash every week to almost anyone who asks for it, even if they're foreigners who have just arrived in the country—'

She raised her hand like a traffic cop. 'Right! That's enough! I knew it! Racist!'

'I beg your pardon?'

She pointed at him. 'Foreigners. You said foreigners. Racist! Fascist!'

'What on earth are you talking about?'

She jabbed her forefinger at him. 'We all know what your sort means by foreigners. Yer mean black people.'

'Not at all—'

'Yes, yer do. Jus' 'cause yer speak all 'igh an' mighty,' she screeched. 'Jus' 'cause yer fink yer better than wot we is. Well, I tell yer somefing for nuffing, Grandad. Yer not, see? You wiv yer airs and graces.'

Behind him he could sense that the queue of 'clients' was riveted by the sight and sound of Sharon in full cry. He felt his face reddening. His ears burned. A warm wave of anger surged through him. 'I want to see your superior,' he said quietly. 'A supervisor, manager, whatever you call him.'

'Woffor?'

Hallam folded his arms and smiled politely. 'Firstly,

Sharon, I'm going to make an official complaint about the way you treat your clients.'

'Wotcha mean? I done nuffin'.'

'And secondly I'm going to complain about the way you have tried to stop me claiming the unemployment benefit to which I am fully entitled.'

'No you isn't—'

'So I want to see whoever's in charge of this place today.'

She glared at him. 'You gotta 'ave an appointment.'

'Fine. Then make one for me, will you? For some time in the next five minutes.'

'She won't see you today. She's busy.'

'Well, I'm not.' Hallam smiled. 'I can sit here all day if you like,' he said. 'I'm not budging from here until I've seen her.'

She stared at him with her little black glittery eyes. She licked her lips. He could almost hear her thinking.

She bent towards her wastebin, retrieved his application form and smoothed it on her desk with her hands.

'P'raps I been 'asty,' she muttered.

'Just get the supervisor, will you?'

Sharon did not move. 'There's different rules when someone leaves 'is job of 'is own 'cord,' she mumbled. 'We 'ave ter ask an independent tribunal to 'judicate.'

'Will you please call the supervisor? Or shall I start making a fuss?'

She stared at him with loathing.

She left her seat and disappeared through the door at the far end of the room. Hallam folded his arms and sat back in the chair to wait.

'Well done, mister,' said a man in the queue behind him. 'She got it coming to her, that one. She been bloody 'umpy with me, an' all.'

'That's right,' said a woman. 'Cheeky cow!'

Several minutes later Sharon returned with a tall, serene-looking woman, who introduced herself as the customer services manager, shook his hand, sat behind the desk and smiled at him. She folded her hands. Sharon stood behind her, looking baleful.

'Sorry to keep you waiting, sir,' said the manager.

That's a bit more like it.

'Sharon has explained the situation to me,' she said, 'and I understand your frustration but I'm afraid the regulations are quite specific. Cases like yours, where there is some doubt as to the exact reason for your unemployment, have to be considered by a tribunal, and that, I'm afraid, can take months, and until they give their ruling we are not allowed to pay you any benefit.'

Sharon crossed her arms and smirked.

'If the tribunal rules against you,' said the manager, 'and finds that you were in any way to blame for your unemployment, then you have to wait for twenty-six weeks before we can pay you any benefit.'

Hellfire: that's six months. How can we survive for another six months?

'In addition, I'm afraid, even if the tribunal finds that you are entitled to unemployment benefit, we do have to subtract from it any mortgage or job-loss insurance payments you may have received.' The manager smiled sympathetically. 'I wish you had come to us earlier. I understand that you didn't do so because you had some savings to live off, and although I admire your independence it was, I'm afraid, a foolish thing to do. Had you come to us right at the start we might well have had the tribunal's decision by now. As it is we have to start at the beginning, as though today were your first day out of work, as though you lost your job only yesterday.'

'I see,' said Hallam. 'In that case I won't waste any more of your time.' He stood. 'Thank you for your explanation, but I can't afford to wait for months. I'm almost completely broke. I'm going to have to find some sort of job, anything at all, no matter what.'

'I'm so sorry,' said the manager. 'We'll process your application anyway and send you a registration card and let you know the date of the hearing. In the meantime there are several other alternatives you could pursue. You could apply to the DSS for income support, housing benefit, dependents' allowances.'

No, never. Not income support and housing benefit, those final refuges of the utterly helpless and indigent. I'm not *that* desperate yet. I'll find some sort of job, even if I have to sweep the streets.

'I'd rather not if I can manage without.'

'It's perfectly customary in cases like yours, you know.'

'I'd still rather not.'

The manager smiled with delicate understanding. 'You're perfectly entitled to it. There's no shame attached to it, Mr Hallam. Just think of it as an insurance policy whose premiums you've been paying for years . . .'

'I'd really rather not, if possible. I'll find something.'

The manager nodded sadly. 'If only more people were as honest as you,' she said. 'Perhaps I can at least arrange for you to have some counselling.'

Counselling? Certainly not.

'No thanks,' he said.

Sharon was glowering at him. Her plastic badge winked at him: 'HI THERE! I'M SHARON, YOUR PERSONAL JOBSEEKER COUNSELLOR (Grade 3b).'

'Tell me, Sharon,' he said, 'what qualifications do you need exactly to become a Jobseeker Counsellor?'

She glared at him again.

The manager made a clucking noise. 'Come on, Sharon, dear,' she said. 'Don't be modest. You tell Mr Hallam. What is it, the one thing we insist on?'

Sharon blinked. She stared at him. 'Yer gotta be good wiv people,' she said.

CHAPTER 8

Thin Ice

When the ice on a sunny winter pond suddenly breaks up beneath your feet, everything happens with terrifying speed: the first alarming pistol shot of warning is matched within seconds by a network of cracks that spreads across the ice so fast that there is nothing you can do to stop yourself plunging into the freezing waters below. Within seconds you are dragged down and away, and trapped beneath a solid sheet of ice. So, too, when the fragile crust of civilisation suddenly gives way beneath you: at one moment you are gliding serenely across the smooth, bright surface of life, the next you are plunged deep into an unimaginable horror from which there seems to be no escape.

As soon as Hallam had spent all his savings, his life crumbled beneath him at a frightening rate. In October he had persuaded his bank, the Millennium, to lend him five thousand pounds but by mid-December most of that had gone and his two credit cards had both reached their five-thousand-pound limit and were beginning to accumulate huge amounts of monthly interest charges. Jenny's application to become a school-dinner lady had been rejected as soon as the headmistress heard her middle-class accent, and all her other attempts to find a job were in vain. She went for interviews at kindergartens, offices, department stores, the town hall and even applied for a job as the receptionist in a massage parlour, but each application was rejected because she was 'not experienced enough' or 'over-qualified' or 'under-qualified' or just 'unsuitable'.

'Perhaps I had better start wafting about in négligees and entertaining elderly gentlemen in the afternoons,' said Monica.

'I could leave school, Dad, and get a job,' said Susie earnestly.

'You'll do nothing of the kind,' said Hallam. 'You're going to go to university.'

They all looked at Matthew, who was sitting on the floor in a yoga position and picking his toenails. He glanced up and glared at them. 'I'm trying, aren't I?'

'Very,' said Monica.

'It's not that easy. Is it, *Father*?'

I'm going to have to lower my sights. I'm going to have to take whatever I can get.

But now that it was almost Christmas it was pointless to try to find any job at all until the second week in January. People are sacked by the thousand just before Christmas – bosses seem to relish firing people during the festive season – but no one is ever hired in December. It was going to mean another month of waiting, of mounting debts and interest charges and desperation.

He approached the Millennium Bank again for another loan. Surely they would let him have enough at least to see him through Christmas? And then he would start afresh in January with several New Year resolutions: to throw off his depression, to start thinking positively again, to tighten his belt, to take any work he could find, anything at all, to give Matt an ultimatum to do the same.

The young woman bank clerk considered him vacantly

through the bullet-proof glass. She was wearing a plastic badge that announced: 'HI THERE! I'm Cheryl Varley, Customer Services Personal Account Operative (Grade IIa)'. She looked about nineteen. He had never seen her before. He had been banking with the same branch for more than twenty years but he had never seen any of the clerks before. They all looked about nineteen. Everyone looked about nineteen these days. Even the Prime Minister nowadays was younger than he was.

'Good-morning-sir-how-may-I-help-you?' said Tracey the bank clerk.

'Hello,' he said. 'I have an account here. I need a loan.'

'Certainly-sir-no-problem-name-please-sir.'

'Hallam. Peter Hallam.'

'Poddern?'

'Peter Hallam.'

'Mr Allen.'

'No, Hallam.'

'Poddern?'

'Hallam with an H.'

'With a haitch?'

'That's right: an H. H-A-L-L-A-M. That's two Ls.'

'There you go. Cheers. Hallam with a haitch and two Ls. No problem. Bear with me.' She tapped at her computer screen. 'Account number?'

He told her.

'Poddern?'

He told her again.

'How big a loan, Mr Hallam?'

'Five thousand pounds?'

'Poddern?'

'Are you a little hard of hearing?' he said.

'Nah. S'yer voice. Yer jus' speak funny, 'at's aw'.'

'Five thousand pounds,' said Hallam slowly. 'Is that better?'

'Brilliant,' she said. 'Cheers. No problem. Bear with me.'

She tapped away at her keyboard, letter after letter, number after number, for at least a minute. Why so long? Why so many numerals? All he wanted was another five thousand.

After a while she stopped tapping and stared glumly at the screen for several minutes.

She looked up.

'Yer account's badly overdraw',' she said. 'Yer gone way over yer limit awready.'

'I know. I'm sorry.'

'So we carn' give yer another loan, Mr Hallam. I'm ever so sorry.'

'What do you mean?'

'Yer overdraw'.'

'Well, of course I'm overdrawn. That's why I want another loan. I wouldn't need another one if I wasn't overdrawn.'

'I'm sorry, Mr Allen, but—'

'Hallam.'

'Hallam. But rules is rules. I'm ever so sorry.'

'But I've never been refused a loan before.'

She shrugged. 'Swot the computer says,' she said.

'I beg your pardon?'

'The computer,' she said, jabbing a finger towards the screen in front of her. 'It won't not give you no more credit, see. It says what you can't not have no more.'

'But I've borrowed thousands here over the years and always paid you back.'

'Swot it says. Carn' argue with the computer. Yer done yer limit, see. I carn' argue with the computer.'

'In that case I'd better speak to the manager.'

She looked at him with pity. 'Manager? We don't not have no managers no more. We got the computer.'

'The *computer* decides who can have a loan and who can't?'

'Course,' she said. She seemed astonished at his ignorance.

'A *machine* decides?'

'Course it do. That's wot computers is for.'

'Well, I'd better speak to whoever's in charge of the computer, then.'

'You doan unnerstan',' she said slowly, as though talking to a child. 'No one's not in *charge* of the computer no more. No way. The computer's, like, in charge of us.'

'Good grief,' said Hallam. 'Like God.'

'Poddern?'

'Never mind.'

Cheryl went into robot close-down mode. 'Thank-you-for-your-application-sir-have-a-nice-day-next-customer-please.'

He tried the building society to see if they would increase his mortgage by advancing him a few thousand pounds. The manager was sympathetic. 'And how would you meet the extra interest payments?' he said.

'I'll get a job soon.'

'Of course. But until then?'

'Well, at first, I suppose, the interest payments would come out of the extra loan.'

The manager looked shocked. 'I'm sorry,' he said primly, 'I'm afraid that would be out of the question.'

'Why?'

He pursed his lips. 'We cannot possibly lend you money to pay the interest on money we have already lent you.'

'Why not?'

'I'm sorry, Mr Hallam. I'm really very sorry.'

Hallam approached a couple of loan-shark companies but their interest rates of more than thirty per cent a year were so extortionate that he quickly shied away from them.

Who else?

Pinky Porter: the thousand pounds. That would at least pay for Christmas.

He telephoned Pinky.

'God! Peter!' said Pinky. 'How good to hear you. But I'm in a hell of a hurry. On the way to the airport.'

'Going somewhere nice?'

'Barbados. For Christmas.' He chuckled. 'Taking a very sassy little thing I met in Rome last week. Swedish, blonde, twenty-nine, huge knockers, goes like a rocket.'

'Pinky . . .'

'I know, I know, that thousand quid I owe you. I promised it before Christmas. I'm terribly sorry, Pete, it completely slipped my mind. Tell you what, I'll stick a cheque in the post as soon as I get back.'

'Pinky, I could actually do with it a bit before—'

'Must dash, Pete. Taxi's waiting. *Ciao*. See you soon.'

Bloody Pinky. The bastard. It's gone for good. I know it. That thousand quid: I'm never going to see it again.

Jenny was often out of the house in December, taking the car, 'shopping', she said. How could she go shopping when she had so little money? Perhaps over the years she had saved a bit from the housekeeping account, or perhaps she was just visiting friends, going anywhere to escape him. The possibility that she was now avoiding him left him bereft. How could they have come to this? Only a year ago people were saying what a perfect marriage they had. How could it all have collapsed so suddenly? She was silent, sullen and no longer smiled at anything he said. She never laughed. When he tried to touch her she moved away and he no longer dared to approach her sexually. Twice he had done so and twice she had rebuffed him. They still shared a bed but the most private part of her was somewhere else. He would lie in the dark and feel her warmth beside him, the slenderness of her back as she faced away from him, her buttocks inches from his groin, the back of her neck slim and white in the darkness, and the nearness of her made him ache with loneliness. One afternoon, when everyone else was out, he lay on the bed and wept aloud for what they had lost, smelling the trace of her perfume on her pillow, sobbing. He haunted the house, drifting from one room to another, picking up books and putting them down again, leafing through old photograph albums. Surely this was just a bad patch, he thought, the sort of cold war that all marriages have to survive occasionally?

Please, God, let her come back to me soon. I don't think I can do this on my own.

Almost as hard to bear was Matthew's relentless scorn. 'Still no job, *Father*? Oh dear. Tut-tut. What a shame.'

And the compassion he saw in Susie's eyes made him feel utterly inadequate.

Why is it, he thought, that men are almost wholly defined by their work? That a man without a job is seen to be a man without balls?

Susie's concern for him pierced his heart. For weeks she scanned the newspapers every day and circled possible jobs for him, but as the employment ads and personal columns shrank in November and December the jobs she circled became less and less impressive. 'You'd make a great librarian, Daddy,' she said brightly. Or 'Look, here's one for a bursar in a prep school.' Or 'What about this one? Garden-centre manager.' He saw the hopeless eagerness in her eyes and his heart turned over. She reminded him so much of the Jenny who had loved him once.

Even Fudge and Jezebel seemed to sense that something was wrong. Fudge followed him everywhere, licking his hand, wagging his tail whenever Hallam looked at him, lying close to his feet when he sat, and Jezebel would sit and stare at him with her cool green eyes for half an hour at a time, head unmoving, eyes unblinking, as though she were trying to read his mind. Only Monica was the same as before, always brisk and cheerful, refusing to admit that anything was wrong, almost as though she had not yet noticed that he no longer went to work but spent much of each day mooching about the house. She played her sixties records as loudly as ever, singing along with the Beatles and the Rolling Stones, lending the house a spurious impersonation of normality. Sometimes he was grateful for her chirpy pretence and, against all the odds, she could still make him laugh. Early in December she was stopped by the police for driving her little Metro at 50 m.p.h. in a 30 m.p.h. restricted area. 'I do apologise, Officer,' she told the two patrolmen breezily, 'but I had no alternative. I'm almost out of petrol so I had to drive as fast as possible to get to the petrol station before the tank runs dry.'

'"Mary had a little lamb,"' she announced one afternoon as she watched him digging in the garden, '"and it tasted delicious."'

'You're not still working on those blasted nursery rhymes.'

'Of course I am. They're going to make me a fortune. I can't expect to win on the horses every week but you'll see, the book'll be a bestseller. My stars said so. It'll all be tickety-boo. "Humpty Dumpty sat on a wall so now he's got piles, of course."'

He laughed despite himself. She was indomitable. And she was only trying to help, to cheer him up for a moment or two.

He leaned on his spade. 'Got any more?'

'Zillions. "Little Polly Flinders / Sat among the cinders / And she won't make the mistake of doing *that* again."'

He chuckled.

'"There was an old woman who lived in a shoe. Her favourite food was sole."'

He grinned. 'You're quite mad, Miss Porridge,' he said.

She beamed. 'That's the nicest thing you've ever said to me.'

Occasionally her relentless optimism made him want to throttle her, and then he felt guilty for being intolerant and ungrateful. She knew very well how much he was suffering, but she came from that wartime generation which believed that the best way to face adversity is to treat it with contempt. She was only trying to help.

As the days grew shorter and colder he felt increasingly restless cooped up in the house, but he could no longer afford to play tennis and he resigned from the club to save on the subscriptions. He tried to escape from the house every day, walking the streets for hours to exhaust himself enough for sleep, but the dampness of those grey December afternoons, with their mists and dripping leaves and echoing footsteps, filled him with gloom. He sat on park benches, wrapped in raincoat and muffler, until he realised that he looked like a tramp or an alcoholic. In the park he stood and watched the children playing on the swings and slides until he saw one young mother staring at him and moving her children protectively away. *Dear God, she thinks I'm a child molester.* He sat in the reference room of the public library, scanning the daily papers and the magazines, but after a few days he became aware that the librarian was watching him with an air of condescension.

He had always slept well, at least seven hours every night, but now he was waking regularly at two or three o'clock and failing to go back to sleep. He would lie in the dark for three or four hours, staring into the blackness, his mind a turmoil, painfully aware of Jenny soft and warm beside him, listening to the rhythm of her breathing, not daring to move in case his restlessness might drive her to sleep elsewhere. If that happened it would surely be all over between them. At least while they shared a bed there was still some hope.

He developed a nervous tremor in the big toe of his right foot, which would suddenly start trembling and twitching uncontrollably for no reason at all. When he rose each morning his arms and legs felt insupportably heavy. When he went for his long walks it seemed as though he had to drag his feet to move them along the pavements. He started to develop afternoon headaches, and when he woke in the early hours his heart was often pounding at twice its usual speed. Often during the day he experienced sudden palpitations that made him catch his breath. He went to see the doctor, who sent him to hospital for various tests: the ECG, X-rays, the treadmill. They even drained some fluid off his spine to test for multiple sclerosis.

'There's nothing wrong with you,' the doctor said, when the results of the tests came through. 'Nothing physical, at any rate. You haven't got MS, thank God, and your heart's fine.'

'But these palpitations?'

'They're perfectly normal, you know. Everyone gets them to some extent.' He chuckled. 'It's when your heart *stops* pounding that you need to start worrying.' He cleared his throat. 'Is everything all right at home?'

'Fine.'

He thinks I'm a neurotic, that it's all just psychosomatic. How do you tell your doctor that your wife no longer loves you?

'Sex life OK?'

'Sure. Fine.'

'Your job?'

'I'm actually in between jobs at the moment.'

'Ah. Unemployed.'

'Only temporarily.'

The doctor nodded. 'Of course,' he said, without conviction, 'but these things can sometimes have strange effects. Would you like some tranquillisers?'

'No thanks.'

'They do some excellent tranquillisers these days. No side-effects.'

'I don't believe in taking pills unless it's absolutely necessary.'

'That's *very* old-fashioned.'

'I am.'

'Well, what about counselling?'

'Certainly not,' said Hallam. 'Bloody mumbo-jumbo.'

'Not at all,' said the doctor. 'Times have changed, Mr Hallam.'

Not only does he think I'm neurotic: hell's bells, even the doctor's younger than I am.

For the first time in thirty years he began to doubt all the things he had taken for granted for so long: Jenny, his family life, his principles, his own abilities. Perhaps Matt had been right: perhaps he had followed the wrong bright star all his life and now he was paying for it. Maybe he had never really been much good at his job after all: if he had really been as good as he had always thought then surely some other company would have snapped him up by now. Maybe he had survived so long as sales manager simply because Andy Unwin and Fred Parker and Joe Mullaly had all been just too kind to get rid of him.

No, that can't be true. I was bloody good. I know it.

But now it was six months since he had left his job and no one had shown the slightest interest in employing him.

He approached two other banks to see if he could shift his overdraft to them but neither was interested in taking on his debts. 'But isn't that how banks make their money?' he asked one bank official. 'Out of lending money to people like me?'

The banker smiled delicately. 'Not quite, sir,' he said. 'We make money out of lending it to people we think will be able to pay it back.'

He made another trip to the building society to try to increase the mortgage. The manager was still sympathetic. 'The insurance people still refusing to pay your mortgage?'

'Yes. They say they're only liable if you're sacked or made redundant but not if you resign. I've tried to explain but they refuse to listen.'

'That's insurance companies all over.' The manager shook his head. 'The small print, Mr Hallam,' he said mournfully. 'There's always the small print. Look, I'll tell you what we can do. I can't possibly increase the loan but I can allow you to postpone any repayments for three or four months. That would give you a breathing space.'

'Thank you. I'm very grateful.' At least we'll still have a roof over our heads for another three or four months.

But the thin ice of Hallam's life was cracking up around him now with a frightening ferocity. Two days later a computerised letter arrived from the Millennium Bank demanding immediate repayment of his overdraft as well as the five-thousand-pound loan he had taken out in October.

Nearly eight thousand pounds in all.

Eight thousand pounds. Just before Christmas. What bastards.

His heart started pounding rapidly. He felt weak and light-headed. He sat down on the edge of the bed, frightened, really frightened, physically frightened, for the first time in decades. He put his head between his knees. His heart hammered against his chest. Eight thousand pounds? Where was he going to find eight thousand pounds?

The world seemed dark around him.

His heart danced. It thundered in his chest. He felt dizzy.

It was impossible. Where was he going to find eight thousand pounds?

After a few minutes the dizziness faded. Eight thousand pounds! It was not only impossible, it was outrageous. How *dare* they do this to him, out of the blue, so suddenly? How *dare* they?

He telephoned the bank. As the double ringing tone

purred at the other end of the line he began to feel increasingly angry. How *dare* they suddenly pull the plug on him, just like that, without any warning, after more than twenty years?

The call was answered.

A click, a hollow echo, a recorded voice: male, slow, smooth, reassuring.

Dear God, now the computer speaks. And it speaks like a child psychiatrist.

'You have reached the Millennium Bank, your caring financial enabler for the twenty-first century. Good morning. Thank you for your call.'

Get on with it.

'If you are already a customer of Millennium Bank please press one. If you are . . .'

Hallam jabbed at the button on his telephone.

A click.

More distant ringing.

Another connection. The same sleek, sleepy, computerised voice. 'Thank you for pressing one. You have reached the current customer services department of the Millennium Bank, your caring financial enabler for the twenty-first century. Should you be a business or corporate account holder please press one. Should you be a personal customer account client please press two. Should you be—'

Hallam jabbed at button two.

Another click.

More ringing in the distance.

Another click. That bloody voice again, like oil oozing. 'Thank you. You have now reached the personal account call station of the Millennium Bank, your caring financial enabler for the twenty-first century.'

Dear God.

'Thank you for your call. Thank you. Bear with me. Please hold a moment.'

Some buzzing.

More clicking.

And now a computerised female voice.

A miracle! The computer has a girlfriend.

'Hi there!' said the female computerised voice. It sounded determinedly jolly, like a TV talk-show hostess, all teeth and tits. 'Thank you for calling. Please state your name and account number – slowly, clearly and distinctly – after the tone or alternatively—'

'H-a-l-l-a-m,' said Hallam.

'—you can spell out your name and account number—'

'Nine-eight-four-five-two—'

'—by punching the relevant letters and numbers on your telephone.'

I'll punch them all right: I'll bloody well murder the buggers.

There was a momentary silence.

'Sir or madam?' said the computer anxiously. 'Are we still in connection, please? We seem to have a small problem of non-recording. Please bear with me.'

There was another moment of silence.

'May we please repeat the previous process?' said the computer. 'Bear with me. Please speak your name and account number – slowly, clearly and distinctly – or alternatively you can spell out your name and account number . . .'

Hellfire.

'. . . by punching the relevant numbers . . .'

Yes, yes, get on with it.

'. . . on your telephone. Would you please try that again for me? Thank you.'

'H-a-l-l-a-m,' said Hallam tightly.

When did all this nonsense start, talking to machines instead of people? And why is it that nowadays the machines sound like real people and real people sound like machines?

'Nine-eight-four-five,' he said, 'two-eight-one-six-three-four.'

A couple more clicks on the telephone line.

A humming noise.

Another click.

'Thank you – Mr – Allen,' said the computer.

Oh, for God's sake . . .

'I just want to speak to a human being,' said Hallam crisply.

'Bear with me, Mr – Allen. I am now in the process of processing your call, Mr – Allen.'

'JUST GIVE ME A HUMAN BEING! PLEASE!'

'I am about to connect you to one of our customer services personal account operatives, Mr – Allen.'

More ringing tone, more double purring, on and on for at least a minute. The female computer again, apologetic. 'I am sorry, Mr – Allen – sir – but our customer services personal account operatives are all engaged at the moment . . .'

'Impossible!' bellowed Hallam. 'No man in his right mind would look at any of them twice.'

'. . . but I will connect you as soon as one is available. Please bear with me. We are doing all we can to connect you as soon as possible to a free customer services personal account operative. In the meantime here is a selection of international white noise and mood music for your entertainment and pleasure.'

Please no. Not white noise. Not mood music. Please!

Soothing sounds and rhythms wafted down the telephone line: surf breaking on a beach, seagulls calling, a flute trembling, a drum replying, an infant chuckling, the soaring voice of some tribal Ethnic Woman crying high and loud *aieeeeai-ai-ai-aieeeeai*, as though she were suffering some terrible pain in some distant century before the development of speech.

The girlie computer again. 'I am sorry, Mr – Allen – sir – but all our customer services personal account operatives are still engaged with other customers. We do apologise for this delay. I will, of course, connect you with a customer services personal account operative as soon as one is available but in the meantime did you know that the Millennium Bank, the caring financial enabler for the twenty-first century, offers a broad and deep range of financial and economic services that will cosset you and comfort you through life?'

Hell's bells.

'The Millennium Bank, the caring financial enabler for the twenty-first century, can smooth every economic transaction you ever need to make, from pocket money to pensions, from marriages to mortgages, from weddings to wills. The Millennium Bank, the caring financial enabler for the twenty-first century. The Millennium Bank: Tomorrow's Future Today.'

More musical noises. More rhythms. Torrential rain in a tropical forest. Rolling thunder. Lightning crashing. A million frogs croaking, *rimick-rimick-rimick*. Soft, sad chords on a classical guitar. The sudden sounds of a silent night. Rustling leaves. A mouse squeaking. The roar of a lion. Some Ethnic Woman howling high and plaintive *aaieeeeai-ai-ai-aaieeeeai* as though she had just discovered sex in some distant century before they discovered the Female Orgasm.

And then suddenly, without warning, another robotic voice: 'Good - morning - sir - or - madam - this - is - Marleen - your - personal-account - tele - operative - at - your - service - thank - you - for - calling - how - may - I - help - you?'

For a moment Hallam was baffled. A real woman? At last? 'You're a real person?'

'Poddern?'

'Not a computer?'

'Yer what?'

'Thank goodness for that. My name is Peter Hallam and I have an account with you.'

'Good morning, Mr Allen.'

'Hallam. With an H.'

'Hallen with a haitch. Cheers. There you go.'

Never mind. Let it pass.

'I need to speak to whoever's in charge of closing accounts if they go too far into the red.'

'It's the computer what does that, Mr Hallen.'

'No, Marlene, I need to speak to a human being. Isn't there a manager, a supervisor, someone like that?'

'And to what would be the purpose of this enquiry, Mr Hallen, if I may ask?'

'I need to ask whoever's in charge to give me a little more time before making me bankrupt.'

'No problem. Bear with me, sir. I shall make enquiries.'

Why did they all keep saying, 'No problem,' and 'Bear with me,' and 'Cheers,' and 'There you go'? After a while it could drive you mad, like those damned car window stickers saying, 'Baby On Board.' So what if there is? What the hell are you supposed to do about it? Smash into the car if there *isn't* a Baby On Board?

More soft noises down the telephone. A river gurgling. A gentle wind sighing in trees, the hollow repetitive boom of some primitive aboriginal instrument. A cat purring. Violins soaring. A cello weeping. Some bloody Ethnic Woman shrieking *aaieeeeai-ai-ai-aaieeeeai* as though she had just been punched on the nose by an enraged customer of the Millennium Bank.

'Mr Hallen, sir, you still there, sir?'

'I seem to have been here for the best part of a couple of months.'

'Yes sir sorry sir bear with me Marleen again I have our Mr Dean Castle for you sir thank you sir.'

'Who's Mr Castle when he's at home?'

'Mr Heller?' A smooth male voice, silky, unctuous, condescending.

'*Hallam*. Peter Hallam. I have an account with you.'

'Ah. Yes. So what seems to be the problem, then?'

'And you are . . . ?'

'Mr Castle.'

Why do I distrust men who call themselves 'Mr'? Like old soldiers who still insist on calling themselves 'Captain' or 'Major' years after leaving the Army.

'Mr Dean Castle.'

'And your job is . . . ?'

'I am the senior duty executive enabler today.'

'So you're a big cheese, then?'

Castle chuckled in a worldly fashion. 'The ultimate Gruyère, sir.'

'At last. In that case perhaps you can explain to me why I've just had a letter from you . . .' Suddenly he was tongue-tied. He struggled to find the right words, the appropriate level of protest, and found himself floundering. Should he be angry, abusive, icy? What was the most effective way to behave when your bank was about to make you bankrupt?

'You've sent me a letter calling in my overdraft and loan.'

'Yes? Perhaps you would be good enough to give me your account number, Mr Heller.'

'Hallam.'

'Of course you are. The number?'

Hallam told him.

'Bear with me,' said Castle. He called up his records on the computer. After a minute or so he coughed discreetly. 'Ah, yes. I see. Most unfortunate.'

'I want to know why.'

Castle cleared his throat. 'I regret to say that you are no longer a Grade A risk, Mr Hallam. Eight thousand pounds is a great deal of money.'

'Come off it! Not to a bank like the Millennium.'

'Ah, but where would we be if every one of our customers owed us eight thousand pounds? We would be bankrupt ourselves. And the computer has identified that in your case there is now a perceived risk that our capital may be in jeopardy. It is six months since any payments were made into the account except for receipts from a building-society savings account. No salary payments, nothing. You see our problem, Mr Hallam.'

'And what about mine? I've lost my job and now—'

'Ah. Really? That makes the situation even more serious. I don't think the computer knows yet that you are unemployed.'

'And what will it do when it does know? Send me its condolences? A Christmas card, perhaps?'

'Very droll, sir.'

'Look, Mr Castle, quite frankly I resent your sudden threat to bankrupt me. I need your help, not threats, and I feel I'm entitled to it. I've been with your bank for more than twenty years.'

'Is that so? Most commendable.'

'Doesn't that count for something?'

Castle's voice leaked down the telephone line like gravy. 'Of course, we are greatly gratified by your adherence to this bank, Mr Hallam, but unfortunately loyalty does not pay any bills. We have to be more concerned nowadays with customers who may stay with us for the *next* twenty years rather than those whose relationship with the bank is history.'

'*History?*'

'What is past is past, Mr Hallam. The future is what matters.'

'But how can you justify this high-handed behaviour without even giving me any notice?'

'Well, of course it's the computer, not I, that has called in the debt, and if you look at the terms and conditions of our original overdraft and loan agreements—'

'Sod the small print, Castle. I'm talking about decent behaviour. Fair play.'

'Ah. Well, there you have me. I'm only a banker, sir,

not a moralist, and the first rule of banking is not to lose money.'

'So you're saying there's nothing you'll do to give me more time to repay you?'

'Nothing I *can* do, sir. You have breached the parameters of our standard credit agreements. The only outcome of that is to minimise our risk by calling in our loans to you.'

'But I can't pay you. Not now. Not this very minute. It's stalemate. So what do we do now?'

Dean Castle cleared his throat again. It was a disconcertingly metallic sound, as though some eighteenth-century executioner were testing the guillotine. 'You did offer a percentage of the value of your house as collateral, sir.'

'I beg your pardon?'

'We have a lien on part of the value of your house.'

Hellfire.

'You mean you'd force me to sell it?'

'There is always that regrettable possibility, yes.'

'You can't be serious. You'd chuck me and my wife and family out of our home and force me to sell it just so that I can pay you a few thousand lousy pounds?'

'They may be just a few thousand lousy pounds to you, Mr Hallam,' said Castle, 'but they are *our* few thousand lousy pounds.'

'I never thought I'd see the day . . .'

Hallam began to stammer. He was losing his train of thought. His mind was clogged with overload.

I'm starting to babble, he thought. I'm beginning to panic. Stop panicking. Settle down. The man's only human, after all. He's bound eventually to see reason.

'For years you've been bombarding me with letters and leaflets and pamphlets and God knows what urging me to borrow money when I didn't need it but now, when I really do need a loan, you won't let me have one and even want the old one back immediately. My old bank manager would have let me have one. Mike Richards – he'd know that I've always been an excellent risk.'

'I doubt it, sir. Mr Richards retired about two years ago.'

'But he can't be a day over forty even now.'

'Probably not, sir, but it was then that we introduced computerised telephone banking, which required the early retirement of many older members of surplus staff, especially those who were not prepared to alter their style of working.'

Poor old Mike. Given the boot at thirty-eight. On the scrapheap at thirty-eight!

'How old are you, Dean?'

'Twenty-seven, sir.'

'You'll go far.'

'Thank you, sir. I intend to.'

'You're exactly the right sort of person for modern business.'

'I like to think so.'

'Just make sure you do it in the next six or seven years,' said Hallam bitterly, 'because by the time you're thirty-five they'll be sacking anyone over thirty-four. By then your precious computer will have taken over your job as well.'

Dean Castle chuckled. 'I don't think so,' he said. 'My uncle owns the bank.'

Christmas was dreadful. Hallam had always loved Christmas but this year the house was tense with silences and gloom. He bought a tiny, crippled tree, a fraction of the size of their usual seven-footer, and it cowered unhappily in the corner of the living room, scrawny and misshapen, bowed down by the weight of baubles that were much too heavy for it and blinded by its own lights.

The stores and streets were jammed with shoppers and bright with lights and cheery winter window scenes and carols in the early dark afternoons. 'God rest you merry, gentlemen, Let nothing you dismay.' He haunted the chilly streets like the ghost of his old self, staring into shop windows with regret, ashamed at how little he could afford to spend on presents this year.

Next year, he swore, next year it will all be different. It'll be like it was before. Better. When Jenny comes home again.

They sent out nearly a hundred Christmas cards, as many as ever. 'I'm not cutting back on the list,' said Jenny coldly. 'People will think we can't afford to send them.' But by Christmas Eve they had received in return only thirty cards: for two-thirds of their old friends and acquaintances they seemed to have ceased to exist. Five came from members of his old sales-department staff, Leila Roberts's with the message 'Well done, Mr Hallam, and good luck. We all wish you were still here.' Another card was signed, in straggly writing, 'Ron Doggett (ex-comisionare they saked me mr hallam now i'm working for the scrapyard up bolton st way).'

For the first time in twenty years they did not throw their usual open-house party on Christmas Eve and Jenny refused to go to the midnight carol service.

'But we always go on Christmas Eve,' he said hopelessly.

'Not this year.'

'Please, Jen. It's always lovely. You always love it.'

'Not this year,' she said.

He went with Susie and found himself wiping his eyes as the choir sang 'Silent Night' and one of Jenny's favourites, 'The Candlelight Carol', with a terrible sweetness. How dark the world was nowadays, he thought. How cold it can be without love.

'Don't cry, Daddy,' whispered Susie. 'It'll be all right in the end. I know it will.'

He did not trust himself to reply.

She squeezed his hand.

At least I have Susie. Some people have no one at all. Like

Monica. How does Monica feel alone on Christmas Eve after all those years? Does she weep silently in her room? Perhaps. Maybe you never stop missing someone you really love.

Christmas Day itself was a grim endurance test. After breakfast they opened their presents with a quiet desperation and he was ashamed of the cheapness of the presents he had bought. They say 'it's the thought that counts' but that's simply untrue: the price is equally important. Last year he had bought Jenny an alarmingly expensive brooch and when she had opened it she had thrown her arms around him and cried. This year he had been able to afford only the latest hardback novel by one of her favourite writers, Joanna Trollope. She glanced at it, said 'thank you' far too politely and put the book aside. *And that's the Christmas present she will always remember: the book, not the brooch.* His own present from her was a dark, sober business tie. Sarcasm? A heavy hint? She had never given him a tie in all their years together.

He crossed the room to kiss her. 'Thank you, darling,' he said.

She moved her head away at the last moment so that he kissed her clumsily on the ear.

'I love you,' he said.

She said nothing. She looked away.

Who is this woman? Where has she been hiding all these years?

His throat was tight when he saw what Susie had bought him: a box of three expensive bottles of wine. 'You shouldn't have, Susie, darling, you really shouldn't. It's far too generous.'

'You deserve it. Doesn't he, Gran?'

'Of course he does,' said Monica.

'I'm going out for a walk,' said Jenny crisply.

Matthew announced that he was going to eat a vegetarian Christmas dinner elsewhere – 'I can't stand the atmosphere in this bloody house' – and although Susie, Monica and Hallam did their best to be bright and cheerful at lunch, wearing paper hats and reading out corny cracker jokes, Jenny's face was as stiff as granite. Her mood infected the whole house with unhappiness. The turkey was overcooked, the vegetables burned, the wine cheap and corked.

'Let's play charades,' said Susie eagerly afterwards.

'Lovely,' said Monica. 'And then that word-game, the one where you have to make up definitions.'

'I've got a headache,' said Jenny. 'I'm going to bed.'

Come back, Jenny. Please come back. I can't bear this any more.

Boxing Day was just as bad. Jenny disappeared for the whole day, announcing that she was going into town for the sales.

How can she go to the sales? How can she afford to buy anything?

She returned in the early evening, flushed and tired. She had bought nothing. 'There was nothing worth buying,' she said. 'I'm going to bed.'

For the first time in his life he understood why more suicides are committed at Christmas than at any other time of the year.

Worst of all was New Year's Eve. In the past they had always gone out to a party with friends but this year she refused to go.

'You go on your own,' she said.

'Jen.'

'Well, why not?'

'I can't.'

She shrugged. 'Suit yourself. I'm going to bed early. Let's hope next year is a damned sight better than this one.'

Matt and Susie went out to parties and only Monica sat up with Hallam to share a bottle of champagne that she had bought and to watch television until after midnight.

'I'm so sorry about my bloody daughter,' said Monica suddenly. 'She's behaving disgracefully.'

'She's afraid. I can understand that. It's not much fun not knowing where the next penny is coming from.'

'She should be giving you support. Taking some of the pressure off your shoulders, not behaving like a selfish, moody little cow. I've told her so.' Monica shrugged. 'Not that it did any good at all. She's changed. I hardly know her any more.'

To his horror he found that tears were suddenly pouring down his cheeks.

'Oh, God,' he said. 'I'm so sorry.'

'Why? You don't have to be.' She handed him a handkerchief. 'It's about time you let it all out. I don't know how you've kept going for so long.'

Later, when he had recovered, she said, 'I know how difficult things are for you at the moment, Peter. I'd like to lend you some money until you get a job.'

His eyes stung. Monica, of all people. 'That's awfully . . .'

'I don't want to argue about it, Peter. You're desperate, I know, and there's no need to be. Apart from David's pension I've got about twenty-one thousand in the building society. And I've still got my shares in your old company – eight hundred of them. I could always sell those. So how much do you need to clear your debts? *Your* debts? What am I saying? They're *our* debts. We're all in this together.'

He blinked. Hellfire, I'm going to start weeping again, damn it. 'Monica . . .'

She leaned across and put her hand on his arm. It was so good to be *touched* again. 'Please let me help you. Please.'

'I . . .'

'It would give me so much pleasure, Peter. Please.'

'Well, if you're absolutely sure . . .'

'I am. I really am.'

He hesitated. It would hurt her to say no – and, in any case, how could he afford to say no?

'About eight thousand,' he said, 'to clear the immediate debts.'

She nodded. 'And what about the bills for the rest of the winter? The heating. Electricity. Food.'

He cleared his throat. 'I'm going to have to take any job I can get, no matter how humble or dreary it is. I've got to earn some money somehow. I'll drive a bloody taxi if necessary.'

She looked at him with unexpected fondness. He had never seen her so affectionate.

'Dear Peter,' she said softly. 'I'm so sorry. It's so unfair.'

'Well, yes, but it's no good whining about it. I've got to stop fooling myself about the sort of job I might be able to get. That's my New Year resolution: I have to face facts, and the facts are that nobody wants to employ me any more. I'm only forty-five but it seems that I'm too old for the sort of jobs I'd like to do, so I've got to lower my sights.'

'But in the meantime you need to pay off the debts. Clear the decks. Start afresh.'

'That would be wonderful. Monica . . .'

She stood, went up to her room, returned with a cheque and handed it to him.

He looked at it.

Ten thousand pounds.

Ten thousand pounds.

'That's far too much,' he protested, handing it back to her.

She waved him away and sat in the armchair. 'Nonsense. You're going to need every penny.'

'I only need eight thousand.'

'A couple more will go very fast, believe me, just on everyday living, just paying the bills. And I can afford it, Peter, and I've still got those shares. I can always sell them if I need to. And anyway, it's only a loan. You'll pay me back, I know. Eventually.'

'I will. Of course I will. I promise.'

He stood, moved towards her, bent and hugged her clumsily. 'I don't know what to say.'

'Thank you will do.'

'Thank you, Monica. I'll repay every penny. I promise.'

'Of course you will.' She smiled. She raised her glass of champagne. 'Happy New Year,' she said. 'And I know it will be. I've been reading your stars and they say you're going to have a fantastic year.'

Then she shook her head. 'That bloody daughter of mine doesn't know how lucky she is.'

He took huge pleasure in sending the cheque to Dean Castle personally at the Millennium Bank together with a cold letter retrieving the balance, closing his account and telling him precisely what he thought of the bank for treating an old customer in the way that he had been treated. He added that he was sending a copy of the letter to the bank's chairman: it did not matter that the chairman might probably never see it; at least someone at the branch would have a sleepless night or two.

But Monica's ten thousand pounds was no more than a tiny, temporary lifeboat. The ice was cracking far and wide around him now. In the first week of the new year a letter arrived from one of the credit-card companies, asking why he had failed to make any repayments for two months and why he had allowed his debt to exceed his five-thousand-pound limit. It instructed him that his card was no longer valid and should be cut in two and returned to them immediately with a cheque for the full amount of the debt: £5,289.62. Three days later a similar letter arrived from his other credit-card company demanding £5,137.07. The following day the usual huge winter gas bill arrived, followed a day later by a frighteningly large bill for electricity.

He felt helpless. It was useless trying to battle on like this. Even if Monica lent him her last penny it would still not be enough. Even if he did find some lowly job – as a minicab driver, waiter, barman – he was never going to be able to stay afloat. The crisis he had dreaded all along would finally have to be faced.

He was going to have to sell the house.

CHAPTER 9

Goodbyes

'What do you mean, sell the house?' said Jenny.

'I'm so sorry, Jen,' he said, 'but it's the only way we'll ever pay off our debts.'

He offered her his hand. She ignored it.

'*Our* debts?' she said. Her face was tight. '*Your* debts, you mean.'

Something seemed to break inside him. She would never come back to him now. 'If that's how you want to look at it,' he said.

She stared at him defiantly. 'Are you really telling me that in a few weeks we may have nowhere to live?'

'Come on, Jen. Don't overdramatise it. Of course we'll have somewhere to live. It'll just be somewhere smaller, that's all, a flat, perhaps.'

'A *flat*?' The shape of her lips was ugly. 'I haven't lived in a flat since I was a student. A teenager.'

'Be reasonable, Jen. It'll only be temporary, only until I get another job and start saving a bit.'

She laughed sarcastically. It sounded like the crowing of a raven.

'And what about Matthew and Susie? And Mother?'

He felt so old. Even his bones were tired. He felt about seventy. Perhaps they were right: perhaps he really was past it. 'We should be able to make a bit of a profit on the house. We should be able to have a room for Susie.'

'*Should* be able? I should bloody well hope so. She's only sixteen. You're not thinking of throwing her out on the street at sixteen, are you?'

'Come off it, Jenny.'

'I wouldn't put anything past you at the moment. And what about Matthew? And Mother? And Fudge and Jezebel?'

So even the animals were more important than he was now. He had never felt so weary. He wanted to sleep. He sighed. 'I don't know, Jen. Perhaps we can find enough room for Monica, or perhaps she'll have to go into some sort of sheltered housing.'

'I *beg* your pardon? My mother in some old folks' home? Some council hostel?'

'I don't know. I'm just thinking aloud.'

'And Matt?'

'Matt's going to have to start fending for himself,' he said.

'What the hell does that mean?'

'He's going to have to start taking responsibility for his own life. He's going to have to grow up, get a job, find a room of his own somewhere.'

'There aren't any jobs,' she snarled. 'You of all people should know that.'

'There are more jobs for youngsters than there are for people our age.'

'Who says?'

Hallam was threatened by a surge of irritation. 'He can wash the dishes in a bloody restaurant, for all I care.'

'Your own son!'

'Apparently.'

'What the hell is *that* meant to mean?'

'Nothing, Jen. I'm just tired. Depressed.'

'That's not good enough. What did you mean? That Matthew isn't your son?'

'No, Jen, I—'

'That's what you said.'

'No, I just—'

'Well, fuck you, sunshine.'

She stood and made for the door. 'If you sell this house I'm leaving you,' she said viciously. 'Do you understand? I'm not living in some poky bloody flat.'

'Don't threaten me, Jenny.'

She laughed sourly. 'Oh, it's not a threat, I assure you: it's a promise.'

Her eyes glittered, as hard and shiny as mica.

Dear God, she actually *hates* me. So it's true about love and hate: they're not opposites at all; they're twins. 'So what would you do instead? Where would you go?'

Her face was ugly. How could her face be ugly? It had always been beautiful.

'I'll tell you what I'd do.' Her lips were twisted. 'I'd find myself another man, a proper man, someone who could look after me properly. That's what I'd do. And you'd better bloody believe it.'

She left the room and slammed the door behind her.

It's not just that she no longer loves me, he thought, not even that she hates me. It's that she despises me, that she looks at me with contempt. I might just be able to handle the loss of love but not the death of respect.

Three estate agents came to estimate the value of the house.

'Mmmm,' said the middle-aged woman with the damp, beaky nose. 'Not bad. A hundred and ninety-five thousand. Give or take.'

'Not much call for places like this at the moment,' said the mournful young man with halitosis. 'Too many of them on the market already. A hundred and ninety thou if you're lucky.'

'Oh, very nice,' said the cheerful young man from Boggitt, Burlap and Boggitt. 'Very nice indeed. Yes, we shouldn't have too much trouble with this one. A hundred and eighty-five K.'

'No more than that?' said Hallam.

'One eighty-seven if you're lucky.'

'I need a quick sale, a very quick sale.'

'You'd have to drop the price a lot for that,' said the woman with the beaky nose. 'Nobody buys anything in January and February.'

'It's a very slow market at the moment,' said the mournful young man, sucking his teeth. 'Never picks up until Easter – March, April. Could take months.'

'I can probably find you a purchaser within a week,' said the cheerful young chap from Boggitt, Burlap and Boggitt.

A week? In that case it would be worth taking less if necessary: £185,000 now would be just as good as £190,000 in six months' time.

'Tell you what I'll do,' said the cheery young man. 'Since it shouldn't take long I'll do it for half the usual commission. I'll only take one and a half per cent.'

Three thousand pounds' commission instead of six: enough to clear more than half the debt on one of the credit cards.

'You're on,' said Hallam.

They shook hands. 'Lee Yeomans,' said the estate agent. 'Tell you the truth, I've got a punter already who might be just right. He's been looking for ages for something just like this. I'll bring him over. Tomorrow afternoon? Three-ish?'

'Fine.'

'Brilliant.'

'So you're selling the house,' said Matthew. He was sitting

on the kitchen table with his boots up on the work surface between the fridge and the cooker. There was wet mud on the tiles. His jeans were stained with oil. Three of his friends were sprawled across the chairs in the living room, watching television. One had purple hair.

'Yes,' said Hallam. 'I'm sorry. I just can't afford to keep it going any more.'

'And what am I supposed to do? Where am I supposed to live?'

'Well, I hope—'

'You don't give a toss about me, do you?'

'Matt—'

'I might just as well doss down in a shop doorway for all you care.'

'Matt—'

'You and your bloody bourgeois principles. You make me sick. For more than two years you've been sneering at me because I can't find a job and now you can't find one either so you just back off from your responsibilities and chuck us all out in the street. That's great. That's really great. Thanks a bunch, *Father*.' He swung his legs off the work surface and slid off the table.

'You're twenty, for God's sake,' said Hallam. 'How long am I supposed to be responsible for you? You've got the vote. You've got a driving licence. You can get married, join the Army, emigrate. You collect the dole. You could probably get housing benefit, or rent a room for a while with one or two of your friends. You're a man, Matt, so why do you expect me to support you?'

Matthew turned on him. 'I can't *believe* you said that. Because you're my fucking father, that's why. Because that's what fathers do. I know guys who are nearly thirty who still live at home with their folks.'

'That's sad.'

'Why shouldn't they? You seem to think that kids are

second-class citizens but we've got rights too. This is meant to be a democracy, isn't it?'

'You're hardly a kid.'

'But there's no democracy here, is there? Not in this bloody house. When you decide to sell our house, our home, you don't put it to the democratic vote, do you? You just make a high-handed unilateral decision. You're a shit, not a proper father, for all your high-flying principles. You're not a proper man, are you? No wonder Mum's thoroughly pissed off. I'm amazed she's stayed with you as long as she has.'

So now my son despises me too. 'If that's the way you feel then I suggest you sod off right now,' said Hallam. 'I was hoping to rent a flat big enough for all of us but if that's what you think of me then you can just sod off.'

Matt stared at him. His eyes were bloodshot, his hair tangled.

I don't like you either, thought Hallam miserably. You're my son and I can't stand the sight of you.

Matt looked away. 'I've got nowhere to go,' he said.

'Fuckin' selfish, mate, that's what I call it,' said the friend with the purple hair.

Yeomans brought his prospective purchaser around the next afternoon: a skinny man in his mid-thirties, hungry-looking with short, oily hair, a suspicious expression and the name Sheepshank. His nose twitched constantly.

I don't want you to buy my house, thought Hallam suddenly. It's not just a house, it's our home. We've been happy here for years. I don't want it to belong to anyone else.

'So you're really selling it?' said Jenny in a voice of ice.

'What else can we do?'

'I'll refuse to sign the papers. I do own half of it, you know.'

'Of course you do. But we really do have no alternative, Jen. What else do you suggest?'

She stared at him with violence in her eyes. Had she ever loved him? Really? Of course she had. For years. Hadn't she? It was difficult to believe.

'I'm going out,' she said, 'and I'm taking the car. I may be some time.'

'Oh, Daddy,' said Susie, when she heard. She had tears in her eyes. She hugged him. 'Oh, Daddy.'

Monica waited until they were alone. 'Would it help if I lent you the rest of my savings?' she said.

Yes, a bit, for a while, but I couldn't ask that of you. 'That's incredibly generous of you, Monica,' he said, 'but it's gone too far now. It's beyond repair. I can't pay the mortgage and the credit card companies are threatening to sue me and to sell the house over our heads if we don't sell it ourselves. But it's incredibly generous of you to offer. And you mustn't worry. We'll always have a room for you, wherever we are, even if we have to go into a flat. We'll find something, don't worry.'

She straightened her shoulders. 'Don't you fuss about me. I can look after myself.'

Sheepshank glared at the small hallway, the cupboard under the stairs, the living room. His head poked in and out of them like a nervous turtle's. His nostrils twitched. 'Needs a bit done to it,' he said grumpily.

'Here and there,' said Yeomans diplomatically, 'but otherwise it's a very nice property. Compact. Cosy. Got a nice feeling.'

Cosy? thought Hallam. *It's got four bloody bedrooms!*

Sheepshank looked balefully into the kitchen. 'Could do with some decent modern units,' he said, 'them stylish jobs, all dark-wood cabinets.'

'No problem there,' said Yeomans. 'I know just the guy to do it for you. Cheap, too.'

'Needs a bit of paint.'

'No problem. Just a lick here and there.'

'Can't stand that wallpaper.' Sheepshank lowered his voice and spoke in a hoarse whisper that could be heard all over the house. 'How can people live with wallpaper like that? Is that damp?'

'Where?'

'There.'

'Nah, just a stain in the wallpaper. Dodgy glue.'

'You sure?'

'God's truth.'

'Looks like dog's piss.'

I don't want this man to buy my house. I don't want this person sleeping in my bedroom and lying in my bath and sitting on my lavatory seat. Please go away and buy somewhere else.

'We'd have to knock down the wall to the diner. Bit poky otherwise.'

Yeomans tapped the wall in question. It echoed. 'No problem,' he said jovially. 'Not load-bearing. Have it down in a jiffy.'

They disappeared into the garden. Their voices were muted out there but it was still impossible not to hear what they were saying.

'Bloody hell, there's grass everywhere,' said Sheepshank, tiptoeing fastidiously across the lawn as though it were covered in dog droppings. 'And mud. Can't stand grass in a garden. I'm more a terrace-and-patio man myself.'

'Quickly dig that out, then, no trouble at all,' said Yeomans. 'Lay down some nice slabs, a few tubs and pots.'

'I like those coloured tiles,' said Sheepshank. 'The big red and yellow ones.'

'Oh, yes,' said Yeomans. 'Very tasteful.'

'They look brilliant with gnomes.'

'Gnomes?'

'I love gnomes. I got lotsa gnomes, all sortsa gnomes. I gotta butcher gnome with a cleaver and blood all over his apron; I gotta policeman gnome with a truncheon. I even gotta Father Christmas gnome. They do pop-star gnomes with guitars, now, too.' He sniggered. 'I even gotta coupla rude gnomes. One's a flasher wearin' a mac. Cor!'

'Fantastic.'

'Gnome sweet gnome, that's me, har har har.'

'Har har har.'

'You can buy lady gnomes now, too.'

'Really? I never knew there were lady gnomes.'

'Yeah. They do girl gnomes with miniskirts, tits, the lot. They even done a Gnomus de Milo what's got no arms.'

'With the little pointy hat on?'

'Course. They all got the pointy hat. You ain't a gnome at all unless you got the pointy hat. Without the pointy hat you'd be an elf or something. A goblin. A lepercorn.'

'A fairy.'

'Yeah, they got them too. I seen a gay gnome once down Brighton way.'

'How'd you know he was gay?'

'He were wearin' an 'airy chest, a pink vest, a pair of tight black leather shorts and a bunch of keys dangling from his belt.'

'Yeah, that sounds a bit fruity, all right.'

'They got one gnome down the garden centre looks just like Maggie Thatcher. Even got the big bulgy eyes and the handbag.'

'Wicked.'

'Yeah, a garden's not a garden unless it's got a few gnomes. Gawd, what's that? A pond?'

'Yeah. Nice, eh? Little waterfall, few goldfish. Relaxing.'

'Can't stand garden ponds. I'd have to fill that in.'

'No problem – few bricks, bit of rubble.'

'How much you say he wants?'

'Hundred and eighty-five K.'

Sheepshank thought. 'Tell him I'll give him a hundred and seventy.'

Sod off! thought Hallam, with sudden asperity. *Bloody cheek!*

'I wouldn't insult him, sir, by even putting your offer to him,' said Yeomans loudly, with unexpected dignity.

I should damn well think so, too. Thank you, Yeomans. Well done.

'The price is a hundred and eighty-five,' said Yeomans, 'and not a penny less.'

'I'll go to a hundred and seventy-five, then,' said Sheepshank, 'but that's my top offer. There's a lot needs doing to the place.'

'I'm sorry, sir,' said Yeomans. 'My client's price is a hundred and eighty-five. It's a fair price and he's not accepting anything less.'

'I bet he will,' said Sheepshank. 'Cash. In readies.'

Yeomans shrugged. 'You can try,' he said dismissively, 'but I'll advise him to hold out for a higher offer. This is a class property, this. Bound to get a higher offer eventually, month or two.'

Another month or two of huge credit-card debts? Eleven thousand pounds mounting up each month at 2 per cent a month? No money to pay the bills, to buy petrol, nothing even for food? £180,000 now would be better than £185,000 in two months' time.

Sheepshank and Yeomans came back into the house, Sheepshank wearing the smug expression of a man who is about to clinch a bargain.

I really should discuss this with Jenny first, thought Hallam, but what's the point? She'll never agree to anything unless I go ahead and do it and I can't afford to delay.

Sheepshank licked his lips. He looked devious. 'I'll give you a hundred and seventy-five grand,' he said, in a croaky voice.

It was all a game: Mickey Mouse money, utterly unreal, thousands of banknotes tossed about as if they were autumn leaves. People who counted their change after buying a newspaper would blithely add or subtract five or ten thousand when buying or selling a house without thinking about it. Just building-society money, that's all it was, just words on a contract, not like real money at all, not like the sort you have to work for, the sort that takes you months to earn.

'I really can't afford to take less than a hundred and eighty-five,' said Hallam.

Like an Arab *souk*, like a Middle Eastern bazaar.

'Told you,' said Yeomans.

Sheepshank looked crafty. 'I'll go up to one seventy-seven,' he said, 'but that's my final offer. Place needs doing up. Needs money spending on it.'

I don't want you to buy it. Not someone like you. This is my home. 'One eighty-three,' said Hallam.

'One seventy-eight and that's my top whack.'

'One eighty-two.'

'One seventy-nine and not a penny more.'

'Oh, all right,' said Hallam. 'One eighty.'

'One eighty?'

'One eighty.'

'Mmm,' said Sheepshank, thinking. 'One eighty.'

'In cash,' said Hallam.

'One eighty, eh?'

'In cash.'

Sheepshank nodded. 'See,' he said, leering at Yeomans. 'Told you he'd take less for cash. OK, mister, a hundred and eighty it is.'

They shook hands on it.

'A hundred and *eighty*,' said Yeomans. 'Top score in darts.'

Three days later Jenny left him. He returned from his long morning walk to the park to find her loading two suitcases and several large black plastic bags into the car. She looked so small, so vulnerable. He wanted to kiss the back of her neck. He wanted to hug her. He wanted to hold her hard. He was suddenly engulfed in a huge black hole of loneliness. He had never felt so alone.

'Don't do it, Jen,' he said.

'You can't stop me.'

'I can try.'

'Waste of time.'

'Please don't do it. Please.'

'Don't crawl. I hate crawlers.'

'I'm not crawling. I'm just asking you to stay.'

'I'm not living in a bloody flat,' she said, stuffing another plastic bag into the car. 'No way.'

He felt helpless. 'Don't leave me, Jen.'

She looked at him as if he were a stranger. 'And why not?'

'I love you.'

She made an explosive noise with her lips. It sounded like *pfwh*. 'Love!' she said.

'It's true.'

'You always were pathetically romantic. All those bunches of flowers, anniversary presents, cards on Mother's Day. Pathetic. Did you think you could buy me?'

'I thought you liked them, little things like that.'

She stared at him, almost through him. 'Yes, you did, didn't you? But you didn't know me at all, did you?'

No. Not if you can do this. No, I didn't know you at all.

He felt useless, inadequate. A few months ago even her touch had made him shiver; now his touch made her shudder.

'We'll manage, Jen. Don't go.'

She turned on him with a vicious expression. She actually bared her teeth. '*Manage*? I don't want to *manage*. I want to *soar*. I want to *live* before I die. And I'm taking the car. I need *something* out of this bloody marriage.'

How could she talk like that, after all these years? How could she end it just like that?

There was no point in arguing any more, no point in fighting. He was beaten. And maybe she would be back. Of course she would be back. This was just a lovers' tiff. All marriages have their dark moments. In some small dim corner of his mind there flickered still a tiny flame of hope: *don't worry, one day she'll be back, when you're on your feet again, when she's got it out of her system.*

'So where will you go?' he said.

She straightened her back and turned towards him. She swept her hair away from her eyes with that old gesture that he had always loved.

'I'm going to live with Jim,' she said.

Jim?

Jim?

'Jim?' he said.

'Yes.'

'Jim who?'

'Who d'you think? How many Jims do we know?'

'Jim . . . Donaldson?'

'Of course. Who else?'

'Jim Donaldson?'

'For Christ's sake, *yes*! Jim Donaldson.'

'But . . .'

She shook her head with impatience. 'You haven't a clue, have you?'

'I . . .'

Jim Donaldson?

'We've been having an affair for two months.'

'You . . .'

'You had no idea at all, did you?'

'I . . .'

'He's been wonderful ever since you lost your job.'

'But he . . .'

'A real support. A tower of strength.'

Jim Donaldson? Jim? My old friend Jim?

'But he's . . .'

'Sandra?' She sneered. He had never seen her sneer before. 'They haven't been happy for years. Anyone could see that. Didn't you realise that? Anyone could see that. Anyone except you, of course.'

Jim Donaldson?

'She's gone back to her mother.' She laughed harshly. 'Typical. Poor old Sandra, scuttling back to Mummy.'

She stowed the last plastic bag in the back of the car and turned to face him. She flicked her hair away from her eyes again. He wanted to hug her. He wanted to hold her tight, to squeeze her to him. He wanted her to say that it was all a terrible mistake, wake up, the nightmare's over.

Jim *Donaldson*?

She stared at him. Those eyes. That nose. That mouth.

Jen?

She looked at him as though she would never see him again, as though she were trying to remember him.

Jenny?

'Goodbye,' she said. 'You'll be all right.'

Goodbye? Just that? Goodbye?

She turned and opened the car door.

Just that? You'll be all right? After twenty-three years?

She climbed into the driver's seat and started the car.

Not even a kiss? Not a hug? After twenty-three years?

Tears flooded his eyes.

Oh, Jenny, my Jenny, my Jen.

She climbed into the car and flicked her hair again. His vision was blurred, his cheeks wet. He wiped his chin with the heel of his palm.

Jenny. Jen. My darling. My love. You can't do this. Don't do this. Don't.

The car coughed, belched, farted.

She did not even look at him as she drove away. She did not look back once. His eyes were awash. He watched the car turn left at the watery gate and slip like a fish beyond the Evanses' watery hedge and out of sight. Everything wavered as though the world were underwater. There seemed to be a huge black hole where his heart had been. His head was empty.

He was suddenly aware that Matthew was leaning against the wall behind him, his arms folded. 'So now you've lost your wife as well,' he sneered. 'Careless bugger, aren't you? Not quite so perfect after all, perhaps.'

Not now, Matt, please. Please, not now.

'Arsehole,' said Matthew.

Jim Donaldson.

Jim Donaldson.

For two months. Ever since November.

The shit. What a bastard.

My best friend.

Judas.

When?

All those Saturdays and Sundays when she had disappeared for hours with the car. Jim Donaldson. And Jenny. Illicit lunches. Hotel rooms. Afternoon beds. *My Jenny. My wife. My love.*

For days jealousy tormented him. He lay on his bed during the afternoons and thought about them together, Jenny and Jim. Then. Now. Together *now*. How could he bear it? Jenny. *My love.* With him. With Donaldson. Judas Donaldson. The bastard.

At night he tossed in bed, unable to sleep. They would be in each other's arms now. He would be holding her. Touching her. That wonderful smell of her. That taste. Donaldson, the bastard.

'She'll be back,' said Monica. 'I know her, the selfish little slut. She'll come crawling to you and then I hope you'll have the guts to refuse to take her back.'

'I'd take her back at any time,' he said.

'I know. The stupid, stupid woman.'

Sandra Donaldson rang a couple of times but he did not want to talk to her. She had a keening voice. Listening to her, he was appalled to realise that he could not blame Donaldson at all for dumping her: what man would *not* have preferred Jenny to Sandra Donaldson?

'They've been doing it for months,' she said, in her whiny voice. 'Didn't you suspect anything?'

'No.'

'I did.'

'Yes?'

'He started showering a lot. Bought new underpants. I knew there was someone. Well, you do. A wife does. Didn't know it was your bloody Jenny, though.'

'I'm sorry. She's been—'

'She was always so sweet to me. Butter wouldn't melt. The bitch.'

'I'm so sorry, Sandra.'

'What about a little drinkie some time?'

She was wheedly, that little-girl voice, the one that had always driven him mad, the one that probably drove her bloody husband into Jenny's arms.

'Or what about lunch?' she said. 'Cheer ourselves up.'

Hell's bells: *lunch*?

'Or even dinner?'

Dinner. Legs touching under the table. Getting their own back. Consoling each other. Two cast-offs. Also-rans. Second-raters. Sandra naked. The classic Mercy Fuck. Taking some sort of pathetic revenge and hating themselves and each other afterwards.

'Uh . . . no thanks, Sandra. I'm not quite up to it yet . . .'

Her voice cracked. 'Suit yourself.'

'Later, sometime, perhaps . . .'

Later, sometime, never.

And then he felt guilty. She was crying when he replaced the receiver.

You mean swine, he said to himself. You could at least have bought her lunch. And then he laughed with a hopeless bitterness. Bought her lunch? he thought. With what?

Susie clung to his neck and wept. 'Oh, Daddy.'

He held her close. She felt so small, so soft.

'I don't want to go and live with her,' she sobbed. 'I want to stay with you.'

He hugged her tight. Her tears were wet on his neck. 'I know, darling. I wish you could. But Mummy can give you a proper home and I can't at the moment. Later, when I get a job. I promise. As soon as I get things together again.'

'I hate Jim Donaldson.' She sniffed.

'No, you don't.'

'I don't want to live there.'

'Just for a while.'

'I hate her too.'

'That's not true.'

He kissed her temple where the fine hair curled towards her ear. 'I love you so much,' he said.

On the morning that Jenny was due to come and pick up Susie – and Fudge and Jezebel – Monica took to her room, refusing even to speak to her. 'She expects me to go and live with her and her fancy man,' she told Hallam. 'Damn cheek. As if I would. Does she think I've got no pride at all? No standards? May I stay here with you until the house is finally sold?'

'Of course.'

Susie walked slowly all over the house, saying goodbye to it, touching cupboard doors, stroking window-ledges, as though they were alive. She had lived here all her life. She had never known another home. She had stopped crying now, which made it almost worse, for a heavy sadness shadowed her from room to room. The tears had been clean and wholesome but this new, silent misery squeezed his heart. She was locking her memories away one by one and slamming tight the bolts on her grief. When she left they stood together in the kitchen and clutched each other. He could not bear to go outside with her. He could not bear to see Jenny again. Not yet. Not so soon.

Donaldson. Judas. Donaldson.

'I promise,' he said, with a tight throat. 'I promise.'

'Oh, Daddy,' she said. 'Oh, my dad.'

Fudge nuzzled his thigh and whimpered. Hallam fondled his ears. Fudge knew, and Jezebel, who had suddenly disappeared to hide somewhere in the garden. How did they know?

When Susie had gone he sat alone in the living room, staring at the wall, tormented by the sound of their voices outside. Matthew was talking to Jenny by the garage. 'But why can't I come with you?' he was saying. 'He doesn't want me, does he? Your sodding boyfriend.'

'Of course he does, darling, it's just . . .'

Her voice. Jenny's. His Jenny's voice. A bird singing. Just there. Outside. So close. So far away.

'He doesn't like me, does he? He's another boring, stuck-up old middle-class fart.'

'Matthew!'

'Tell him to go fuck himself. See if I care.'

'Oh, darling, you'll come over for meals, for weekends . . .'

'What, like some bloody in-law or granny? I can't believe you said that. Do me a favour, Mother. The man's a pompous prat. He's no better than Dad is. You must be mad going to live with him.'

'I love him.'

'Yeah, sure.'

'You'll understand one day, darling.'

'Oh, sure. I understand now, very well indeed, and you'd better understand something too. Just don't come whining to me when you're old and grey and feeble and you need some help because you'll get fuck-all from me.'

'Oh, Matthew . . .'

Susie's voice, heated, angry: 'You bastard! What's wrong with you? God, you're a horrible person. How can you be my brother? You're disgusting, you are.'

Susie. My Susie. At least I'll never lose you.

And then Matthew again, full of bitterness and contempt: 'Well, I don't need you, any of you, so don't think I do. Ben's folks have said I can sleep in a tent in their garden, so fuck the lot of you. And thus endeth the typical idyllic, bourgeois, nuclear family, hypocritical to the end.'

So now it's just Monica and me, and nothing will ever be the same again.

Monica took charge of the kitchen even though Hallam had always been a reasonable cook when it came to producing simple, basic meals. 'Go away,' she said, flapping her arms at him. 'Shoo! This is women's work.'

'That's very old-fashioned, Miss Porridge,' he said, 'and sexist and politically incorrect.'

'I am.'

She refused to cook anything in the microwave, claiming that microwaves make food radioactive.

'Stands to reason,' she said, 'all those invisible atoms and neutrons and things whizzing about.'

'Any sort of heat is invisible, Monica.'

'Ah, but microwaves aren't hot at all, they're cold. You'll see. Eventually people who've been eating microwaved food all their lives will start to glow a luminous green in the dark.'

Whenever he opened the fridge he would find himself

confronted by cups half filled with congealed, discoloured liquids and dishes of mould and platefuls of tired old teabags – 'They work much better on the eyes when they're ice-cold' – and Monica insisted that they could save electricity if only he would shorten the cable on the toaster so that it was nearer to the plug and if he would put the electric kettle in the oven to warm up before filling it with water to boil. 'It's obvious, a hot kettle is bound to come to the boil much quicker than a cold one.'

She moved Hank the cactus down from her bedroom and installed him in a corner of the kitchen – 'I like company when I'm cooking' – and whenever she prepared a hot meal she wore a black leather biker's helmet and goggles 'to keep the smells out of my hair and eyes'. She also spent much of the time discussing the finer points of cuisine with Hank.

'Hank's a whizz when it comes to Mexican food,' she said. 'Beans, chilli, tortillas, that sort of thing. Well, he would be, wouldn't he, coming from Arizona?'

'Where on earth did you get the helmet and goggles?' asked Hallam.

'Rafe Richardson gave them to me.'

'Who?'

'Rafe Richardson.'

'The actor?'

'Of course. Who else? Dear Rafe, such fun – liked nothing better than to roar up the M1, doing a ton on a bike, even when he was seventy.'

'I see. Ralph Richardson, eh? And when did you know him, then?'

'Oh, for years. Nearly thirty years, I suppose, on and off. We bumped into each other in New Zealand in 'fifty-four or 'fifty-five.'

'And what was he doing in New Zealand in 'fifty-four or 'fifty-five?'

'On tour, of course. I think I might well have married him, had I not just met Jennifer's father in Wanganui.'

'And what on earth were *you* doing in New Zealand?'

'Looking for wombats.'

The dishes she produced were equally startling: boiled chicken with kiwi fruit and raw broccoli, sardines with lentils and sliced bananas, garlic sausages with marmalade and peanut butter.

'I'm compiling a new cookbook,' she said. 'I'm going to call it *Classic Twenty-first Century Cuisine*.'

'How can it be classic when we haven't even got there yet?'

'Don't be such a pedant, Peter.'

'You've given up the limericks and nursery rhymes, then? Very wise.'

'Not at all. I wrote one yesterday about Hank.'

'Don't bother,' he said hurriedly, 'I think I can guess.'

'*A cheeky young cactus called Hank* . . .'

'I don't think so, Monica. Really.'

'It's quite clean.'

'I doubt that very much.'

'Oh, very well. You're such a stick-in-the-mud. But what about this one?'

'I really don't—'

'You'll like this one, I know:

> 'There was a young lady from Bude
> Who walked down the street in the nude.
> One chap remarked, "Whattum
> Agnificent bottom,"
> And pinched it as hard as he could.'

Later Hallam looked Ralph Richardson up in *Chambers Biographical Dictionary*. 'Toured Australia and New Zealand in 1955,' it said.

'Cuckoo!' called Monica up the stairs. 'Cuckoo! Grub's up.'

They say that the four most stressful things that can happen to you are the death or loss of someone you love, divorce, the loss of your job and moving house – and I've managed to clock up three out of four, thought Hallam, and moving house is almost as bad as the others. Sheepshank's surveyor arrived and his architect, builder, plumber, electrician, carpenter, gardener, interior decorator and second-cousin-once-removed. It seemed as if every one of Sheepshank's acquaintances was tramping through the house and poking noses into cupboards, lifting carpets, shaking heads, muttering, sucking teeth. And then, just before the contracts were due to be signed and exchanged, Sheepshank suddenly decided to reduce his offer.

'What do you mean, he says he'll only pay a hundred and seventy-seven?' said Hallam furiously.

'That's what he says,' said Yeomans. 'It's diabolical.'

'But we agreed a hundred and eighty.'

'He says he's discovered a lot of things wrong with the place.'

'Balls!'

'Says he's going to have to spend several K to renew all the electrics, the plumbing, fix up the dry rot.'

'What dry rot? Where?'

'His surveyor found some dry rot in the roof.'

'Hellfire. What if I refuse to go any lower?'

'He says he'll pull out of the deal.'

'Slimy little toad. Do you believe him?'

'Yes.'

'So what do we do now?'

Yeomans sighed. 'Normally I'd say tell him to get stuffed and wait for a better offer. But you need a quick sale, and you've spent quite a bit already on the lawyer, and it's cash in hand and you might not get another cash offer, which would mean waiting for someone to get a mortgage and sell his own place and then you might be in a chain where they all still have to sell their own places . . .'

Hallam felt a surge of despair. Three thousand pounds less, damnation; three thousand that he needed badly. 'Sod it! I've got no choice, have I? Tell bloody Sheepshank yes.'

'Seems best. Sorry about this.'

'The man's a crook.'

Yeomans hummed in agreement. 'This business is full of them,' he said. 'Happens all the time, gazumping, gazundering, ducking and diving. Happens all the time.'

So now he would get just £177,000, which would dwindle to £173,000 once Yeomans and the lawyer had taken their cuts and then fall to £73,000 once the mortgage was paid off. He reached for his calculator. Then there were the credit-card debts, nearly £11,000 now with all the extra interest, and the £10,000 he owed Monica. In the end there'd be just £51,000 left, and half of that had to go to Jenny. That was only right: whatever she had done, she still owned half the house, but it meant that they'd get only £25,500 each, that was all. £25,500 to find himself somewhere to live: far too little to buy a flat, even a tiny one-room 'studio'. He flicked hopelessly through the property advertisements in the local paper. You couldn't buy even a garage for that these days. And £25,500 in the building society at 5 per cent after tax: that would bring in just £24.50 a week in interest, that's all. You wouldn't be able to rent a dog kennel for that.

He telephoned Pinky Porter to ask him yet again for the money he had borrowed. Pinky's answerphone was on but somehow Hallam suspected strongly that someone was listening at the other end, monitoring his call: there seemed to be a presence there, a sort of knowingness behind the silence down the line. He left a forceful message. 'Pinky,' he said, 'I'm getting a bit desperate. I really do need that grand you owe me. Could we meet, please? Today? Tomorrow? I really do need it now. I'm absolutely skint.'

The machine seemed to sigh as he replaced the receiver.

He telephoned the Job Centre again to see if there was any hope yet of collecting the dole.

'Yeah?'

Sharon. The one who was meant to be good with people. Even her voice sounded as if it were wearing bovver boots.

'So wotcha want me to do abaht it?' she said.

'I thought you might be able to chase up my application, see how it's going, whether the tribunal has fixed a date for the hearing.'

'You trying ter jump the queue?'

'Of course not, I just—'

'There's lotsa people waiting for tribunals, mister, not just you.'

'Yes, I'm sure, but—'

'Takes time, tribunals does. Takes mumfs. Why d'yer fink you should have special treatment?'

'I don't. Of course I don't—'

'They'll let you know when they got a date. Now I'm busy.'

She crashed the receiver down.

For a moment Hallam was suffused with an unaccustomed fury.

'You jumped-up little bitch!' he yelled at the deaf receiver. 'Hell's bells, one of these days—'

'That's better,' said Monica. 'Much better. It's about time you started to get angry. If I were you I wouldn't just be angry, I'd be aching by now for revenge.'

Revenge? What was the point of revenge? That wouldn't change anything. That wouldn't make it all better again.

For several days he scanned the personal column advertisements in the local paper every day. It was useless now going for any of the jobs he might once have wanted. Now he was reading the ads for barmen, waiters, cleaners. Anything at all would have to do, anything just to put a roof over his head.

How has it come to this? I've always been straight, honest, hard-working. I've always paid my taxes, taken out insurance, given to charity, helped old ladies across the road. And it's done me no bloody good at all. I have to get a job. Something. Anything. I *have* to get a job.

His forty-sixth birthday came and went, unnoticed by Monica, a day of echoing emptiness: just one birthday card, from Susie, who caught two buses to come over to see him in the evening after school and who gave him a Joe Cocker CD and cried. Forty-six. Another year gone. Just nineteen more till the old-age pension.

He tried all his old business contacts again but a couple had moved on by now to other jobs themselves and none of the others returned his calls. Why should they bother? He was yesterday, a has-been, history.

Remember Pete Hallam?

Haven't seen him for ages.

Poor old Pete.

Whatever happened to him?

Wife left him, you know. Poor bugger. Carrying on with his best friend.

No!

Yes, some bugger called Donaldson: been slipping her one for months, apparently.

Poor sod. Time for another one?

Why not?

Just one for the road, then. Cheers.

Chin-chin.

He tried the local libraries again: at least they would be

warm to work in, their clients reasonably intelligent; but they said they had no jobs available and in any case you had to have the right qualifications and to be a member of the union. He approached a local minicab firm to see if they needed a driver. At least he had one skill that no one could argue about: he had a driving licence.

The boss was so fat that every heavy breath seemed to be a major achievement. The flesh on his neck wobbled when he spoke. 'You been a cabbie before?' he said.

'No.'

The man made a snorting noise that rumbled from the back of his massive throat and down his vast nostrils. 'Yer know yer way around town?'

'I've lived here for twenty years.'

'So's most of our punters but they wooden know 'ow ter get from Basil Street ter Parson's Green.'

'I'd go down French Street, right into Derby Crescent, right again into Urquhart Avenue, down to the roundabout, take the third left, along Lionel Street, fourth right into Parson's Green.'

The cabbie looked up at him. 'Not bad,' he said. 'OK, 'ow'd yer get to Porter Street from here?'

Hallam thought. 'I'd go down Argyll Lane, turn right into the square, second left along Malvern Avenue, right at the T-junction, left at the roundabout.'

The cabbie nodded. 'Fair enough. So yer got the knowledge. But yer gotta be respectable to be a cabbie. You respectable?'

'I like to think so.'

'Any form?'

'I beg your pardon?'

'Form. Convictions. You been in prison?'

'Certainly not.'

'Safe with the birds?'

'Eh?'

'Crumpet. Women. Late at night. Some guys get ideas, alone with a bird in the cab, midnight maybe, she's 'ad a coupla drinks, know what I mean?'

'Do I look like a rapist?'

'None of them do, squire.'

'Thanks very much.'

'Okay, guv'nor, okay, keep yer hair on. We gotta be careful these days, thassall. Lotsa pre-verts out there these days. Know what I mean? You gotta clean licence?'

'Yes.'

'No endorsements?'

'No.'

'Hmm. What wheels you got?'

'Wheels?'

'What motor?'

Motor. He hadn't thought of that. He needed a car. They expected him to use his own car. Of course. How bloody stupid.

'Ah . . . I don't actually have a car at all at the moment.'

The man gazed at him. His cheeks trembled. His eyes seemed to be almost pink. He jerked his head towards an open doorway behind him. ''Ere, Morry,' he called.

'Yeah?'

'Wanna laugh?'

'Always do wiv wunna them, Charlie.'

'Geezer 'ere wants to be a cabbie.'

'Nice to 'ave ambition.'

'But 'e got no wheels.'

'Yer kidding.'

'Never.'

'No motor at all?'

'Nuffink.'

'Not even a bike?'

The owner fixed him with an amused, watery stare. 'You gotta bike, mister?'

'Uh . . . no.'

'Not even a bike, Morry.'

In the back room Morry barked like a seal. 'Wooden be much good anyways. You wooden get old Missus Roberts on the back of a bike.' He started wheezing. 'P'raps 'e god wunna them rickshaws, then,' he wheezed, 'her-her-her-her-her.'

Charlie fixed Hallam with his pale eyes again. 'You godda rickshaw, guvnor?'

Hallam rose to leave. 'I'm sorry, I've obviously made a mistake.'

The boss nodded sagely. Even his ear lobes wobbled. 'Tricky bein' a cabbie wivout a motor,' he said.

Hallam felt himself blush. 'I – uh – rather thought – you . . .'

'Me, guv? Yer think I got a fleet of cars jus' waitin' fer drivers? Eh? Yer think I'm made of money?'

Hallam shrugged. 'I'm sorry. I've made a mistake. I'm sorry to have wasted your time.'

'Time?' said Charlie. 'I got plentya time, guv'nor. I just ain't got no motors or drivers or money.'

'I'm sorry. I've made a mistake. Goodbye.'

As he closed the door behind him he heard Morry wheezing in the back room. 'Gaw blimey, Charlie.'

'Some people.'

'Tykes yer bref awye, dunnit?'

Get real, he told himself. The time has come to be beyond shame, beyond embarrassment. It's a cold world out there, alone, and there's nobody else. This is it: just you and the universe.

Pinky Porter never replied to the answerphone message. He must be away again, thought Hallam, enjoying somebody else's thousand pounds, lying on some fat, white, hot beach with some thin, brown, hot woman.

He walked the streets for days, following a newspaper trail of personal-column advertisements across town, fiddling with bits of small change in draughty telephone boxes, holding conversations with answerphones, leaving messages that were never returned, catching buses, hanging around for hours in windy bus shelters, knocking on doors, attending interviews. He applied for jobs as a school caretaker, warehouseman, security guard, park labourer and was rejected for them all. Potential employers looked at him suspiciously as though he were up to no good. 'Over-qualified,' they said. Too middle class, they thought. Too posh. Too well spoken. Too old. He was judged unfit to be a van driver, part-time barman, door-to-door salesman or lollipop man, and the ridiculously youthful manager at the local supermarket was wary when Hallam answered his advertisement for an external services manual operative, whose job consisted of sweeping the supermarket car park, collecting rubbish, rounding up abandoned metal trolleys and wheeling them back in long rows to park them in queues beside the entrance doors.

The manager looked about sixteen. His cheeks were pink. They had fluff on them. His office was a cramped little cubicle behind the fresh-fish counter. The fresh-fish counter smelt decidedly off.

'What's your game, then, mister?' said the manager, glancing at Hallam with distrust down the length of his sharp little nose.

You'd think I'd asked him if I could sleep with his granny. 'I just need a job.'

The manager's face carried a pinched expression. 'But you got heducation,' he said. 'Why d'you want a job like this?'

'Well, I do actually need a job quite badly.'

The manager looked at him without conviction. 'You'd only get a hundred and ten quid a week. You could earn . . . oooh, four, five hundred, easy, somewhere else.'

Five hundred? A few months ago I was earning more than double that, more than a thousand a week.

'Well, it's not that easy, not for a man of my age.'

'You what – thirty-five? Thirty-seven?'

'I'm forty-six.'

The manager stared at him sceptically. 'You don't look a day over thirty-seven.'

'Well, that's very kind of you, but—'

'So what's your game, then? You been sacked, ain't you?'

'Well, I—'

'Thought so. Fraud?'

'Certainly not.'

The manager nodded. 'That's the usual with your sort, heducated men. You a dodgy accountant?'

'Absolutely not. I used to be a sales manager.'

'Ah!' The manager nodded thoughtfully. 'Gear off the back of a lorry.'

'I beg your pardon?'

'You done time?'

'What?'

'Prison.'

'Good grief, no.'

The manager pushed his chair imperceptibly backwards. 'You got Aids? You infectious?'

'Certainly not.'

The manager looked crafty. 'You a drinker, then?'

'Well, I like a drink, but not the way you mean it.'

The manager sat back smugly and crossed his arms. His eyes gleamed. His expression was as pointed as his nose.

He thinks I'm an alcoholic and that's why I can't keep a job. He thinks I'm a down-and-out. And in a way he's right: I'm down, all right, and I'm certainly not In.

'Sorry, mister,' said the manager. 'No chance.'

'I'm not an alcoholic, you know,' said Hallam.

The manager sniffed.

'I just like a couple of whiskies now and then.'

The manager looked po-faced. A shutter seemed to have come down behind his eyes. 'That's your look-out,' he said. 'It's a free country.'

'I'm only asking for a chance.'

'Sorry, mister. More than me job's worth. Send the next guy in, will you?'

The 'next guy', who was standing beside the fresh-fish counter and smelling almost as shifty, was a burly young man with a narrow forehead, a florid face and heavy tattoos on his arms and fingers. Tattooed on the knuckles of one hand was the word L-O-V-E, on the other H-A-T-E.

He'll get the job without a doubt, thought Hallam hopelessly. He's a natural. So now I'm just an also-ran to a youth with 'DORIS' on his biceps.

On the sixth day, in desperation, he applied for a job as a night porter in a three-star hotel called the Unicorn. The hotel manager was a smart, well-spoken young woman, who could not have been much more than twenty-nine. She had a frank, open face and a brisk manner. 'I don't want to be impertinent,' she said, 'but why would a man of your age, education and experience apply for a job as a night porter?'

'I'm allergic to sunlight,' he said.

She smiled. 'Lost your job?'

He nodded.

She looked sympathetic. 'Redundant?'

'Sort of.' He shrugged. 'More a clash of personalities, really. My boss had a thing about anyone over forty-five.'

'And you are?'

'Yes. Forty-six.'

'You don't look it.'

'Thank you.'

'In fact, you look far too young to be a night porter. They're usually old men.'

He laughed sadly. 'So you're going to turn me down because I'm too *young*?'

She chuckled. A nice chuckle: throaty, with a hint of wickedness. 'Of course not. But I must warn you that it's a pretty dreary job. You'd have to wear one of our uniforms, start work at ten o'clock every night except Sunday, serve drinks to any residents who want them for as long as they want them, even if they want to stay up until two in the morning, and then when everyone's gone to bed you'd have to lock up, tidy and Hoover all the public rooms downstairs, clean any shoes that the residents might have left outside their doors, stay awake all night, register any late arrivals, answer any calls, do the rounds now and then to check all the external doors and windows, go out and buy the newspapers at about six o'clock, prepare and serve breakfast for any residents who want to be served in their rooms . . .'

'Sounds great. When do I start?'

She gazed at him. Her eyes were cool. 'You really want it?'

'Yes.'

'You haven't even asked what wage I'm offering.'

'I'm desperate,' he said, 'completely broke, so whatever the pay is it has to be better than nothing. I can't get any other work anywhere. There just aren't any jobs for men of my age. I'm having to sell my house. My wife has left me. My family has broken up. I'm going to have to move into a bedsitter. Believe me, being a night porter in a decent hotel like this would be paradise by comparison with all that. What *are* you paying, anyway?'

'A hundred and fifty pounds a week. With breakfast thrown in.'

'Full English breakfast or Continental?'

Her eyes twinkled. 'Full English, the works, as much as you can eat.' She was really very attractive. Twenty-eight, twenty-nine. What a shame: far too young for a man of forty-six, even if he did look younger.

'Sounds perfect,' he said.

She leaned forward, her elbows propped on her desk. Her eyes were clear and frank. 'But what's in it for us?' she said. 'Why do you think you'd be any good at the job?'

'Because I'm intelligent, honest, hardworking . . .'

'. . . and modest.'

She laughed.

'. . . and very keen to get the job and keep it,' he said. 'I'm reliable, you see. Oh, yes, I've always been wonderfully reliable.'

'You've been used to a much bigger salary.'

'A long time ago. In a different life.'

'You'd resent the customers. Some of them can be very demanding. Condescending. Patronising. Offensive. Rude, even.'

'So were some of mine when I was a sales manager.'

'You wouldn't like being a servant, fetching and carrying for people.'

'I've been fetching and carrying all my life. You do when you've got a wife and children.'

Her lips twitched. 'You'd hate having to wear a uniform. It's got a big white unicorn on the pocket.'

'I used to wear a suit every day. What's the difference?'

'People notice you in a suit. It gives you status and respectability. They don't notice you at all in a hotel servant's uniform.'

'That would be a huge relief,' he said. 'I could do with a spell of anonymity.'

'You'd hate taking orders from me.'

'Not at all. My daughter has been bossing me about for years.'

She laughed again.

Make a woman laugh and you're half-way there. Who was

it who had told him that? *Don't be ridiculous: she can't be a day older than twenty-eight.*

'You'd have to take orders, too, from the housekeeper,' she said. 'The head barman. The head waiter.'

'And I wouldn't have to give orders to anyone else. It sounds like bliss, the ultimate simplicity.'

She looked at him with her head cocked slightly to one side, curious, as though she were studying some new species. Please, he thought. *Please*. But he was not going to say it. He did not need to say it. She looked into his eyes. They spoke to her. *Please*, they said.

She thought about it. 'OK,' she said, 'you've got the job.'

'Really?'

'Really. But don't say I didn't warn you. When can you start?'

He was stunned. After all these months. A job. A lousy job, but a job all the same. A hundred and fifty pounds a week. Peanuts, but at least it would be a regular wage. At last. And breakfast every day, the works, as much as he could eat: eggs, bacon, sausages, fried bread, toast, marmalade. The full monty. He would eat a monstrous hotel breakfast every morning and he would need little more all day.

'Tomorrow?' he said. 'Friday?'

'No need. The present night porter isn't leaving us until the week after next. Would that do? The twenty-sixth?'

'Perfect.'

'Good.' She smiled. She had a lovely smile. And her eyes sparkled.

Don't be so bloody stupid. Don't screw it all up by getting absurd ideas.

She rose from behind her desk. Slim waist, trim bottom, nice legs. 'Right, let me introduce you to a couple of people,' she said, 'show you the ropes, give you a list of your duties.'

He stood. 'What do I call you? Madam? Miss? Ms?'

Her eyes sparkled. 'Mrs Forsyth, of course.'

'Mrs?'

'Forsyth.'

'*Mrs* Forsyth?'

'What else?'

'You're married.'

'Of course. Why wouldn't I be?'

She was teasing him. He felt his face reddening. 'Of course,' he said. 'How stupid of me. It's just—'

She chuckled. 'I know. I'm young enough to be your daughter. Now let's go and meet the housekeeper first.'

'Probably an alkie,' said the head barman to the barmaid after Hallam had left the hotel. 'Guys that age, bit of education, talks proper but no experience. Stands to reason. What's a guy like that doing working in a hotel? Night porter? Don't give me that. Better watch the optics, Dolly, when he starts. And keep a sharp eye on the till.'

And then, suddenly, everything was happening at once and the sale of the house was going through amazingly quickly. 'Cash sale, you see,' said Yeomans. 'No mucking about with banks and building societies. Just straightforward.' Yeomans went to see Jenny, somehow persuaded her to sign the contract, and suddenly there were representatives from removal companies tramping through the house and a man from the auctioneers to value the furniture that Hallam would now be forced to sell.

Monica had decided to go and stay with her old friend Liz for a week or two while she looked at the possibility of finding a room of her own or perhaps a small flat in a sheltered housing unit, and a week before they were due to leave the house Hallam found a tiny bedsitter in a seedy part of town, in Halcyon Road, to rent for a hundred and ten pounds a week. It had just one large room with a bath in one corner and a small cooking area behind a curtain in another. There was no telephone and only one lavatory, along the corridor, that had to be shared with the other tenants. The window-frames were rotten: a draught stirred the flimsy net curtain. He had lived in a place like this when he had been eighteen. Twenty-seven years evaporated as though they had never been. He was back where he had started. The only thing that was different now was that then he had had hope.

'I'm so sorry it's come to this,' he said.

Monica touched his arm gently. 'So am I. That disgraceful daughter of mine. I feel responsible.'

'It's hardly your fault.'

'She's my blasted daughter. I'm so ashamed of her.'

'You've got nothing at all to be ashamed of. You've been fantastic, Monica. I'll pay you back, every penny.'

'I know you will.'

'As soon as the house is sold, I promise.'

'Don't worry about it. Whenever you're ready. And you've been fantastic yourself, Peter. The way you have taken me in, made me welcome, never complained about it. I know all the jokes about mothers-in-law.'

He laughed. 'I've told a few myself, I can tell you.'

She smiled. 'You're a good man. Jenny must be mad.'

'Will you be all right?'

'Oh, yes. I'm a survivor. I'll manage, all right.'

Where did they find their indomitable courage, this dying generation of Englishwomen, bred in battle and tempered by war and hardship? 'I know you will. You're amazing.'

She gave him an affectionate smile. 'So are you. A night porter in a hotel. I admire that, Peter, more than I can say. You're a survivor too.'

He kissed her cheek. She squeezed his hand. How odd that after all these years it was Jenny's betrayal that had made them friends at last.

She had decided to leave the house a couple of days before he did, and on her last night she invited him up to her room. The furniture was still there, awaiting the auctioneer's van the next day, but her two suitcases were packed and lying open on the floor and her own few possessions were stacked in a couple of boxes: a few ornaments, some pictures, books by H. E. Bates, Georgette Heyer, Eric Linklater, Daphne du Maurier, Jean Plaidy, Alec Waugh. Who remembered them now except old ladies like Monica? And her records, too, LPs from the earliest days of rock 'n' roll: Fats Domino, Bob Dylan, the Everly Brothers, Buddy Holly. With a jolt he realised that Monica had been a young mother in her mid-thirties, younger even than Jenny was now, when the Beatles had enchanted and seduced the world. No wonder she played their songs over and over again: they reminded her of her prime.

She was sitting in her armchair by the window, wearing her leopardskin hat and gloves and leafing through an old photograph album that she was holding on her lap. Hank was in his pot on the window sill behind her, peering over her shoulder. She looked up as Hallam came into the room. Her eyes were damp. She gave him a watery smile. 'So long ago,' she said, shaking her head. 'So very long ago.'

'May I?'

She nodded.

He stood behind her chair and looked over her shoulder. She was looking at her wedding album. The photograph beneath her gnarled old fingers showed her as a girl in her early twenties, nearly fifty years ago. She had been quite beautiful, with eyes like laser beams. There was no mistaking who she was: she had been Jenny mark 1, the harbinger of Jenny, her prototype. Had Hallam met Monica in the 1940s he too would have fallen for her, for Jenny-to-be.

Suddenly his own eyes were stinging. *Come back to me, Jen. I can't bear it any more. I need us to be like we were before. I can't go on like this.*

'You were very beautiful,' he said.

'Yes.' Monica nodded. 'Yes. I was. Everyone said so.' She sighed. 'I hate being old,' she said. She blew her nose briskly. 'Weren't the styles ugly, though, in those days?' she said. 'Look at that awful dress! And my hair! That hat! We had no money then, of course, just after the war. Everything was rationed.'

'You looked wonderful,' he said. 'I can see where Jenny got her looks.'

He put his hand on her shoulder. She patted it.

'Thank you, dear,' she said. 'And I know you mean it.'

'I'll bet you were chased by all the boys.'

She laughed gently, sounding like a young girl. 'I did have a couple of beaus,' she said.

She looked down at the album again. 'Dear David,' she said. She brushed her fingertips lightly across the young face of her dead husband. She touched the photograph as though it were a lover. 'Dear David.'

Hallam looked at the man in the photograph: a nondescript man, not particularly good-looking, nothing obviously special about him, but so happy, so optimistic, so much to look forward to, so very dead. But his wife had loved him and she loved him still, just as Jenny had loved him too once. What can a photograph reveal against the memories of the heart?

'He was always so kind to me,' said Hallam, 'and Jenny adored him.'

She stroked the paper. 'I thought I'd die when he died. Is it really nearly five years ago? There seemed to be no point in going on. But now that all his pain is over I'm glad he died when he did, before he got too old. David would have hated being really old. And I'm glad he never saw me as I am now.'

'You still look fantastic.'

'You're very sweet, Peter, but you're a terrible liar.'

Then she laughed, a sudden cackle. 'Oh, he could be so funny! We never wore any pyjamas and I remember once when he got out of bed one morning and went into the bathroom and saw in the mirror that during the night my HRT patch had come adrift and had somehow got stuck on his own bottom. He panicked and started dancing around the bathroom, trying to flick it off, yelling that he was going to turn into a woman. Oh, my! I can see him now! His terror! His bony knees! His feet! The way his hands were flapping!'

She hooted with laughter.

Another photograph of her husband was propped up on the bedside table: his face the first thing she saw when she woke each morning, the last thing she saw before she fell asleep. She probably kissed the glass each night. He hoped it brought her some small comfort. The loneliness of widowhood must sometimes seem quite insupportable. At least Jenny was still alive: at least there was still a chance.

'He would not want you to be unhappy,' he said.

How bloody fatuous and condescending.

'No,' she said, 'but at least that's one thing you do learn as you get older, not to let yourself become either too happy or too unhappy. Both joy and misery are such frightening traps: they make you so terribly vulnerable. It's much safer just to settle for contentment and acceptance.'

There was an old smell in the room, the sort of geriatric odour that you find around elderly people: not anything particularly physical, nothing especially unpleasant, just a sort of mustiness, a quintessential *ancientness* that seems to permeate the rooms and clothes and lives of the old, a hint of history, of other-worldliness. It was not the sort of smell that he had ever previously associated with Monica. She had always seemed so lively, so absurdly youthful. Now she seemed shrunk. But perhaps it was not her smell at all: perhaps it was the house itself that was dying.

'You've been so kind to me,' she said. 'You won't lose touch, will you?'

'Of course not.'

'And don't give up hope. Never give up hope. You'll come back. You'll bounce back. I know it. Your stars say so.' She stared at him. 'And forget about Jenny,' she said. 'She's not worthy of you. She's not worth a moment more of your grief.'

His eyes brimmed. *Oh, shit, I'm going to weep again.*

'She's not worth any more tears, either,' she said. 'And as for the others you ought to be thinking of revenge.'

Revenge? What would be the point?

'People like Skudder,' she said. 'The bank, Jim Donaldson. When people do you down you should never let the bastards get away with it. "An eye for an eye," that's what it says in the Bible, "a tooth for a tooth."'

The Bible, yes: she could be some Old Testament prophet herself, indomitable, eyes blazing, crying in the wilderness.

'I mean it,' she said. 'Don't let the bastards grind you down.'

'I'm going to miss you, Miss Porridge,' he said.

She smiled. 'That's the nicest thing you've ever said to me.'

An icy, dirty sleet was blowing on the evening of his own last night at the house. Darkness fell early, wrapping the place in gloom in the mid-afternoon. Monica telephoned from her friend's house to wish him luck with the move and to ask him to forward the address book that she had forgotten and left behind. 'Another Little Senior Moment,' she said. 'Uncle Al seems to be moving in permanently upstairs.'

Hallam lit a small fire with the last of the logs and sat up late staring into it, remembering too much, surrounded by half a dozen large removal boxes packed with the few possessions he had decided he had room to keep. Most of the furniture had been removed already to the auctioneers' warehouse and the empty rooms looked large and alien. They echoed. He gazed into the flames and the tears leaked uncontrollably. Images swam into his head as clear as photographs: Matt as a baby splashing in the bath upstairs; Susie as a toddler staggering across the lawn; their eager little faces smeared with chocolate at Easter; midsummer barbecues by the goldfish pond; children's birthday parties with jelly and ice-cream and balloons; Hallowe'ens with terrifying masks, Matt jumping out of cupboards in the dark; Christmases with the sounds of carols filling the room and glittering tinsel dancing in their eyes and the dogs and cats and rabbits and hamsters of their childhoods excited and unnerved by all the unaccustomed activity. And Jenny. Always Jenny: Jenny smiling, twinkling, laughing, flirting, touching, loving. Here, for so many years, in this very room, Jenny and him, so warm and close, and now it was all over: all the memories evaporated, the dreams no more than phantoms. Tomorrow all this, all the faded memories and silent laughter, would belong to a greedy little toe-rag called Enoch Sheepshank.

Just before ten o'clock Susie telephoned. 'I love you, Daddy,' she said. 'Please don't be sad.'

He lay awake for most of the night, unable to sleep, mourning the loss of Jenny's warmth in the bed, feeling her absence as though it were a tangible object. He thought he could still trace a faint whiff of her perfume on her pillow and he hugged it to his face, breathing her essence, and in the misery of his loneliness in the early hours he toyed with himself desperately for relief, something he had not done for more than twenty years, savagely at the end, as if to punish and degrade himself, as if to drag himself down to the lowest point of all, praying for exhaustion and oblivion. Perhaps it felt like this when you were dead.

* * *

In the morning, just before the removal men were due to arrive, he walked around the house and garden like a zombie, saying goodbye. How could he be going? How could it be that by tomorrow this place would no longer belong to him? The rooms were cold and threatening as though they had forgotten him already. His footsteps echoed. The paint and wallpaper looked tired, almost slovenly, with grubby marks where the pictures had hung for years. How had he never managed to get around to fixing that loose floorboard, that squeaking hinge, that jammed cupboard door? Suddenly they took on a great significance, as though by his forgetfulness he had forfeited any further claim on the house. Outside the lawn was soggy, a carpet of dead black leaves rotting into the grass. The patio was stained with mud, the trees gaunt with winter, the goldfish pond murky. Sheepshank was going to fill the pond with rubble, concrete over it. Sheepshank would change almost everything: in a year the place would be unrecognisable. Sheepshank was about to hijack his past and bury his memories.

Suddenly he could not bear to stay in the place a moment longer. Other ghosts would haunt this house, not his.

It took less than a quarter of an hour for the removal men to clear Hallam's things: the sofa, the TV set, a couple of chairs, a picture or two, some photographs, the CD player, two suitcases of clothes. There would be no room for much more in the bedsitter.

It was drizzling when they finally reached the place in Halcyon Road. In the grey February murk it looked even more forlorn and down-at-heel than it had before. The removal men looked at each other; one coughed. An envelope was waiting for him: a cheerful greetings card from Susie hoping that he would be happy in his new home. It showed on the front a drawing of a thatched cottage in the country with roses growing around an old oak door.

It took them just twenty minutes to carry the stuff in.

He looked around the room and was ashamed. He reached for two five-pound notes to tip them. They looked embarrassed. 'No need for that, guv,' said one. 'Service included in the price.'

Whoever heard of a removal man refusing a tip? So this is it, the ultimate humiliation. And now they shuffle out, amazed at their own compassion, and I'm alone at last, completely alone for the first time in twenty-three years. And the tap is dripping in the bath like the sound of a lifetime of seconds swiftly ticking away.

He wrote out a cheque for £25,502.67 and posted it to Jenny at Donaldson's address with a note explaining how he had arrived at the figure and giving her his new address. He posted another cheque, for £10,000, to Monica to clear his debt to her, and he invested his own £25,502.66 in the building society in the hope that it would earn just enough interest to cover a few small luxuries, a cheap week's holiday before too long, perhaps, a rare game of golf or tennis now and then, birthday presents for Susie and Monica, those little things that bring with them a hint of civilisation.

The wind moaned at the windows, rustling the thin curtain.

He had never felt so lonely in all his life.

Four days later a letter arrived in an envelope that was thick and luxurious with a rich, creamy texture. It was from a firm of fashionable solicitors. The envelope crackled as he opened it, sounding almost like a chuckle. The black embossed lettering at the top of the page slid smooth beneath his fingers. The huge, sprawling signature at the bottom was obviously that of a man with soft, pink hands and fat, sleek fingers. The paper smelt of caramel.

Jenny wanted a divorce. She accused him of selling the

house too quickly and too cheaply. She claimed that her share of the sale of the house was not enough to keep her in the manner to which she had become accustomed. She wanted the entire proceeds of the sale as well as all the furniture. In addition she wanted maintenance payments, and all his life-insurance policies, and half of his pension fund.

He stared at the letter and read it again, and again, the slimy legal words slithering like worms before his eyes: 'Unless . . . disgraceful . . . unacceptable . . . whereas . . . heretofore.'

Donaldson has put her up to this. Bloody vulture. Legalised vampire. Jim Donaldson. You bastard.

Something ice-cold entered his soul then. For one terrible moment he knew that he might one day be capable of torturing or killing another human being.

Revenge. Oh, yes. I've had enough. You're quite right, Monica. I want revenge. Oh, yes. I do. At last.

PART THREE

CHAPTER 10

A Five-Day Haddock

Skudder first. That's where it had all started, this whole nightmare, all this injustice and humiliation: Jason bloody Skudder. That's the first target for revenge: Skudder, who stole my job, status, peace of mind, savings, home, family, future. Skudder, who has tarnished my tolerance and decency. Skudder, who has degraded and coarsened me so that now I have started to use foul language again and can even contemplate revenge. No more 'Mr Nice Guy', eh, *Jyce*? No more 'turning the other cheek'. You always loved a cliché, didn't you? Well, here's another one: 'Revenge is sweet.' Ex'lent! Why should decent people keep on behaving properly when they are being kicked in the teeth again and again? 'Revenge is sweet,' eh, *Jyce*?

So Jason Skudder first, then his precious sidekick, Shane Thing – Whatsisname – Gorman. Shane Gorman. And Melody too, just for the hell of it: pretty little contemptuous Melody with the big blue eyes and the big pink tits and the ludicrous memorandiums. And Jim Donaldson: oh, yes, Jim Donaldson, all right, *especially* Jim Donaldson. And the Millennium Bank: let's not forget the Millennium Bank. What was that smoothie's name, the boss's nephew? 'The ultimate

Gruyère'? Dean Castle: that's right; the owner's nephew, the condescending little shit; perhaps it's time you felt a bit of a banker's draught whistling around your patronising battlements. And Sharon in the Job Centre: oh, definitely, Sharon too – hi there, Shar, you've got yours coming, and soon. And Pinky: ruddy Pinky Porter and my thousand quid; somehow, some way. And Jenny. Of course. Jenny as well. Why not? Jenny the worst of the lot, the most disloyal, the biggest betrayal, the least forgivable. How dare she behave like this towards me? When I loved her so much for so long? When I really adored her? When she *knew* how much I loved her? How *dare* she?

But Skudder first. Jenny can wait. Revenge is a dish best eaten cold, they say, and Jenny is still hot in my humiliation. Jenny can wait. Skudder first. All the heat has gone out of my hatred of Skudder: as far as Skudder is concerned I have for him only a very sharp splinter of ice in my heart, a frozen dagger.

There was a coin-box telephone in the hall downstairs but Hallam did not want the other tenants to overhear his conversation. He pulled on his overcoat, wrapped a scarf around his neck, found a pair of gloves and walked out instead into the winter morning and down to the public telephone box that stood on the corner three blocks away. The sky hung low and grey across the grimy rooftops, the clouds heavy with a winter resentment. A dampness seeped up from the concrete beneath his feet and into his soul. He shrugged his overcoat closer around his shoulders and settled his neck deeper into his scarf. The wind sliced down Halcyon Road between the dark terraced buildings. It stabbed at his ears. Halcyon Road? Do me a favour. They must have had a keen sense of humour when they named it Halcyon Road. The uneven pavement was decorated with dog turds, some of them several days old, dark and crusty. Weeds struggled through the cracks between the paving stones. The gutters were garnished with garbage: empty cigarette packets, a banana skin, sweet wrappers, a twisted wire clothes hanger, a shrivelled apple core, a polystyrene fast-food container, loose newspaper pages flapping in the chill wind. In the gutter on the corner a used condom lay pink across the grating.

He opened the door of the telephone box. The glass was damaged, a network of cracks surrounding a small hole. The air inside stank of stale cigarette smoke and urine. The floor was littered with slime and cigarette ends. The sides of the box were aerosol-sprayed with bright purple graffiti. Stuck up behind the telephone receiver was a row of lubricious cards with fluorescent telephone numbers and lewd photographs of prostitutes. The wires between the receiver and the coinbox had been wrenched apart so that they hung loose and fragile, bright red and green. The bloody thing was probably out of order: almost every other public telephone in this area was out of order, vandalised. Why did they do it, like pigs fouling their own sty? Some joker had jammed a plug of tired chewing gum into the telephone mouthpiece where it had dried and hardened into a smooth grey bullet. He hoicked the gum out with the end of his biro. The mouthpiece was encrusted with grime, the earpiece sticky against his fingers.

He lifted the receiver. Relief. The reassuring purr of the dialling tone. He dialled George Pringle's number, feeling guilty. He should have telephoned George long before this to ask how he was, see whether he'd managed to find another job. And Elsie: he should have called her too. And Doreen and all Skudder's other victims, just to see how they were, just to give them a kindly word of friendly encouragement. But failure brings a silence with it and a need to hide. As the months had gone by he had always put it off. How was he to admit to them, to his own staff, that he was still unemployed? And in his heart he had to admit that he had not wanted to know their news, especially if it was bad news and even more especially if it was good.

'Hello.'

'George?'

'Yes?'

He forced a light chuckle into his throat. 'A voice from the past.'

'Yes?'

'Guess who.'

'Mark?'

'Peter Hallam.'

'Mr Hallam, sir.' He sounded genuinely pleased.

'Peter, please.'

'How good to hear you, Mr Hallam.'

'*Peter*. And you. How are things?'

The telephone line hissed.

'George? You still there?'

'Yes, sir. Well, things are not all that good, sir, to tell the truth. Can't find a job anywhere. Given up trying, really. On income support now and housing benefit. Just gets me by. But there's not much left for extras.'

'I'm so sorry, George. They treated you atrociously.'

'And you.'

'All of us. What about Elsie?'

'I haven't heard from her for some time. Well, you don't, do you? You lose touch, specially when there's not much to spare for bus fares and things. You have to be careful. Last I heard she'd managed to get a part-time job in a laundry.'

'Elsie? In a laundry?'

'Serving in a dry-cleaner's shop or something. Wicked, isn't it?'

'Bloody disgraceful.'

'And you, sir?'

'Peter, *please*.'

'Yes. Peter. And how's tricks with you, sir? You got a job?'

'Yes.'

'Well, of course you have. Stands to reason. You would have been snapped up quick. At Framlingham's? Or Young and Feather?'

'No.' Hallam hesitated. 'I thought I'd try something completely different. I've gone into the catering business.'

'Catering?'

'Yes.'

'Well . . .'

'Yes.'

'That's nice.'

'Yes. It is. Look, George, I was wondering if you still keep in touch with anyone back at the office. I don't know anyone there any more – well, not anyone I could approach, really. I need some information.'

'Information?'

'Just to catch up on what's been going on since we left. Anything, really. About Skudder. The company. About what's been going on there, morale, sales, anything.'

There was a moment's silence.

George knows. He's not a fool. He knows something's up. But I can trust him. Of course I can trust him. That was one of the great things about George and Elsie in the old days. They were both as honest and loyal as Labradors.

'Funny thing,' said George, 'apart from my old chum Harry Dunlop in Marketing, the only person from the old days who has kept in touch has been young Keith Smith.'

Keith: the sales-department jester; the jungle of wild hair, the manic expression, the huge, bulbous, lugubrious eyes.

Hallam smiled. 'Good Lord. Keith Smith.'

'He rings every two or three months to see how I am. Nice of him, really. We weren't especially close in the office but he's turned out to be really kind. Took me out to lunch once. Rang Elsie, too, she said.'

'He's a good man. I always liked him.' *But he never rang me*. Well, of course he wouldn't. I was his boss: you don't ring your boss months after he's been fired to see how he is – he'd be insulted. 'So Keith's still there,' said Hallam.

'Yes. Doing well, too. Says Skudder seems to have taken a shine to him. He's made him Shane Gorman's deputy sales manager.'

'So Gorman's sales manager now, is he?'

'Yes, but Keith says he's useless. And Skudder too. He can't wait for Skudder to do something seriously wrong and for him to be fired. He says sales are falling and Skudder's running the company into the ground. Keith's convinced something dodgy's going on.'

'Like what?'

'Something he can't quite put his finger on. Like a bad smell, he says, and you don't know where it's coming from.'

'Why doesn't he get out, then?'

'Can't afford to resign – wife and two kids. And Skudder's paying him well. Too well, he says – he's even given him a company car. He says the money feels like a bribe.'

A tremor of excitement tickled the back of Hallam's mind. *Something dodgy going on, eh? A bad smell, eh?*

'Can you let me have Keith's number?'

'Of course. His home number. But don't ring him in the office. He says that every phone call in the office is recorded now and Gorman listens to them at random.'

Suddenly Hallam was haunted by an awful recollection of the worst of his last days at the office. They rose like monsters in his memory: the hatred, aggression, fear; the sheer nastiness of Skudder's office politics; the impossible demands; the casual carelessness with other people's lives, as though Skudder were an Ancient Roman emperor giving a bored thumbs-down in the arena of the Colosseum. Above all, he could smell the burning memory of something utterly foreign, as though Skudder and Gorman were creatures from some alien world that simply did not understand the usual standards of honesty, decency and fair play.

'Keith's number,' said George, and gave it.

'Thanks. I'll call him. George . . .'

'Yes?'

'We must get together some time. Have a drink, a meal.'

'That'd be nice, Mr Hallam.'

'Peter.'

'Peter. I don't get out much.'

'Nor do I, and it's about bloody time we did.'

He telephoned Keith Smith's home and spoke to his wife, a young Welsh woman with a sweet little sing-song voice, who said that he was usually home by about eight thirty though nowadays it seemed to be getting later and later. He telephoned Elsie's number but there was no reply. She was probably at work. In the dry-cleaning shop. Elsie working in a laundry! What a terrible waste. He would call her again in the evening. It would be good to see her again.

It had started to rain lightly but relentlessly again as he left the telephone box and walked back to the bedsitter, his shoulders hunched against the drizzle, his head tucked into his scarf like a turtle.

Why do we live here, where the weather's so bloody awful? Why don't we live somewhere warm and dry, where the sun shines and people smile in the streets?

The damp lurked everywhere, loitering behind his neck, testing the soles of his shoes. And yet he felt strangely excited. A sense of purpose seemed to invigorate him. He was no longer helpless, no longer just a victim. It seemed as though the long slide down into an unimaginable pit had stopped at last. *Something dodgy going on*. Oh, yes! *A bad smell*. Oh I do hope so, so very much. Because now he had a mission, something to aim for once again. The moment you determine to fight back is the moment of liberation.

Skudder.

Jason Skudder.

Jyce.

Just thinking the name gave him a sensation of power, as though the mere knowledge of his victim's identity gave him some sort of control over him. Like the primitive tribes that used to believe that if you photographed them you would capture their souls. Like the medieval witches who swore that if you could collect the clippings of somebody's toenails you could will them to misery or death simply by wishing it so.

I'm going to have you, Skudder. Somehow, sometime, somewhere, and when it happens I'm going to savour every glorious minute of it.

Like a trembling Christian slave in the Ancient Roman arena when the lions suddenly leap into the audience and advance snarling on the emperor in the imperial box.

'An eye for an eye', eh, *Jyce*? 'A tooth for a tooth.'

Ex'lent!

He settled quickly into an unexpectedly comforting routine at the Unicorn Hotel. Because he worked at night he met few of the other staff except for the kitchen breakfast shift: a cheery Scots chef, a couple of incredibly polite, well-spoken Pakistanis and a noisy, jovial Irishwoman. He would arrive at the hotel by bus each night at about nine forty-five, changing into the dark maroon uniform with the big white unicorn on the pocket, surfacing discreetly behind the reception desk at ten o'clock on the dot to take over from the late receptionist and the second-shift porter. Becoming a servant did not bother him at all. A few of the customers were loud, arrogant or dismissive, but he treated them with an exaggerated subservience that made them wonder if he was taking the mickey, and the uniform protected him, like camouflage. Until eleven o'clock he had nothing to do except register late arrivals, carry their luggage up to their rooms and take orders for early alarm calls, morning newspapers, breakfasts to be served in the rooms, but once the bar was closed at eleven and the bar staff all went home he was left alone to deal with any late orders for drinks or snacks. Sometimes a group of residents would sit up drinking for an hour or two. On one occasion a boozy gang of rugby supporters stayed up until three in the morning, bellowing regularly for sandwiches and more pints of beer, but afterwards they left a huge tip, twenty pounds, two of them slapping him drunkenly on the back, and he felt no shame in accepting it. It seemed right to be tipped: he had worked for it, hard; and afterwards he accepted the few tips that came his way gracefully and with gratitude. Why not? People like to tip waiters. They want to. It makes them feel good. It relieves the guilt of being served and caters to something deep in the capitalist soul.

Two or three times, when business was really quiet, Hallam found himself listening to the drunken ramblings of lonely businessmen who were staying at the hotel on their own. One of them asked him if he could supply a prostitute, as though hotel night porters should be connoisseurs of depravity. It was disconcerting to discover how openly some strangers would talk to him, unburdening themselves in the most intimate way and discussing their most private problems as though he, of all people, were a psychiatrist or marriage-guidance counsellor. 'You've got an honest face,' a maudlin drunk told him one night. Perhaps the uniform had something to do with it, as though it made him more impersonal. But usually the bar and public lounge were empty by midnight and a welcome silence fell across the whole hotel. It would take him no more than an hour to empty the ashtrays, dust the surfaces of chairs and tables and hoover the public rooms, and then he would pour himself a whisky, always paying for it, and relax for four or five hours in one of the comfortable chairs in the lounge.

During these hours he started to read again, not just

newspapers and magazines but books that he had always promised himself he would read but had somehow never got around to starting: Conrad, Dickens, Greene. How could he have reached the age of forty-six without reading *Lord Jim* or *Bleak House* or *The Power and the Glory*? The older you became the more you realised how little you knew. Just a couple of years ago, for instance, he had understood one morning in a moment of astounding revelation that he could make life much easier if he always put his clothes away in his cupboard with the hooks on top of the hangers facing away from him. That way they were always easily retrieved without becoming snagged in each other. Yet it had taken him forty-three years to realise it. How could it take anyone forty-three years to make such a simple discovery?

During those early-morning hours, in the silent public lounge of the Unicorn Hotel, Hallam began to feel a tranquillity that had eluded him for nearly nine months. The warmth and quiet wrapped about him, healing his wounds and strengthening his determination. He liked to sit in the empty lounge in the early hours and listen to the creaking of the old building and the sighing of the wind on gusty nights and the ticking of the grandfather clock near the reception desk. When he made his rounds of the hotel at two and four o'clock to check that all the outside doors and windows were secure, he enjoyed the stillness of the empty corridors, the faint sounds of snoring behind locked doors, the whisper of his footsteps against the carpet, the humdrum routine. Here, at last, he was useful once again. People relied on him. They slept and put their trust in him, the only man awake in this little world, the ruler of a little universe. He did not even mind the chore of cleaning the residents' shoes overnight. Why should he mind? Shoe polish has an honest, wholesome smell about it, and he derived a curious pleasure out of making the shoes gleam, brushing and brushing them until they shone. Doing something well: that was it; the pleasure of making something right again. And which was the more demeaning: cleaning other people's shoes or working for someone like Skudder? The dark, lonely silence of the early hours brought with them a glorious sensation of liberty. Alone he was free. He owed and owned nothing and nobody. Life had been reduced to its simplest essentials, uncluttered, straightforward. It felt clean.

And during those long small hours he thought often of revenge. Browsing one day at a second-hand bookstall he came across a book about it, *Sweet Revenge: 200 Delicious Ways to Get Your Own Back* by Belinda Hadden and Amanda Christie, and each night for a week he dipped into it and discovered with delight dozens of examples of determined retribution. He could order a mountain of wet concrete or horse manure to be dumped in Skudder's driveway, or a hearse and undertakers to knock reverently on his door every day for weeks, or for dozens of pizzas to be delivered by noisy motorcyclists at one o'clock in the morning for months on end. He could send Jim Donaldson a series of forged hospital letters asking him to return for 'another VD test', or a letter on Unicorn Hotel writing paper 'returning' a pair of lady's knickers. One furious avenger had waited until her victim went away on holiday for a couple of weeks and then had broken into his house, sprinkled mustard and cress seeds all over his living-room carpet, watered them liberally, turned the central heating up high and walked away, locking the door behind her. An angry bank customer hired a strongroom deposit box in the bank, filled it with dead fish and put it back in the strongroom: it took the bank several weeks to find the stinking fish because deposit boxes can only be opened with the written agreement of each customer and by the time all those had been obtained the bank had had to be closed for weeks because of the terrible stench.

Women were especially brilliant at taking revenge. One

jilted ex-mistress cut all the crotches out of her man's trousers. Others had cut the arms off suits, dialled the talking clock in Los Angeles and left the phone off the hook, filled shampoo bottles with hair remover, topped up aftershave bottles with paraffin, stuffed curtain rails with rotting prawns and filled underpants with itching powder. One enraged woman had crammed dozens of plastic paddling pools into every room of her ex-lover's house and had then filled each to the brim with the contents of hundreds of tins of soup, gravy and custard. Another went through her husband's telephone contacts book and changed every 3 to an 8 and every 1 to a 4. Another left a live cow in her ex-lover's basement: cows will walk down stairs, you see, but they refuse to walk up them.

Hallam laughed aloud. Yes! Brilliant! And the lottery scam: oh, yes, that one was magnificent. And just right for Pinky Porter.

Oh, Pinky, me old mate, I can't wait to try the lottery scam: this one's just perfect for you.

And how right it was, how proper. Monica was absolutely correct: why should anyone suffer abuse and indignity in silence? Why should the brutes and bullies be allowed to get away with it? Revenge: sharp, clean and healing. And Keith Smith: my Trojan horse, the key to vengeance.

I'm coming for you, Skudder. Oh yes. You'd better believe it, 'sunshine'.

Keith Smith lumbered into the pub twenty minutes late. It was nearly nine o'clock at night. He looked like an angry walrus, his hair wild, his huge, lugubrious eyes bulging more than ever so that they looked as if they might burst out of his head.

'Sorry I'm late, Mr Hallam,' he said, dumping his damp overcoat across a chair.

Hallam rose to greet him. 'Hello, Keith. Peter, please.'

'Right. Pete. Bloody Skudder kept us all in late again.

You'd think we were kids in school. And you know why he kept us all in? Because someone in Dispatch had made a small mistake in one of the customers' addresses so Skudder decided that everyone in the sales department should stay in until every client address had been triple-checked. Someone's going to murder the bugger some day and I have a feeling it might well be me.'

'What are you having?' said Hallam. 'Pint of bitter?'

'Great.'

Hallam went up to the bar, bought the drinks and carried them back to the table. 'It's good to see you again,' he said, raising his glass in salute.

'And you. It's been a long time.'

'Nine months.'

Keith looked startled. 'You're joking. Already? Bloody hell, it seems like yesterday. Well, no, in fact it seems like ten years. Like another century.'

'Skudder?'

'And Gorman. It's become a nightmare in that place.'

'George told me.'

'He doesn't know the half of it. Skudder's a nightmare but Gorman's just a joke. Sales manager? Bollocks. *You* were a proper sales manager. Gorman couldn't sell a cabbage to a vegetarian. He couldn't sell a hot-water bottle to an Eskimo. The only thing Gorman can sell is the rest of us down the river. He never stops plotting with Skudder and whispering in his ear. And he's so *thick*. I don't think he's ever read anything in his life, not even a newspaper. He thinks there's a Jewish poet called Rabbi Burns. He thinks that "A Natural Woman" is sung by somebody called Urethra Franklin. We had a small order in the other day from the Faeroe Isles and he insisted that they're in Egypt. "No, they're Danish," I said, "north of the Shetlands, near Iceland." "How can they be near Iceland?" he said. "They got no snow on the Pyramids." I mean, can you believe it? You're badly missed, Peter.'

'Kind of you.'

'Kind nothing. I mean it. Gorman isn't fit to kiss your arse, let alone sit in your chair.'

'What a horrible thought.'

'He does bugger-all, and he's always skiving and out of the office pretending to be ill. If it's not his 'pulpytations' it's his gout or his dodgy knee or his so-called migraines. They're not migraines, they're bloody hangovers. And he's at Skudder's elbow all the time, flattering him, agreeing with everything he says, crawling, grovelling, pouring poison into Skudder's ear, spreading false rumours about people. When I was first promoted Gorman even tried to get me to agree to spy on people for him. Every week the two of them go gunning for some poor sod in the office, making his or her life a misery, sneering at them, giving them impossible things to do, encouraging people to treat them badly. It's almost as though Skudder and Gorman don't believe they're alive unless they've got someone to hate and gang up against. Every week there's another target who gets bullied and victimised and the previous target is so relieved that the spotlight's no longer on him that he slinks away with relief and does nothing at all to fight back.'

'How could he fight back?'

'God, I don't know, but at least people don't have to look so feeble and behave so pathetically. Nobody argues even mildly with Skudder or Gorman, not even the directors. Directors? That lot couldn't direct a porno movie in a knocking shop. Gorman told Polly Maguire from Accounts to go out and buy him some raspberry-flavoured condoms in her lunch hour the other day and instead of telling him to get stuffed, she did it. She said she'd never been so humiliated, but she did it. I'd have told him to go fuck himself, with or without his bloody raspberry-flavoured condoms. They're all so terrified of being victimised or losing their jobs. And he never leaves the girls alone. You know the sort? He's always touching them, brushing past them, patting their bums, making suggestive remarks. He's known as Fingers Gorman in the office. Someone's going to smack him one of these days.'

'The place sounds worse than ever.'

'It is. Harry Dunlop used to work for Robert Maxwell back in the eighties and he says the atmosphere in the office now is exactly the same as it was then. Skudder behaves just like Maxwell, swaggering around, throwing his weight about, waving his arms, refusing to listen to anyone, coming up with the most extraordinary schemes, issuing orders one minute, changing his mind the next, constantly moving the goalposts so that people don't know where they are or what they're supposed to be trying to achieve.'

'Disorientation,' said Hallam. 'That's how you destabilise people, make them vulnerable, then cow them into submission.'

'That's it. Skudder's constantly building people up then undermining them, making impossible demands, insisting that they should work thirteen or fourteen hours a day or at weekends, keeping them in the office later and later at night, wheedling one minute, shouting and threatening the next.'

'Classic stuff. Pavlov's dogs.'

'Come again?'

'Pavlov. Russian physiologist. Trained dogs to be submissive by keeping them in suspense. One minute he'd treat them terribly badly, the next he'd spoil them, and then he'd treat them badly again. The animals never knew where they were. They ended up as trembling wrecks.'

'That's it! Exactly. It's like something out of the Middle Ages, like a feudal lord surrounded by his terrified serfs.'

'But not you, Keith. Not you.'

'Well, not yet. I'm a bolshie bugger, don't like being pushed around. But most of the rest of the staff are on the verge of nervous breakdowns. Skudder's doubled his own salary and he's paying Fingers fifty per cent more than you were paid and you should see how much Skudder lets him claim in expenses – five hundred a week!'

'Hell's bells!'

'Fingers is right: fingers in the bloody till. And most of it's spent on wining and dining his tacky little girlfriends. They're just milking the place dry, yet sales are down by ten per cent on a year ago and falling. They haven't a clue. They haven't the foggiest about how to run anything. Skudder couldn't run an umbrella stall in a thunderstorm.'

'How the hell do these people get such powerful jobs?'

'Search me, Pete.'

'And how are they getting away with it?'

Keith grimaced. 'God knows, but there's something fishy going on, I'm sure of it.'

'Like what?'

'Search me, but it stinks like a five-day haddock. I'm working with Gorman in your old office, as you know, and whenever he's discussing finance or even sales on the phone his voice drops and he looks shifty. He actually swivels his chair and turns his back on me and cups his hand over the mouthpiece while he mutters into it. He and Skudder seem to be desperate to raise more money and to find new investors. They keep going off to meetings at the bank.'

A shadow flickered across Hallam's memory. 'Who handles the company account there?' he said.

Keith swigged at his beer. 'Some smooth bugger called Castle – Gene Castle, something like that.'

'Dean Castle?'

'That's it.'

Ah, yes. Oh joy. Dean Castle. The ultimate Gruyère – and probably just as full of holes.

'You know the guy?' said Keith.

'I've met him, yes.'

'He's an arrogant bugger, isn't he? "Castle here, get me

Gorman and be quick about it." That sort of thing. Someone's going to stick one on him one day, and I suspect it might be me.'

Keith stood. 'The other half?' he said.

Hallam consulted his watch. 'Yes, great,' he said.

Dean Castle. And Jason Skudder. And something smells.

'I'd love one,' said Hallam. 'A quickie. A vodka and tonic this time, I think. With plenty of ice.' No one will know at the hotel. There's no smell in vodka. Just the one. For celebration.

Keith went off to the bar.

This is my chance, perhaps my only chance. I have to persuade him to help, to make him see it as a moral duty and not just a personal revenge. He's a good man: honest, decent, loyal, and that may not necessarily count in my favour. He's going to feel loyal to the company, for a start. Perhaps I'm going to have to make him feel sorry for me. Swallow your pride. Look pathetic, if necessary. But just don't blow it: this is your only chance.

Keith returned with the drinks. 'George tells me you've gone into catering,' he said.

Hallam smiled uncertainly.

Keith sat. 'So. Catering. Sounds adventurous. What is it? Hotels? Restaurants?'

Hallam hesitated. *This is where it starts: with honesty.*

'I'm a night porter,' he said, 'in a hotel.'

Keith stared at him, his eyeballs more bulbous than ever. 'Oh, bloody hell,' he said.

'They shouldn't be allowed to get away with it,' said Hallam. 'Nobody should treat other people like that and get away with it, this mindless contempt for ordinary workers, this belief that any sort of ruthless behaviour is justified if it leads to greater efficiency and profits. No one should treat his staff like dirt, not even a sort of genius like Robert Maxwell, let alone Jason bloody Skudder. People like Skudder need to get their comeuppance. They need to be smacked. Hard.'

'You can say that again.'

'But I need help, Keith. On the inside.'

Keith looked at him without expression, his eyes as round and still as goldfish bowls.

'I need to know what they're up to. I need to know *why* it smells.'

Keith looked at Hallam and then across the bar. It was beginning to fill up with the late-night crowd, the just-three-for-the-road-before-bedtime lot.

'Is that what all this is about?' said Keith. 'This drink?'

'Yes.'

Keith stared at him. His eyes were hypnotic. 'So it's not just a chat for old times' sake?'

'Of course it is. That too. It's really great to see you again.'

'But there's more to it than that.'

'Yes.'

'You want me to spy on Skudder.'

Spy? Such a melodramatic word. Such an old-fashioned concept. Spies went out with the Cold War.

'Yes,' said Hallam.

'Like Gorman.'

'Well, I wouldn't put it—'

'So what's the difference?'

'The difference is that I'm the good guy and so are you and they're not.'

Keith nodded. 'OK.'

'Between us, with the right information, we might actually be able to get rid of the bastards.'

Keith took a sip and frowned. He thought about it.

'You're worried about loyalty,' said Hallam. 'Skudder's promoted you, he's your boss, he's treating you better than most, so you think you ought to be loyal. Quite right, too.

Absolutely right. But there's a greater loyalty too, you know. To yourself, your family, your colleagues, the shareholders, the integrity of the company. Skudder isn't the company: he's just the present caretaker of the company. It's the company that pays your wages and gives you your car, not Skudder. Your loyalty is to the company and your colleagues, not to Skudder. And if he's damaging the company then he needs to be stopped before he destroys it and all your livelihoods.'

Keith thought about it some more.

'Yes, it's dangerous,' said Hallam. 'If they found out they'd sack you on the spot. They might even sue you for industrial espionage.'

Keith pinched his nose, scratched his cheek, tapped the table with his fingers.

'But sometimes you have to take risks,' said Hallam. 'You have to stand up for what you believe.'

And end up like you: a night porter in a three-star hotel.

He could see the doubt in Keith's eyes. He had to smother it. 'It's fashionable nowadays to say that nothing is black and white,' said Hallam, 'that no one is wholly good or bad, that no one is ever completely to blame for anything. But it's balls. Some people really are rotten, a few of them are maybe even evil, and Skudder's one of them.'

Keith thought about it some more. He sipped his beer. He nodded slightly.

I've got him. Hallam glanced at his watch. 'Look, think about it,' he said. 'I've got to get off to work.'

Keith shook his head. 'You, of all people. A porter in a hotel. Do you wear a uniform?'

'Yes. Maroon. Quite smart. With a big white unicorn on the pocket.'

'Fuck me.'

Yes: I've got him. Hallam shrugged. 'I couldn't get anything else. I tried everywhere, for months. No one wants old men of forty-five any more – not even their wives.'

Keith's shaggy eyebrows moved. They glided across his forehead like giant caterpillars.

'She's left me,' said Hallam.

'God, I'm sorry . . .'

'For Jim Donaldson.'

'Donaldson?'

'Jim Donaldson. Yes, the legal director.'

'Shit!'

'Used to be my best friend. Now he's hers. She wants a divorce, the house, everything. I've had to sell the house, the furniture, split the family up. I'm living in a bedsitter.'

'Bloody hell . . .'

Yes! Hallam went on, 'It's no good whining about it, but that's what Skudder has done to us. That's why I want revenge. People like Skudder should be made to realise the consequences of their behaviour. People like Skudder should be punished.'

He stood and raised his hand in farewell. 'So think about it,' he said. 'Let me know. It's been great to see you again, Keith. You know I always rated you and I'm glad you've been promoted. It's well deserved.' He grinned wryly. 'At least Skudder's got something right. But let me know. And just remember that one day it could be you. One day it probably *will* be you.'

He turned to leave the pub.

'I'll do it,' said Keith. 'Of course I'll do it. Bloody hell, how can I possibly say no?'

For the first two or three weeks Hallam had trouble sleeping during the day when he left the hotel at eight o'clock each morning and caught the bus back to the bedsitter in Halcyon Road. It seemed all wrong to eat a huge hotel breakfast of porridge, eggs, bacon, sausage, tomato, baked beans, toast, marmalade and tea and then to catch a bus across town with crowds of people on their way to work. It seemed bizarre to go to bed in the morning to sleep for six or seven hours while it was still light. It felt almost indecent.

It was cold in the room in Halcyon Road. The draughts kept him awake and a weak daylight loitered beyond the thin curtain, making it difficult to take sleep seriously. He would toss and turn, trying to find the most comfortable position. As a child he had always loved to sleep on his front with his head turned to one side, his arms and legs in the shape of a swastika, but now if he lay on his front he could never settle properly: the mattress seemed to resent his chest and stomach and eventually he was always forced to roll back again on to his side. Noise from the world beyond leaked in through the windows: an electric milk float whining along the street; someone kicking a stone along the pavement; a passer-by whistling out of tune; a car chortling past, its pounding radio rattling the window-frame; a cheerful team of dustmen calling to each other as their garbage truck clanked and rumbled down the road. From within the house, too, came the sounds of other lives: the muffled noise of a television set; a child crying in a distant part of the building; a man sneezing triumphantly; footsteps echoing in the stairwell; a woman raising her voice; somebody farting; the flushing of a nearby lavatory. How intimate it was, distant lives so close and yet unknown, as remote from his own as if they were on Mars. That was what he missed the most now: not Jenny, Monica, not even darling Susie. What he missed most was privacy.

He was polite but cool with the neighbours: the elderly black couple on the ground floor; the young single mother on the first floor looking sluttish, a slack look about her lips, her skin a greyish colour as though it had been bruised; the pale, anorexic homosexuals in the room across the landing. He smiled and nodded, said good morning and goodnight, but otherwise they had nothing in common, nothing but failure. All they shared was a sense that society had abandoned them and that they had no stake in it. One afternoon he woke with a start and suddenly understood why people like this might become criminals. Why not? What loyalty did they owe to a society that had rejected them?

One evening Susie came to see him but she was strained, her face drawn, and she clung to him and wept to see how he was living. He decided that she should never come here again, that in future he would have to meet her somewhere in town instead, a pub or coffee bar. He could no longer afford to take her out for a meal and that hurt, too, wounding something fundamental in his pride: he could not even buy his daughter food.

'How's your mother?'

She made a snuffling noise.

'Is she happy?'

'I don't know. Don't care. I hope not. Oh, Daddy . . .'

He held her close while she wept again. His heart trembled to know that she was so miserable. 'Of course you care,' he said.

'I don't. I hate her. And him.'

'That's not true.'

'It is. He doesn't like me, I know.'

'Of course he does, Suze. You and he have always got on brilliantly.'

'Not any more. Not now I know what he's like. Not now I know what she's really like.'

I must not criticise Jenny, not to Susie. I must never allow myself the indignity of spite. Jenny will always be her mother, whatever she does. Parents should never enrol their children in their little wars.

'You've got to make the most of it,' he said. 'She's your mother. Is she going to marry him?'

Susie started crying again. 'I'll leave if she does,' she wept. 'There she is living in luxury, with *him*, and you have to live like this.'

'Don't feel sorry for me,' he said. 'I'll get it all together again one day. I promise, Suze. This is just a hiccup.'

She whimpered, pressing her face into his chest. 'Oh, Daddy,' she said, 'I do love you.'

He hugged her again, stroking the back of her head. 'I know, and that's the best thing in the world.'

When she had run out of tears they caught a bus into town and he took her into a café for a coffee. The table was smeared with grease, the ashtray full, the windows dribbling with condensation. With a shock he realised that he was probably the oldest person there: none of the other customers looked over thirty. Nobody these days ever looked over thirty.

'Do you ever see Matt?' he said.

She had cheered up considerably. No one can weep for ever. 'Only once. A few days ago. He's been staying with some of those awful friends of his, dossing down on people's sofas.'

'He always did.'

She smiled sadly. 'This time, though, they keep kicking him out. His friends' parents get fed up with him after a couple of days and tell him not to come back. He says he's looking for a squat, some empty house that he and his mates can move into and take over. He heard somewhere that if you find some house that isn't being used you can stay there for months and the owner can have terrible trouble trying to get you out.'

'I believe that's true.' Hallam shuddered, imagining what it would be like to find your house occupied by a squad of squatters like Matt and his friends. What a nightmare. You wouldn't wish that on anyone, not even Skudder. It didn't bear thinking about.

Not even Skudder?

No, not even Skudder. Skudder deserved something much more horrible than that.

* * *

He telephoned Monica to see how she was. She sounded as cheerful as ever.

'I'm winning on the gee-gees again,' she said. 'Four winners in a week.'

'Well done, Miss Porridge.'

'And Liz is letting me stay on with her as long as I like,' she said. 'I had a look at three or four of those sheltered places but I didn't fancy any of them at all. It was like being back at school. Or in jail. Isn't that nice of her?'

'Very.'

'We go back a long way, Liz and I. Friends in the sixties. You should have seen us in our miniskirts! Well!'

'I'm sure you were gorgeous,' he said. 'So what's her surname, then, this Liz? Taylor, I suppose.'

She giggled. 'Don't be cheeky. Now, what about you?'

He told her.

'Oh, I'm so sorry, Peter,' she said. 'I can hardly believe it. What a greedy little bitch.'

'I can't afford to get a lawyer,' he said. 'These divorce lawyers cost more per hour than I earn in a week.'

'Can I lend you some money again? You shouldn't have sent it all back to me until you were back on your feet again.'

'That's very sweet of you, Monica, but it would just be throwing good money after bad. There's no point. I haven't got anything, anyway, so why hire a lawyer to protect nothing? If Jenny wants to sue me I'll just stand up in court myself and say I've got nothing more to give her, and it's true. Why hire a lawyer to tell the truth for you? The only point of lawyers is when you need them to lie for you. They're very good at that.'

He rang Elsie again, and Doreen, re-establishing contact, as if he were emerging at last from some long hibernation. He no longer needed to hide. He had joined the world again.

Letters arrived from Jenny's lawyer. He replied to the first two by explaining that he had nothing left to give her, but when they still kept coming with increasing menace he simply ignored them, tossing them out each week to sweat in the rubbish bin under the cracked eggshells and breadcrumbs and congealed baked beans. He liked to imagine the lawyer's impotent frustration as each letter went unanswered. What could they do to him? Bankrupt him? What for? He was all but bankrupt already.

After five weeks at the Unicorn Hotel he was called in to the manager's office one morning just after breakfast to see Mrs Forsyth.

Rosie Forsyth.

Rosie.

She was, too. He had always left the hotel each morning before she arrived and she had always gone by the time he started work again in the evening, so he had forgotten how attractive she was. She really was very attractive indeed: that smile; those eyes. That was something else that had come alive again, he thought: he had not looked at another woman, not properly, not like *that*, for years. She was much too young and much too married. Twenty-eight? Twenty-nine? Much too young. But it made him happy when she looked at him and smiled.

She looked at him and smiled. 'I keep hearing good reports about you,' she said.

'That's nice.'

'I've even had comments from a couple of the guests, which is almost unheard-of. People just don't notice night porters, generally, let alone praise them.'

'That's kind of them.'

She glanced at a piece of paper in front of her. '"Courteous, efficient, obliging, always smiling."' She looked up. 'That's from one of the guests. I congratulate you. Well done, Peter.'

He loved the way she said his name, the shape of her mouth as she said *Peter*, the small explosion of her lips.

'Thank you.'

She sat back in her chair. The thin April sunlight caressed her hair, framing it with a halo. It was very soft. 'I need a deputy,' she said.

A deputy. Sheriff Forsyth. Rosie Get Your Gun.

He said nothing.

She tapped a pencil against her front teeth. They were very white. Her lips were very pink and soft. 'I need someone to stand in for me when I go to HQ for the day or to group meetings and conferences,' she said. 'Someone to stay on a bit later at night when we have some special function on. Someone to be my right-hand man. Would you like the job?'

More money. A reasonably decent place to live again. Proper daylight working hours. A job where people look at you again.

'Fifteen thousand a year,' she said. 'What do you say?'

Three hundred pounds a week: almost a living wage again. Occasional lunches with Susie. Perhaps even a holiday.

'What about the juniors in the office?' he said.

Her eyes were cool. 'What about them?'

'Young Dave Wilson. Wouldn't he resent it if I were promoted over his head?'

'Probably, but he's not ready yet for the responsibility. None of them is, whereas you could do it in your sleep.'

Do I really want responsibility again? It's so wonderfully restful without any responsibility at all.

'I need a diplomat, someone efficient who also gets on with everyone, someone who can charm the cleaning women as well as Head Office, someone who's been about a bit. Dave's still a bit raw, a bit unsure of himself. That's not surprising – he's still pretty young and some jobs are still better done by older people. Don't worry about Dave. I can explain it to him. This is one place where age doesn't matter. Here we promote on merit.'

Age doesn't matter? Is she trying to tell me something?

'What do you say, Peter? You don't really want to go on being a night porter, do you?'

'Of course not. It's just . . .'

'That's decided, then. Great.' She smiled. 'Can you start next week? Of course you can. On Monday. Do you have a suit? You'll need to wear a suit.' She laughed. 'Of course you've got a suit. You've probably got a cupboard full of suits.'

'I've become rather fond of the uniform. The maroon matches my nose.'

She chuckled: a throaty chuckle, slightly naughty, fun. She winked. 'Take it home then and wear it secretly at weekends. I won't tell anyone.'

'Fifteen thousand a year?'

'That's right.'

A quarter of what he had earned as sales manager; but twice as much as he was making now, and maybe just enough to live again respectably. 'And breakfast?' he said.

She laughed. 'And breakfast and lunch and dinner if you want.'

I shouldn't be doing this, not working quite so closely with her. We'll be together almost every day. I shouldn't even be thinking of it. This could end in disaster. 'On Monday, then,' he said.

'Great.' She came around the desk and shook his hand. Her fingers were cool: long, slim and capable. He did not want to let them go.

Don't be such a bloody fool. She's only twenty-nine. She's married.

'We'll put another desk in the reception office,' she said, 'and then it shouldn't take you much more than a week or two to learn the basics. It'll be a doddle for someone like you, with your track record.'

Back off. Now. Change your mind. Don't be such a damned

idiot. 'Thank you,' he said. 'Thank you so much. I won't let you down.'

She looked at him straight between the eyes, a look to weaken him. 'Oh, no, I know that,' she said. 'I know that very well indeed.'

Back in the bedsitter in Halcyon Road he found that a note had been pushed under his door.

'kEEf sMIf foned,' it said.

Adrenaline surged through him. Keith. At last. News. Information. Maybe the chance he needed. He wanted to telephone him immediately but of course it was impossible: he would be at work by now. He would have to wait until this evening.

Hallam slept badly, disturbed by sunlight through the thin curtains and noises outside, a children's game in the street, and he kept dreaming that Fingers Gorman was pursuing Rosie Forsyth through a dense jungle that eventually turned out to be Keith Smith's hair. She was laughing helplessly.

He waited until nine o'clock that night, knowing that Keith was unlikely to return home much earlier than that, forcing himself to be patient, fighting his increasing excitement.

At nine o'clock he could no longer contain himself. On his way to work he telephoned Keith from the kiosk down the road.

Please let him be there. Please don't let him be out.

Keith answered the telephone himself. He sounded tense. 'I've got it, Pete,' he said. 'Skudder and Gorman. I've found out what they're up to and it sure ain't Postman's Knock.'

CHAPTER 11

Pinky and the Grand

They met for lunch in a smart restaurant a long way from the office, one that neither of them had used before.

'Lunch is on me,' said Keith, 'and I promise I won't charge it to expenses.'

It was oddly exhilarating to be eating again in an expensive restaurant. In the old days Hallam had lunched in places like this a couple of times a week, taking the luxury for granted, but for months now he had eaten only in cheap cafés where the knives and glasses were smeared with grease, or in the kitchen at the Unicorn Hotel, or at home out of tins or packets of frozen food. With a twinge of nostalgia he noticed now, with new appreciation, the texture of the linen napkins between his fingers, the gleaming silver, sparkling glasses, the deference of the waiters with their black bow-ties, the muted voices, the stylish air of quiet discretion. Occasional self-indulgence is good for the soul, he thought. Some people like to pretend that it's better to be poor, that somehow the lives of the rich are tainted by their wealth, that the poor are somehow hallowed by their poverty, but who could ever really believe it? Try telling that to the inhabitants of Halcyon Road.

Keith unfolded his napkin. 'Skudder and Gorman are massaging the figures,' he said. 'They're exaggerating sales and orders. They're overestimating the value of stock. They're underestimating costs and debts. By cooking the books they're making it look as if the company is still making a decent profit instead of a socking great loss.'

'Hellfire. So that's it. How did you find out?'

Keith grinned. His eyebrows danced. 'I broke into Gorman's computer files two nights ago after everyone had gone home.'

'My God, that's dangerous.'

'Well, it would be if anyone found out, but I waited till nearly ten o'clock to do it. When Skudder left the office at nine thirty he put his head around the door as he went by and seemed impressed that I was still working so late. He told me I'd go far.'

A waiter arrived with two menus and a smile. Keith ordered a bottle of white wine. Hallam relaxed: a good sign, that, wine at lunchtime. Thank goodness it wasn't going to be one of those modern po-faced lettuce-leaf and fizzy-water lunches that had withered the soul of the City for far too many years.

'So how did you get into Gorman's files?' he asked. 'Doesn't he use a password?'

'Sure, but the man's even more of an idiot than I suspected. You were right about your old desk – they haven't changed it since you left so I was able to open the drawers with your keys and there, under some papers in the bottom drawer, was his computer password. What a prat. I told you, the man couldn't organise a Mr Midget contest at a dwarfs' reunion. And you'll never guess what his password is.'

'Go on.'

'Sex.'

'What?'

'Sex. That's Gorman's password. It's one of the corniest and commonest personal-computer passwords of all. Millions of people use it. Pathetic, isn't it? Trust Fingers to choose it. No imagination. Absolutely typical. What a wanker. Let's order.'

They studied the menu. Monkfish. Sea bass. Duckling. Venison. Too much. Too rich, after all these months. Poverty can spoil you too.

'What makes it all worse,' said Keith, 'is that the bank manager knows all about the figures being massaged.'

'Castle?'

'Yes. In Gorman's computer files there are copies of letters he's sent to Castle that make it quite clear that Castle knows all about the figures being fiddled. In one of them Fingers asks about the company's revolving line-of-credit loan . . .'

'Revolving what?'

'Line of credit. It's a rolling working-capital loan that Skudder has arranged with the bank, based on the company's expected future income from customers and the value of the company's stock: raw materials, work in progress, finished goods and so on. In one letter Gorman asks Castle what will happen if the company's figures turn out to be not as good as they were when the bank granted the original loan and not enough to cover the loan – and in the next letter he's grovelling with gratitude because Castle has said that he will keep the loan going even though the collateral no longer justifies it.'

'But that's madness. The bank could lose its money.'

'Right.'

'Hellfire. So the bank manager's in cahoots with a client?'

'Looks like it.'

'So what's in it for him?'

'A bribe? Backhander? Share options? Something dodgy, anyway. D'you know, they even managed to hide the correct sales figures from me until I started rooting about in Gorman's computer files. From *me*, the deputy bloody sales manager! Now that everything's on computer it's almost impossible to find out what's really going on unless you're a computer freak yourself, and Skudder's sacked all the geeks we used to have.'

'Geeks?'

'Computer nerds.'

The waiter arrived with a bottle of white wine and a sweating silver bucket of ice. With a twirl he brandished the bottle under Keith's nose, offering the label as though he were a conjuror who had just pulled it out of a hat. Keith peered at it, nodded and grunted. The waiter, all fingers, wrists and flourishes, flaunted a white napkin over his arm, assaulted the bottle with a corkscrew, popped the cork with a couple of twirls, handed it to Keith to sniff then twisted the metal foil on the neck of the bottle into a little circle, into which he tucked the cork with a gesture of triumph. He swaggered the bottle towards Keith's glass, poured a tiny mouthful for him to taste and stepped back with a supercilious little smile and his feet angled at ten to two like an entertainer awaiting applause. Keith fingered the glass suspiciously, holding it delicately by the thin stem, twirling it, raising it towards the light, staring at it from several angles, swirling the puddle of wine around the bottom of the glass, tipping it towards him, inserting his nose, sniffing twice, frowning, sniffing again, sipping the wine as daintily as a maiden lady, gazing at the ceiling, puffing his cheeks, swirling the wine around his mouth and swallowing it. He clicked his tongue. He gave the air a faint kiss.

'Crap,' he said.

'Sir?'

The waiter looked shocked. He shook his head slightly and hung it a little to one side as though he suspected that something must be wrong with his hearing.

Keith grinned. 'Just joking. It's really very good. Pour away.'

'If Sir has any complaint . . .'

'No, no. Just a bad joke.'

The waiter gave a tight smile. He poured a mouthful of wine into each of their glasses. Even his elbows looked aggrieved. He returned the bottle to the silver bucket with a titanic crash of ice.

Come off it, thought Hallam. Stop being so pompous. Even we waiters can at least have a sense of humour.

'Is Sir ready to order now?'

'Could you give us a couple of minutes?' said Keith.

'Of course, sir. Whatever Sir wishes. No hurry at all, sir. Sir.'

The waiter retreated.

'Here,' said Keith. 'Was he taking the piss?'

Hallam chuckled. 'Yes.'

'Naughty of me, I suppose, but I can't resist it when they start all that poncing about with the wine. It's pretentious bollocks. Do you do it in that hotel of yours?'

'Not any more. They've just made me deputy manager.'

Keith looked delighted. 'Bloody marvellous,' he said. 'Well done. So that makes it a double celebration.' He raised his glass. 'Here's to your promotion,' he said, 'and Skudder's comeuppance.'

They drank. A warm glow investigated Hallam's fingers and toes. It's all going to be all right again, he thought. I know it. This is where the comeback starts. 'So what do we do about Skudder cooking the books?' he said.

'Search me.'

'Have you got copies of the letters? Printed them out?'

'Not yet. I thought I'd better not. The office computer records the date and time each file is printed out and the number of the terminal that gave the command.'

'I never knew that.'

'Well, it didn't in your day. It's one of Skudder's latest refinements so that he can keep tabs on everything we do. There are even alarm clocks on the lavatory doors that ring if you've been sitting there for more than three minutes.'

'You can't be—'

'Absolutely. Scout's honour. So Skudder would know very well who printed out the files of the letters if I did because he knows that I was the only person who was still in the office at ten o'clock that night. And even if I printed out the letters and showed them to the chairman he'd probably sack me for snooping in Gorman's files. Gorman is still my boss. They'd call it disloyalty, gross misconduct, insubordination, something like that.'

Hallam thought about it. He nodded. 'Mulliken probably wouldn't believe you, anyway. He's a hundred per cent behind Skudder. When I went to him months ago and told him precisely how Skudder was treating the staff and how morale had plummeted he almost bit my head off. Mulliken wouldn't notice if Skudder and Gorman staggered out of the building right in front of him with bags of gold marked "swag".'

'Well, it's no good going to any of the directors. They're utterly useless. We could wait for the next AGM, I suppose, put it to the shareholders.'

'Risky. And that's not for another six months. Skudder could have brought the company to its knees by then. And who's going to believe us? They'd say we've both got axes to grind.'

'Not me,' said Keith. 'I haven't.'

'They'd say you were after Gorman's job, hoping for promotion. No, somehow we need to get them to trip themselves up. We need to let them hang themselves.'

'How?'

'I'm thinking,' said Hallam. He thought. 'I'm buggered if I know,' he said. 'We're going to have to work on it.'

The waiter hovered. He sniffed. 'Are we ready to order, gentlemen?' he said.

A week after starting his new job as deputy manager at the Unicorn Hotel, Hallam left Halcyon Road with relief and moved into a furnished two-bedroom flat in a better part of town where the walls were not all daubed with graffiti and nobody spat in the gutter. Miraculously the threatening legal letters suddenly stopped arriving. How easy it was to escape: you just moved house and didn't tell anyone. There must be fifty ways to leave your lawyer.

The flat had its own kitchen and bathroom, its own telephone, a living room with a view of trees, a television set, a proper dining-room table. How strange that he should find such comfort in such ordinary little things just as he was beginning to believe that he no longer needed possessions. Possessions do matter: they define us; they confirm our identity. One morning he heard a woman singing in one of the neighbouring flats. He had never heard anyone singing in Halcyon Road.

He began to enjoy his new job more than he had expected. It was good to rejoin the normal world and to work during the day again and to sleep at night. He revelled in the old-fashioned formality of the hotel, the sense of order and hierarchy, the tidiness, the rituals, the daily rhythm, the feeling that he was helping to make other lives a little more pleasant. Above all, he was comforted by the certainties: that meals would be served at exactly the proper times, that the sheets would be changed regularly, that someone was always behind the reception desk. It was like living in a warm cocoon, like becoming a child of the 1950s again, when everything still seemed safe and nothing was unsure.

Nor was it all that different from being a sales manager: you faced similar challenges of management, organisation, forward planning, of coaxing the best out of your staff, of selling yourself as well as the product. And here he went to work each morning in anticipation of Rosie Forsyth's nearness: her smile, her sparkling eyes, her perfume. Her laugh sounded like birds singing. Yes, of course it was impossible: she was far too young; she was married; but she lit up his life.

It was enough that she was near each day and that she smiled at him. As the weeks went by he found that the pain of Jenny diminished. Her face became blurred in his memory. How could he forget it, after all these years? He had to remind himself by looking at a photograph, and even there her face was the face of a stranger. *I don't love her any more*, he thought, with a sudden wild sense of recognition. *At last I'm free.*

One spring morning, when the flowering cherries were bursting with pink and white blossom, he caught himself humming as he came through the swing doors into the hotel lobby. Hell's bells, he thought. I'm happy. I'm actually *happy*. For the first time in nearly a year.

And then he thought of Skudder. What the hell was he going to do about Skudder? It was useless going to Mulliken, the directors, the shareholders, the bank. Who else was there? The press? No, too soon: they wouldn't touch it; too risky; libel. Who else? No one. Somehow Skudder and Castle had to be made to trip themselves up. They had to walk into it. For the time being Skudder seemed to be as secure as a steel vault in an underground nuclear bunker.

Pinky, then, first: Pinky Porter. Get Pinky and the thousand quid.

Okay, chum, here's how we do it.

As soon as Hallam was settled into the new flat he wrote a letter to Pinky. There was no point at all in telephoning him: Pinky had long ago disappeared behind the electronic smokescreen of his echoing answerphone.

Dear Pinky,

Long time no see and I hate to think that we've lost touch completely and maybe all because of that stupid thousand pounds. Look, I've got a better job now and a decent flat at last, and I don't need the money right away any more, so can we please make it up and you just pay me back some time whenever you're ready? There's no hurry. I'm not skint any more and I don't want to lose our friendship just over a lousy grand. So what about us reviving the old Saturday card school? Perhaps you and Bob and Mike and Charlie could come round here for a few hands one Saturday night, have a few drinks, a bit of supper, a sort of flat-warming. Please say yes. It would be great to see you again. Pete.

You're a ruthless bastard, Hallam. Oh, yes. At last.

Two evenings later Pinky telephoned. 'Hell, Pete,' he said, 'I'm so sorry about that grand. It's been preying on my mind for ages. I keep meaning to send you a cheque but then something else crops up.'

Yeah, sure. 'Don't worry about it,' said Hallam. 'There's no hurry. It's good to hear you.'

'To tell you the truth,' said Pinky, 'I'm still a bit strapped. Pamela's been a bit slow with the maintenance again this month, so it could be . . . well, maybe another month or two before I can pay you back, if that's OK . . .'

'Sure, fine. Three months would do. Four, five, whatever.'

'Well, that's great. And yes, I'd love to revive the card school. It's been too long.'

Yes!

'That's marvellous, Pinky. What about Saturday night?'

'This Saturday?'

'If I can get Bob and Mike and Charlie.'

'OK, fine.'

'Six-ish, then? Start with pontoon and a couple of beers, move on later to the hard stuff?'

'Sounds great.'

'Ex'lent. See you then. Here's the address . . .'

Round one to me. Ex'lent – and now I'm even sounding like Skudder.

* * *

There was no embarrassment at all when the five of them met on the Saturday evening even though they had not seen each other for months and Hallam was now living alone in a small flat. They had all been friends for far too long for the atmosphere to be strained. Men can be good at pretending not to notice things. They joked about him being a bachelor again, and Pinky winked and nudged and promised to introduce him to 'a real cracker who goes off like a rocket'. Within ten minutes it was just like old times: the cracking of rings on beer cans, the gurgle of liquid in glasses, gossip about acquaintances, jokes and anecdotes, the slapping of playing cards on the table. Pontoon first – black jack, 21s, *vingt-et-un* – with Pinky as the banker to put him in a good mood since the banker doesn't often lose.

After an hour and a half, by seven thirty, Pinky was well ahead: thirty quid up for openers, and then they broke for something to eat and something stronger than beer.

'You guys get stuck into the Scotch,' said Hallam, 'and I'll make a start on some supper. Sausages, beans and mash okay? With ice-cream afterwards?' *Comfort food: the ambrosia of bachelors.*

'Great,' said Mike, pouring himself a deep whisky. 'Just the stuff.'

'Proper job,' said Charlie.

'Nectar,' said Bob.

'God, it's good to be back together again,' said Pinky. 'I've missed these Saturday nights of ours.' He leaned back in an armchair, kicked off his shoes, stretched his legs and sighed contentedly.

Fantastic. It's coming along brilliantly. It's going to work.

Hallam stopped in the kitchen doorway and turned towards them.

'Oh, I nearly forgot,' he said. 'I've got a little flat-warming present for us all to celebrate us getting together again.'

'A present?'

'It's nothing much: just a lottery ticket each for the draw tonight. A little flutter.'

'Hey, nice idea,' said Pinky.

'Rock on,' said Bob.

'Great,' said Charlie. 'Thanks.'

Hallam fumbled in his shirt pocket and handed them each a one-pound National Lottery ticket, each printed with six numbers. 'These bloody things never win, of course,' he said, 'except occasionally you may get three numbers right and win a tenner. But if by some incredible chance your ticket does win a decent prize then I wouldn't mind a grand or two as a sort of commission.'

'Yeah, sure.'

'Course.'

'Fair enough.'

They tucked their tickets into their pockets and forgot about them.

'Anything on the box?' said Pinky.

Hallam flicked at the remote control and the screen fizzed into life. He tossed the control across to Pinky. 'See what you can find,' he said, and disappeared into the kitchen in search of sausages and mash.

Just half an hour more and then I've got the bastard.

Pinky, Charlie and Bob watched the end of a comedy and then a half-hour game show and they talked all the time, and just before eight o'clock Hallam emerged from the kitchen, wiping his hand on a towel and pursued by a rich smell of spicy sausage. The game show was just coming to an end, amid an hysterical crescendo of shrieks and applause. 'Let's watch the lottery draw,' he said. 'It's on at eight.'

'Yeah, great.'

'Sure.'

'Why not?'

'Mind you,' said Pinky, 'I never win a bloody thing, not even in the church tombola.'

They reached for their tickets and Hallam took the remote control and zapped the TV on to a different channel. He hardly dared to breathe. *Ah, God, it's going to work. This is when you get yours, Pinky baby.*

The face of a pretty young blonde was filling the screen, the studio floodlights sparkling in her eyes and glinting on her teeth. She was dressed all in white, like a vestal virgin, and tossing her long hair.

'God, look at those knockers,' said Pinky. 'And look at those legs. I wouldn't mind giving her one.'

A shaggy young man stood beside her, wearing a floral waistcoat and smiling inanely. Some of the studio audience were shouting. The band started a noisy fanfare.

'And now this week's winning numbers!' the blonde twittered excitedly.

Drums thundered. Trumpets blared. The shaggy young man in the floral waistcoat gazed into the wrong camera, gave a nervous smile and pressed a button. On the stage beside him a huge plastic drum that was filled with coloured numbered balls began to spin, the balls bouncing against each other like bubbles. As the plastic drum spun faster and faster a bright red ball suddenly dropped out of the bottom of the drum and rolled down a chute. It carried the number 21.

'Twenty-one!' cried the blonde unnecessarily.

'*Vingt-et-un*,' said Pinky. 'I'll give you *vingt-et-un* any time you like, darling, and *soixante-neuf* as well.'

A cheer went up from the studio audience. 'Twenty-one! Key of the door!'

'Hey, twenty-one!' said Pinky. 'That's one of mine. First time lucky.'

And the rest, sweetheart. Oh, yes, I'm going to love every minute of this.

A blue ball fell out of the drum and rolled down the chute to nestle beside the red.

'Forty-three!' shrieked the blonde.

Someone in the audience whooped. 'Forty-three! Scones for tea!'

'So's that,' said Pinky. 'That's one of mine too.'

A green ball followed.

'Five!'

'Five!' yelled the audience. 'Snakes alive!'

'That's one of mine,' said Bob.

'And mine!' said Pinky. 'Hey, I've got three numbers. That's worth a tenner, isn't it?'

'Lucky bastard,' said Charlie.

'Jammy sod,' said Mike.

Another red ball.

'Three!'

'Three!' howled the audience. 'Housemaid's knee!'

'Mine,' said Charlie.

'Bloody hell!' said Pinky. 'That's mine too.'

'Hey!'

'What?'

'How many's that, then?'

'Four.'

'Four! Bloody hell. Four out of four? Jeez, you can win a hundred quid with four.'

The crowd was roaring now, the blonde simpering at them, slim, pure white, an untouched priestess of greed worshipped by millions.

A yellow ball bounced down the chute, glowing with promise. Will this one make you rich? Is this the key to all your dreams and fantasies? And how will it make you happy?

'Thirty-eight!' squeaked the blonde.

'Thirty-eight!' bellowed the audience. 'Don't be late!'

Pinky Porter's face suddenly drained of blood.

'Fuck me,' he whispered. 'That's mine as well. Christ! Five. I've got five.'

'Here, let's see,' said Bob, reaching across for Pinky's ticket.

'Not bloody likely,' said Pinky, clutching his ticket. 'Oh, God. Please. Let the last one be seventeen. Please let it be seventeen.'

A pink ball rolled down the chute.

Hallam could barely breathe.

Now, you bastard. Now! Got you at last.

'Seventeen!' squawked the blonde, jumping up and down as though she were about to achieve an orgasm.

'Oh, Christ,' said Pinky.

He closed his eyes.

He squeezed them tight.

He opened them again.

He stared at the screen, checking the winning numbers against the numbers on his ticket.

'Seventeen!' howled the audience. 'God save the Queen!'

'Oh, Christ,' he croaked. 'I've got all six. I've won the jackpot.'

The final ball rolled down the chute, a purple ball with the number 45.

'And last but not least,' shrieked the vestal virgin, 'the extra bonus ball. Forty-five!'

By now the audience was hoarse with ecstasy. 'Forty-five! Duck and dive!'

Pinky gazed at the screen and then at his ticket again.

His lips moved silently. He nodded to himself.

Three. Yes, three.

And five. Yes, five.

Seventeen.

Twenty-one.

Thirty-eight. That's right: thirty-eight. Three-eight.

And forty-three. Four-three.

All six.

All six winning numbers.

'Six,' he croaked.

'What?'

'All six.'

'All six?'

'You what?'

'I've got all six,' he whispered. 'Oh, God, I've won the jackpot.'

Bob exploded from his armchair, reaching Pinky in two strides, stretching for the winning ticket, wrestling for it. Porter grasped the ticket firmly, refusing to let it go. For one terrible moment Hallam feared that between them they might tear it in two. Bob peered at the numbers, at the screen, at the numbers, at the screen. *3, 5, 17, 21, 38, 43.*

'Fuck me!' he shouted. 'He's right. He's won the fucking jackpot.'

The seven coloured balls on the television screen were suddenly rearranged in ascending order, the red nestling against the green, the green against the pink, the pink against another red, the yellow, the blue, the purple. Seven numbers, the first six enough to win several million pounds if there were only one or two winners, enough to alter someone's life for ever, enough to make you believe in God.

'All six?' said Charlie.

He jumped out of his seat and bent over Pinky's shoulder, checking the numbers against those on the screen.

'My God,' he said, 'you're right. All six. My God, Pinky, you've won millions.'

'Hellfire,' said Hallam.

He, too, bent over Pinky's shoulder. Then he stood back and stared at him with awe. 'Millions,' said Hallam.

'Bloody millions,' said Bob.

Pinky stared at them like a zombie.

'I never win anything,' he croaked, 'not even the church tombola.'

'Well, now you can buy the church itself,' said Hallam, 'including Westminster Abbey, the Archbishop of Canterbury and the Bishop of Bath and Wells.'

The studio audience's applause was by now hysterical. 'So here are this week's winning numbers,' squeaked the blonde. 'Three, five, seventeen, twenty-one, thirty-eight, forty-three – and the bonus number is forty-five.'

The numbered balls skittered across the screen: 3, 5, 17, 21, 38, 43 with the extra ball, 45, tacked on to the end.

'Jesus wept!' said Charlie.

'Oh, God,' said Pinky.

His voice sounded like water gurgling down a drain.

'Oh, Christ,' he said.

His face was like parchment.

He looked at his ticket again, and again at the screen, frowning, moving his lips, touching the numbers on the ticket as though they might be unreal.

'Pinky?'

'You OK?'

His face was ashen.

He looked at them with horror. His face was frozen. He seemed to have difficulty moving his lips.

Hellfire: he's going to have a heart-attack. The shock is going to kill him. Not now, you bastard, not yet.

And then Pinky jumped out of his chair, clenched his fist and punched the air. 'Yes!' he bellowed. 'Yes! I'm a fucking millionaire!'

Hallam grinned. *Got you, you bastard! Got you at last!*

'I'll ring the lottery people and make a claim for you,' said Hallam. 'You have to claim if you win one of the big prizes.'

Hallam took his own lottery ticket towards the telephone, lifted the receiver, consulted the claims number on the back of the ticket, punched out a telephone number, waited, spoke.

The others listened in silence, struck with wonder.

'Yes, that's right. Yes. Three. Yes. Five. Yes. Seventeen. Twenty-one. Thirty-eight. Yes. Forty-three. Porter, Michael Porter. Yes. Have there been any other claimants yet? Oh, God. Right. Yes. Tomorrow, then. Yes. Fine. Right. Counselling? What? Counselling? No, I don't think so, thank you. No. All right. Yes. Goodnight. Yes. Monday. Right. Yes. Goodbye.'

They watched him, mesmerised, as he replaced the receiver and turned back towards them.

'Yes?' said Pinky.

'Yes.'

'How much?'

'They can't say yet but so far there's been no other claim. You may be the only winner.'

Pinky looked frightened. 'Jesus!' he said.

'You could have won as much as twenty million. Hell-fire!'

Pinky looked terrified. 'Twenty million!'

'Maybe more.'

'Twenty.'

'Million.'

'Maybe more.'

And then Pinky delivered himself of another huge cry. 'Fuck me! I'm rich! I'm a fucking millionaire! Champagne! Let's get some champagne! Christ, we'll go on a cruise! All of us. All five of us. And Concorde! Let's go to New York by Concorde for the day. Or Rio! Fuck me, a dirty weekend in Rio. Just the five of us. The classiest call-girls in Brazil. They wear ostrich feathers. Nothing else. On the beach. Copacabana. A thousand quid a night. Who cares? I'm rich. I'll have two of them at a time. Three! One black, one white, one yellow. And the best hotels. Private planes. Fuck me! I'm a millionaire!'

'I just happen to have some champagne in the fridge,' said Hallam. 'I'll open a bottle.'

'*One* bottle?' yelled Pinky. '*Four* bottles. *Eight* bottles. *Twelve* bottles. Until we fall down. Fuck me! Twenty million! Jesus!'

'I've only got one bottle,' said Hallam.

'Stuff that! We're going out on the town. Of course. On me. Everything's on me. Dinner at the Ritz. A nightclub. Some tarts. That's it. That's the way to celebrate. Ring for a cab. Two cabs! We're going up West, on the town.'

'Bloody marvellous,' said Bob.

'Fantastic,' said Mike.

'Get a cab! Ring the Ritz! Book a table! Now! Fuck me! I'm a zillionaire!'

The Ritz was fully booked but they drank champagne in the bar, and whisky again, and moved on to eat in an expensive Italian restaurant in the West End with white wine, red wine, brandy, more champagne, taking with them a riotous atmosphere wherever they went. People stared. Some smiled, laughed, happy to touch the edge of happiness.

'Everything's on me!' yelled Pinky, flourishing his credit card. 'It's all on me!'

By midnight he was very drunk, slurring his words, staggering when he rose to go to the lavatory, patting waitresses, leering at women sitting at other tables. By twelve thirty he was insisting on a visit to a strip-club before going on to a night-club. 'Let's all get laid,' he said. 'Shit, I haven't had a decent leg-over for a week.'

Oh, baby, are you going to have the mother of all hangovers tomorrow.

Pinky stared at Hallam with sudden intensity. His eyes softened. 'Pete,' he said gently. 'Pete. My old friend. Pete.' He nodded with a sage expression. 'Pete. Love you very much. I owe you. Grand.'

'We'll talk about it tomorrow.'

'No. Bollocks tomorrow.' Pinky was adamant, with a sudden stubborn, drunken insistence. 'Owe you. Grand. Should've paid you months ago. Out of order. And another grand. For tonight. Lottery ticket. Promised. Jesus!'

He gazed at Hallam with amazement. 'If you hadn't given

me that ticket tonight . . .' He shook his head slowly, as though in deep debate with himself. 'Ten grand, twenty grand, that's what I'll give you.'

'Just one would be fine,' said Hallam. 'I don't want any more.'

'Twenty. Least I can do. Soon as I get the lolly. How much?'

'Maybe twenty million.'

'Fuck me. Monday. Pay you then.'

'That's really not necessary, Pinky,' said Hallam. 'Just one thousand would be fine.'

Pinky gazed at him in wonder. 'You could have won,' he said, 'if you'd kept the ticket yourself.'

Hallam shrugged. 'Well, win some, lose some. That's life.'

Pinky gazed at him. There were tears in his eyes. 'I love you, Pete,' he said. 'You're a gent. You're a real sportsman. Fair play, Pete, I'm gonna give you a cheque right now.'

He fumbled inside his jacket pocket.

Here it comes. At last. A cheque for a thousand pounds. And about bloody time too.

The chequebook appeared, a biro.

Pinky looked at the other three. 'We're old friends, you know.'

They nodded.

Pinky nodded in unison. 'We're very old friends, Petey and me. Go back a long way. Old muckers. Old fuckers. Yeah.' Pinky looked at him blearily. His voice was thick. He flourished his biro, waving it above the chequebook. 'Just two K, then? You sure you don't want twenty? Thirty? I'm loaded, you know. I just won the lottery. What about fifty K? I'm a multi-millionaire.'

Hallam smiled encouragingly. 'Just a thousand, Pinky, if you really insist. That's all. That's plenty. And it's very good of you. That'd be great.'

'*Two* grand,' said Pinky. 'You bought me the ticket. You could have been a contender.'

Slowly he wrote out a cheque for two thousand pounds, concentrating hard, his tongue protruding from between his lips.

At last, you bastard. I've got you at last.

Pinky looked up at him, gave a crooked smile, ripped the cheque from the book and tore it up, scattering the pieces on the floor.

Oh, no! He's—

Pinky gazed at him craftily. 'Not two thousand quid,' he said magnificently, 'two thousand *and one*.'

'What?'

'Two thousand and one. You paid a pound for the ticket. Fair's fair. I owe you another quid. I ought at least to pay you back for the ticket.'

He wrote out another cheque, painfully slowly, biting his tongue again.

Dear God: his bank's going to query the cheque. It's been written too carefully. The handwriting is wobbly. The signature's too careless. It's probably illegible. He'll get the date wrong.

'What's the date?' said Porter.

'The sixteenth.'

'Fifteenth.'

'That was yesterday. It's after midnight.'

'Sod it.'

He tore out the cheque with exaggerated care and flapped it at Hallam as though he were waving goodbye.

Hallam took it, glancing at it, checking it, then tucked it into his own inside jacket pocket. 'Thanks, Pinky,' he said. 'That's very kind.'

'No, *you*'re very kind,' said Pinky, with flabby lips. 'If you hadn't given me the ticket . . . You're the kindesest person I've ever met. Isn't he the kindesest person, Billy?'

'Bob,' said Bob. 'Definitely.'

'Absolutely,' said Charlie.

'The kindesest, kindesest person ever,' said Pinky. 'Even Billy says so. And thingy there. He could have won, you know.'

'Yes.'

'If he'd kept the ticket himself. He could have won. He could have been a zillionaire but he can't be now 'cos I am instead.'

'Do you think it's time to go home?' said Hallam.

Pinky glared at him with sudden belligerence. 'Home? Bollocks to that. We haven't started yet. It's my party. I'll cry if I want to. Fuck that! I haven't had a fuck yet.'

'I'll cry if I want to.' Oh, yes. Oh, sure. Tomorrow, without any doubt. Tomorrow, you bastard, when you find out you've been had.

Hallam slipped away unnoticed at one thirty, leaving the others carousing in a club where they had fallen in with a group of rowdy rugby supporters for whom Pinky had insisted on buying a magnum of champagne. As Hallam left they were singing 'The Ball of Kirriemuir'.

Back in his flat he set the alarm for nine thirty and slept for seven solid hours. Then he took a taxi to the Sunday-opening branch of his bank to pay in the cheque. 'I need special express clearance straight away on this one,' he said. 'Can you do that on a Sunday?'

'No problem,' said the clerk. 'We got twenty-four-hour banking nowadays every day of the year. Mind you, I gotta charge you fifty quid to make the special clearance.'

'Fine.'

'And it could take ten minutes, fifteen maybe.'

'OK. I'll wait.'

'Right. No problem. Bear with me.'

Hallam laughed. By the time Pinky woke this afternoon with a mighty hangover and remembered what had happened and grabbed the Sunday papers to see how much he had won and to check his numbers yet again it would be too late. His £2,001 would be gone and tucked safely away in Hallam's own bank account. Guilty about the extra grand? Sod that: just think of it as interest.

Hallam laughed again.

'Sir?' said the clerk.

'No problem,' said Hallam. 'Bear with me.'

It was late afternoon before Bob Jackson telephoned. He sounded seedy. His voice was thick. 'Pete? My God, what a night,' he said. 'What a fan-bloody-tastic night.'

'You went on somewhere after I left you?'

'God, my head! When did you leave? I didn't even see you go.'

'About one thirty. I couldn't take any more.'

'I'm not surprised, you poor bugger. Stands to reason.'

'You were in the Pink Pussy at the time.'

'Where the hell was that?'

'The lap-dancing place. Where the girls were wearing postage stamps and Pinky was buying magnums of champagne.'

'Christ, we went on for *hours* after that. For some reason we seemed to have half a dozen other blokes with us.'

'Rugby fans.'

'Really? God knows where they came from. Or where they went to, come to that.'

'Wales.'

'Jeez, well, that explains it. I've never seen such thirsty buggers. Then we went on to a casino in Mayfair, then a late-night drinking club, then a brothel in Pimlico, and Pinky paid for the lot.'

'That makes a nice change.'

'He must have spent thousands, all on his credit card. He even wanted to treat us to the hookers, and a couple of the

Welsh guys got stuck in, but Charlie and Mike and I weren't too keen, to tell the truth. You never know, do you? Not these days. So eventually we got him home about six this morning. God, I feel knackered. Thank God it's Sunday. Mouth like a Sumo wrestler's jockstrap. Anyway, I just wanted to find out how you are, you poor sod. You must be feeling bloody depressed.'

'Depressed? Why?'

'Well, losing all that bunce.'

'What bunce?'

'The lottery jackpot. I mean, aren't you seriously pissed off that you gave that ticket to Pinky? Shit, I would be, giving that ticket to him and then watching him win millions with it. Come to think of it, why the blazes didn't you give the ticket to me? Bloody hell, Pete! If you'd kept that ticket yourself it'd be *you* collecting millions tomorrow.'

Hallam laughed. 'No, it wouldn't.'

'What do you mean? Of course you would. Six winning numbers. Why are you laughing like that?'

'That lottery draw,' said Hallam. 'It wasn't this week's. It was last week's.'

'What?'

'You all thought we were watching the live draw on the TV last night but we weren't. We were watching a video recording of last week's draw. Those numbers all won last week, not last night.'

'What the hell do you mean?'

'I mean that Pinky has owed me a thousand quid for nearly two years and he's kept refusing to pay me even when I was really broke, so to get it out of him I recorded last week's lottery draw on the video, then I bought you tickets for this week and made sure that the numbers on his ticket were the same six numbers that had won *last* week.'

'You mean . . .'

'Yes.'

'So . . .'

'Yes. He hasn't won a bean.'

Bob started laughing. 'Ow!' he cried. 'My head! Don't make me laugh.'

He laughed some more. 'My God, Pete, you're a devious bugger.'

'I like to think so,' said Hallam.

And about bloody time, too.

Susie came round to the flat and enthused about the view of the trees, the new paintwork, the furniture, the little kitchen.

'Wow, Dad, this is great,' she said. 'Fantastic. You're really getting it together. The other place was horrible. Can I come and stay for a few nights now you've got two bedrooms?'

'I'd love you to. Whenever you like.'

'Next weekend? Maybe Friday to Monday? I don't want to be at Mum's and His next Friday. It's His birthday and she's giving Him a dinner party.'

Donaldson's birthday?

'I can't stand it when she's all over Him,' said Susie. 'He's so pompous and arrogant. He doesn't love anyone except Himself but she makes such a fuss of Him. It's creepy. I hate it.'

So Donaldson's forty-five on Friday and I bet Skudder doesn't know yet. But he will. Oh, yes. That's it. How nice. How neat.

After Susie had gone he found the ad in the local evening paper and telephoned them.

'On Friday,' he said. 'Yes, a guy called Donaldson, Jim Donaldson. He's forty-five. You'll find him at about eleven a.m. in the managing director's office, a nice guy called Skudder. Sixth floor, Jason Skudder.'

And I only wish I could be there to see it.

* * *

Monica came to lunch at the Unicorn Hotel. She looked as though she were going to a wedding. She was wearing a fussy pink hat with a cluster of bows and frills and she tottered along on a tiny pair of pink shoes with heels at least four inches high.

'What fun!' she said. 'I haven't eaten in a smart hotel for years.'

He introduced her to Rosie.

'What a nice gel,' said Monica archly afterwards. 'And she seems very fond of you. You could do much worse than her, you know.'

'Come off it, Miss Porridge. She's far too young. And married.'

She gave him her laser look. 'What's that got to do with it? So was Jenny.'

'You ought to be ashamed of yourself,' he said. 'Just read the menu and stop causing trouble.'

'You need a woman,' said Monica. 'You're the sort of man who does.'

They ordered their food and a bottle of wine.

'There's something you ought to know,' she said. 'The house is up for sale again.'

'What house?'

'Ours. Yours. The one you sold two months ago. I drove past there yesterday and it's still empty and there are two for-sale boards up outside. And it's the same estate agent selling it.'

'Boggitt, Burlap and Boggitt?'

'That's it.'

For a moment his brain shifted into neutral. Yeomans selling the house again? Already? After just two months? Surely not. It's just not possible. Sheepshank was going to knock walls down, modernise the kitchen, fill in the pond, concrete over the lawn. Why would he be selling it already?

'Perhaps they just haven't taken the for-sale boards down yet,' he said.

'No, there are two boards up now. There was only one

when you were selling it.' She darted a quick glance at him. 'And this is the worst bit,' she said. 'I telephoned them this morning and pretended to be interested in buying the house. They're asking two hundred and nineteen thousand.'

He stared at her.

'They're selling it for forty-two thousand more than you got for it.'

Two hundred and nineteen thousand pounds? There must be some mistake.

'Come again?'

'Two hundred and nineteen thousand.'

Forty-two thousand more than Sheepshank paid us for it.

'Did you say two one nine?'

'Yes.'

Nearly 25 per cent profit in just two months: more than five thousand pounds a week. And Yeomans is handling the sale again, so Lee bloody Yeomans must be in on it. So that's how he found us a purchaser so quickly. Sheepshank and Yeomans: friends; perhaps partners in crime. He even persuaded me to drop the price to one seventy-seven. Of course he did. *Lee bloody Yeomans was in on it right from the start.*

He shook his head. No. It was not possible.

'They've stitched you up,' she said.

Yes.

'We can't let them get away with it,' she said.

No.

'I'd like to make a suggestion,' she said.

'Yes?'

Her eyes glittered. 'Susie tells me that Matthew and his friends are looking for an empty house to squat in. I think we ought to let him know that the house is still empty.' She cackled.

Oh, magnificent. Hallam gazed at her with admiration. Brilliant. Sheepshank and Yeomans will never know what's hit them if Matt and his friends decide to squat in the house. By the time they get them out the place will be a wreck.

'You're fantastic,' he said. 'The bastards! What bastards! Will you ask Susie to let Matt know?'

'I'll ring her tonight.'

And now Skudder. She's full of ideas. Monica will know what to do about Skudder.

'I've been thinking,' he said. 'You're quite right about revenge. It's clean and healthy and therapeutic. It's much better than feeling sorry for yourself and bitter and harbouring a grudge. And it's good for the victim too – if you've behaved badly it's good for the soul to be punished.'

He told her about Pinky Porter and the thousand pounds and the lottery ticket, and she clapped her hands with delight and her eyes danced with appreciation. He told her about how he dreamed of taking revenge on Skudder and the bank and Jim Donaldson, and even on Jenny. He told her all about Skudder and the bank and the massaged figures, the revolving line of credit, the lack of collateral.

'Skudder's the one who really deserves to be damaged,' he said. 'It was Skudder who started all this, but I just don't know what to do about it.'

She gazed at him with a little smile. Her eyes were wonderfully clear. Forget the wrinkled skin: her eyes looked as if she were no more than twenty-five.

'Well, that's easy,' she said.

'Yes?'

'Of course it is. I've still got my shares in the company, haven't I?'

'Your shares . . .'

'Eight hundred of them,' she said. 'Just leave it to me. I'll put a bomb under the little sods. I'll put the fear of God into them and then we'll sit back and watch them sweat. Just leave it to me.'

She lit a cheroot. 'Any chance of a glass of port and brandy? And then I must put a fiver on Parson's Nose in the three twenty at Newmarket.'

CHAPTER 12

Vengeance

Dean Castle swivelled his big black leather chair away from the desk in his tenth-floor office and slid it round to face the huge plate-glass window with its stupendous view across the City. He crossed his legs contentedly and gazed at the horizon. The office buildings towered on either side, their rows of windows as blank as dead men's eyes. Their solid chunkiness gave him a warm sensation of power. The river glinted far below, slipping silver between the feet of the skyscrapers like a snake. The morning sun was hazy in the mist but there was already a hint of summer in the air, a smudge of green about the branches of the tiny trees below. Everything seemed to be going right these days. He had reached that magic time of life when everything you touch seems to blossom. His shares were booming. His uncle was hinting at a huge new job in Head Office, which meant that he would almost certainly be a millionaire before he was thirty. The stunning girl from Goldman Sachs, the one with the red hair and tits like coconuts, had just agreed to spend the weekend with him in Paris. Damian Morgan had promised to lend him his island in the Caribbean for two weeks. Darren Simmonds had just gone bust after burning his nasty little fingers on some over-heated South American futures. And now Jason Skudder had just sent him yet another fat envelope crammed with brownbacks. Life was wonderful. Dean Castle was very pleased with himself. No doubt about it: he'd cracked it.

The intercom telephone buzzed. He swivelled back to his desk, admiring his fleeting reflection in the huge glass window. He was bloody good-looking. There was no doubt about it: he was *bloody* good-looking. He punched the button on the intercom.

'Speak,' he said.

'Mrs Monica Partridge to see you, Mr Castle.'

'Say again?'

'The lady who called last week? For investment advice? You told me to make an appointment.'

Castle smiled thinly. Ah, yes: the old widow with the £20,000 to invest; the one who refused to talk to anyone but him. He smiled at his reflection in the window and smoothed his hair with his free hand. He always got on well with old widows. They always flirted with him, baring their false teeth at him. With any luck one of them might leave him everything in her will one day. Mind you, there wasn't much you could do with twenty K these days: buy a little car, perhaps, or a garage in the outer suburbs. Still, it was better than nothing. I'll have it off her quicker than a whore's drawers, he thought.

'Wheel her in,' he said.

He smoothed his hair with both hands and shot his shirtcuffs, flashing the gold cufflinks. Old widows liked that sort of thing: cuffs, cufflinks, hair.

There was a knock at the door.

'Come!' he called.

She was not at all the sort of little old lady he had been expecting. She was small, all right, she was tiny, but she was also wearing a red golfing cap, a purple anorak, an emerald sweater, bright leggings splashed with half a dozen garish colours, a pair of tangerine trainers and an eager expression. She bounced into his office as if she were stuffed to the gills with HRT and steroids.

'Hi there, Dee-Anne,' she said, in a voice encrusted with decades of gin and tobacco.

'Dean,' he said.

She bounded towards him and shook his hand. Her grip paralysed his fingers.

'Funny name for a man, Dee-Anne,' she said.

'It's *Dean*. Dean Castle.'

Her eyes widened. 'Oh, you poor boy. What an unfortunate surname.'

'*Castle*,' he said, 'with a C.'

'You must forgive me, dear,' she said. 'I'm a little hard of hearing.'

He smiled. He had a knack of making his eyes twinkle when he smiled.

'Mrs Partridge,' he murmured in his brown, reassuring voice. It moved slow and gentle, like molten molasses.

She gazed up at him.

He smiled.

'You've got a big wet bogey hanging out of your nose,' she said.

He stepped back, disconcerted, turned away, fumbling in his pocket for a tissue. 'Uh . . . sorry,' he said.

He wiped hurriedly at his nose.

'Now it's stuck to your lip,' she said.

'I—'

He wiped.

'The other one,' she said. 'It's a big green bogey.'

'Excuse me.'

He hid his cheek with his handkerchief and turned away towards the mirror on the wall. He peered at his reflection. Nothing.

'It's probably fallen on to the carpet,' she said, sitting on the fat sofa. 'Never mind, Dee-Anne, the cleaning woman will find it. *Squelch*.'

She cackled.

She delved into a pocket of her anorak, withdrew a small packet of cheroots and lit one.

'Mrs Partridge. I'm afraid we don't—'

She blew a cloud of smoke.

'I'm afraid this is a non-smoking—'

'Strange word, *bogey*, don't you think?' she said, leaning back on the sofa, crossing her ankles and resting her tangerine trainers on a plump cushion. 'Very odd when you look at it. B-O-G-E-Y. *Bogey*. It doesn't look English at all. It looks like Hungarian or something.'

'Mrs Partridge . . .'

'Do you play golf, Dee-Anne?'

'Dean. It's not—'

'It's a golfing term too, you know. My husband used to play a lot of golf so I know a thing or two about bogeys. They're something to do with the number of strokes you play. Maybe that's why *bogey* means snot as well.'

'Mrs Partridge, you—'

'Holes in the nose, you see, Dee-Anne: nostrils. In golf the bogeys drop down into the holes and in noses they drop down out of them.' She nodded. 'Awful for Humphrey Bogart, of course. Remember Bogart, the Hollywood actor? No, I don't suppose you do. You're too young. It must be very odd being so young, not knowing anything.'

'Mrs Partridge—'

'They used to call him Bogey. Not nice, that, having the same name as a piece of snot. You wouldn't call someone Snot, would you, Dee-Anne? Or Mucus. But they called poor old Bogey Bogey. Mind you, there are worse names, I suppose, like your own surname, you poor boy. Have you never thought of changing the pronunciation? You could call yourself *Arsolly*, perhaps, or *Azole*. That wouldn't sound quite so . . . *raw*.'

She took a drag on her cheroot, rolling the smoke around her tonsils and blowing a perfect ring.

'Mrs Partridge, I really do think we ought—'

'I love words, don't you, Dee-Anne? Spellings, rhymes, palindromes, onomatopoeia, things like that. And limericks. Do you like limericks, Dee-Anne?'

'I'm not sure this—'

'I made one up this morning specially for you.' She winked. 'Oh, yes, you'll like this one.'

'Mrs Partridge—'

> 'A pompous, promiscuous banker
> Discovered his tool had a chancre.
>   He got such a shock
>   From his ulcerous cock
> He turned into a born-again wanker.'

'Mrs Partridge! I really . . .'

She gave a rasping laugh. She looked around the room and waved her cheroot. 'Got an ashtray?' she growled.

'I'm afraid not. This is a non-smoking building.'

'How terribly self-controlled of it,' she said. She smiled dangerously. 'No wonder it's managed to grow so big and tall.'

She flicked ash on to the carpet.

'Mrs Partridge!'

She waved her hand. 'Tobacco ash is excellent for carpets,' she said, 'which is why all Persians are heavy smokers. Unless the carpets are cheap, synthetic ones, of course, in which case it hardly matters if they are ruined.'

'It's a disgusting habit, Mrs Partridge.'

'So is banking.'

'I beg your pardon, madam?'

'I bet you're one of those revolting hypocrites who force their employees to huddle outside the building on the pavement if they need a cigarette, even on a winter's day, as though they were second-class citizens, yet you're only too happy to do business with crooks, conmen, drug-dealers, rapists and child-molesters so long as they have a bit of money.'

'Mrs Partridge, I deeply resent . . .'

She gazed at him with her bottomless eyes. 'You're not denying it, I hope?'

'I am indeed, madam. I . . .'

'Very well, then,' she said. 'Let's get down to the evidence. I have several hundred shares in a company run by one of your dodgy clients. I'm decidedly dyslexic when it comes to maths and numbers but I know enough about them to be able to tell you that this client of yours is undoubtedly a crook.'

Castle stood and pressed the intercom buzzer. 'I'm afraid I can see no possible purpose in continuing this conversation,' he said.

'Oh, I think you will, Dee-Anne,' she said.

She lay back on the sofa and blew another smoke ring.

'Let's talk about Jason Skudder,' she said.

Matthew Hallam climbed over the garden gate, wrenched at the *FOR-SALE* sign that was fixed to the fence, tore it down and tossed it aside on the grass. Ben, Nigel and Mickey followed him over the gate and approached the house.

Already the place seemed somehow to have shrunk. It looked forlorn and lonely in the chilly afternoon, as if it knew that it was no longer loved. The garden path was soft beneath their feet and wet with rotting leaves. The grass was shaggy. A dead goldfish floated on the surface of the pond. Why shouldn't he come back and live here again? thought Matthew. It was obvious that nobody else wanted it. Bloody capitalist property speculators: this was his home; this had been his home all his life, for more than twenty years. He knew every blade of grass, the slight bump on the far right-hand corner of the lawn, the mossy patch to the left of the patio, the charred earth where his father had sometimes lit a bonfire, that hole in the fence that had never been fixed. It was just over there, behind the greenhouse, that he had tried to smoke his first cigarette when he was ten. It was there that he had whispered his deepest childhood secrets to the blushing tomatoes, there that he had hidden as a child to sulk after rows with his father. He and the greenhouse were confidants, so how could it possibly belong now to someone called Sheepshank? Once he had been happy here. It seemed a very long time ago.

He crossed the slimy patio to the kitchen door. They had not bothered to change the locks. How strange that people should spend hundreds of thousands buying a house but fail to change the locks.

He used his old key to open the door. It was damp and gloomy inside the house, with a musty smell. The floor was bare, the windows uncurtained. There was a chill inside that was more than simple coldness: it seemed to enter the soul as well as the bones.

Mickey shivered.

'Let's hope they haven't cut off the electric,' said Ben.

'We'll soon have it put back on if they have,' said Matt. He found the main electricity fuse box under the stairs and pulled the mains switch. A lightbulb lit up behind them in the corridor.

'Magic!'

Matthew grinned and rubbed his hands together. 'Now we just nail up the doors and windows and sit tight,' he said. 'They won't be able to get us out for months.'

'Where are we going to find some wood?' asked Nigel.

Matt looked at him and shook his head: sixteen stone and

as thick as a dinosaur. 'The floorboards, of course,' he said. 'We just pull a few up and nail them in place.'

'We've got no furniture,' said Ben. 'We'll need some chairs and stuff.'

Matt sighed. Didn't they know anything at all? Sometimes he wondered whether he ought to be mixing with a better class of dosser.

'We just ask the social services, don't we?' he said. 'They have to give us chairs and tables, beds. We're unemployed, aren't we? We're homeless.'

Ben gave a huge grin. 'Not any more, we aren't,' he said.

'You're brilliant, Matt,' said Mickey. 'Give us a kiss.'

Jason Skudder's telephone rang. He reached for the receiver. 'Skudder.'

'It's me.'

Dean Castle. He sounded breathless.

'Yeah?'

'Scrambler.'

Skudder pressed a button on his telephone. You couldn't be too careful: nowadays you could eavesdrop on private conversations from half a mile away. He'd done it himself.

'Scrambler on,' he said.

'You sure?'

Skudder's pale, lashless eyes glinted with impatience. His bald head glistened. 'Course I'm sodding sure. Shoot.'

'There's been a leak,' said Castle nervously. 'The figures. The collateral on the loan. I've just had a mad old woman in here asking about your shares and she seems to know all about it.'

Skudder's naked eyelids flickered. 'What?'

'Everything. The real sales figures, orders, stock valuations, the loan. She thinks there's something dodgy going on. She asked me if I thought she should go to the police.'

'Fuck me!'

'I put her off, of course. Smoothed it over. But she's on to us, somehow. If anything goes wrong . . .'

'Who the hell is this old bag, then?' snarled Skudder. He cracked his knuckles. The sound was like pistol shots.

'Search me, Jace. One of your shareholders, she says, a Mrs Partridge.'

'Partridge?'

'Monica Partridge.'

'Never heard of her.'

'I've looked her up in the list of shareholders. She's there, all right, eight hundred shares, an address out in the sticks.'

'Partridge. Jewish, you think? Sounds like a yid. The bastards are everywhere.'

'She didn't look Jewish, Jace.'

'What's that mean, for God's sake?' snapped Skudder. 'They don't aw' walk round wiv long noses, you know. Some of them even look like peopoo. So how did she find out, for fuck's sake?'

'She wouldn't say. Very cagy about that. But someone's grassed and it has to be someone your end.'

'Bollocks. More likely to be your end.'

'Come off it, Jace. Are you mad? Nobody here knows a thing about it. I wouldn't last five minutes if they did.'

'Well, nobody here knows nuffing except me and . . .'

Gorman.

Yes.

Shane Gorman.

'And . . .'

Skudder thought about it. Shadows lurked in the sockets of his eyes. 'Gorman.'

'It's got to be Gorman, then,' said Castle. 'It's obviously not you or me.'

Gorman? Never. Surely not. Not Shane Gorman. Never.

'I'm going to have to call in the loan, Jace,' said Castle.

Skudder's face twisted with anger. 'You what?'

'You've got to repay the loan. Now. Before it all goes pear-shaped. If they know how over-exposed you are . . .'

'And how the hell am I meant to do that?' he snarled.

'Look, Jace, I don't care how you do it but I'm giving you just twenty-four hours to repay that loan. I haven't got any alternative. If you can't do it by this time tomorrow then I've got to report to Head Office that we no longer have enough collateral to cover our loan to you.'

'Oh no you don't, sunshine.'

'What else can I do? Be reasonable. It's either that or I get the chop, and how's that going to help either of us? Don't you see? My bloody neck's on the line if this gets out. Turning a blind eye to your cash-flow deficit? I wouldn't last five minutes.'

'Come off it, you bastard. You're not just going to dump me like that. I need more time. Renegotiate the loan wiv someone else.'

'For God's sake, Jace, the shit could hit the fan at any minute and I'm the one—'

Skudder's eyelids flickered. 'We're in this together, sunshine. I need at least three days. Gimme four.'

'No, I—'

'Four days,' snarled Skudder, 'otherwise we go down Shit Creek together.'

'Oh, God.'

Skudder laughed sourly. 'Just 'cos the scrambler's on, mate,' he said, 'it don't mean the tape-recorder ain't.'

He slammed the receiver down.

He cracked the knuckles of both hands.

He pressed the button on his intercom. 'Get Gorman in here,' he barked, 'pronto.'

Shane Gorman breezed into Skudder's office with all the cheerful bonhomie of a man who was about to attend his mother-in-law's funeral. 'You wanted me, chief?' he piped in his little falsetto voice.

'Too fucking right I do,' said Skudder.

Gorman looked wary: it appeared that the mother-in-law was about to sit up in her coffin.

Skudder was wearing his red bow-tie and matching waistcoat. That was never a good sign, the red bow-tie. Skudder wore the red bow-tie only when he was feeling especially rabid.

Skudder stared at him. 'You been blabbin', Gorman? About us and the bank?'

'Blabbin'? Course not.'

'About the sales figures? Exports?'

'Never.'

Skudder stared at him. His eyes were cold with suspicion. He punched his right fist into the palm of his left hand with a sickening smack. Gorman closed his eyes. He felt weak. Any minute now he was going to have another attack of the pulpytations.

'Someone's been blabbin',' said Skudder. 'Somebody's on to us. Castle's calling in the loan. He's shit-scared. He's running around like a chicken with its 'ead cut orf. So who's been blabbin'?'

'Not me, Jyce. Honest.'

A black expression drifted across Skudder's gleaming brow. His eyes simmered with disbelief. He jabbed a bony finger at Gorman. 'Don't yer start playing "silly buggers" wiv *me*, Sonny Jim,' he said, twitching his fingers in the air like quotation marks. 'There's only free of us what knows about the sales figures and the bank loan and one of us has been blabbin' and it ain't me.'

Gorman looked frightened. 'It must be Castle, then, what's 'pilled the bees,' he squeaked. 'I never trusted Castle. Honest, Jyce, it weren't me. I ain't not told no one nuffin'. My lips is healed.'

Skudder glared at him. He shifted in his chair. He cracked his knuckles.

Gorman flinched.

Skudder glowered at him. 'You sure you didn't blab it out some time when you was pissed?' he said.

'Who, me?'

'Yes, you, Turd Features,' snarled Skudder. 'You're always pissed these days. If you been blabbin' when you was pissed . . .'

Gorman grovelled. 'It weren't me, Jyce, honest,' he twittered. 'Scouse honour. Cross me 'ark and 'ope to die. I wouldn't do nuffin' like that.'

Skudder pinned him with his eyes. 'You better be telling the troof,' he said, 'or I'll have yer guts for braces.'

'I am, Jyce, honest. Would I lie to you?'

'You'd lie to yer granny if it suited you, yer little toe-rag.'

'Not you, Jyce,' trilled Gorman. 'We're old mates, in't we, me an' you?'

Skudder sneered. 'Mates? Don't make me laugh. Whatever gave you that idea? I'm the managin' d'rector and you're just the sales manager, and doncha ever forget it. And you better keep your sodding mouf shut, or else. Nah sod off. I'm busy. And if I fine you been lyin' to me . . .'

Skudder cracked his knuckles again. 'Sod off,' he said.

On the Friday morning Melody Canter was sitting at her desk outside Skudder's office, chewing gum and filing her long pink fingernails, when the two uniformed policewomen arrived.

The security guard sitting outside Skudder's door leaped to attention with a look of alarm. He wore the expression of a man who has perhaps had rather too many encounters himself with the law over the years.

'This Skudder's office?' said the shorter policewoman. 'Jason Skudder?'

Melody nodded. 'Yeah, but 'e's in a meetin'.'

'Too bad. We need to see him. Urgent.'

Melody looked nervous. *Police?* She reached for the intercom.

The shorter policewoman put out a hand to restrain her. 'No, don't call him,' she said. 'We don't want him doing a runner.'

Melody smiled apprehensively. 'So what can I do for you ladies?' she said.

'Oh, we ain't ladies,' said the taller policewoman.

The shorter one grinned grimly. 'No way,' she said. 'Never.'

She unclipped a pair of handcuffs from her belt. 'We'll go in, then.'

''E said not to disturb 'im,' Melody stammered.

The shorter one smiled sourly. 'It's a bit late for that.'

'He should have thought of that before,' said the taller one, 'before he started being a naughty boy.'

'But . . . 'e's in a meetin'. 'E's got aw' the 'eads of department, like.'

The policewomen looked at each other and nodded. 'All the better, then,' said the taller one. 'It's always best to have some witnesses.'

The policewomen approached Skudder's door. The security guard stood uncertainly in front of it.

'Move,' snapped the taller policewoman, 'or I'll have you an' all. It's an offence to obstruct police officers in the course of their duty.'

He stood aside, opening the door for them, standing back.

There were five men and two women with Skudder in his office: Gorman, Donaldson, Frobisher, Prendergast and the other heads of department. They were sitting in a circle in front of Skudder's desk like infants in a kindergarten. Skudder himself was wearing a blue and black striped bow-tie and matching blue and black braces, and was striding up and down in front of them, waving his arms, haranguing them. The neon lighting glinted off his naked skull, casting hollow shadows beneath his cheeks. His eyes had almost sunk out of sight. Their sockets were like dark caves.

'It's not fuckin' good enough!' he was saying, swaggering in front of them and slapping the palm of his hand with his fist. 'If you don't all "pull your fucking fingers out" some heads are gonna roll and that's a promise.' He twitched his fingers. 'There are too many sodding passengers in this place, too many lazy bastards what are not "pulling their weight".'

He turned, disturbed by the opening of the door.

'Mel!' he bellowed. 'I fought I said I weren't to be disturbed.'

The two policewomen came into the room. They advanced towards him, the shorter one with her handcuffs dangling loose from her left hand.

Skudder's pale face turned a thin yellow in the neon light. The flesh seemed to fall off the bones of his skull. His eyelids flickered like a lizard's.

'Skudder?' said the taller policewoman. 'Jason Skudder?'

'No,' he said in a weak voice. 'No, I can . . .'

The policewomen advanced towards him.

'You're *not* Jason Skudder? I must warn you that . . .'

He cleared his throat. It sounded like a digger shifting gravel. 'Yes, yes, I'm Jason Skudder. I just meant . . . I can explain everyfing.'

He raised his hands in supplication, the palms facing towards them. He stepped back a couple of paces as though in retreat. He licked his lips.

'It were all Dean Castle's fault,' he said. 'The bank manager. He made me do it. I can explain everyfing.'

His eyes flickered. The heads of department sat rigid in their seats, not daring to blink.

'I never knew it were illegal,' said Skudder.

The shorter policewoman frowned. 'Dean Castle?' she said. 'Who's he?'

A moment of hope flickered across Skudder's face. So they didn't know everything, then: not yet, anyway. In that case he could probably do a deal with them, come to some sort of compromise, turn Queen's Evidence, give them Castle, give them Gorman, in exchange for a light sentence for himself.

'Perhaps we should talk about this "in private",' said Skudder, twitching his fingers. 'Down at the station, p'raps.'

'What the hell are you talking about?' said the taller WPC. 'It's not you we want. It's Donaldson.'

Eh?

'James Angus Robbie Donaldson,' she said. 'Your legal director.'

Not me! They're not after me at all! They want Jim Donaldson! 'He's there,' said Skudder swiftly, jabbing his finger towards Donaldson sitting in the middle of the row of heads of department. 'That one, 'im there; the one wiv the poncy specs. 'Ere, Donaldson, what you been up to, then? You been misbehavin', then? Dippin' yer fingers in the till, eh?'

Donaldson stood up. 'Certainly not.' He turned towards the policewomen. 'What's this all about?'

'James Donaldson?' said the shorter WPC.

'Yes.'

'James Angus Robbie Donaldson?'

'That's me.'

She flourished a document. 'James Angus Robbie Donaldson, I have here a warrant for you undressed. You are not obliged to say anything but everything will be taken down and may be used in evidence against you.'

'What on earth are you talking about?' said Donaldson.

The heads of department seemed to be frozen in their seats. Melody and the security man hovered nervously in the doorway, mesmerised.

'Hooray!' cried the smaller policewoman, grabbing Donaldson's tie and beginning to undo it.

'Surprise, surprise!' cried the larger policewoman, starting to unbutton his shirt.

'Get off!' said Donaldson, trying to push them away.

The smaller WPC hurled away his tie and reached for his belt.

'No!' bellowed Donaldson. 'Help!'

'Here!' said Skudder. 'What's going on?'

A gasp came from the heads of department. Somebody sniggered.

Simon Frobisher giggled. 'It's a strippergram!' he said. 'They're not the police at all, they're strippers.'

'Strippers?' roared Skudder. 'In my fucking office? In the middoo of a meeting?'

'Surprise, surprise!' trilled the girls, prancing around Skudder's desk, unbuttoning their uniforms, tossing their caps aside, their jackets, skirts, blouses, stripping down to their underwear, suspender belts and black fishnet stockings.

'Fuck off out of it!' bellowed Skudder. 'Fucking scrubbers. Here, guard! Security! Get them out of here!'

'This is an outrage,' spluttered Donaldson, stepping back, fastening his belt, buttoning up his shirt. 'How dare you break into this office? This is trespass. Assault and battery. Public indecency.'

'Security!' chuntered Skudder. 'Guard! Guard! Where's that flaming security guy?'

The strippergram women began to sing, dancing around Donaldson as they did so: 'Happy birthday to you, happy birthday to you, happy birthday, dear Jimmy, happy birthday to you.'

'Get those fat old slappers outta here!' bellowed Skudder.

The strippers clapped as they sang, circling Donaldson as he tried to tuck his shirt in, his face turning crimson.

'Forty-five today, forty-five today, he's got the key of the door, never been forty-five before . . .'

'Fordy-five?' said Skudder. His eyes swivelled like billiard balls. 'Fordy-five?' he said, nosing the air like a hunting dog.

'Forty-five today, forty-five today . . .'

The security man grabbed one of the strippers by the arm and twisted it behind her back.

'Oi!' she yelped.

Donaldson and Frobisher seized the other girl.

'Leggo!' she squawked. 'It's only a bit of fun. Leave off!'

'Get those old tarts outta here,' bellowed Skudder, waving his arm like a tic-tac man. 'Ring the pleece. Bring charges. Frow the book at them.'

Prendergast retrieved the bits of discarded police uniform and they bundled the women out of Skudder's office, hustling them out to the lift.

'Here, leave off!'

'Not so rough!'

'Where's your sense of humour?'

'Bunch of poofs, the lot of yer.'

Their voices gradually dwindled beyond Melody's office, fading as they were frogmarched down the corridor, growing fainter as they disappeared towards the lifts.

Skudder was breathing heavily. He smoothed his bald head with his fingers. He paced up and down behind his desk, brushing his waistcoat with his hands. He straightened his bow-tie. He tweaked at his braces, just to be on the safe side. His fingers twitched. His mind boiled. *Stone me, that were close! One minute later and I would of told them everyfink. Donaldson! It were aw' Donaldson's fault. Just a few more seconds and I might of confessed everyfink.*

Skudder glared at the heads of department. They had resumed their seats and sat again in a semi-circle in front of his desk, as meek as waxwork dummies.

Donaldson had made him look a fool. Donaldson had very nearly jeopardised everything. And Donaldson was forty-five: over the hill, past it.

'Stand up, Donaldson,' he snapped.

'Me?'

'Is there anyone else here called Donaldson?'

'No.'

'So who the fuck d'yer fink I mean, then?'

Donaldson stood. The silence was as brittle as a frosty morning.

Skudder stared at Donaldson. He cracked his knuckles. 'You're a disgrace,' said Skudder.

Donaldson raised his eyebrows. 'Sorry?'

'Yer bought the company into dispute,' snapped Skudder.

'What?'

'You're guilty of gross misconduct, Donaldson.'

'I beg your pardon?'

'Insuborduration.'

'Come again?'

Skudder smacked his palm with his fist and then counted his fingers. 'One, bringing them old slappers in here. Two, letting them cavort about wiv no bleeding cloves on. Free, lettin' them disrupt an' heads of department meeting. Four, making me look a laughing shmuck. That's unforgivaboo.'

'But I didn't—'

'You're sacked,' said Skudder.

'I'm what?'

Skudder's eyes glinted. 'Don't you not speak no English no more, sunshine? I said you're sacked. Fired. Axed. Dismissed. Discharged. Let go. Laid orf. "Booted out." Given the bullet. The push. The chop. The heave-ho. "Yer marchin' orders." OK? Got it now, skipper?'

Donaldson shook his head. 'You can't do that.'

'I can. I have.'

Donaldson gave his lazy, superior, lawyer's smile. 'You can't, you know. I've got a contract, a two-year—'

'Not any more you don't, sunshine. Gross misconduct, insuborduration, bringing the company into dispute. That's sackable offences wivout compensation free times over.'

Nobody dared to breathe.

Skudder leered. His grin resembled the smile of an undertaker. 'Oh, yeah,' he said, 'and many happy returns of the day.'

CHAPTER 13

Unlucky for Some

Three days later, on the Monday morning, Jim Donaldson strode confidently into the chairman's office on the forty-eighth floor of the Group's towering headquarters in the heart of the City, swinging his briefcase and humming a little tune. As he crossed the thick white carpet high in the sky he felt as if he were walking on cloud. That little shit Skudder was not going to get away with sacking him just like that. No way: Donaldson knew enough about Skudder to have him out on his ear before the sun went down. And who were they likely to appoint to take Skudder's place as managing director?

Donaldson smirked.

Who else?

The chairman looked grim. He waved Donaldson towards a chair beside his desk.

'Morning, Willie,' said Donaldson brightly.

'No, it's bloody not,' said Mulliken. 'It's a bloody awful morning. It's a stinking mess. I've just seen the true figures. How the hell could Skudder have run the company into the ground so quickly?'

Donaldson crossed one pinstriped leg over the other and gave a tight little smile. 'Because he's completely incompetent,' he said. 'And because he's also paranoid he got rid of all the really talented and experienced people so that they wouldn't show him up. He fired so many key people that he was left with hardly anyone who knew what they were doing. He seemed to think that anyone who was any good was a threat to him, so he sacked them.'

Mulliken fixed him with a meaningful stare. 'He kept you on,' he said.

Donaldson looked uncomfortable. 'Well, he didn't get rid of *everyone* who was any good.'

Mulliken grunted. 'You say you've got more evidence of misbehaviour by Skudder?'

'Lots.'

'Like?'

Donaldson snapped open his briefcase and retrieved a sheaf of papers. 'Not only was he fiddling the figures and lying to you and the board and in cahoots with the bank manager, he was also using the identical collateral in the company to borrow money to pay himself bonuses to buy himself shares.'

'But that's . . .'

Donaldson nodded, pleased with himself. This would crucify the little bastard. This would teach Skudder to meddle with him.

'And that's not all. He was up to his neck in hypothecation, he was using standby letters of credit and he was piggybacking his own private investments on the back of the company's investments.'

Donaldson handed the file across Mulliken's desk. Mulliken opened it and began to flick through the papers. Donaldson allowed himself a little smile. That stuff would sink Skudder once and for all. That would put his bow-tie into a final fatal spin. It might even send him to prison for a couple of years. How dare Skudder try to sack him, the jumped-up little swine?

Mulliken scanned several sheets of paper, looking increasingly horrified. Donaldson experienced a warm glow of satisfaction. They would surely promote him after this. There would surely be a fat bonus, a salary increase, the top job at last. Who else was left who could do it?

'When the company's collateral began to go down the tubes,' said Donaldson, 'even the bank manager eventually refused to lend Skudder any more, not even to finance raw materials, so Skudder started paying for them by using standby letters of credit, which he got from some dodgy financier who'd been involved with Robert Maxwell years ago.'

Mulliken frowned. He shook his head. 'God, what a nightmare,' he said.

'He was siphoning cash off the pension fund. He was piggybacking his own cash on the back of the company's investments so that he could increase his own rate of interest and buy more shares in the company. He was giving himself thousands of unjustified share options. And he was planning to sell all his shares just before the next audit so that he could make a killing before anyone realised the true situation and the value of the shares collapsed.'

'Bloody hell, Jim. How long have you known about this?'

'A couple of months, maybe three.'

'So why didn't you blow the whistle on him weeks ago?'

Donaldson looked shifty. 'I wasn't sure you'd believe me. Well, he was your appointment . . .'

'The bank's.'

'Well, yes.'

'The Millennium head-hunted him for us, as you know, but that's no reason to let Skudder wreak havoc on the company for so long. You should have come to me yourself, long before this.'

'I thought I needed more evidence to convince you.'

Mulliken fixed him with a beady stare. 'Are you saying it's *my* fault?'

'Good God, no, of course not . . .'

'How much more evidence did you need? The man is patently a crook. He's been robbing us blind for months.'

Donaldson said nothing.

'You were accumulating evidence for so long that the company nearly went bust?'

'I was about to come to you any day.'

'Too bloody late, Jim. You should have come to me long ago.'

Donaldson bristled. 'Well, why didn't anyone else do anything about it? Why didn't *you* do something about it?'

Mulliken looked aggrieved. 'I've got half a dozen companies to run, Donaldson, not just one. And do you know how many other boards I'm on? Seven. Yes, seven. I can't be expected to know precisely what's going on in every piddling little corner of every one of them. That's what I pay people like you for. To keep your eyes open. To blow the whistle.'

Donaldson took a deep breath. Now was the time to be bold, to show Mulliken that he had leadership qualities. 'Come on, Willie, you knew things weren't right. Peter Hallam told you for a start, months ago, nearly a year ago.'

Mulliken frowned. 'Hallam . . .'

'Yes. But you wouldn't listen.'

Mulliken nodded slowly. He was thinking. 'Good man, Hallam. I'm sorry about him. What happened to him? We should have protected him.' He looked up suddenly. 'Hear his wife's moved in with you.'

Donaldson looked at him defiantly. 'Yes.'

'You were friends, I seem to remember.'

'Once.'

Mulliken shook his head. 'Don't approve of that sort of thing,' he said curtly. 'Colleague's wife. Friend. Bad form. Messy business. Shows lack of judgement.' Mulliken brooded. 'Skudder's out, of course,' he said. 'I shall dismiss him today.'

Donaldson simpered.

Mulliken stared at him.

Here it comes, thought Donaldson, *the top job at last.*

'And so are you,' said Mulliken.

'What?'

'Out.'

'Me? Out?'

'Yes.'

'But I'm the one who—'

Mulliken grunted. 'Come on, Donaldson, you should never have let things get to this stage. You really should have come to me weeks ago. We might have been able to limit the damage if you had. As it is, the company is in deep clag. It's going to need a serious rescue operation and that's going to mean a completely fresh start.'

'That's bloody unfair. I bring you all the ammunition you need to get rid of Skudder and you reward me by sacking me too.'

Mulliken sighed. 'But you were the legal director. You knew that Skudder was behaving illegally. By failing to blow the whistle on him you were guilty of gross dereliction of duty. You could almost be accused of aiding and abetting, of being an accomplice.'

'Come off it, Willie. These things go on all over the place. The City's full of dodgy characters like Skudder, they just don't get found out.'

'They do if they nearly destroy their companies.'

Donaldson gave a sour laugh. 'Oh, that's great. So immoral behaviour is OK as long as it makes a profit?'

'I didn't say that.'

'You didn't have to.'

Mulliken closed the file and placed it in a drawer in his desk.

Donaldson held out his hand. 'I'll have that back, thank you,' he said.

'No.'

'Yes. It's my property.'

Mulliken folded his arms. 'No, it's not. It's company property and it's evidence, but it's not the sort of evidence that we can afford to let fall into the wrong hands, like the hands of the police.'

Donaldson held his hand out again. 'Hand it over, please, Willie. It's my dossier. I put it all together.'

'You put it together as an employee of the company, for which you have been very highly paid. You have now brought it to me, and on behalf of the company I have relieved you of it.'

'Give it back, Willie. It's my bargaining counter.'

Mulliken raised his eyebrows. 'Bargaining? You're in no position to bargain about anything.'

'What a shit you are.'

'I don't think this is getting us anywhere.'

'Oh, yes, it is. It's going to get us into court. If you persist in trying to sack me I'm going to sue you, Willie. You can't get rid of a loyal old employee just like that, a director. Not any more, you can't. This isn't the eighties.'

'That would be very foolish,' said Mulliken. 'Think of all the dirt that would come out – your collaboration with Skudder, your failure to blow the whistle on him. It would do your reputation no good at all. You'd never work in the City again.'

He stared at Donaldson. 'Oh, don't worry,' he said, with the trace of a sneer. 'I'll make sure you get a nice fat pay-off. You won't go hungry. It's only the inoffensive little guys who get booted out without a penny. The shits and the incompetents ride off into the sunset with bags full of gold, just to keep their mouths shut. Don't worry, you'll get your bunce. So what shall we call it? Redundancy? Early retirement? Moving on to seek fresh challenges?'

'That's not good enough.'

Mulliken gave him a cold smile. 'Well, it's all there is,' he said, 'unless you're foolish enough to make a nuisance of yourself, in which case there will be nothing and you will have to risk a fortune taking us all the way to the High Court.' He waved a hand at Donaldson. 'And now I've got things to see to,' he said. 'Skudder, for one. Count yourself fortunate. I'm not going to give Skudder a penny.'

'You're a bastard, Willie.'

Mulliken smiled. 'Of course I am. How else would I have got where I am today?'

Hallam, thought Mulliken. *Of course. Peter Hallam. The very man. The only one of them with the balls to stand up and speak out right from the start. Hallam, who else?*

'I've made a terrible mistake,' said Jenny. She stared at Hallam with a beggar's eyes. 'I realise that now. I want to come back. Can you ever forgive me? Please forgive me. I'd like to come back.'

They were in the coffee shop where he had taken to meeting Susie regularly. Jenny's eyes were as dark as storm clouds, swollen with unshed tears. She looked much older, weary, disillusioned. She looked like a stranger. Twenty-five years between them, two children, a million memories, and now they were nothing.

'Jim doesn't love me,' she said. 'I thought he did.'

She looked furtive as she said Donaldson's name, glancing quickly at Hallam and then away again, as though she had uttered an obscenity. *Jim*. Odd, that, he thought: once the sound of Donaldson's name had burned a hole in his heart, lighting a blaze of jealousy, yet now it was nothing to him. *Jim:* it was just another name and a rather silly one, at that, as though it were sort of unfinished.

She played nervously with her coffee spoon, twiddling it between her fingers, turning it over and over.

'He never really loved me, I know that now,' she said, 'not like you did.' She looked at him again. 'Not like you.'

Monica had been brutal on the telephone: 'She only wants to come back to you because he's lost his job and he's got huge debts. His wife's divorcing him and even though he's getting a big pay-off the irony is that the bigger it is the more he'll have to give his wife. She's also demanding the house, most of his insurance policies, half his pension and huge amounts of maintenance. And he can't pay her off by selling his house because of the collapse in the market. Nobody's buying houses at the moment. Peter, I know Jenny only too well and so do you. She's got no balls, she runs away from trouble. That's why she left you and that's why she wants to come back. I'm sorry to have to say it about my own daughter, but if you ever hit another bad patch she'd be off again.'

'Mummy's frightened,' Susie had told him. 'He's started shouting at her. She cries.'

Jenny was toying compulsively with the handle of the coffee cup. Her fingers were trembling. 'I'll get a job,' she said. 'I'll help, I promise. I won't be a burden.'

She looked at him with a desperate hope. He could not bear the vulnerability of her eyes, the knowledge that she was prepared to accept any sort of indignity. 'Please, Peter,' she said. 'Please, darling. I don't know what came over me. I'm so ashamed of myself. I always loved you. Always. Please.'

It would have been so easy to say yes: to hold her tight, to kiss her brow, savouring that long-beloved perfume of her hair, to taste her lips again. But it would have been too easy: the coward's way. It would have been dishonest. How could they lie to each other like that? Everything had changed and nothing could be the same again.

I just don't love her any more, he thought, and pity is no substitute for love. To pity her would be an insult.

To take her back just like that would be a betrayal of what

they had had before. Forgiveness cannot be switched on and off like electricity. A year ago he would have taken her back without any hesitation, with joy, with relief, but now he was no longer the man he had been. Jenny had changed him. Jenny's betrayal had created someone else. Even the sound of her name no longer tore his heart.

'I can't, Jen,' he said. 'I'm sorry.'

She stared at him, her eyes so sad and old, so bruised, the misery spilling down her cheeks in tears of regret at the waste of it all. He wanted to take her hand in his but he dared not for fear of giving her false hope. He must not lie to her. That would be the cruellest thing of all. At least this monstrous year had spawned a brutal honesty.

'You nearly destroyed me,' he said.

'Oh, God.'

He nodded. 'I very nearly went under. I came so close that it terrifies me to think of it. I'm never going to take the risk again.'

She wept properly then, great racking sobs, head bowed, shoulders shaking. The other customers glanced across and looked away, embarrassed.

Dear God, the things we do to each other.

The kindest thing he could do for her now was to force her to stand on her own feet, to take responsibility for her life. She was still only forty-two, after all. 'I'm so ashamed of myself,' she had said – but what was shame except just another self-indulgence? Shame is no substitute for pride. For too long she had depended on others: she needed now to stand up straight, alone. And then . . . one day . . . perhaps . . .

Except that he knew it would never happen. 'She's got no balls,' said Monica, and Monica was right as usual. Jenny would go back to Donaldson and spend the rest of her life with him in a silent cocoon hollow with regret. What a terrible revenge: that Donaldson and Jenny should now be shackled to each other for life, condemned to make each other miserable, unable to escape; poetic justice, perhaps, yet he felt no sense of triumph, only a deep emptiness. He looked at her, that face he had loved so much, and felt nothing. He mourned for himself, for that part of him that was gone. The death of love is as tragic as death itself.

'I'm sorry, Jen,' he said. 'I'm so very sorry.'

Jason Skudder was wearing a dark three-piece suit and a pink bow-tie when he entered the chairman's penthouse office on the forty-eighth floor of the Group's headquarters in the heart of the City.

He swaggered into Mulliken's office with a confident smile. His teeth glinted. His bald head gleamed with credibility.

'Don't bother to sit,' said Mulliken. 'This won't take more than a minute.'

Skudder sat. He crossed his legs and smiled.

'I said, don't bother to sit, Skudder.'

'Nah,' said Skudder. 'It's aw' just a misunderstanding, Mr Chairman. I can explain everyfink.'

'I doubt that very much,' said Mulliken.

'Froo the chair, then, Mr Chairman,' said Skudder, looking trustworthy, 'it's them bank loans what's bothering you, innay?'

'Among other things.'

Skudder spread his hands wide and smiled broadly. 'Froo the chair, Mr Chairman, there's nuffink dodgy about them. Not at aw'. Me and the bank manager just fought it were in the interest of the company to tell a few "fibs" about the collateroo for the loans.'

'A few *fibs*?'

'Yeah, a bit of the economicals wiv the troof, see. We fought it were better to massage the figures a bit to keep the company going till fings improved rather than tell peopoo we was in trouboo.' He twitched his fingers. 'We was only being sorta "economicoo wiv the actuality", like the geezer said.'

'Let's get this straight,' said Mulliken grimly. 'You've sacked almost every one of the most talented and experienced members of staff. Consequently the company is a shambles and sales have fallen by nearly twenty per cent in a year. To cover your incompetence you've been fiddling the books, lying to me and the board, deceitfully using company collateral twice over to cover private as well as company loans, giving yourself unjustified bonuses and share options, raiding the pension fund, piggybacking your private investments, resorting to standby letters of credit and doing God knows what else that we have yet to discover and you still have the gall to say that you did it all in the interest of the company. Is that right?'

'Well, I wouldn't put it quite like that, skipper,' said Skudder.

'I bet you wouldn't.'

'I never done the pensions fund for starters.'

Mulliken treated him to a grim smile. 'Hear this, Skudder: you're sacked, as of this minute. You're sacked without a penny, for gross misconduct, for criminal negligence, for abuse of office, for anything else you care to imagine, and if you try to make a fuss about it the whole file goes straight to the police. I am tempted to send them the file in any case, except that it would do the company an immense amount of damage if you were prosecuted and if it were revealed that our managing director was a crook.'

Skudder grinned. His pale, greasy skin was stretched tight across the bones of his skull. He leaned back casually in his chair and clasped his fingers behind his head. 'You can't do that,' he said. 'You're out of order, Mr Chairman.'

'Oh, yes?' said Mulliken. 'Watch me. And you will not return to the office after this interview either, Skudder.

You've done enough damage already without being allowed a chance to do any more. I have given instructions that you are not to be allowed back into the building. Your personal effects will be sent on to you – after they have been screened by the security staff.'

Skudder smiled. 'Froo the chair, Mr Chairman, on a point of order, but I got a free-year rolling contract.'

'You'll get a three-year rolling prison sentence if you're not careful.'

Skudder chuckled. It sounded like sewage gurgling underground. He shook his head. 'Nah, I don't fink so,' he said. 'You see, I can prove that everyfink what I done were done wiv your agreement.'

'What are you talking about?'

'I kept you fully informed of everything what went on. Course I did.'

'You did nothing of the kind.'

Skudder nodded. 'I sent you aw' the documents, Mr Chairman, aw' the memos. I done nuffink wivout your permission.'

'You're mad, Skudder. Now get out.'

Skudder leaned forward. His eyes glittered. The bones of his skull jutted like tombstones. 'I got copies of everyfink,' he said, 'and I got two secketries and a sales manager what'll give me sworn affidavids that I consulted you on everyfink and you give your approval. Anyfink I done you done too.'

He sat back and smiled. 'Froo the chair, Mr Chairman, course.'

Mulliken stared at him.

Bluff. It had to be. Of course. Any decent counsel would destroy Skudder's 'evidence' in half an afternoon. A couple of silly young secretaries and a junior executive? A decent QC would slaughter them.

But think of the expense of a court case, the distractions,

the time wasted, the damage to the company and its reputation. Months of hassle, argument, suspicion. And some people would believe that Skudder was telling the truth. There were always people who preferred to believe lies, especially in the City. How could he *prove* that Skudder was lying? 'No smoke without fire,' people would say knowingly. 'Always thought that Mulliken was a bit too smooth by half.'

'P'raps you was always too busy running aw' yer other companies,' said Skudder. 'P'raps you never had time to read aw' the stuff what I sent yer.'

He smirked.

The bastard's got me by the short and curlies.

'How much do you want?' said Mulliken.

Skudder smiled. His eyes skulked dark in their sockets. He cracked his knuckles. 'Fair's fair, Mr Chairman,' he said. 'I don't want no more than what's due under me contract. That's free years' pay. That's five hundred and twenty-five K.'

More than half a million pounds!

No, thought Mulliken. Never. Impossible. Over my dead body.

But how much would a court case cost? At least half a million, if all the preliminaries were dragged out for more than a couple of years, as they often were in a case like this. And what about the time and effort wasted trying to assemble evidence, combing through files, interviewing witnesses, meetings with lawyers, sworn statements? And all the people who might choose to believe Skudder rather than him . . .

And the man had a contract. It was there in black and white: three years' notice; a legal undertaking. This had nothing whatever to do with morality: this was the law, which was not the same thing at all.

Mulliken blenched. 'Very well,' he said. 'I shall instruct

Halliday to send you a cheque as soon as possible in exchange for a signed legal undertaking never to reveal any of this to anyone and I mean anyone.'

Skudder gave a broad smile. Something glinted in the cavern of his mouth.

'Ex'lent!' he said.

He's going to get away with it, thought Mulliken bitterly. I've got no option. But at least Dean Castle has been punished properly: Castle is being banished to run the Millennium Bank's branch in Zaïre. At least there's some justice in the world.

'Tell me, Skudder,' said Mulliken, 'is it true that Castle's your brother-in-law?'

'So what if he is?'

'So it *is* true.'

'Yeah, he married me sister. Got her up the duff.'

'So that's why Castle recommended you for the job, because you're his brother-in-law.'

Skudder raised his chin defiantly. 'So what's wrong wiv that, eh? We was old school-mates.'

'You and Castle went to school together?'

'Yeah, Eton.'

'*Eton?* Good God!'

'Never fought it were up to much, meself. We called it Slough Comprehensive.'

'You went to *Eton*? So why do you talk like a yob?'

Skudder's eyes narrowed. 'Wotcha mean?'

'Why don't you speak properly if you went to Eton?'

Skudder frowned. 'Here, moosh! I do talk proper, same as what everyone else do. It's only a few old wrinklies and crumblies like you what talk aw' snooty. Your day's over, mate. Your time's up. You're finished. It's us what's in charge now. The Peopoo.' He snapped his fingers.

'God help us all,' said Mulliken.

Skudder stood to go. 'Just one more fing, skipper. The

public announcement. We both say I'm leaving at my request, OK? I'm leaving for "postures new" and to find "exciting new challenges", yeah?' He twitched his fingers.

'Sod off, Skudder,' said Mulliken, 'and I very much hope that you get yours one day.'

Skudder laughed. 'I wouldn't bank on it, sunshine,' he said. 'I wouldn't bank on it at aw. *Ack-ack-ack-ack-ack*.'

When Skudder had swaggered out of his office Mulliken crossed the room to the drinks cabinet and poured himself a stiff whisky and soda. He needed it very badly indeed. He would have opened the window for some fresh air if that had been possible, but windows on the forty-eighth floor of skyscrapers in the heart of the City are sealed just in case there's another depression and tycoons are tempted to jump: you simply have to put up with the smell inside, however unsavoury it might be.

Three years' pay. Five hundred and twenty-five thousand pounds. It was shocking: insupportable; a thundering disgrace. But what was the alternative?

He took a hefty gulp of Scotch and buzzed his secretary.

'Get Peter Hallam for me, will you?'

Hallam: the obvious choice, staring him in the face. Why hadn't he ever thought of him before?

Lee Yeomans was sitting at his desk by the big front window of Boggitt, Burlap and Boggitt and writing the sales blurb for a house that was nearly falling down ('charming character property, needs some refurbishment') when Enoch Sheepshank telephoned him.

Sheepshank was not happy. 'We got squatters,' he said.

'Hell.'

'Yeah. Four of them. Two white layabouts and a couple of darkies.'

'Sod it!' said Yeomans.

'So how do we get them out? They've changed all the locks.'

'Did they break in? Was it breaking and entering?'

'Doesn't look like it. Can't see any damage.'

'Damn! They must have used a key. In that case, since it wasn't forcible entry, you've got to get a court order.'

'Shit! How long will that take, then?'

'It can take weeks, maybe months.'

Sheepshank's voice hinted at hysteria. 'There'll be nothing left of the place by then,' he said. 'They're trashing it already. There's several broken windows, the outside light's smashed and they've nailed what looks like floorboards over the doors. In the living room there are smoke marks all over the wall where they've lit a fire.'

'Bloody savages.'

'So how do I get a court order?'

'You have to make a court application, then there's a hearing before a Master in the High Court.'

'Sod that for a game of soldiers. How much is all that going to cost?'

'Lawyers, bailiffs – hundreds, maybe a grand or more.'

'Shit!'

'If all goes well the Master gives you an order to get them out. Then you've got to go through a complicated service procedure: you have to go very carefully by the rules laid down in something called the *White Book*. You have to do all the right things in the right order, otherwise you have to start all over again. The bailiffs go in and in theory the squatters have to get out and leave quietly. That's in theory. If they resist, then . . . well, that's best not thought of, really.'

'Bloody hell.' Sheepshank's voice rose. He sounded panicky. 'I can't hang around for months before I sell the place. I need to sell it soon. I can't afford to keep the loan going much longer. You said we'd be able to sell it quickly.'

'I'm sorry, Knockers, but the market's collapsed. It's all

changed in the last few weeks. People just aren't buying at the moment.'

Sheepshank exploded. 'But we're going to lose all our profit on the place at this rate. What's wrong with the bloody law, eh? It's trespass, isn't it? Just walking into someone else's property and taking it over? That's plain theft, isn't it? So how do they get away with it?'

'Crooks everywhere,' said Yeomans. 'It's shocking.'

'How can people just break the law and get away with it?'

'Search me. Happens all the time. Bent buggers everywhere.'

'What makes it worse is one of them's Hallam's son.'

'What?'

'Hallam. The geezer we bought the place off. His son is one of the squatters.'

'No!'

'Yes: ugly bugger, hairy. Wears a fur coat and a curtain ring in his ear. Ought to have a bone through his nose. I recognised him when I looked through the window. Dirty, too. The place already smells like a polecat's shithouse. By the time we've got them out of the place we'll have to have it repaired and repainted and fumigated and we'll be lucky to make any profit on it at all.'

'Hallam!'

'So much for you saying "we'll make a killing out of this, this sucker Hallam is desperate to sell."'

'Well, he was, wasn't he? We got the place for peanuts, didn't we? I didn't know this was going to happen.'

'You told me he was a mug,' snapped Sheepshanks.

'Yes, it's terrible,' said Yeomans sadly. 'You can't trust no one nowadays.'

Matthew Hallam locked the door of the squat behind him, shouted to Ben to jam the floorboards back across it, and caught a bus into town to sign on for the dole. It was almost like a club down there at the Job Centre: they were all there, the usual crowd, the Fs to Js, queuing as always for the eight windows and shuffling forward every minute or two to sign the forms asserting that they were unemployed, that they had earned nothing at all in the previous two weeks and had spent hours every day looking for work and applying for jobs. It was all lies, of course, and everyone knew it, from the clerks behind the windows to the supervisors in the little offices behind. Joe Greenfield over there, for instance, ran a very successful little business as a window-cleaner but had been collecting the dole for years. Fred Iliffe was a free-lance plumber, Mike Johnson a carpenter, Rachel Kenton a part-time whore in a massage parlour. The shortest queue stood at the ninth window, on the far right, where a few honest souls declared that they had indeed earned something during the previous fortnight and that therefore they were not entitled to unemployment benefit. Everyone else in the room thought they were idiots.

Standing a few places in front of Matthew in the same queue was Sharon Jennings, the Job Centre clerk. He did a double-take. Sharon? Queuing up for the dole? What on earth was she doing here? She was usually behind one of the windows up front and bellowing at one of the unem-ployed. Now she was shuffling forward with the rest of them, hefty and resentful in an anorak decorated with a red Aids ribbon. She was wearing a T-shirt with the somewhat confusing slogan FUCK MEN and a lethal-looking pair of black bovver boots.

Wicked. Sharon the dole clerk in the queue for the dole herself.

'Here, Shar,' said Matthew.

She turned and glared at him. 'Wotcha want?' she said.

'What are you doing here? In the queue?'

'Mind yer own naffin' business.'

'You on the dole yourself, then, Shar?'

'What if I am, hey? What's it got to do with you?'

'You've lost your job, then?'

She made a sound that resembled the growl of a Rottweiler. She turned away.

'But they never sack civil servants,' said Matt. 'Civil servants have got a job for life.'

She turned back towards him, baring her teeth. 'Not any more,' she snarled. 'They changed the rules, didn't they?'

'So you've been sacked?'

She looked away. 'This old bitch called Monica Partridge come in here yesterday to say she wants to sign on . . .'

Monica! Signing on the dole?

'. . . and when she says she's seventy-two I tells her she's too naffin' old for the dole and to naff off down the income support but then she says, "Don't you talk to me in that tone of voice, young lady," and I says, "Don't you call me a lady, you old bag, and I'll talk to you any naffin' way I like," so she reports me to the supervisor and the supervisor says I been rude to clients once too often and I'm out. I never been rude to no one, least of all to that Partridge bitch, the old bag. If I ever see her again . . .'

Monica!

'She's my gran,' said Matthew, 'and a right old bitch she is, too.'

'I'm rather enjoying this revenge lark,' said Monica cheerfully. 'I think I might take it up as a career. I could get my own back on all sorts of people – traffic wardens, people who ride bikes on the pavement or drop litter in the street or let their dogs crap everywhere. That'd be a good one: you could post the dog turds through their letter-boxes. Or kids with ghetto-blasters. Or motorists who keep those awful red plastic charity noses on the front of their cars all the year round. Beggars who don't need to beg at all. Car alarms that howl all night. People who use mobile telephones in restaurants. Can you imagine what all those radio waves do to everyone else's food? And they complain about smokers. Grey Rage Rules! What do you think, Hank?'

The cactus seemed to consider the matter but it made no reply.

'Dad,' said Susie, 'now that you've got two bedrooms, can I move back in with you? Permanently? I hate living with Mum and Him. I hate the atmosphere there.'

Her eyes are so clear and eager, her love of life so open, her love for me so genuine. How can any man not love his daughter? But then how can any man not love his son as well? These things are mysteries. But I must make it up with Matt some day, somehow. All this will pass, and Matt and I will one day be friends again. He hugged her. 'Of course you can,' he said.

'You're the obvious choice, Peter,' said Mulliken. 'You're far and away the best candidate to clear up Skudder's mess.'

Hallam gazed beyond Mulliken's shoulder. It was a lovely summer day. High up here on the forty-eighth floor, beyond the thick plate-glass window, the sky was a deep blue, the clouds no more than wisps of cotton wool, the birds gliding free. Life was going on out there as though nothing whatever had happened. What happened in here had little to do with life.

'If anyone is going to turn sales around again it's you,' said Mulliken. 'You were always a brilliant sales manager.'

So why did you let Skudder get rid of me? Where were you when we all needed you?

'I must apologise,' said Mulliken. He looked humble. 'I treated you abominably when you came to see me to warn me about Skudder. I was unforgivably rude to you. I'm sorry. Please forgive me.'

Hallam shrugged. It no longer seemed to be of any importance. Somehow Skudder and Gorman and Mulliken himself had shrunk and had come to seem of little consequence. Mulliken, Skudder and Gorman: they sounded like a firm of dubious solicitors.

'I should have listened to you, Peter. I regret that deeply now. You were the only person in the entire place with the balls to stand up and be counted and we treated you disgracefully. I'm determined to make it up to you. But that's not why I'm offering you the top job. It's because you're undoubtedly the best man for it. The staff trusts you, too, Peter. I've taken soundings and they'd be right behind you all the way. So would I. And the board. We'd do everything we could to give you anything you need to turn the company around.'

Managing director. The top job. A swanky salary. A swanky car. The challenge, the excitement, the sense of achievement. It was something of which he had often dreamed when he was younger, when he had still allowed himself to dream. But now?

Do I really want all that? Yes. No. Maybe.

'We'd need an urgent renegotiation of the bank loan,' he said.

'Yes,' said Mulliken, 'I'm working on that already. Millennium are being extremely helpful. They're deeply embarrassed about what has happened. Dean Castle has been banished to the wilds of Zaïre. Let's hope the pygmies eat him.'

Hallam smiled. 'We'd need to restructure several departments. Change two or three of our usual suppliers – some of them always overcharged us, even in Andy Unwin's day.'

'Whatever you think is necessary.'

'We'd need to slim down some of the production process. It's unwieldy. And I'm sorry to say that I'd have to get rid of a few people.'

'Well, of course.'

'Some of the dead wood that Skudder brought in with him. There's a fellow called Gorman, the sales manager . . .'

'Whatever you say, Peter. You're the boss.'

'And I'd want George Pringle and Elsie Benson reinstated.'

'Who?'

'Two excellent old sales-department colleagues. Skudder sacked them for no reason at all.'

'Of course, whoever you want.'

'And Nathan Solomons. Asoke Gupta. And my old secretary Doreen Bailey, if she wants to come back. And half a dozen others.'

'You can have anyone you want. You have only to say.'

Anyone you want. The top job at last, after all these years, and a free hand, and now I'm not at all sure that I want it after all.

'I'm going to need forty-eight hours to make up my mind.'

'If it's money, Peter . . .'

'It's not money.'

'We were paying Skudder a hundred and seventy-five K a year.'

Hellfire. Hell's bells.

'We could go a bit higher if necessary.'

What would be the point? Most of it would probably end up in Jenny's pocket after the divorce. Even worse, it could end up in Donaldson's pocket.

'I'm not thinking about money. I need to go back, to get my bearings again. I need to look at the books and talk to the staff, meet some of the new people there. Skudder's new people. Take the pulse.'

'Of course. Good idea. Tomorrow?'

'Fine.'

'Nine o'clock?'

'Suits me.'

I'll telephone Rosie at the hotel and tell her that I need to take the day off work and I'll tell her why. I'll tell Rosie everything. She'll understand. She might even be proud of me.

'Excellent,' said Mulliken. 'My chauffeur will pick you up at nine o'clock. Prendergast is holding the fort at the office for the time being. I'll tell him to expect you.'

'Right.'

But do I really want this job? I'd be able to sack Shane Gorman. And that snooty little cow Melody Canter. And that bitch in Personnel, Skudder's disgusting girlfriend, what's-her-name, the one who took Fiona's place. And I could make Keith Smith up to sales manager. And promote some of the best of the youngsters – Mary Flanagan, Harry Forbes, Jemima Richards. It's all very well turning the clock back and reinstating some of the old members of staff but you have to look forward as well. The future depends in the end on the young. And by taking this job I could show that nice guys can win, sometimes, that the shits don't always get away with it. But do I really want it any more? Hallam rose to leave.

'We need you,' said Mulliken.

'I know,' said Hallam. *But do I still need you?*

Mulliken's chauffeur arrived at one minute to nine to drive Hallam to the office. It felt strange to be wafted through the streets in quiet luxury in the soft back seat of a limousine after so many months of travelling by foot and public transport. The real world seemed to be a distance away, as though he were separated from it by some invisible wall. Is this why presidents and prime ministers and chairmen of great companies so often lose touch with reality? If he did agree to do the job he would find himself travelling like this all the time. There would be no more commuting, no more pushing and shoving on buses and trains, no more elbowing through the crowds on the pavements, anonymous in the crush. He would be wafted off to work each day by a chauffeur of his own, in a smart company car of his own, and when he reached the office he would be whisked up to his eyrie on the top floor with the views across the river and the soft carpet and the smiling secretary. He would lift the telephone and people would scurry to do his bidding. He would smile and they would smile, frown and they would frown. Once, long ago, he had dreamed of making it to the very top but did he want it any more? Did he really want to separate himself from reality? How stupid to think that the top job was now at last within his grasp and yet maybe he no longer wanted it.

It was odd to enter the building again after so many months and to find it so familiar and yet also quite different, as though Time had slipped sideways. Billy Prendergast was there in the lobby to meet him as he came into the front hall.

'Billy.'

'Peter.'

They shook hands.

'It's good to see you again.'

'And you. Welcome back. We've missed you.'

They took the lift to the top, to Skudder's office, Andy Unwin's office – *his* office, if he wanted it.

Melody Canter and the creamy redhead were still sitting there in their little outside office. Melody rose from her chair and gave him a ravishing smile. For the first time ever she looked at him properly, deep into his eyes. He had forgotten how stunningly good-looking she was, how blue were her eyes. She looked fresh and mischievous. The tiny blue dolphin tattoo cavorted on the back of her little wrist.

'Welcome back, Mr Hallam,' she gushed. 'It's reely great to see you again.'

'Melody,' he said.

How can I possibly sack a girl like her? What would be the point? The Melodys of this world are not worthy of revenge.

In Skudder's office he could not bring himself to sit in Skudder's chair. It stood forlorn and empty behind the desk, much smaller now than he had remembered. Its seat sagged. The office was noticeably shabbier, the carpet threadbare in places, the walls in need of a coat of paint, the windows smeared with a hint of grime. The desk was still by the window, the sofa along the right-hand wall, the paintings and prints as unattractive as ever. His own life had been turned completely upside down but here even the smell was the same: it smelt faintly of dust. Could this possibly once have been the lair of a monster? Why had everyone been so afraid of him? On the desk stood a silver-framed photograph of a young woman with two small children. Hallam picked it up.

'Skudder's wife and kids,' said Prendergast. 'We'll send it back to him.'

Hallam stared at the photograph. Skudder married? Skudder a father? Somehow it did not seem possible. Did Skudder's children love him? Of course they did: he was their father. It did not bear thinking about.

'I'll go walkabout now,' said Hallam.

'Do you want me to come with you?'

Hallam shook his head. 'I just want to drift, gauge the atmosphere. I want to listen to the heartbeat of the building.'

Prendergast smiled. 'It really is very good to have you back again,' he said.

He wandered the corridors he had known for so many years, poking his head at random into offices, greeted warmly by those he knew already, introducing himself to those he did not. Two of the secretaries in the sales department came up and hugged him. One of them was crying. How could a man like Skudder, a man with a wife and children, be able to make so many people so miserable? How had he managed to get away with it for so long? Greed at the top, that was it, and callousness, and a complete lack of morality in modern business. Profit was everything nowadays, misery of no account. If people had nervous breakdowns, who cared? There were plenty of unemployed workers who would be only too happy to take their place. Once there had been strong trade unions and professional associations to protect employees from bosses like Skudder but not any more. The unions had been shackled. The pendulum of power had swung too far the other way.

In Hallam's own old office Shane Gorman greeted him with exaggerated deference: Fingers Gorman, the scourge of the girls in the sales department, now nervous and twitchy. He rose from his desk red-faced and breathing heavily and smiled oleaginously as Hallam came into his office.

'Mr Hallam, sir,' he piped, in his treble voice. 'How very good it is to see you again.'

Hallam nodded. 'Gorman,' he said.

Gorman offered his hand. Fingers' fingers. Hallam ignored them.

I could sack him now, if I chose, this very minute. Fingers Gorman: lazy, lying, corrupt, drunken, dangerous; a man deserving punishment. Yet somehow the mood for revenge had weakened already. Monica would have the determination to carry on with it. Monica would wreak vengeance all the way, right to the end, but my own appetite is already satisfied. When it comes to hatred Monica would say that I'm a wimp.

'Too many crooks spoil the broth, eh, Gorman?' he said.

'Pardon me?'

'You heard.'

His old office was smaller than he remembered, almost poky. It seemed dark and gloomy. Had he really spent so many years of his life cooped up in this place? He was overwhelmed by a wave of melancholy, a sense of waste.

Keith Smith was standing beside Doreen's old desk in the corner: Keith, who had given him the ammunition to bring Skudder down; his secret weapon.

'Keith,' said Hallam, shaking his hand warmly.

'Mr Hallam.'

'Peter, please.'

'Peter. Welcome back. It's so good to have you back.'

'Thank you.'

How can I abandon these people?

'I'll need to talk to you later, Keith,' he said. 'In the MD's office. So don't go home too early. Stick your head round the door first.'

Gorman stood beside his desk, glowering.

'You can go home whenever you like, Gorman,' said Hallam. 'I won't be needing you.'

For several hours Hallam wandered the building, stopping to talk to people, asking about their problems, the company's difficulties, their hopes, their ideas for improvement. An air of despondency hung over the place, an unexpected seediness. Somehow everything had been contaminated. Skudder's ghost haunted the corridors: only success would be able to exorcise the memory of Skudder and his regime.

As the evening spread a soft darkness over the city he sat on the sofa in Skudder's office, gazed out at the twilight and thought about his options. A blanket of depression as gloomy as the gathering night settled on his shoulders.

I don't want this job at all, he thought. I've had enough. You should never go back. It would be a huge mistake. I've changed so much and so has the company. We no longer belong to each other.

And yet . . .

Oh, sod it! Duty. Always that sense of duty, that bloody

feeling of responsibility, of the importance of doing the right thing. Why do I always have this puritan belief that any man of worth has unavoidable obligations? Somebody has to be big enough to take this job on and put it right again and there's no one else but me. They're depending on me: not Willie Mulliken or the directors or the fat cats in the City but the ordinary people on the staff. How do I just turn round and abandon them and walk away?

As the moon rose pale above the river he sat at last in Skudder's chair at Skudder's desk and telephoned Monica for advice. Monica would know what he should do. Monica was the wisest person he knew.

She listened to him, thought about it, listened some more.

'I think you ought to walk away from it,' she said eventually. '*No* is a wonderful word. It's so clean and so uncomplicated. We should all learn how to say *no* much more often.'

Yes.

'And if you're still after revenge then the best revenge of all would be to say *no*. Living well is supposed to be the best revenge, but even better than that is the revenge of utter independence, the revenge that says, "Sod off, you can't buy me." Saying *no* is the ultimate freedom.'

Yes?

She laughed, her voice rumbling with half a century of self-indulgence. 'And this is my own little revenge on you,' she said, 'that after all these years you should come to me for advice. You used to laugh at me, didn't you, Peter? In the old days. You thought I was a bit of a card, a waste of space. I was just mad old Monica, goofy Granny, the barmy mother-in-law. But now you come to me for guidance. I'm so glad. And now we can be real friends.'

'You're the wisest person I know, Miss Porridge,' he said. 'You don't give a damn what anyone thinks of you. You just don't give a toss. I really admire that. Mind you, you're still barking mad.'

She gave a gravelly cackle. 'I've got some news for you,' she said. 'Matthew's got a job at last.'

'A miracle. Hallelujah! Praised be the Lord!'

'Not a bad job, either. In an office, clerk, with prospects. And Susie tells me that he wants to marry that girlfriend of his.'

'Matthew? *Marry?* What girlfriend?'

'The one who always used to come to the house.'

'What girl? Was one of them a girl?'

'Yes. Not easy to tell, I admit. The one called Mickey.'

'Good God! The skinny one.'

'Yes.'

'Good grief! Well, thank God for that. I thought Matt had become a homosexual.'

She cackled. 'I can't *believe* you said that.'

He laughed.

'And here's something else,' she said. 'He's thrown his other two layabout friends out of the house. He says they're untidy, that they never help with the washing-up.'

Hallam laughed.

OK, Matt, OK. This is where we start all over again. Welcome back to the human race.

'Tell me, Monica: you started to tell me one of your limericks once, about the Garden of Eden, and I was rather rude and just walked away so that I never heard the last line. I'd love to know the last line. It was something about Adam, something about him stroking Eve in the Garden of Eden. How does it go?'

She chuckled.

> 'In the Garden of Eden lay Adam,
> Complacently stroking his madam,
>   And loud was his mirth
>   For on all of the earth
> There were only two balls – and he had 'em.'

Hallam laughed. 'Trust you,' he said. 'Filth, sheer filth. So what's your favourite limerick of them all, then? Something disgusting too?'

'Not at all. It's absolutely clean: *The Dowager Duchess of Dee*.'

'A clean limerick? From *you*? This must be a record, Miss Porridge.'

'Don't be cheeky.'

'So how does it go, then, this Duchess of Dee?'

She cleared her throat.

> 'The Dowager Duchess of Dee
> Was stung on the neck by a wasp.
> When asked, "Does it hurt?"
> She replied "Not at all,
> It can do it again if it likes."'

She hooted with mirth.

'But it doesn't even—'

'Of course not,' she said. 'That's the whole point.' She hesitated. 'Peter,' she said, 'I've got a confession to make.'

'Yes?'

'Those limericks. I pinched some of them out of a book, a collection of limericks by a man called Legman. I made some of them up myself but the rest were his.'

'I guessed,' he said. 'I don't suppose you really knew any of those famous people you keep mentioning, either, did you?'

'Of course I did. Would I lie to you about that?'

'Almost certainly.'

She giggled. She sounded like a young girl. How can a woman in her seventies sound like a girl? 'Please don't lose touch, Peter. I'd be awfully sad if we did. And please find yourself another woman. You need a good woman. You're the sort of man who does.'

'You can't just find one anywhere, you know, Miss Porridge, not just like that.'

'Of course you can,' she said. 'They're all over the place if only you'd look at them properly. Tickety-boo.'

He still had twenty-four hours to make up his mind about the job. He would take the problem to Rosie: she would know what to do. She was only twenty-nine but Rosie was wonderfully sensible.

The following morning just before he set off for work at the Unicorn Hotel as usual a letter arrived from the Employment Service to say that a date had finally been fixed for the hearing of the tribunal that would decide whether he had been sacked or had resigned, and consequently whether he was entitled to the dole or not. Typical, he thought: about six months too late. He threw the letter into the bin.

At the hotel he left a message with Rosie's secretary that he would like to see her when she was free. It was so restful to be back in the hotel, an oasis of calm and comfort, away from all the tensions and demands of Mulliken and business life and the office. Here, by contrast, the atmosphere was one of quiet civilisation. Here the aim of work was not simply the restless pursuit of profit but the pursuit of comfort, happiness and relaxation. Why should he exchange this intelligent existence for a life of stress and confrontation?

Half-way through the morning Rosie called him in to her office. She looked sad. Her face was drawn. She looked tired. His heart went out to her. He hated to see her like this. He hated to see her unhappy. He wanted her to smile. 'You all right?' he said.

'I'm getting a divorce,' she said.

His heart turned over. *Don't be so ridiculous! She's only twenty-nine. You're forty-six, you stupid old fart. That's much too much; the gap is far too big. You're a wrinkly and it's time you accepted it.* 'I'm so sorry,' he said.

She shrugged. 'I'm not. It's been pretty rough for some time. We've been going our separate ways for a couple of years.'

'I'm so sorry. I never knew.'

A wisp of her hair had come adrift and was hanging down the side of her cheek. He wanted to touch it, stroke it, to tuck it back in place again. 'Your husband must be out of his mind to let you go.'

She smiled fondly at him. 'Dear Peter,' she said.

He wanted to hold her, to kiss her. If only . . .

Why was life so bloody unfair?

'So what are you going to do?' he said. 'Is there anything I can—'

'I'm moving in with Johnnie Campbell,' she said. 'We've been seeing each other for several months.'

Of course: another man. A woman like her. Of course, inevitable.

He felt a pain deep beneath his ribs. 'He's a lucky man,' he said.

She smiled. 'Thank you.'

'Congratulations.'

'So I'm giving up the job. We want to start a family straight away. I'm getting on a bit: thirty this year. Thirty! The biological clock, ticking away. I'll soon be too old if I'm not careful. Let's hope I haven't left it too late already.'

Children. Of course she wanted children. He could never have given her those. He could never have gone through all that again. He was forty-six, a wrinkly, too old for children.

'You ought to apply for my job,' she said. 'You'd be brilliant at it. You'd get it, too, if you wanted it.'

He looked at her with grief in his eyes. *I don't want anything except . . .*

She rose behind her desk and came towards him: so young, so fresh, so *fine*.

The pain sat like a lump in his guts.

She put her hands lightly on his shoulders and kissed him on the cheek. Her lips were like butterflies. 'I know, Peter,' she said. 'I know. I'm so sorry.'

He was going to need a few hours more to make up his mind about the job. He had promised Willie Mulliken a decision within forty-eight hours but he needed another night to think about it. Decisions are so often best made by the empty mind, in sleep. He needed to sleep on it, to let it fester in the compost of his subconscious.

Just one more night. He could not decide now, not just like that, not after Rosie's news. He needed more time to make up his mind. At forty-six you need to know where you're going.

He disconnected the telephone and went to bed.

He would let Willie Mulliken know in the morning.

Acknowledgements

I would like to thank Dean Bachelor, Bryan Clough, Nathan Dony and Dick Sargent for their invaluable advice about various nefarious financial and business matters. And Belinda Hadden and Amanda Christie for some splendid stories in their book *Sweet Revenge: 200 Delicious Ways to Get Your Own Back* (Headline, 1995) and especially for the lottery scam I have used in Chapter 11. And *The Limerick* (Bell, 1964 and 1969) edited by G. Legman, for some, but not all, of Monica's naughty rhymes. The limericks taken by Monica from Legman's book were copied by Legman himself from two unpublished, oral collections assembled informally in manuscript, mimeograph and card index form by students at the universities of Ann Arbor (Michigan) in the 1930s and Berkeley (California) in the 1940s. The students themselves copied the limericks from even earlier sources, so none of these limericks can be attributed to any individual author. They are all by 'Anon'. As Legman says in his introduction, the paternity of bawdy limericks has been admitted by very few of their creators and they are part of oral erotic folklore, free and owned by no one.